THE WILD HUNT

THE WILD HUNT

Elizabeth Chadwick

MICHAEL JOSEPH

LONDON

MICHAEL JOSEPH LTD

Published by the Penguin Group
27 Wrights Lane, London W8 5TZ, England
Viking Penguin Inc., 40 West 23rd Street, New York, New York 10010, USA
Penguin Books Australia Ltd, Ringwood, Victoria, Australia
Penguin Books Canada Ltd, 2801 John Street, Markham, Ontario, Canada L3R 1B4
Penguin Books (NZ) Ltd, 182–190 Wairau Road, Auckland 10, New Zealand

Penguin Books Ltd, Registered Offices: Harmondsworth, Middlesex, England

First published in Great Britain 1990

Copyright © Elizabeth Chadwick 1990

Printed and bound in Great Britain by
Richard Clay Ltd, Bungay, Suffolk
Set in Monophoto Bembo 11/13pt

A CIP catalogue record for this book is available from the British Library

ISBN 0 7181 3423 0

To my parents for their support, to Alison King for all her help, to my husband for his understanding and to my agent Carole Blake and my editors Maggie Pringle and Barbara Boote for making dreams come true

CHAPTER 1

The Welsh Marches
Winter 1098

NOW, DRIVEN BY a biting November wind, flurried against Guyon's dark cloak then swirled past him towards the castle glowering down from its crag overlooking the spated River Wye. The weary horse pecked and lumbered to a sluggish recovery and Guyon tugged his mount's ears and slapped the muscular neck. The light was fading fast and the weather was vicious, but at least shelter was within sight.

The grey destrier almost baulked at the icy, hock-deep water of the ford, but Guyon touched him lightly with his spur and, snorting, the stallion lunged forward, splashed through the dark, fluid ice and gained the muddy, half-frozen village road.

The crofts were lit from within by cooking fires and the fatty sputtering glint of rushlight. As they passed the church, a cur ran out to snap at Arian's heels. Shod steel flashed. There was a loud yelp, then silence. A withy door opened a crack and was quickly thrust shut in response to a sharp command from the depths of the hut.

Guyon rode on past the mill and the oily black gleam of the leat and began the steep climb to the castle. Once he paused to stare up through snow-spiked lashes at the solid sandstone keep, and grimaced as if a mouthful of wine had suddenly become vinegar. On their arrival, Arian would be given a rub down, a warm blanket and a tub of hot mash to content him through the night. Guyon wished fervently that his own concerns could be dealt with as easily, but he bore tidings that made such a thing impossible.

The drawbridge thumped down to his hail and the grey paced the thick oak planks, hooves ringing a hollow tocsin, for beneath lay a gully of jagged rocks and debris, foraged only by the most nimble of sheep and the occasional cursing shepherd in less than nimble pursuit.

He pricked Arian to a trot so that they passed swiftly beneath the fangs of the portcullis and emerged through the dark arch of the gatehouse into the open bailey and, drawing rein, swung from the stallion's back. His legs were so stiff that for a moment he was unable to move and stood clinging to the saddle until a groom came running to take the horse.

'Evil night m'lord,' the man remarked, sucking his teeth, eyes bright with unspoken curiosity.

Guyon released his clutch on the saddle tree and steadied himself. 'Worse to come,' he answered grimly, not entirely referring to the weather. 'Look at the shoe on his off-fore Sim, I think it's loose.'

'Aye m'lord.'

Guyon slapped Arian's dappled rump and went across the bailey, slowly at first until the feeling returned to his thighs, his dark head bent into the wild, white-flaked wind. He gave greeting to the guards at the forebuilding entrance and, stripping his gauntlets, went up the steep staircase to the hall on the second level.

The dinner horn had but recently sounded and the trestles were crowded with diners. At the sight of their lord's heir, jaws ceased chewing, hands paused half-way to dishes, eyes grew round and swivelled like marbles to view his progress up the hall, the men marking his long, impatient stride, the women marking, with a different look entirely, the breadth of his shoulders and the arrogant, striking beauty of his face.

Looking neither left nor right, Guyon strode up the room to the dais table where sat his father with the senior knights and retainers of the household and also, he noticed

2

with a certain irritation, his half-sister Emma in the lady's customary place.

Miles le Gallois glanced, startled, then rose to greet his son, his expression concerned. 'Guy! We had not looked for you so soon.'

'A man rides quickly when the devil snaps at his heels,' Guyon answered, bending to kiss his sister and stepping over the trestle to take the place they had hastily made for him. His legs suddenly felt as if they had turned to water. The room swam and wallowed before his eyes.

'The wonder is that you did not fall off. Guy, you look dreadful!' Emma gave a peremptory signal to one of the lads serving their table.

'Do I?' He took the cup of wine she thrust at him. 'Well, perhaps I have good reason, Em.' He was aware of them all looking at him, anxious as rabbits with the scent of a ferret in their nostrils.

'Surely the King did not refuse you your uncle Gerard's lands?' asked his father incredulously.

Guyon shook his head and stared into the bloody, opaque wine. 'The King was pleased to acknowledge me the heir and grant me all rights and privileges pertaining,' he said in a flat voice that, far from reassuring his father, well and truly unnerved him.

It was three months since Gerard had died fighting the Welsh on the Island of Mon that some called Anglesey. He had been a childless widower and Guyon his named heir, but King William Rufus had been known to abjure the laws of heredity in favour of the laws of money. Guyon had gone to Rufus in Normandy in order to claim the lands, but the manner of this, his return, filled Miles with foreboding. His son's eyes were as densely black as the deep waters of the mill leat, and as grim. Part of it, he could see, was fatigue. Part of it was something that Guyon was holding back, throttling his spirit.

Miles glanced at Guyon's compressed lips, the taut grip of

3

his fingers on the goblet stem, and then ranged his gaze over the other men at the board. Whatever it was, Guyon was not going to make of it a public announcement. He drew breath to suggest that they retire to the solar, but was forestalled by his daughter who, God bless her, had also noticed Guyon's condition.

'Jesu!' she scolded, putting her hand over his. 'You're frozen stiff! What were you thinking of to make a journey in weather like this? Surely it could have waited! And do not look at me like that. I'll have the servants prepare a tub in the solar and you'll come there now where it's warm!'

Some of the blackness left Guyon's eyes. A spark kindled. Emma still viewed her three years' seniority over him as a licence to command his obedience, more so since his mother had died of the sweating sickness two winters ago. While her husband travelled with the court, a senior assistant to the chamberlain, she played chatelaine in the marches, terrorizing servants and family alike with her demands for a state of rigid domestic order.

This time he did not, however, kick against the traces but, after one look, let her have her way. 'You had better stir the cooks to provision for my men,' was all he said as he rose to follow her. 'They will be here within the hour and cursing me to the devil, poor sods.'

Emma started to scold him about the folly of outriding them when the marches were so dangerous and unsettled. Guyon let the words tumble away over the top of his head.

Once the steaming tub was ready, Guyon began to disrobe and Emma dismissed the maids with an autocratic snap of her fingers, causing him to lift his brows before striving to tug his hauberk over his head.

Miles dropped the curtain behind the two girls. 'I doubt that Guyon has any designs on ravishment just now, Emma,' he remarked dryly.

'Do you? From what my husband tells me of the court,

Guy would have designs on ravishment even if he were tied down and bludgeoned half unconscious.' She snatched the hauberk from her brother, eyes accusing.

'Half the tale and a fraction of the truth,' Guyon defended and then yelped as she jerked overly hard on his gambeson to draw it over his head and almost tore off his ears.

'Vixen,' he complained, rubbing the back of his head, then ducked with coiled agility beneath her cuff of rebuke, straightened and seized her wrist to pull her hard against his unyielding length to snatch a kiss.

Emma glared up at him, her mouth twitching despite her best effort to keep it straight. 'And you are surely a cur!' she riposted, adding, as he pressed his lips to the clenched knuckles of the hand he held captive, 'You need not attempt your courtier's tricks on me. I know them by rote!'

Falsely crestfallen, Guyon released her with a sigh and began to unlace his shirt. 'I suppose you do,' he said, and suddenly the teasing look was gone from his face to leave it the grim mask of his arrival. 'But I needs must hope they still have their effect on other women.'

Emma's brilliant eyes narrowed. 'Not within this keep,' she said with asperity.

'I was thinking further up the march. Maurice FitzRoger's daughter, to be precise.'

'What?' Miles, who had been lounging against an inlaid coffer was suddenly alert.

'Judith of Ravenstow,' Guyon said neutrally and, drawing off his chausses, stepped into the steaming tub. 'On the King's order.'

'Rufus offered you Maurice of Ravenstow's girl?'

'He did not offer. He said marry her or else.' He looked at his stunned father with bleak and bitter eyes. 'He also sold the earldom of Shrewsbury to Robert de Belleme for three thousand marks.'

'What!' Miles said for the second time, concern transmuted into consternation. 'Surely the King would not permit him

5

to inherit that. Considering what he owns already and the kind of man he is, it is much too dangerous!'

Guyon took the soap and cloth that Emma silently handed him. 'Every man has his price and de Belleme has calculated Rufus's to a nicety,' he said with a grimace. 'He wanted Ravenstow as well, being as it belonged to his late half-brother. He might have had it, too, if FitzHamon had not remembered that the heiress was a ripely marriageable sixteen and unbetrothed. The King chose to bestow her himself, and not without a little malicious amusement.' He began vigorously to wash as if to purge himself of the thoughts chasing round his mind.

'You cannot do it!' Emma's mouth twisted with revulsion. 'If you marry the girl, it will make you blood kin to that monster. Everyone knows how evil he is. He robs and tortures for sport and impales those who displease him on greased poles and smiles as they die. God's mercy, he keeps his own wife locked up in the cells below Belleme with only the rats for company!' She shuddered and hugged her arms. He did not accuse her of hysterical over-reaction. In an age when brutality ruled, brutal men were horrified by the sadistic cruelty of Robert de Belleme, eldest son of the late Roger de Montgomery, Earl of Shrewsbury.

It was not his treatment of serfs that caused distress — their lives were expendable — but his torture of noble prisoners quite capable of paying ransom, and he had no respect for any authority but his own.

'If I do not accept this match, Em, I forfeit uncle Gerard's lands too and the both will go to one of the King's Flemings.' He floated the dish across the tub and watched it rock. 'I am caught in a cleft stick. Not only does Rufus force a wife into my bed, he makes me pay for the privilege too — five hundred marks. Nowhere near three thousand, I know, but enough to make my tenants squeal when I squeeze them for its payment. It is fortunate for de Belleme that he does not have a conscience as to how he goes about raising his own relief.'

Emma shuddered and crossed herself.

'And of course,' said Miles, eyes narrowing, 'the lands you gain with this match, added to what you own and what you will inherit, make you a suitable counterbalance in the middle marches to whatever schemes of advancement de Belleme may choose to plot.'

'Oh yes,' Guyon said darkly. 'I am to pay for that privilege too, mayhap with my life.'

There was a taut silence. Into it Emma drew a shaken breath that might have been the mastery of a sob and, murmuring something about food and wine, fled the room.

Miles sighed and sat down on a stool, his movements smooth. As yet, his fifty-four years sat lightly on his body which remained, through vigorous activity, firm and taut, if perhaps a little more stocky than in his lissome youth.

'I know the girl's mother,' he murmured thoughtfully. 'Alicia FitzOsbern, Breteuil's sister. She was pretty at fifteen, very pretty indeed. If I had not already been married and satisfied with your mother, I might have offered for her myself.'

Guyon grunted. 'I always understood you had no liking for the FitzOsbern clan.'

'The male stock, no. They all were – and are, when you consider Breteuil – snakes, but Alicia was different. She had such a courageous, gentle nature and eyes like wild violets. She never forgave her menfolk for selling her in marriage to a brute like Maurice de Montgomery.'

Guyon reached for the towel that Emma had left conveniently to hand and stepped from the tub. 'Reason enough for any woman to hate, I would warrant,' he remarked drily, thinking of the former lord of Ravenstow who had resembled nothing so much as a glutted boar atop a dung heap.

'As I remember, Judith was born late into the marriage after numerous slurs of barrenness had been cast in Alicia's direction,' Miles reminisced, folding his arms. 'I doubt it was all her fault. As far as I know, for all his lechery Maurice sired no bastards.'

7

Guyon pulled on a furred bedrobe and called entry to the two servants who came to empty the water from the tub down a waste shaft in the corner of the room.

'At least Ravenstow is a formidable keep from which to base your dominance,' Miles remarked towards Guyon's silence, thinking of the solid new fortress towering over the River Dee. 'Whatever other sins lie on de Belleme's soul, he is a master architect.'

'And I have the suspicion that one way or another he will attempt to annex it to his earldom. Ravenstow guards the approach to the Chester plain and all roads east.' Guyon flicked him a look from beneath locked black brows. 'Ideally suited to the purposes of robbery and extortion, would you not say?'

Miles eyed him, recognizing the uncertainty behind the flippant façade. It was a trait inherited from himself.

'There is always the Holy Land, I suppose,' Guyon added with a twisted smile. 'Freedom from Rufus and de Belleme, and the glory of slaughtering infidels to gild my soul!'

'Guyon stop it!'

'Would you rather that I wept and clutched the altar cloth, gibbering for sanctuary?' he snapped.

'Perhaps I would,' Miles retorted, undisturbed by the flash of anger in the hot brown eyes. Guyon possessed a royal temper when roused but also the control to throttle it down. 'At least it would be better than . . .' He broke off and drew a deep breath as Emma re-entered the room followed by a maidservant bearing food and wine.

Guyon's lips tightened. He subsided onto a hard-backed chair.

'Rhosyn is in the hall,' Emma announced as she dismissed the woman and poured the wine herself. 'You will have to tell her.'

Guyon eyed his sister warily as he took the cup and drank. 'What of it? Last I saw her at Michaelmas she refused to stay, made it plain that she wished to take it no further than the occasional meeting between the sheets. She has no cause to baulk.'

'She might not have had a cause at Michaelmas, Guy, but she certainly has one now,' Emma replied darkly.

Guyon's wariness sharpened. 'Meaning what?'

'Meaning that she is not so skilled a herb wife as she thought and the rounding of her belly proves it. Midsummer I would say, to look at her.'

Guyon glanced from his sister's pursed disapproval to his father's blank surprise. He took another swallow of wine and shrugged. 'All right, I'll speak to her tomorrow, but I do not see that this marriage will change anything. Willingly I will acknowledge and provide for the child, but you know Rhosyn – a wild law unto herself.'

'I am not thinking of wild law, but Welsh law,' Emma said, as he reached for a piece of bread. 'A man's first-born son, even begotten out of wedlock to a mistress, has equal rights with the other legitimate heirs of his body.'

Guyon chewed and swallowed and, after a pause for con-sideration, discarded the notion with a regretful shake of his head. 'I am Norman born, Em and Welsh rights do not pertain this side of the border, more's the pity. Oh, I daresay there are a couple of holdings I could cede to a chance-gotten child without too much hue and cry, but never a piecemeal portion of my honours. Besides, the babe is yet unborn and if it lives may well be a daughter. The last one I got on a kitchen wench at Windsor was a girl.'

Emma's full mouth tightened. 'When was this?' she enquired glacially.

'Last spring before the Welsh campaign. The babe died before it was a week old.'

'Not niggardly with your favours, are you?' she snapped. 'Do you and Prince Henry keep tallies to compare the results of your ruttings?'

'Oh don't be such a prude Emma!' he growled. 'You know

9

the ways of the court. I'd rather go to hell for the sin of fornication than for the sins of sodomy or regicide.'

Colour flooded her face. Her husband, as assistant to the chamberlain, knew most of what transpired in the immediate circle surrounding the King; the scandals, the petty power struggles, the prevalent vices and Guyon, with his arrogant features, disregard for propriety and hint of Welsh and marcher barbarity was a magnet to which all three were drawn whether he wished it or no.

Miles eased tactfully to his feet and stretched like a cat uncoiling. 'Time enough for discussion tomorrow,' he said. 'I'm for my bed before the dawn catches me still on my feet.' He gave his daughter an eloquent stare. Guyon had his trencher piled high enough already without her heavy-handed seasoning of moral chastisement and righteous advice.

'A conspiracy of men,' Emma declared with a sniff, and then a tight smile. 'I know when I am beaten.' Going to her brother, she stooped and kissed his stubble-blurred cheek.

'That does not mean you will give in!' he laughed, playfully tugging her thick copper braid.

'Does it not?' She arched her brow at him. 'Let me tell you, I will gladly relinquish the battle to your wife and hope that she has more fortune than I in taming your scapegrace ways!'

'Know when you are beaten, do you?' he chuckled as she went towards the curtain. 'Is that why you always have to have the last word?'

CHAPTER 2

I N THE DIMLY lit great hall, Rhosyn rolled over on her lumpy makeshift pallet and sat up, irritated to discover that yet again her bladder was full. Beside her, oblivious, her father snored. He was a prosperous wool merchant these days, with the beginnings of a paunch to prove it. Complacent. They had fared well since their business dealings with Miles, lord of Milnham and Ashdyke. There was much profit to be had in wool and the cloth woven from the fleeces. Lord Miles bred it raw on the hoof. Her father sold the clip in Flanders and speculated a little on the wider trade markets – spices and leather, silks and Tyrian glass – and they grew rich.

Beside their grandfather, the children of her first, now widowed marriage slept deeply in a puppy huddle. Rhys was ten, a sturdy, dark-eyed replica of his father. Eluned, seven, resembled herself – slender and fey with raven-blue hair, autumnal eyes and a luminous, rosy complexion. This coming child, as yet scarcely realized; well, if a boy, she could only hope by God's charity that he inherited Guyon's beauty married to a less difficult nature.

Stupid, she thought with self-irritation as she quietly left her children and her father to seek out the garderobe. Stupid to have been so easily caught, she who knew all her herbs and simples, or thought she knew because they had always worked before. Too late now, too dangerous, and not the season for the plants that would most definitely and messily have cured her condition.

She had been in two minds whether to make this trip to Hereford with her father, but had reasoned that it would be

11

her last opportunity before the weather grew too difficult for travel, and she needed to purchase linen for swaddling bands that she could stitch during the dark, hall-bound months of winter; and winter's threat was already upon them. The knife-bitter wind and the scudding, fierce snow squalls had caused them to curtail their journey early in the day and seek shelter here at Ashdyke.

Guyon's appearance at dusk had been a surprise, and she was not sure if it was a welcome one. The news of his impending marriage had caused her no grief. She had always known that the day would come, indeed, had held herself a little aloof with that knowledge in mind. He was heir to a considerable amount of land and had a duty to take a wife of his own status and breed up children, a wife who would have more in day to day common with him than she did herself.

Rhosyn's practical merchant origins told her that there was no point in building upon their tenuous relationship. For all the beauty of his body and his skill between the sheets, his fluency in the Welsh tongue and his ability to adapt to Welsh ways, he was only one quarter of the *Cymru* and raised to be a marcher lord who would ride into Wales on the back of a warhorse to ravage the land if his King so commanded. He regarded the towering Norman border keeps as home and refuge, not as grey, enclosing prisons that hemmed in the soul.

The garderobe was cold and stank of its main function, and she did not linger. Instead of making her way back to the hall, however, Rhosyn turned of a sudden impulse in the direction of the private quarters. She knew immediately which chamber Guyon had been given, for his young white bratch bitch, Cadi, was lying outside, nose tucked into her tail, and she rose with a joyous whine of greeting as Rhosyn paused to stroke and make a fuss of her, before reaching to lift the heavy curtain.

Guyon had been soundly asleep, but he came alertly to his senses at the first soft clink of the curtain rings and the muffled whine of the dog. This was the keep where he had been bred up, his welcome here guaranteed, but his mind and body were so conditioned to react to danger and complete security was so seldom his, that he was out of bed and across the room in the minute space of five swift heartbeats.

A shadow flickered across the dim torchlight in the passage. 'Guyon?' it breathed doubtfully, and then uttered a muffled scream as it was seized from behind.

Guyon felt long silky hair toss against his chest. The crown of his captive's head butted upwards, jarring his teeth together and he bit his tongue and tasted blood. A supple body writhed against his and he felt the swell of a generously rounded breast beneath his fingers. The woman strove to bite him. He took his hand away and pulled her round to face him.

'It's me, Rhosyn!' she gasped indignantly, her French bearing the lilting accent of Wales. 'Have you lost your wits?'

'More likely you have lost yours!' he retorted, but with amusement now that he was fully awake, the feel of her soft, slender body against his own sufficient to restore his humour. 'It is a foolish thing to creep up on a man in the middle of the night, *cariad*. Oft-times I sleep with a naked sword at my side. I might have cut off your head!'

'I have seen your naked sword frequently enough for it not to concern me,' Rhosyn replied with spurious innocence and rubbed herself sensuously against him in the darkness, feeling the familiar heady sweetness begin to melt her bones. She tangled her fingers in his thick hair and stood on tip-toe to bite his ear and then whisper into it; 'But mayhap it would be safest to sheathe it, my lord.'

Guyon laughed huskily. 'To the hilt,' he muttered, before bending to taste her willingly offered lips, his fingers busy with the lacings of her gown.

Rhosyn stretched languidly like a cat and then relaxed, a contented little half-smile curving her lips. 'I had forgotten what a pleasure it was,' she purred, eyeing Guyon sidelong across the tossed coverlet in the glow from the night candle.

'Your fault,' he remarked, but easily, without accusation. 'I wanted you to come with me.'

'And I would have stuck out like a sore thumb among those Norman women and been as miserable as sin.'

'Sin is never miserable,' Guyon chuckled, thereby earning himself a slap. He caught her wrist and pulled her across him and playfully retorted the flat of his hand on her neat buttocks. She wriggled upon him, feeling him still half-hard and, after a moment's hesitation while she resisted temptation, she pulled herself away and sat up to study him through the skein of her hair.

He had his Welsh grandmother's olive complexion and black hair, and his eyes were a dark, luminous, peat-pool brown. He could easily pass for one of the *Cymru* were it not for his Anglo-Norman height and breadth.

'What are you looking at?' he demanded, the stubborn mouth softening into a smile.

Her gaze swept the whole of him once more and she laughed. 'I am like a beggar at a feast. The delicacies offered overwhelm my palate!'

Guyon grinned in response, but the expression did not quite reach his eyes which had grown serious. 'I hear that you are with child?' he said softly.

The laughter left her own eyes. Her round chin thrust at him defiantly. 'What of it?'

'Would you have told me?'

Rhosyn bit her lip. 'Probably so,' she said and slid her gaze from his probing scrutiny. 'My father and yours do too much business together to keep the thing a secret and Rhys and Eluned both chatter like jackdaws. You would have discovered sooner or later.'

Guyon regarded her thoughtfully, sensing her reluctance and feeling it tug at his gut. 'My sister seems to think that you will invoke Welsh law on the child's behalf,' he murmured impassively.

14

The beautiful hazel-green eyes widened.

'The son of the handmaiden is equal to the son begotten on a legal spouse,' he said as she continued to stare at him nonplussed.

She shook her head, her expression almost frightened. 'Your sister is wrong. What good would it do on this side of the border where Norman custom reigns? It would be a hobble of broken straw indeed and I am not sure that I would want a child of mine to dwell among *saesnegs* in a great stone tomb like this.' Her eyes roved the comfort of the room with disparagement.

Guyon's jaw tightened. A harsh retort came to his lips – that he was not sure he wanted a child of his to grow up running barefoot over the Welsh hills or huckstering in wool for a living, but he curbed the words behind his teeth, knowing from bitter experience that they too were hobbles of broken straw.

'Emma spoke from the viewpoint of a Norman lady,' he said instead. 'She imagines what she herself would do in your position, and that would be to fight tooth and nail to have that child accepted as my responsibility.' He reached to thread a tendril of her hair through his fingers and a rueful grin curved his lips. 'Also, I think she said it to put me in dread of ever doing the like again. She disapproves of what she sees as my casual fornications.'

Rhosyn pulled a wry face, remembering Emma's frosty glare as they made up their pallets in the hall, and then the grimace was touched with the hint of a smile as she imagined the lady Emma's response could she have but witnessed herself and Guyon a few moments ago.

The night candle guttered and sparked and Guyon tugged the strand of hair gently. 'But our concern is not with Emma, but with you,' he said, gaze ranging her body which betrayed as yet very little evidence of her coming motherhood. Perhaps her breasts were slightly fuller and her belly no longer concave.

Rhosyn's look grew wary before she dropped her lids.

'I try to learn by my mistakes,' he said gently as he saw her fear. 'I will not try to hold you and nor, though it be my greatest desire, is it fitting that I should.'

'Your bride, you mean?' she said without rancour.

Guyon made a face. 'You know about that? Ach, how should you not when my men are below in the hall. Rhosyn *cariad*, you are well out of this coil. Take the road to Wales and in the name of God, do not look back.'

'Guyon?'

He flashed her a look devoid of humour, dark and grim. 'Did you also hear that I am to wed into the house of Montgomery? It is by royal command and the girl's mother is an old family acquaintance. My refusal would put her in mortal danger from Robert de Belleme, the new Earl of Shrewsbury. If he can lock up his own wife in some dark oubliette and put out his own godson's eyes, what need to cavil at tossing his sister-in-law and niece over Ravenstow's battlements? It is about power, Rhosyn, and you are well out of it. When your father has concluded his business in Hereford or wherever, go home, sit close at your own hearth and forget about venturing across the border unless you have a well armed and determined escort. Robert de Belleme and his minions will turn the marches into hell for such men as your father.'

Rhosyn shuddered, wanting to believe that he was exaggerating, but denied that comfort. His tongue might lie – she knew that he could be glib to further a cause – but the expression in his eyes this night was naked truth.

'I will speak with your father tomorrow before our roads part, make sure that he knows to travel only on our land and take no short cuts across Shrewsbury's domain.'

'Is it really so dangerous?'

'Yes. I mean what I say Rhosyn. Either go into the heart of Wales and do not venture forth again, or stay here with me, within the protection of one of my keeps. There can be no middle path.'

She shook her head numbly. He touched her arm and felt how cold she was, and drew her back down beside and against his warmth, pulling the coverlet around them. She pressed herself against him, feeling the solid muscular wall with its illusion of security.

This was the end of it. She could no more live in one of these great, grim fortresses than a Norman lady could sit milking a ewe on the slopes of *Yr Wyddfa*. She needed her measure of freedom and, aside from that, Norman women had entirely different views upon the subject of mistresses and their offspring and she had no wish to feud over a lost cause with Guyon's new wife. If he wanted to see her and the child, then let him come to Wales.

'*Ffarwel fy llewpart du,*' she murmured against his throat, and kissed him first there in the brown hollow and then raised her head to find his lips. '*R wy'n dy garu di.*'

Guyon's arms tightened around her and as the kiss deepened and their bodies took fire he felt the prickling sting of unshed tears behind his lids. 'I love you too, *cariad,*' he muttered thickly, and silently cursed the whole Montgomery clan into the deepest pit of hell.

CHAPTER 3

JUDITH CLENCHED HER teeth and hissed through them as Agnes, her mother's maid, drew the ivory comb down through her young mistress's hip-length tawny-bronze hair and discovered a hitherto overlooked snarl.

'Stand still, sweeting and it won't hurt so much,' said the maid, a hint of exasperation in her voice, perspiration streaking her three wobbling chins. 'Nearly done now.'

'Do not cozen me like a babe!' snapped her charge, who was shifting from foot to foot, fidgeting like a horse with a burr beneath its saddle and behaving with a graceless lack of decorum that would shame them all if she was not curbed before encountering her betrothed.

Agnes's mouth puckered to become another fold in her fleshy face and she turned away to pick up a long rope of polished agate beads. Judith sniffed and blinked, set her jaw and refused to cry. Tears availed her nothing. It was a lesson hard-learned in early childhood. Her father had dismissed them as a female weakness to be despised. Her mother had wept too many herself in grief over lost causes to encourage her daughter in like indulgences.

Judith looked down at her wedding garments. A pale green linen undergown, close-fitting to her slender, almost thin body and an overtunic of a darker green heavy silk damask, gorgeously embroidered with thread of gold at throat and hem and trailing sleeve, and around her waist a girdle of jewel-set bronze links. She felt like the centre-piece at a feast, dressed to be devoured.

In a few hours she was to make her marriage vows in the

18

chapel to a man she had never before set eyes upon. She was to leave her home, go with him, his property to deal with as he pleased; to be bedded by him tonight and perhaps bear his child nine moons from now. She was a week short of her sixteenth birthday and terrified. She knew how much her mother had suffered at the hands of her father before his death in September. The growls, the curses, the frequent slaps, the drunken beatings, the disdain that tore at the foundations of confidence. Her mother had borne the brunt, shielded her daughter from the worst of it, but Judith had known, observed the hell, and could not bear that it should be her own.

'Stand still sweeting,' said Agnes. 'Let me pin these in your hair, there's a good lass.'

The maid's fingers tweaked and tugged, trailing pain in their wake. Resentment flared in Judith's breast, not just at Agnes, but at everything. She uncoiled her fingers, raised her arm and slapped Agnes's hand aside. 'You should have been a butcher's wife, not a lady's maid!' she spat.

Affronted, Agnes started to bluster and cluck like a midden hen.

The curtain clacked gently on its rings and Alicia de Montgomery entered the room, her walk still the graceful long glide of her girlhood. She took in the scene and atmosphere immediately and the faint vertical marks between her brows became slightly more defined.

'Thank you Agnes, you have wrought wonders. Our cygnet is a swan. Will you go and get one of the girls to bring up fresh candles ready for tonight?'

The maid knew a dismissal when she heard one and, indeed, was glad to go. Fond of lady Judith though she was, Agnes acknowledged that these days she was becoming too difficult to handle, wedged in that awkward stage between child and woman and uneasy within both identities.

'Agnes is an old besom at times,' Alicia said when they were alone, 'but that is no excuse to strike out. Is it what I have taught you? You will become no better than your father.'

Judith bit her lip, held her chin rigid to stop it from quivering and blinked hard. 'I am sorry mama,' she said unsteadily, 'but she hurt me and made me feel like a filly being groomed for a horse-coper's approval!'

Alicia's mouth twitched. Before her father, who had believed in female submission, indeed abasement to the superior sex, Judith had behaved as if butter would not melt in her mouth, but Alicia was fully aware of the rebellious spirit that went unquenched beneath the dutiful obedience.

'You should address your apology to Agnes, not me,' she replied, folding her daughter in a warm, rose-scented embrace. 'I know that you do not think it now, but you are most fortunate in this match.'

Judith's response was a stifled sob and arms gripped suddenly tight on her mother's sleeves. 'Mama, I am afraid!' she whimpered.

'Hush now, you'll undo all Agnes's good work.' Alicia kissed her daughter and stroked her hair, and after a moment stood away and, looking into the child's eyes, saw the hopeless misery of a hunted animal brought to bay.

'This match was made for men's political purposes, but it is a blessing for you could you but understand it. The man whose son you will wed . . . I was almost his bride myself. Would to God that I had been so fortunate.'

Judith gulped and sleeved her face and stared round-eyed at her mother.

'He was already married,' Alicia said, turning away and smoothing a crease from her cendal gown. 'Your grandfather FitzOsbern offered me to him when his wife was seized in a Welsh raid, but Miles went over the border and brought her back. Your grandfather was furious to have his plans so thwarted. I was happy for Miles – he loved Christen – but I cried myself to sleep for weeks afterwards.' She picked up her ivory-backed mirror and stared into the shimmering glass, seeing not the attractive, mature woman of four and forty but the green, blossoming girl of fifteen and the dark-avised lord of Milnham who had no eyes except for his flaxen English wife.

She had never quite recovered from that first, girlhood pang of the heart, made all the more poignant by her marriage at sixteen to Maurice de Montgomery who beat her for the merest transgression and behaved with all the finesse of a stinking, rutting, wild boar.

Occasional baronial gatherings had afforded her glimpses of Miles le Gallois as he grew into middle age. The cat-like grace of his twenties had set, become less lissome and rangy, but in essence remained. Maurice had grown even more to resemble a boar as his waistline overspread the bounds of his belt.

'I know very little of Guyon, but with Miles and Christen for examples I do believe that your marriage will be easier than mine.' She gave a regretful shrug. 'If circumstances had been different, you would have had time to know each other before the wedding, but as it is I would rather you had a strong protector when your uncle Robert comes to claim his earldom. Already the vultures are gathering.'

Judith glanced sidelong at her mother whose expression revealed nothing – too much of nothing. Judith well knew the rumours surrounding Robert de Belleme. The maids delighted in terrifying each other of a night with tales of his brutality and Judith understood more English and Welsh than was seemly for a girl of her high breeding. They said that he tortured for sport and robbed and murdered incontinently without conscience. The more fanciful of them even said that he possessed a forked tail and cloven hooves, but Judith gave no credence to their imagination. What need when the truth was already so lurid?

He had designed Ravenstow personally and loaned her father the money to build it. They were still in his debt to the tune of several hundred marks. She knew that her mother was afraid he would come immediately to claim it, being himself in debt to the King. It was the reason that this marriage had been arranged so quickly – before he had a chance to reach out and seize and strangle.

Judith shuddered. The wedding was supposed to be a quiet affair with a select number of guests and vassals – supposed to be, but de Belleme's brother Arnulf of Pembroke had ridden in yestereve and with him had been Walter de Lacey who was a powerful vassal of de Belleme's, a hunting crony of her father's and former suitor for her hand and the Ravenstow estates. Her mother had been hard-put to find them either houseroom or cordiality, for it was obvious that they were not present for the sake of wishing joy on the marriage, but they could not be turned away and so guested below with those of official invitation such as Hugh d'Avrenches Earl of Chester and FitzHamon lord of Gloucester.

The curtain swished and Agnes reappeared followed by a girl bearing a rush basket of fresh candles. 'They're sighted, m'lady. Be here within the hour, so de Bec says,' Agnes announced and directed her subordinate with a jabbing, fat finger.

The room swam before Judith's eyes and the walls seemed to encroach upon her, caging her in a space so small that there was no room to breathe. She felt hot and sick, but her hands as they clasped each other were like ice. 'Agnes, I'm sorry, I shouldn't have struck you,' she strangled out, swallowing hard.

'That's all right, loveday,' Agnes said comfortably. 'Bound to be a bit strung up today aren't . . .' Her words trailed to a halt. She held out her hand to the child who had gone the colour of curd cheese.

The walls were squeezing so tightly around Judith that she felt she would die if she did not escape. Gathering her skirts in one hand, the other clapped across her mouth, she bolted towards the doorway. The other maidservant, candles in hand, leaped startled out of the way. Both Alicia and Agnes called out to her, but Judith was gone, fleeing heedless of the dangerous, spiralling stairs, fleeing with the wild instinct of a hunted animal to escape. While she was running, she did not have to think. While she was running, she was not fettered.

'Shall I go after her, my lady?'

Alicia gnawed her lip and looked at the still swaying curtain. 'No Agnes,' she said slowly after a moment. 'We have hemmed her about too much today. Let her be alone awhile. It will be her last chance.'

'She ain't ready for this yet,' Agnes said grimly. 'They say he's used to the women o' the court, that he plays fast wi' other men's wives.'

'Gossip!' Alicia snapped. 'And you know better than to listen, Agnes. And do not give me that pitying look. I am not so naïve as to imagine no truth in servants' rumours. I do not doubt he has owned casual mistresses, but these tales are always embroidered to give them colour and I trust to his breeding more than I do to third-hand tittle-tattle. Besides, whatever marriage to him holds in store for Judith, it can be no worse than a fate at the hands of her uncle Robert, or indeed Walter de Lacey. She has to be ready.' And Alicia turned aside from the senior maid lest the expression in her eyes belie her firm tone of voice.

When Judith returned to her senses, there was a tight stitch in her side and she was leaning against a jagged lump of stone, the breath rasping harshly in her throat, her tawny hair dishevelled around her and a dark stain spreading upwards from the hem of her gown where she had splashed heedlessly through a puddle in the bailey. Her gilded shoes were soaked and her toes clung cold together inside them.

Sleet spattered fitfully on her head. The wind was as raw as an open wound. Judith began to shiver. Her new cloak with its warm beaver lining was hung upon her clothing pole in the chamber she had fled, and not for anything would she return to fetch it.

'I cannot do it,' she whispered miserably to herself, knowing that her words were empty. If she did not agree to this marriage then she exposed them all to the threat of her uncle Robert. Sooner or later she would have been contracted to wed anyway, probably to Walter de Lacey, and nothing could be worse than that, she told herself stoutly as she stared out over the grey choppy water of the river below.

Guyon FitzMiles, lord of Oxley and Ledworth. She tested the name on her tongue and tried to envisage the man, but nothing came except a sickening twist of fear to roil her gut. What if his teeth were rotten or he stank? What if he was gross and balding like Hugh, Earl of Chester? The images, undesired, filled her mind, flooding and overflowing and for a wild moment she contemplated flinging herself from the promontory to break like the spume upon the rocks below.

The very notion frightened her and she drew back from the treacherous edge, the wind blinding her with her hair, her breath coming in great sobbing gasps.

A thin, plaintive mew caused her to look around and then down to where a golden tabby cat twined sinuously around her skirts, tail erect, round head butting and rubbing.

'Melyn!' Judith scolded, momentarily diverted from her own unhappy dilemma as she bent to scoop the cat up into her arms. 'In the name of the saints, where have you been?'

The cat, missing for three days, merely purred and gave her a slanted look compounded of smugness and feline disdain.

It was uncommon for cats to be kept as house pets. Usually they roamed the undercrofts and barns, tolerated to keep the vermin at bay, essentially wild. Judith had discovered Melyn two years ago out on this headland, a mangy kitten with a badly cut paw. Alicia had been teaching Judith her herbs and simples and had let her develop her knowledge on the kitten, lord Maurice not being at home to see the little animal destroyed. By the time he did return, Melyn was fully recovered, had become accustomed to life in the bower and had learned manners to suit. Her feline sense of self-preservation sent her either out of the room or into hiding whenever Maurice was in the vicinity.

Following his death, Melyn had stalked the keep like a queen surveying her domain, imperious, regal, untouchable. Her disappearance three days since had been an ill omen. It was as if she knew that a new tyrant was coming to Ravenstow and she wanted no part of it . . . except that now, when his arrival was imminent, Melyn had chosen to materialize.

They stared at each other. Then Melyn suddenly and painfully dug her hind legs into the crook of Judith's arm and clawed herself up onto her favourite perch across her mistress's shoulder. Judith yelped and protested, but bore with the discomfort. She had not known how much the cat's disappearance had preyed upon her peace of mind until discovering her just now.

Judith tugged her hair out of the way. Melyn uttered a strange, whining growl and her claws dug into the back of her mistress's neck. Another cat emerged from the tangled dank grass and walked without haste across their path towards the keep. He was sleek and black as jet, rangy and elegant.

'Oh Jesu!' Judith exclaimed in exasperation, not knowing whether to be annoyed or amused and most definitely concerned. God alone knew how her future husband would react to a bowerful of kittens. God alone knew how her future husband would react to anything.

CHAPTER 4

GUYON DREW REIN and, while the herald rode forward to announce him formally, stared up at the rectangular limewashed keep, gleaming white against the roiling grey clouds and wind-whipped tussocky rocks of its slope.

'I must be mad,' he muttered as the drawbridge thumped down across the ditch and, beyond, the serjeants in the gatehouse made shrift to raise the black fangs of the portcullis and open the doorway into hell. A frisson of foreboding scuttled down Guyon's spine. One of the most impregnable keeps along the whole northern march Ravenstow might be, desirable in the extreme, but for two pins he would have ridden away and left it. Being as there were more than two pins at stake, he gently shook Arian's bridle and the stallion stepped delicately onto the planks. Cadi bounded joyously forward with no such reservations, and Guyon whistled her sternly to heel.

'The Welsh won't take this in a hurry,' Miles said as they turned at a sharp angle to ride between the curtain wall and the palisade of the inner bailey before turning again to enter through the massive gateway.

Guyon grunted and gazed at the formidable defences with a jaundiced eye, appreciating their strength even while he felt the revulsion. If only Robert de Belleme was not so closely connected with the place, he would have been a great deal easier of conscience and mind.

Upon dismounting, they were greeted by an officious little man in a scarlet silk robe that clutched his slack belly, making him look five months gone. Behind him stood a taller, iron-thewed greybeard in full armour and a welcoming party of what looked like the more prominent members of the guard and the household knights.

'God's greeting my lords, and welcome,' said slack belly, hands clasped together like a supplicant. 'I am Richard Fitz-Warren, steward of Ravenstow, and this is our constable, Michel de Bec . . .'

Guyon tightened his lips, but forced himself to listen and look polite as he was introduced one by one to all the members of the group. It was always politic to remember names, since it was a valuable asset when it came to handling their owners, but it gave him cause to wonder what was amiss that the steward should come out to greet them instead of the hostess herself and then keep them here in the wind-knifed bailey, drivelling of matters that could wait.

Glancing briefly beyond the men while he made acknow-ledgement, he noticed a woman hurrying from the forebuild-ing towards them, her manner obviously agitated. Her cloak was fur-lined and her rose-coloured gown shimmered beneath it as she moved. Her braids were a handspan thick and lustrous as jet.

'The lady Alicia,' his father said softly, causing Guyon momentarily to divert his gaze and eye him sharply instead.

'Thank you, FitzWarren,' she said curtly on arrival. 'I know that you have done your best, but it might have been better to bring our guests within and serve them spiced wine instead of freezing them to death out here with one of your sermons!' And then she turned to Miles and Guyon and smiled with her mouth, but not her eyes. 'I apologise for our lack. The more I try, the more caltrops seem to get thrown in my path. Come inside, I pray you.'

'Is there something wrong, my lady?' Miles asked, for it was plain that her mind was preoccupied, and it was not just the cold that was making her face white with strain.

Alicia drew breath to deny, but changed her mind and let

27

it out on a disarming, shrugged sigh. 'Nothing of great import, my lords. The guests are squabbling; the cook has just tipped boiling lard all over the spit boy and the manchet bread is burned; the maids don't know their heads from their heels; my steward when told to baulk you, keeps you standing in the ward in the sleeting rain as I am doing now; and to season the stew, my daughter has taken fright and run off heaven knows where. Otherwise, everything is as normal as you would expect for a wedding so quickly arranged.'

Miles stifled a grin at her wry summary. Guyon started to ask a question, but the words were driven from his mind as the white bratch bitch gave a bark of antagonistic joy and sprang from his side to hurtle across the ward towards a girl who was trying to slink unnoticed around the side of the forebuilding, and would have succeeded were it not for the dog.

The cat that was coiled around her shoulders became a spiked arch of erect orange fur, claws far-splayed, topaz eyes blazing, deep growls rumbling up from her throat. The bitch launched herself across the ward at the girl, who over-balanced as she struck and sat down on the muddy, noisome gravel of the bailey floor. A white-tipped feline paw flashed. Blood sprang to the accompaniment of a horrified yelp. The cat leaped over the dog, avoiding the belated snap of her teeth, whisked around the forebuilding, through the legs of a startled guard and on into the keep.

Hampered by her gown, Judith struggled to rise. A swift glance around made her wish that she had been knocked unconscious. The servants present in the bailey, grooms and guards and kitchen maids on errands were gawping in horrified delight. FitzWarren's stare was a study in open-mouthed, pop-eyed shock. Her mother's face as she bore down upon her was set like a stone. Someone sniggered. She closed her eyes, decided that shutting out the situation was not going to make it go away and opened them again upon a neatly built greying man of middle years who had overtaken

Alicia and had a hand beneath her elbow, assisting her to stand.

'I take this for an omen. You and my son are bound to fight like cat and dog and scandalize the entire neighbourhood!' Miles chuckled.

Judith gaped at him stupidly without the wit to respond. Her father would have beaten her senseless with the buckle end of his belt.

'No more than you and mama ever did!' a younger man retorted amiably, appearing beside them, his fingers gripped around the white dog's collar as she strove, forepaws flailing, to pursue her quarry into the keep. His glance flickered between his father and the wide-eyed frightened child and settled on the latter. 'It is my fault,' he owned with a smile. 'Cadi's still a pup and has yet to learn her manners.'

Judith lowered her lids. He was beautiful and unreal. A courtier, a gilded image with a voice as smooth as dark mead. Her uncle Robert was handsome and smooth too, and rotten to the core beneath the gilding. The wind knifed across the bailey. She shivered and her mother bustled forward, directing FitzWarren to his duties and hustling her daughter away to the bower and Agnes to have the ravages of her escapade repaired.

Miles smiled tolerantly at Alicia's chagrin when she returned to the hall to see to the comfort of her guests. 'It is already to be an irregular wedding. I am sure that Guyon's memory of his first encounter with his intended will remain unblurred for the rest of his life.'

Alicia cast a glance over her shoulder to where Guyon was giving the dog into the temporary care of one of his knights, then looked back at Miles. 'I think you are laughing at me, my lord.'

'Yes.'

Her mouth began to curve. She straightened it. 'Judith is nervous of this match. Tonight she will be a wife, when this morning she was a child.'

29

Miles dropped the humour. He could see that Alicia was worried. 'Guyon has a sister and nieces and is by no means green about women,' he said.

'So we hear,' Alicia replied a trifle sharply and then lifted her shoulders. 'And no surprise when you consider his looks and the ways of the court.'

'I am not at court now, my lady,' Guyon said in her ear.

Alicia spun round, stifling a gasp and had to crane her neck to look into his face. He was smiling, but his eyes were cool. 'You need not fear. I promise I will treat her with every respect and courtesy.'

'Judith is young, but she is quick to learn and quite capable of managing a household. If she appeared in a bad light just now, it is because she has been unsettled by her father's death and this sudden change in her situation.'

In other words, Guyon thought wryly, she was a resentful, frightened little girl who would take a deal of delicate handling if anything was to be salvaged from the morass.

The wine arrived, and with it Hugh d'Avrenches, Earl of Chester, thus sparing Guyon the need to make Alicia a reply.

'It is bound to be difficult at first,' Miles murmured softly to her as Guyon lent a relieved ear to what his neighbour had to say concerning the Welsh clans of the region. 'Given a conventional arrangement, there would have been the time we all need.'

'Given convention,' she said with a sidelong look at Guyon, 'there would have been no arrangement at all, would there?'

Lost for a reply, Miles lifted his cup and drank.

Guyon looked at the girl to whom he had just bound himself in Ravenstow's freezing, dark chapel, his vows committing him to her protection for the rest of his life, no matter how short that might now be. Her own voice making the responses had been faint and tremulous and more than once swallowed in tears.

He was aware of the daggers in men's eyes knifing the fine

woollen cloth of his wedding tunic. Arnulf of Pembroke had barely been civil in greeting; Walter de Lacey had been sneeringly hostile, slinking around the edge of Guyon's vision like a lone wolf.

Judith had her face turned obediently towards him now, awaiting the sacrificial kiss of tradition, a freckled, pale oval with high, flat cheekbones that gave a distinctly tilted cat's expression to her eyes which were a peculiar mingling of brown upon grey like spated water.

Oh God, he thought, what have I sold myself into? Most likely an early grave was the immediate tart response from the cynical side of his mind. He slid his arm around her waist, feeling her rigid and trembling beneath the glowing green damask, a grown woman's gown hanging incongruously on her thin, child's frame, and knew that he could no more bed with her tonight than he could with one of his nieces.

He kissed her on the cheek as he would a vassal, the touch brief and impersonal. Her skin smelled faintly of herbal soap, her hair of the rosemary and camomile in which it had been washed for the wedding.

Judith shuddered at the contact and Guyon immediately released her. She choked down her terror and turned with him to receive the congratulations of the guests and witnesses, few in number because of the hasty arrangements, but seeming to her a claustrophobic press of enormity.

The whole thing was a nightmare endured through a fog. Now and then the mist would lift to reveal a sharply coloured tableau with herself bound helpless at its centre. The awful moment when the dog had sent her flying, her entrance into the chapel, the faces turned expectantly towards her with their myriad expressions, all of them stamped with speculation and now, clearly, she could see her own hand resting upon her husband's dark sleeve, the twin rings of Welsh gold proclaiming his ownership. She was as much his property now as his horse or that dog, to be used as he chose, abused as he chose.

The mist thickened again. She made all the proper responses, accepted the felicitations with a smile, behaved impeccably, her facade of mechanical propriety carrying her through the nightmare that had yet to begin, and her blind eyes did not see the look that Walter de Lacey cast over herself and Guyon as they walked past.

The guests mingled in the great hall. Below the dais they danced in honour of the newly wedded couple. Guyon watched his wife tread a measure upon the arm of one of Ravenstow's neighbours. Ralph of Thorneyford was another of de Belleme's vassals, a thoroughly disagreeable, parsimonious old ferret who, according to Alicia, was only here in order to eat and drink at another's expense. Being as his borders marched with Ravenstow's on the immediate Welsh boundary, it had been necessary to invite him lest he take offence. His wife, apparently, was a dumb half-wit and left at home tended by her women. At least, Guyon thought half-smiling, if Ralph of Thorneyford was only here to eat and drink and escape his wife, he was a deal more welcome than certain others claiming the right of hospitality at his wedding.

he dance progressed and Judith was passed onto the arm of Arnulf of Pembroke. He had skin like a pitted stone and features similarly appealing. Guyon winced at the knowledge that the man was now his uncle-by-marriage. Arnulf de Montgomery owned none of Robert's charisma or genius, more a kind of low, dull cunning. Not possessing the inventiveness to scheme, he was sufficiently shrewd to attach himself to the schemes of others if there was benefit to himself — a man to be watched from the eye corners, frank confrontation not being his style. But how did one look before and behind and to the side at one and the same time?

Arnulf of Pembroke swept his niece into the clutch of Walter de Lacey waiting at the end of the line. The younger man pulled her against his whippy strength, caught her wrist and turned her around. Judith's face wore a fixed, mammetlike smile. His hand lingered on her waist and he murmured something against her ear.

'More oil than you'd find in an entire olive grove,' said the Earl of Chester. Guyon looked round and up. Hugh d'Avrenches, also known as Hugh le Gros on account of his enormous height and girth, was quite the ugliest man Guyon had ever seen and, even now, long acquaintance had not bred the indifference of familiarity.

He had triangular eyes of a brilliant pale blue beneath which his cheeks hung like two huge, red-veined bladders. His nose was economical and hooked, his mouth small and soft with a sweet, surprisingly child-like smile, the similarity enhanced by the black gap where his two upper front teeth had once resided. He cultivated a jolly, bumbling personality to match his gross bulk and the unwary stepped in, never thinking of the dangers lurking beneath the shallows. A good friend, an implacable enemy.

'Enough to slip his feet from under him, I would say,' Guyon confirmed.

Hugh d'Avrenches folded his arms and regarded Guyon with twinkling, thoughtful eyes. 'Good soldier, though. He led a competent command on the Mon campaign.'

Guyon's lip curled. 'As I recall, he also amused himself with torture and the rape of girls not old enough to be women.'

'So?' The Earl shrugged. 'We all have our own little foibles and sometimes tortured men can be made to sing a very pretty tune.'

Guyon's nostrils flared. 'Yes,' he said without inflection.

'Oh, Christ's arse!' Chester laid an exasperated hand on Guyon's shoulder. 'Son, you're too finicky and you can't afford the luxury of principles in the present company.'

Walter de Lacey set his hands on Judith's hips and swung her round. The stiff smile on her face slipped sideways. 'I know, Hugh,' Guyon bleakly replied. 'He offered for the child himself shortly before her father was killed and he had de Belleme's sanction to the suit.'

Chester pursed his soft, small lips. 'Did he so?' he said with interest, eyeing the dancers. 'He'll bear watching then, because it doesn't look as though he's willing to concede you the victory.'

Guyon turned his gaze and narrowed it angrily. The music had finished on a flourish and Walter de Lacey had pulled Judith hard to his chest and was kissing her full and passionately on the mouth, one hand roving and probing the curve of her buttocks. Guyon muttered a terse oath, thrust his wine into the earl's hastily held out paw and stalked across the room to reclaim his bride.

'The privilege is mine, I believe,' he said quietly to de Lacey as he stepped between him and Judith. 'I would not like our other guests to grow confused as to the true identity of the bridegroom.'

De Lacey flushed at the barb and threw Guyon a fulminating glare. 'Horseplay,' he said, snarling a smile. 'Too much wine. I fear it has gone to my head.'

'Like delusions of ownership?' Guyon answered with an equally false smile. 'Mind with whom you drink.' The words were spoken softly so that only de Lacey heard, and Guyon snapped his fingers at the hesitant musicians who fumbled and then struck up a lively jig to cover whatever mild altercation had occurred. Guyon held out his arm to Judith.

She pressed her lips together and shook her head. 'I cannot dance,' she muttered from between clenched teeth. 'My lord, I . . . I think I am going to be sick.'

Her face reflected the green of her gown. Guyon took her arm and propelled her out of the hall, ignoring salacious remarks and concerned enquiries alike.

Outside it had begun to snow. Judith leaned miserably against the wall of the forebuilding, thoroughly nauseated but not quite to the point of actually vomiting. The feel of de Lacey's tongue slithering slug-like around her mouth filled her with shuddering revulsion. She could still taste him, feel his hand digging into her buttocks, forefinger slyly seeking, and the hard thrust of his pelvis against her stomach and loins.

It had been horrible. In less than three hours she had to endure that and worse in her marriage bed.

'Did he hurt you?'

She shook her head dumbly, unable to respond.

'There are always men like him,' Guyon said contemptuously. 'It was thrown down to me by way of a challenge. I am sorry that he chose to use you as his gage.'

Judith bit her lip and wished that he would go away. The snow floated down.

'You need not be afraid of me, child,' he said gently, tipping up her chin on his finger. 'I will do you no harm.'

'I am not a child!' she snarled at him gracelessly and, jerking away, sleeved her eyes and wondered if he would hit her.

'And you are not yet a woman grown,' he answered, not as a retort, but stating a fact. He touched her shoulder and felt the tremor course through her body and wondered at the treatment she had received in the past to make her this terrified. 'I know it is hard for you.'

Judith gritted her teeth at the patronizing, gentle tone. In a moment he was going to pat her head as though she were a dog. 'Do you, my lord?' she asked flatly.

'You have been forced into a match made for the purposes of others and to a partner you had not even set eyes upon before today. How should you not be afraid and resentful? I understand more than you think.'

Judith flicked him a startled look over her shoulder. Whatever she had expected, it was certainly not this candid, rueful approach. It had not occurred to her that the resentment was mutual, that he might not want her rich dower and lands and the passel of burdens that accompanied them, not least herself.

He applied gentle pressure to her shoulder with his fingertips until she turned hesitantly to face him, her heart jumping erratically in her throat.

'I said that you need not fear me for any reason . . . The bedding ceremony, it worries you?'

Judith looked down, wondering where all this was leading. She did not desire a lesson in enlightenment, no matter how kindly bestowed.

Guyon took her downcast silence for modest assent. 'The first part is something that will have to be borne. The second we can abandon. Rape has never appealed to me.'

'I . . . I know my duty my lord,' she stammered bravely.

'I have no doubt, but it would be rape all the same and I prefer the pleasure to be mutual. In your own time *fy cath fach.*' He lightly brushed a strand of hair from her cheek. She lifted her lids, eyes torn with relief and doubt.

'You truly mean that my lord?'

'I would be a fool if I did not. There is enough on your trencher already without burdening your body so young.'

Judith wiped her eyes again, impatiently. 'I am not always such a wet fish my lord, truly,' she excused. 'It is just that I was so afraid. Before you came, I almost threw myself off the headland . . . And then, when I saw you . . .' she looked at her toes. The snow whispered down. 'I was even more afraid.'

'But why?' He looked nonplussed. 'I gave you no cause, surely!'

Judith bit her lip. She could not say that she knew how a flower must feel when it turns towards the sun only to find its blaze too hot to be endured. 'I did not know what you would think of me, sprawled in the mud at your feet.'

'Unique,' he chuckled. 'No girl has ever tried to claim my attention like that before!'

As if on cue, something brushed against his legs and mewed plaintively. Before Judith could bend and scoop up her cat from the settling snow, Melyn came to her own decision and sprang with practised ease onto Guyon's shoulder, hooking her claws firmly into tunic and shirt to retain her grip. Guyon winced.

Judith caught her breath, eyes wide and dismayed.

'You live dangerously puss,' he addressed the cat, but made

no move to dislodge her and turned towards the steps. 'Your mistress values your life, but I am not necessarily of the same mind. You may keep your claws to yourself.' He looked at Judith over his unoccupied shoulder and winked. She had relaxed at his amiable tone and was even smiling slightly.

'Come,' he coaxed with a smile of his own, 'let us see what our guests think of my new fur collar.'

Alicia saw Guyon enter the hall with Judith at his side and breathed a heartfelt sigh of relief. Whatever he had said or done outside had obviously been the right thing. The rigidity had left Judith's body and her eyes had lost some of their staring terror.

'What in God's name has Guyon got on his shoulder?' Miles demanded, a laugh in his voice.

Alicia transferred her gaze and gave a cluck of amused annoyance. 'That cat has no sense of propriety whatsoever, although how she came to be there I have no idea. Usually she avoids men. They tend to kick her or bellow when she gets underfoot.'

'A good sign then.' He looked at her sidelong.

'Not necessarily. I have heard that women are particularly susceptible to your son's brand of charm. Melyn is just another she-cat bedazzled by her instincts.'

Miles grinned at the barb, but shook his head. 'Guy's reputation far outmatches his deeds,' he defended. 'I'm not saying he's as pure as the driven snow, far from it, but tales become exaggerated in the telling and part of it when at court is pure self-defence, the King being what he is.'

Alicia made an irritated gesture. 'Pay no heed to me, my lord. Only this morning, I rebuked Agnes for listening to gossip and here I am no better. It is only a mother hen fussing over her chick.' She bent her head and suddenly resembled nothing so much as a wilting flower. The rose hue of her damask gown had reflected a false warmth into her cheeks and, close as he was now, Miles realized that in fact she was waxen, with grey smudges beneath her fine eyes.

'Guyon will treat her with all honour,' he placated gently, leading her to a bench set into the thickness of the wall near a hide-covered arrowslit.

'I am sure he will.' Alicia paused, looked at Miles and suddenly blurted her main concern. 'But she is young and inexperienced. Even if more than half the tales told of Guyon are moonshine, that still leaves a wealth of living in the other part and he is a full twelve years older . . . a man. What do I do if she comes screaming to me on the morrow that she will have no more ado with him? It will wring my heart. I remember leaning over the garderobe, sick with revulsion and praying to die. Like her I was sixteen, a little more wise in the ways of the world, but hopelessly unprepared for a stranger's violent invasion of my body.'

'Then Guy's experience is surely all to the good. He will not force her and, as you have seen, he is capable of charming the birds – or cats – down from the trees if he so chooses.' He frowned at her. 'Have you said anything to Judith to give her a distaste for coupling?'

'I am not stupid. More harm than good would come of that, although I fear her attitude has been tainted by her father's behaviour. Slaps and curses and drunken rough handling have not led her to view marriage in a very favourable light. She may find joy, and I hope she does, but it is a fickle world.'

'You have little cause to like men, either of you,' Miles murmured compassionately.

'I do not need your pity, my lord,' Alicia said, suddenly proud. Her head came up and her eyes went to Judith where she stood at Guyon's side. The tawny hair had taken on a fiery glint from the glow of the candles and, with that half-smile on her face and the way her head was tilted, Alicia saw Judith's father for a fleeting instant most clearly. 'No,' she said, her voice hard and steady, her lips curving at some secret triumph. 'Do not pity me. I have had my moment of glory and it pays for all that Maurice ever did to me. My concern is with Judith now. I can see that she has a leopard by the tail and must either tame it or become its prey. I know her capable, her blood dictates it so, but she is young for the challenge, perhaps too young.'

Miles gave up. She was speaking in riddles and acting very strangely, shifting from uncertainty and chagrin to smiling defiance and back to uncertainty in less than the flicker of a candle flame. He wished that Christen or Emma were here; they would have known immediately what to say or do, but the former was beyond him forever and the latter was summoned to the court by her husband.

'I'll fetch wine,' he muttered, and went to accost a servant.

Alicia drew several deep breaths and sternly took a grip on herself, aware that Miles was regarding her as he might a skittish horse. If she gained that kind of reputation, she would be shunned or sold off in marriage and then locked up, conveniently labelled insane like Ralph of Thorneyford's poor wife.

Miles returned with the wine. She took it from him and looked out over the assembled guests. 'I am not usually hysterical,' she said ruefully.

'I did not think that you were.'

'Nevertheless you panicked.' Her mouth twitched. She darted him a glance.

Miles grinned and rubbed the back of his neck. 'A little,' he admitted.

Alicia sipped the wine and set it down. She needed a clear head, for as hostess she was required to mingle among the guests and there was still the bedding ceremony to be organized. The humour left her face at thought of that, but she controlled her movements. Her eyes roved the hall. Melyn had settled herself comfortably around Guyon's neck, her eyes half-slitted, totally secure. He had his hand lightly around Judith's waist. She was saying something to him. His head was cocked attentively, but his eyes were elsewhere, sifting and assessing, paring beyond the disguise of flesh and bone, coldly narrowing on Walter de Lacey and Arnulf of Pembroke even as he answered Judith with a smile. Alicia shivered and offered up a silent prayer. A leopard by the tail indeed.

Judith stood obediently calm, raising and lowering her limbs as Agnes dictated until she stood naked in the bridal chamber that had belonged to her parents. The bed had been aired and made up with crisp new linen sheets. Dried herbs to perfume the clothes and promote fertility had been liberally strewn over the bed and the priest had sprinkled holy water everywhere. The droplets on her body made her shiver. Agnes paused in brushing down her hair and, clucking, draped a bedrobe around her shoulders.

The female guests, few though they were, crooned and chooked around her, turning the room into a fowl run. Judith stared at the wall, feeling as numb as part of the furniture. Someone giggled a piece of advice in her ear. Someone else of a more practical mind thrust a pot of dead nettle salve into her hand, an ointment used to soothe the female passage after childbed and other rough treatment.

'I won't need this,' she said and looked round in surprise at the laughter. Fear returned to claim her, and uncertainty. She did not know if she could trust Guyon. What if he went back on his word? What if he used her as brutally as her father had been wont to use her mother? Men lied. An involuntary whimper escaped between her clenched teeth.

Anxiously, Alicia tried to comfort her, but the curtain was flurried aside and the room was suddenly full of men, most of them less than sober, their jokes bawdy, crude and raucous. Judith withdrew into the fastness of a far corner of her mind. She did not hear the jests. She did not feel them removing her bedrobe and tugging her to the bed, nor the cup of spiced hippocras that was pressed into her hand to replace the pot of salve. The pink silk of her mother's embrace was a haven. She clung to it desperately, but it was abruptly torn away with a noise very much like a suppressed sob. Sounds faded to silence. She stared blankly at the wall. The cup of hippocras shook in her hand.

Guyon leaned over and gently removed the cup. Judith blinked and refocused. Like herself he was naked, his torso lean but powerfully muscled and marked with minor battle scars. Her gaze skimmed over and fled from the curling mat of dark hair at his groin and its nestling occupants. He set the cup down beside the pot of salve, quirking a brow at the latter, then swung on his heel and padded to the curtain. She heard him speak a command in Welsh and then an endearment and her interest sharpened.

'Cadi might hate cats, but she makes an excellent guard dog,' he explained with a grin as he returned to the bed. 'Not that she'll bite anyone, but she'll greet them with such enthusiasm that we'll have warning enough of eavesdroppers.'

Judith smiled wanly. Her eyes flickered again to his crotch. Guyon sought out the bedrobe they had pulled from him, put it back on and handed Judith her own from an arm's length distance.

Judith struggled clumsily into the garment, feeling all fingers and thumbs. Aware that his proximity was the reason for her nervous fumbling, Guyon paced over to the narrow window and pulled back the hide covering to look out on a slit of whirling white darkness.

'I meant what I said, *cath fach*,' he murmured without turning round. 'You need not fear me.'

The logs in the hearth crackled and settled. 'I am not afraid,' Judith lied valiantly, clutching the bedrobe across her breasts.

'No?' He gave her a half glance over his shoulder.

'Well, only a little. I know mama and the others meant well, but they overwhelmed me with their good advice.'

'Such as pots of salve,' he contributed gravely and, pinning back the hide, turned around. She was watching him anxiously, like a dog desiring desperately to please. The tawny hair tumbled over the coverlet and took on red–gold highlights from the fire, and was really quite attractive. Her eyes were as grey and brown as the muddy water churning beneath the battlements and equally full of currents and undercurrents. A veil of honey-gold freckles dappled her face and throat and, for an infinitesimal moment, she reminded Guyon of someone else. The impression, however, was too fleeting to be caught and she moved her head, changing the play of light on the angles of bone.

'Mama is skilled in herb lore,' she said.

'So it would seem,' he said drily. 'Do you have the same competence?'

'Mama has taught me what she knows.'

He poured himself some wine from the flagon left on the chest and, returning to the bed with it, seated himself on the end and considered her. 'So if I cut my arm open with a dagger, what would you do?'

'Self inflicted? I would dose you with valerian to rectify your disordered wits!' she answered pertly, and then at his silence, sobered and lowered her lids, thinking that she had gone too far. The sound of his appreciative chuckle snapped her eyes wide.

'Nay, inflicted by the blade of my wife's tongue!' he laughed. 'Which I hazard is as keen as a sword once un-sheathed!'

Judith looked at him warily, but saw nothing in his face to contradict the honesty of his amusement. 'If it was a deep wound,' she said, 'I would sprinkle it with powdered comfrey root to ease the bleeding, then stitch it and bind it with a piece of mouldy bread.'

'Mouldy bread!'

'It is a remedy handed down from Grandma FitzOsbern and it usually works. Deep wounds heal cleanly without going proud or filling with pus. The main danger is from the stiffening sickness. If the wound was only a scratch, I would clean it with water in which pine needles had been steeped and then smear it with honey and bind as necessary.'

Guyon studied her as she spoke so earnestly and fought a

battle to keep his amusement from showing on his face. In itself, the information was interesting and her obviously detailed knowledge showed that Alicia was justified in commending her daughter's skill. It was just so incongruous that this slender, willow-twig of a girl with all her innocence and uncertainty should hold forth like a grey-haired matron of sedentary years.

The incongruity continued to deepen as he further explored her knowledge of matters domestic. He learned the best way to salt beans and hang sausages, exactly how many pine needles were required to dye homespun cloth a rich shade of golden-red, the correct ingredients to make a venison ragout, how to buy spices without being cheated. He almost choked on his wine when she began to explain to him the best way to go about honing a sword.

'Your mother taught you that too!'

'Of course not!' she retorted, tone indignant now that she had gained a spark of confidence. 'De Bec showed me last winter when we were snowed in. He taught me how to fight with a poniard too . . . Are you all right my lord?'

Guyon wiped his streaming eyes, speechless between laughter and coughing. 'Jesu!' he croaked at last. 'When I said that this marriage would kill me, I never thought that you would be the hazard!'

'My lord?'

He waved her away as she leaned towards him, her face full of concern. 'Do you number riding among your many talents too?' he asked after a moment, the residue of mirth quivering in his voice.

Judith shook her head regretfully. 'No my lord. Mama prefers to travel by litter and papa said that it was a waste of time for a girl to master a saddle when she should be at her distaff. I know a little, but not enough to venture out on more than the most docile rouncey, but I am willing to learn.'

'All to the good.' He wiped his eyes again. 'There are

several estates in my honours that are not negotiable by litter.'

'You intend taking me, my lord?'

He lay full length on the bed, plumping up the bolster and pillows to support his back. Judith moved away, but with more wariness than fear. 'My parents always went together and the people have become used to the arrangement. Besides,' he added, bending one elbow behind his head, lips twitching, 'there is nothing quite like the imminent visit of a chatelaine to set a keep humming with industry.'

Judith stirred uneasily. 'My lord, I fear I will not be equal to the burden you lay on me.'

'If you can sharpen a sword and dagger-fight your way out of a corner, you are wholly capable of handling anything else I ask of you!'

She shook her head doubtfully. True, she could manage Ravenstow efficiently. It had been drilled into her without surcease since her third year day, but to venture further, tackle people and situations she did not know, that was daunting. It was easy for him to speak. He was a marcher lord with access to the royal ear, his experience far beyond hers.

'Trust me,' he said, seeing the expressions fleet upon her face like the eddies of a river current, twisting in tidal flow, and kissed her cheek lightly as he might have done to a child. The gesture magically bolstered her flagging resolve and she sat up, her lips thinning at being so obviously patronised.

Her bedrobe gaped open. Guyon flickered his glance over the slight mounds of her breasts, scarcely raised from her narrow rib-cage. Judith blushed, the colour scorching her face and throat, and clutched the garment together.

There was an uncomfortable silence, Guyon biting his tongue to avoid being unkind. He would need to be desperate before his loins would fill at sight of her meagre flesh.

'Do you have a mistress, my lord?'

'What!' Once more he found himself gaping at her, slack-jawed, completely thrown off balance. 'What kind of question is that!'

'Oh, do not be angry with me, my lord!' She held out a supplicating hand. The fingers were long and fine-boned and not at all the hands of a child. 'It is only that I do not want to make any foolish mistakes. Mama once threw out one of my father's women because she did not know he had taken a fancy to her and raised her from the kitchens to his bed. He beat mama nearly witless when he found out.'

'God in heaven,' Guyon said, lip curling with intense disgust. 'Your father was a fool to end all fools. I am surprised that with all your knowledge of simples, one of you did not seek to salt his food with monkshood.'

'And have uncle Robert assure our welfare? How long do you think we would live?'

Guyon shook his head and finished the wine. 'No, *cath fach*, since you ask, I do not have a mistress. We parted last month. The borders are no longer safe for her to travel in her father's wool train and, being Welsh, she would not be constrained within one of my keeps.' He shrugged and looked down at his hands, remembering them lost in the black waterfall of Rhosyn's hair. 'A marcher lord and a hill-bred girl. Such matches are at the most ephemeral. It never was.'

Judith swallowed, wishing that she could recall the question and jail it behind her teeth.

'Even if Rhosyn had agreed to live a Norman life, there are still such things as courtesy and discretion,' he said after a moment. 'It is neither considerate nor far-sighted to have a mistress and a wife beneath the same roof. Grief is bound to come of it.'

Judith nodded sensibly. It never occurred to her to think that Guyon would be faithful. Her father had been as lecherous and indiscriminate in his ruttings as a dunghill cock, the friends and vassals who dined at his board, the same. Discretion was not a word they knew. Gratitude was an emotion that Judith seldom felt.

45

'You are very patient with me, my lord,' she murmured, lowering her lids.

'Well, I learned patience with women in a very hard school,' he replied, the easy humour back in his voice. 'My sister has three girls, all of them hoydens – not in front of their mother of course. Em would kill them if she knew the half of it. And Rhosyn's daughter, Eluned, is not far behind them in devilry!'

Judith looked at the thick white candle on the pricket, watching the yellow flicker of the flame. He spoke with such obvious affection of his womenfolk that another shard of fear was broken from the frozen lump at her core and dissolved away.

'Will you tell me about your family my lord? The marriage was arranged so quickly that I am very ignorant.'

Guyon obliged. It was safer ground by far than talk of mistresses, or so in his ignorance he thought. Indeed, all went sweetly until he spoke of his half-sister Emma and how she had married a royal official. From there, the conversation drifted into the murkier waters surrounding life at court.

'De Bec says that the King . . .' Judith caught herself just in time from committing another *faux pas*. As foul in his preferences as a blackamoor's back passage was not a safe remark.

Guyon had not missed her sudden dismayed check. His lips twitched, for he could well guess the reason. Rufus's tendencies were common guardroom scandal and one did not learn how to sharpen a sword and fight with a poniard without ingesting much of the former.

It was not really amusing, not when the King, who was short and scarlet of feature, preferred his partners to be of above average height, lean and dark-avised. On more than one occasion the very personal royal jewels had stood in imminent danger of severe damage by dint of Guyon's knee. That had been in the early days before he discovered the amicable company of the ambitious Prince Henry and that the occasional night spent carousing with him amid women of doubtful character and wine of opposite excellence, was sufficient to dampen Rufus's ardour and send him in pursuit of more cooperative game.

'. . . De Bec says that the King spends more money on clothes in one week than mama would be allowed to spend in an entire year.' Judith amended, regarding him anxiously. He did not appear to have noticed her near mistake, so stumblingly corrected, but something had caused his eyes to narrow and his jaw to clench.

'Not necessarily,' he said and then chuckled. 'Rufus likes to think that he spends more on his wardrobe than other men, but he is outwitted by his own vanity. Last time I was at court my brother-in-law, who was dressing him, fetched him a pair of gilded leather boots. Rufus asked how much they cost, so Richard told him. Rufus was furious and demanded that he go away and find a pair that were worth a full mark of silver, claiming that those he had been offered were fit only for shovelling dung.' His laughter deepened. 'I do not tell a tale like Richard. God, he had the tavern in uproar!'

'What happened?'

'Richard duly went away, found a red pair with green fringing that were thoroughly hideous and cost less than the first pair and took them to the King, telling him that they were the most expensive boots he could lay hands on.'

'And Rufus swallowed the bait?'

'Well, he paraded round all day in them, thinking himself a peacock and looking like a Southwark pimp and Richard pocketed the profit. God knows if the tale has got back to him yet. I should hate to be in Richard's *boots* when it does!'

Judith made a face at his weak pun and then giggled, the sound a delicious feminine tumble of notes, as surprising to him as the delicate strength of her hands.

'Tell me about de Bec,' Guyon said at length when they had ceased laughing at the royal vanity. 'How long has he been here at Ravenstow?'

'He came not long after the main keep began to go up, the year before I was born, I think. Papa was away fighting the Welsh and it was mama who employed him.'

'And he has been her man ever since?'

'Where it has been possible. If he had interfered when my father beat her, or me, he would have been straightaway dismissed and he is too old to travel the roads with his sword for hire.' She gave him a look of swift concern. 'You do not intend to turn him off, my lord? He is most loyal and he knows this keep better than any man alive . . . saving my uncle Robert of course.'

'Of course,' he said grimly, and then, 'No, I do not intend turning him off, not unless he proves unsatisfactory to my own assessment. Seventeen years of service are not to be dismissed lightly.' And then he laughed with something less than amusement. 'I am not so sure, however, that I cannot manage without the services of that steward.'

Judith tossed her head. 'Oh FitzWarren's all right. Dry as dust and too full of his own importance by half, but he's loyal and very efficient. He can conjure a feast out of nothing – I've seen him do it, and his accounts are meticulous.'

'I am sure they are. It just troubles me as to where he obtains the wealth to clothe himself in scarlet sarcenet.'

'It was my father's, new last Candlemas. He and FitzWarren were much of a height. Mama gave it to him after the funeral. You can see the account rolls on the morrow if you want . . . Oh, do you read and write?'

'Both. Do you?'

'A little my lord.' Actually, it was considerably more than a little, gleaned from the household scribe on cold winter days and polished in private moments to an astute skill, but most men preferred their women to dwell in ignorance, or at least in more ignorance than themselves.

Guyon's own tuition had been somewhat more regulated and he had a particularly keen eye for tallies and accountings and the juggling of numbers. It was a craft that fascinated him and which he had already put to good use in wringing the marriage relief from his vassals.

'After the hunt tomorrow you can show me – I don't want FitzWarren standing at my shoulder watching the direction of my eyes and quill, even if he is honest.' He glanced towards the shutters. '. . . If there is a hunt with all this snow blowing about.'

Judith stretched and yawned. The wine had made her eyes heavy and it was very late.

Guyon glanced at her. He was not averse to the prospect of sleep himself, for the day had been long and fraught and the morrow seemed set to continue the same. He leaned over and pinched out the night candle and in the darkness removed his bedrobe. Fabric slid silkily against skin as Judith shed her own garment and burrowed down beneath the covers.

'*Nos da cath fach*,' he said compassionately.

'*Nos da fy gwr*,' she replied, her own Welsh impeccable.

Guyon mentally added the skill of language to her other numerous talents and wondered mazily to himself how in God's name Maurice FitzRoger had managed to beget a child like this, a silk purse from a pig's ear. His last thought before sleep claimed him and not to be remembered in the morning, was that perhaps Maurice had not begotten her at all.

CHAPTER 5

JUDITH BLEARILY OPENED her eyes in response to the persistent thrust of a small, cold nose against her cheek and a thunderous vibration in her ear. Opal-agate eyes peered into hers and then blinked slowly. Melyn uttered a prrt of greeting, barred orange tail waving jauntily aloft. Judith groaned and buried her face in the pillow. There was an ache behind her eyes that spoke of an excess of wine and an insufficiency of sleep. The room was lit by weak grey light penetrating the membrane screen across the arrow slit. Given the time of year, it must be well beyond the hour of first mass which meant that there was no time left to turn over and go back to sleep.

Judith pushed Melyn aside, gathered her hair and sat up. The cat stalked across the pillow to the turned brown back, sniffed the rumpled black hair and then patted a playful sheathed paw on the man's face.

'Rhosyn,' Guyon murmured, opened his eyes and received a cold, wet kiss that dispelled all dreaming illusions. 'God's blood!' he swore and jerked upright, seeking his non-existent sword – a man did not come thus armed to his marriage bed. The cat, having achieved her purpose, leaped nimbly to the floor and commenced an inquisitive investigation of Guyon's baggage.

Her father would have hurled the flagon at Melyn, splattering dregs and sharp fragments everywhere. Guyon uttered several foul epithets and, scraping his fingers through his hair, glared withheld murder at Melyn's graceful form. Judith decided that he was suffering from her own malaise and best

50

left in peace to gather his wits ... except that this morning there was no time.

She sought her bedrobe and put it on. Guyon continued to swear softly and pressed his face into his hands. Tactfully, Judith left the bed, scooped up Melyn and went to the arrowslit.

'It is not snowing now, my lord,' she remarked. 'And the clouds are high. The hunt can be held. We are short of fresh meat and it will prevent quarrels from developing. There was a terrible fight last Christmas when mama's niece got married. The groom's cousin lost three fingers and an ear and the hall was completely wrecked.'

Guyon surfaced slowly from the depths. He was not usually a sluggard, but the past weeks had drained him and the hippocras had been a potent soporific. 'God forbid,' he said with a wan smile and stretched.

Judith judged that it was now safe to return to the bed, although she deposited Melyn at a distance. 'Watch Walter de Lacey today,' she warned. 'I suppose you must know that he offered for me before papa died and he is one of uncle Robert's friends.'

'I did not think your uncle Robert had any,' he riposted and began to assemble his clothing. 'Do not worry, *cath fach*. I know well he is one of the *Cwmni Annwn*. I will tread most softly.'

'The what?'

'Hounds of hell,' he translated, tugging on his shirt. 'The wild hunt. Appropriate, would you not say?'

It was a barrier, the lightness. His father would have recognised it immediately and cut brusquely beneath it. Judith stood blocked, floundering, unsure as to the best course to follow. She watched him dress. He had laid aside his wedding finery for a warm, fur-trimmed tunic of green plaid wool, thick chausses and tough, calf-high boots.

Melyn leaped onto the bed. Judith's eyes were momentarily distracted to the cat where she had settled to wash herself on

51

the white linen undersheet. White as the snow that had fallen in the night. Pristine. Unstained.

'My lord!' Panic gripped her voice. Any moment now they were likely to be disturbed by their guests and the first task of the morning would be the display of that sheet to all and sundry, stained with the sanguine proof of her virginity . . . or lack of it.

Startled, Guyon left off buckling his belt and stared round. 'What's the matter?'

'The bed . . . the sheet. They will think that I am impure, or else that you were unable.'

He gaped at her.

'There is no blood!' she almost shrieked at him.

Enlightenment tardily dawned and with it a glint of amusement. 'Oh, I see what you mean. I don't make a habit of deflowering virgins.' He shot her a sour grin. 'I wonder which choice they would settle upon.' Pushing Melyn to one side, he drew his meat knife from the sheath at his belt and, forcing up his left sleeve, made a shallow cut upon the inside of his forearm. As the blood welled in a thin, bright line, he smeared it over the centre of the sheet.

'Self-inflicted,' he remarked with wry humour. 'I beg a cup of valerian to mend my disordered wits, and a pot of honey to smear this slit in my hide.'

Judith handed him the jar of nettle salve. 'This will serve just as well for the nonce.'

'And have all the women condemn me for a clumsy oaf and risk your mother's extreme displeasure? I have a reputation to keep up, you know.' His tone was self-mocking.

Judith blushed, for she had not thought of how others would misconstrue the finger marks in the ointment.

'It has stopped bleeding now anyway.' He pushed down his sleeve and grinned at her. 'I daresay it is not the last wound I'll take defending a lady's honour.'

Before Judith could decide how to reply, there came a warning whine from without the curtain, followed by a series of joyful barks and a human squeal of indignation. On the bed Melyn became a stiff horseshoe of growling orange fur.

Guyon tugged a strand of Judith's hair, gave her a conspiratorial wink and went to draw aside the curtain and wish good morning to his mother-by-marriage, the small entourage of female wedding guests in her wake and the fat maid bearing a ewer of warm, scented water.

Cadi greeted her master boisterously. He commanded her down and she obeyed somewhat reluctantly, her forepaws dancing the floor, her whole body tense and quivering with precariously subdued enthusiasm. Alicia returned his courtesy coolly and entered the room. Beside her another, older woman, a cousin or some such as he remembered, was fastidiously brushing white dog hairs from her dark blue gown.

Alicia looked from the bloodied sheet to her daughter who was clutching the salve pot in her hand. Judith flashed a dismayed glance at Guyon, caught her underlip in her teeth and put it quickly down as though it were red hot. Alicia's mouth tightened.

Melyn, surrounded by a gaggle of avid, wide-eyed strangers, and disliking the atmosphere, leaped off the bed. Her movement was immediately spotted by Cadi who took a flying lunge at her with a yelp of savage delight. Guyon stumbled into Alicia. Agnes shrieked. The ewer flew out of her hands as the dog flung past and a warm deluge christened the two women immediately in front of her. Screams and squawks rent the air, intermingled with a cat's snarls and the hysterical barking of the dog. Melyn streaked for the door and, Cadi hot on her heels, scorched up the thick arras curtain to cling yowling at the top, claws fiercely dug.

Guyon seized Cadi's collar, drew breath to speak, saw from the basilisk glares turned his way that it would be a waste of time and beat a hasty retreat with the bitch to the haven of male company breakfasting below stairs.

Judith, tears of laughter brimming in her eyes, went to coax Melyn down from her precarious refuge.

The breaking of fast was an uncomfortable affair, fortunately not prolonged because the men were eager to be out on the trail of the boar that Ravenstow's chief huntsman assured them lurked in the forests on the western side.

The bride tardily appeared as the men were preparing to leave, her manner much subdued, the glances she cast at her husband swift and furtive. When the bloodied bridal sheet was displayed by the women, she almost lost control. Her narrow shoulders heaved and she covered her face briefly with her veil while she mastered herself. Alicia's arm went protectively around her daughter's shoulders and she threw Guyon a look full of glacial murder.

'Why was Judith weeping, were you clumsy with her?' Miles asked disapprovingly of his son as they slowed their mounts to enter a patch of bramble-tangled woodland. Ahead of them the dogs could be heard barking as they trailed the rank scent of boar.

Guyon looked indignant. 'Credit me with a little more experience than that. The blasted wench was laughing. I ought to drown that cat of hers!'

Miles raised his brows, justifiably baffled and more than a little worried, remembering Alicia's fear of the previous evening, his own reassurances and then the look on her face this morning. If eyes could have killed, his son would have been a dead man and himself frozen to stone.

Guyon regaled him with the details of the morning's disaster and Miles's wayward eyebrows disappeared into his hair.

'So there we were,' Guyon said ruefully, 'Judith with the pot of salve in her hand, not daring to look at me lest she laugh, and the sheet all bloody and my mother-in-law itching to geld me . . .' he paused on a breath and turned in the saddle as the constable de Bec rode up to join them on his sturdy dun.

His manner was tangibly cool, his mouth tight within its

neat grey bracket of beard. He too had witnessed Judith's struggle for composure in the hall and had been filled with a protective anger, at first so hot that he had almost enquired of lady Alicia whether she desired her new son-by-marriage to lie in a premature, accidental grave. Almost, but not quite, for as he had been gulping down his bread and wine and preparing to leave, he could have sworn that Judith had smiled at him, a sparkle of mischief in her eyes. Girls distraught to the point of tears did not do such things.

Besides, he had reasoned, if Guyon died, the King would only select another man to fill the position, probably of far worse moral fibre and, when he thought about it rationally, the new lord had only had his right and seemed in public gently disposed towards the child.

'Judith tells me that you have been teaching her to hone a blade and use it,' Guyon remarked pleasantly to the constable.

De Bec rubbed his fist over his beard. 'She asked me so I showed her, my lord,' he said defensively. 'Nothing wrong in knowing a bit about weapons, especially here in the marches.'

'No,' Guyon agreed, mouth twitching at de Bec's stony expression and his father's sudden wide stare. 'Did her parents share your opinion?'

'Lord Maurice had no idea. Lady Alicia had her reservations, but there were times when mistress Judith was wild for to hold and a little free rein with a guiding hand behind it steadied her down with more success than threats and a beating.'

'Nursemaid as well as constable,' Guyon needled gently. 'Devotion to duty indeed.'

De Bec glinted him a look. 'Nearer the truth than your jesting knows,' he replied. 'I was the one who delivered her into her mother's arms and severed the cord that bound them. Lady Judith was born a month before her time, in a charcoal burner's hut half way across Cannock Chase with myself and Agnes in attendance. It is fortunate that I'm a shepherd's son and seen enough ewes drop a lamb to know

55

what to do. Agnes was about as useful as a headless duck. Stupid besom couldn't stand the sight of blood, so it was all left to me.' He sleeved a drip from his nose and his lips curled wryly.

'I suppose that since then I have always felt responsible for mistress Judith. She is the daughter I never had the opportunity to settle down and sire.' There was far more to it than that, but he was not about to recount the words that lady Alicia had screamed in the extremity of her labour. They belonged to secrecy. Locked in his mind and the key far-flung.

His look narrowed on Guyon. 'Do not be deceived by what you saw yesterday. Mistress Judith can be a hellion. Tread very softly my lord, or you may wake up one morn to find yourself gelded.'

'She is maiden still,' Guyon said quietly. 'I do not have a taste for raping children. The blood on the sheets is from my arm.'

De Bec cleared his throat. 'It is your right,' he muttered gruffly into his chest.

'And so it is,' Guyon answered, tone neutral. 'But one I exercise at my peril. I hazard that if I harmed so much as one hair of her head, I'd not wake up at all the next morning.'

Their eyes locked and held, dark-brown upon dark-grey. The older man dropped his gaze to the smooth, flowing muscle of his mount's shoulder, knowing that he had gone as far as he dared with a man he did not know. It had been easy with lord Maurice, the onset of his rages clearly signalled, and fairly simple to divert or avoid. The new lord of Ravenstow was a different prospect entirely and not one he was enthusiastic to tackle unless forced.

Guyon turned his head. Distantly the hounds gave tongue in a new key, a sustained tocsin, belling deep.

'Boar's up and running,' Miles said, jerking his courser around.

Guyon began to swing his own horse.

De Bec spoke abruptly. 'Keep your eyes open my lord. You have as many enemies among your guests as you have allies and when I see men huddling in corners and glimpse the clink of silver in the darkness, I know that no good will come of it.'

Guyon smiled thinly, aware that by disclosing his suspicions when he could have held silent, de Bec had accepted his new master, even if the fact was as yet unrealized. 'I was not blind myself last night, but I thank you for the warning. The sooner this mockery of a celebration is over, the happier I will be.' Gathering up the reins, he set his heels to the red courser's flanks and urged him in pursuit of the dogs. De Bec wrenched the dun around and followed.

Guyon bent low over Rhuddem's neck to avoid the tangled branches that whipped at him. Shallow snow flurried from beneath the chestnut's hooves. The frozen air burned Guyon's lungs as he breathed. His eyes filled and he blinked hard to clear them, and braced himself as Rhuddem leaped a fallen tree in their path. Ahead he could hear the loud halloos and whistlings urging the dogs on and the excited belling of the dogs themselves. At his back, de Bec bit his tongue and cursed as his mount took the fallen tree.

They pressed further into the depths of Ravenstow's forest. Thorns tore at their cloaks and goaded their horses. Hooves thudded eerily in the echo chambers created by the vaulted span of huge beeches, the daylight showing luminous grey through the fretwork of empty black branches.

They galloped across a clearing, the snow fetlock deep, splashed through a swift-flowing stream, picked their way delicately round a tumble of boulders and plunged back into the tangled darkness of the winter woods. A branch snapped off and snarled in Guyon's bridle. He plucked it loose, eased Rhuddem for an instant, then guided him hard right down a narrow avenue of trunks pied silver and black, following the frenzied yelping of the dogs and the excited shouts of men.

The boar at bay was in fact a sow, a matron of prime

years, weighing almost two hundredweight. She had met and tussled with man before. A Welsh poacher had lost his life to her tushes when he came hunting piglets for his pot. The huntsmen had found his bleaching bones last spring when they came to mark the game. The sow bore her own scar from the encounter in a thick ridge of hide along her left flank where the boar spear had scored sideways, turned along bone and wounded her sufficiently to breed an intense hatred for the puny, two-legged beasts who periodically invaded her territory.

She held her ground now, backed against an overgrown jut of rock, raking clods of beech mast from the forest floor. Her huge head tossed left and right, the vicious tushes threatening to disembowel any dog or human stupid enough to come within their reach.

Guyon reined Rhuddem back and flung from the saddle. The chief huntsman tossed him a boar spear which he caught in mid-air as he alighted. It was a stout weapon, broad of blade, with a cross bar set beneath to prevent the boar from running up the shaft as it was speared and tearing the hunter to pieces. Pain brought only mad rage to a wild pig, not fear.

A dog ran in to snap at the sow's powerful black shoulder, was not swift enough to disengage and was flung howling across the path of the other dogs, a gaping slash in its side. Cadi barked and darted. She was a bratch, bred to course hare, not boar, but her narrow-loined lightness made her too swift to be caught like the dying alaunt.

The men began cautiously to draw in upon the sow, their spears braced, knives loose in their belts, every muscle taut to leap, for until the moment she charged no man knew if he was her intended victim.

It was exhilarating, the tension unbearable. She raked the leaves with her trotters, rolled her small black eyes and tushed the ground, smearing her bloody incisors with soil.

'Come on girl, get on with it,' muttered Hugh of Chester into his jowls, and licked his lips. Another man whistled loudly, trying to attract her attention and waved his spear over his head. Ralph of Thorneyford sleeved his mouth, a pulse beating hard in his neck. Walter de Lacey, his face a mask of alabaster intensity, remained immobile, his only movement a darting glance of challenge at Guyon. Guyon returned the look, eyes glittering dark as onyx and crouched, the spear braced. Then he pursed his lips and forced a strange low whistle between his tight-clenched teeth. Miles glanced at him and moved immediately closer, knowing what would happen next, for it was a Welsh trick that he himself had taught him.

The sow paused, quivering; the massive head went down; the damp leaves churned. A squealing snort erupted through her nostrils and she made a sudden powerful lunge from her hams, straight at Guyon.

Driven by her charging weight, the levelled spear reamed her chest. Guyon braced the butt against the forest soil, the muscles flowing and locking in his forearms and shoulders as he strove to hold her. The barbed tip lodged in bone and the shaft shuddered. Guyon heard the wood creak, felt it begin to give as the sow pressed forward, and knew that there was nothing he could do. The spear snapped. Razored tushes slashed open his chausses and drew a bloody line down his thigh. The sow, red foam frothing her jaws and screaming mad with pain, plunged and spun to gore him, the broken stump of the spear protruding from her breast. Guyon rammed the other half of the boar spear straight down her throat. A fierce pain burned his arm. Miles's hunting knife found the sow's jugular at the same time that de Bec's spear smashed her ribs.

Silence fell, broken only by the eager yelping of the dogs and the whimpers of the injured ones. Blood soaked the trampled soil and snow. The chief huntsman whipped the hounds from the still twitching sow, his face grey. He darted a look once at de Lacey and Pembroke behind, and then away. They ignored him.

59

'Are you all right?' Anxiously Hugh of Chester laid hold of Guyon's ripped sleeve to examine the darkly pulsing gash.

Guyon nodded and smiled for the benefit of those who would have been only too pleased to see him seriously injured or killed and wadded his cloak against the wound to stay the blood.

De Bec crouched beside the broken spear shaft and examined it. Then he rose and stalked to the senior huntsman and thrust the stump beneath his nose. The man shook his head, his complexion like whey. De Bec began to shout. Arnulf of Pembroke moved between the two men. Guyon shouldered him aside.

'Let it go,' he commanded. 'There was a weakness in the wood. It could have happened to any one of us.'

'A weakness in the w . . .?' De Bec began indignantly, but caught the look in Guyon's eye and realized that the young lord was as aware as himself that there was treachery afoot. 'Faugh!' he spat, threw down the shaft and stalked to his horse, muttering imprecations into his beard.

'My lord, I did not know, I swear I did not!' stuttered the huntsman, his throat jerking as if a noose already tightened there.

'Oh stop gibbering man, and see to the pig!' Guyon snapped impatiently and turned away. There was time enough later to grill him for details and the wilds of these border woods was no place to hold an impromptu court with tempers high, edged with blood lust.

Miles bent and picked up the shaft, saw how it had broken, and narrowed his eyes.

Guyon whistled Cadi to heel and, stepping over the thin rivulets of pig blood, went to mount up.

Judith was sitting in the solar, distaff in hand, longing to set about her companions with it. They had offered her all manner of advice, both well meaning and malicious and had asked her some very intimate questions that made her realize just how innocent she really was, and all she could do was blush, her embarrassment scarcely feigned. The women's curiosity was bottomless and avid and at least one of them with connections at court knew things about the groom that were better left unsaid. It did not prevent her from relating the information with grisly relish. Alicia parried frostily. Judith retreated behind downcast lids and wished the gaggle of them out of the keep.

Steps scuffed the stairs outside the chamber and the curtain was thrust aside. The women rose, flustered and twittering at the sight of the bridegroom whose reputation they had just been so salaciously maligning. Guyon regarded them without favour. 'Ladies,' he acknowledged, and looked beyond them to Judith. She hastened to his side. There were thorns and burrs in his cloak and a narrow graze down one cheek. There was also, she noticed, a tear in his chausses.

'My lord?'

He reached his right hand to take hers, an odd move since his left was the nearer. 'I need you to look at a scratch for me.'

'Your leg?' Her eyes dropped to his chausses.

'My arm. I fear you may need your mouldy bread.' He spoke softly, his words not carrying beyond the air that breathed them. All the women saw was his hand possessively on hers, the movement of his lips close to her ear and the sudden dismayed widening of her eyes.

'Go to the bedchamber,' said Judith. 'I will bring whatever is necessary. I take it that you do not want them to know.'

'No.'

Her mouth twitched. 'You are begetting a foul reputation, my lord.'

'Not half as foul as their minds,' he rejoindered with a jaundiced glance at the women.

'Is there a difficulty, my lord?' Alicia enquired coming forward, prepared to do battle. She was furious. It was bad enough that he should have used Judith so roughly last night as attested by the sheet and her daughter's trembling fight with tears, but that he should stride in here, dishevelled from the hunt and demand her body again, using her like a whore to ease his bloodlust, was disgusting.

'I should be grateful for a word if you can free yourself from your duties.'

Alicia eyed him narrowly. 'Now, my lord?'

'If you can come above with Judith, I will explain.'

Her eyes flickered with bewilderment as the ground of expectation was swept from beneath her feet. Guyon bowed formally to her, saluted the others with mockery and left the room, drawing Judith after him. Alicia collected her reeling wits, made the excuse that the men were returned from the hunt and she needed to consult them as to what had been captured for the table and left them to think what they would.

Judith snipped away the blood-soaked sleeve from his left arm. Guyon clenched his fist on his thigh and winced.

'Boar?' Judith peered at the jagged tear. It was not deep to the bone, but neither was it superficial enough to just bandage and leave. 'It will have to be stitched.'

He gave a small resigned shrug. 'At least I am testing your abilities to the full.' He gave her a weak grin as she soaked a linen pad in a strong-smelling liquid decocted from pine needles.

'Just pray that they do not fail. It's a nasty wound. What happened?'

Guyon almost hit the battlements as she pressed the pad to his arm and began to clean away the dirt slashed into the wound by the boar's tush.

Alicia walked into the room to hear her daughter breathlessly apologizing, a quiver in her voice.

'Get on with it!' Guyon gasped through clenched teeth, his complexion grey. 'If you stop every time I flinch, we'll be here all day, and that really will set the fat into the fire!'

Judith bit her lip. Alicia looked down at the raw, still

seeping wound. 'You will need the mouldy bread,' she said neutrally.

'I have it, mama.'

Alicia pursed her lips at Guyon, eyes thoughtful. 'I have just been down to the kitchens, my lord. They say the boar spear snapped and that you were lucky to escape with your life, let alone a few small scratches.'

'This is more than a small scratch, mama!' Judith protested, staring round.

'I can see that. I am only repeating what the cook said, and he had it from your uncle's squire.'

'They were both right,' said Guyon.

The women stared at him. After her first startled declaration, Judith's wits had quickened. Obviously Guyon was not disclaiming this tear as a mere scratch just to be manly. He wanted the wound kept a secret, or at least minimized to a nothing.

'Boar spears do not just snap,' she said. 'Papa was always very strict about the state of the hunting equipment, particularly when it came to boar. He had the spears checked regularly.'

'By your chief huntsman?'

Alicia reached for a roll of bandage while Judith threaded a needle. 'Maurice never made any complaints against Rannulf's efficiency,' she said carefully. 'I cannot say that I know him well myself. He came to us from Belleme on Robert's recommendation.'

'Would he be willing to commit murder for the right amount of silver?'

'Truly I do not know, my lord. Anything is possible if my brother-in-law has his hand in the pie.'

'Has someone then offered Rannulf silver to give you a weak spear?' Judith asked to the point.

'Probably. De Lacey was talking to him most earnestly in the hall last night and he's not the kind to mingle with servants unless it be for a specific purpose. I will know more

63

when I have had an opportunity to question Rannulf and . . . ouch!'

'Hold still, my lord and it will not hurt as much.'

'Easier said than done. I think you are enjoying this.'

Judith wrinkled her nose at him. 'Fie, my lord. So much complaint for such a "little scratch."'

'Saucy wench,' he grumbled, eyes laughing.

Baffled, Alicia watched the two of them as she prepared the poultice of mouldy bread. Here was no frightened child flickering nervous glances at the world through a haze of tears and, despite Guyon's obvious pain and preoccupation, he was handling Judith with the automatic ease of a man well-accustomed to women, not one who would deflower her savagely in a fit of unbridled lust.

Guyon gritted his teeth and sat in stoical silence until Judith and Alicia had finished with him, aware of very little save the hot beat of the pain and the concentrated effort it took to hold his arm still while it was stitched and bound.

Judith gave him a cup. He sniffed the contents suspiciously. 'Valerian, yarrow and poppy in wine,' she told him. Guyon tasted, grimaced, put down the cup and began to ease his sleeve over the bandage.

'It will relieve the pain.'

'And dull my wits,' he retorted.

Judith tsked and went across the room to find him a fresh pair of chausses and some salve for his grazed cheek and thigh.

'It seems that I have misjudged you,' Alicia said softly.

Guyon finished arranging his sleeve. She looked at his fingers. They were long and tapering and she could not have imagined them wielding a sword were it not for the fading callouses banded across his right palm, a legacy of the Mon summer campaign. He raised his head, eyes ruefully amused.

'I hope I have enough common sense to realize that rape is not the best way to begin a marriage. I haven't touched her and I won't until she's ready . . .' He stopped and looked round as his father swept aside the curtain and strode into the room.

'Your huntsman's bolted,' he announced starkly. 'Snatched de Lacey's black from a groom and was out over the draw-bridge before anyone could stop him.'

'Hell!'

'That is not the worst of it. De Lacey's gone after him and with every right to kill. Pembroke's with him and Ralph of Thorneyford. Chester's taken de Bec and some of the guard and ridden out in the hopes of preventing a murder.'

Guyon swore again with considerably more colour and reached for his swordbelt.

'I'll meet you in the bailey,' Miles said. 'The grooms have resaddled Rhuddem.'

Guyon struggled to tighten the belt with his injured left arm. Judith knelt to help him. 'Have a care, my lord,' she said anxiously. 'I fear that Rannulf may not be the only quarry.'

He looked down at her upturned serious face and with a faint, humourless smile, gently tugged her braid. 'Well, *cath fach*, forewarned is forearmed, so they say,' he replied. 'I promise you I'll do my best.'

They rode hard and caught de Bec and Chester a little beyond the village and de Lacey upon the forest track that led eventually across the border into Wales.

'I thought I had him!' de Lacey growled, gauntleted fist knotted upon his thigh. 'But the bastard's doubled back on me. Bones of Christ, when I catch him I'll string him up by the balls. Do you know how much that stallion is worth?'

'Nevertheless, I want him alive,' Guyon said coldly.

'God knows why,' Pembroke snorted, eyes shifting like those of the wild boar they had so recently killed. 'First that "weak spear" and now Walter's best courser. The turd's guilty as hell.'

'Yes,' Guyon said, arching a sardonic brow. 'And I want to talk to him about why.'

Stung by the barb, Pembroke flushed. Ralph of Thorney-ford sucked his teeth and looked puzzled. De Lacey drew his sword and turned his remount on the road, momentarily blocking the way.

Guyon and his father exchanged glances pregnant with alarm. Miles dismounted and disappeared into the woods bordering the road on swift, silent feet. He had spent his boyhood among the Welsh hills and, saving the supernatural, could track anything that trod the earth, including a rat that smelled so bad the stench of it was smothering his nostrils.

'Put up your sword,' Guyon said softly, his expression taut, his scalp prickling with unease. 'Rannulf will meet his end in justice, not hot blood, when the time comes.'

De Lacey eyed him narrowly for a moment until stared down. The sword flashed again as he shrugged and began sheathing it. 'This is justice,' he said with a strange, glittering smile.

The unease shot in white-hot warning down the length of Guyon's spine. He began reining Rhuddem about. Simultane-ously there was a warning shout and the whirr of an arrow's flight. He flung himself flat over Rhuddem's neck. The cantle butted his midriff. The horse flung up his head, banging Guyon's nose, and the arrow sang past them to thunk into and shiver a beech sapling on the other side of the road.

De Lacey's blade once more rasped free of its scabbard and he spurred his stallion into the forest. De Bec bellowed and kicked the dun after him while Hugh of Chester rammed his own mount into Pembroke's horse, preventing him from pursuit. Among the trees, someone screamed.

Cursing, his eyes water-filled, Guyon completed circling Rhuddem and spurred him after de Lacey.

He was too late. The huntsman Rannulf was sprawled in sightless regard of the bare winter branches. Walter de Lacey, his tunic splashed with blood, stood over him, his mouth white-rimmed, eyes blazing, whole body trembling with the aftermath of violently expended effort and continuing fury.

Miles was leaning against the bole of a tree, his eyes closed, arms clutching his torso.

'Papa?' Ignoring his injured arm, Guyon flung down from Rhuddem.

'I'm all right,' Miles answered huskily and lifted his lids to allay Guyon's anxiety. 'Winded, I'm not as fast as I was . . . more's the pity.' He flashed a dark look at de Lacey and pushed himself upright.

Guyon glanced him over and, reassured, swung to the other man. 'I said I wanted him alive!' he snarled.

'Should I have let him knife your father and escape?'

'If you were close enough to cut off his head, then you were close enough to have stopped him by other means, but then dead men don't talk, do they?'

De Lacey's sword twitched level and, red-edged, glinted towards Guyon who reached to draw from his own scabbard. Hugh of Chester, moving swiftly for a man so fat, placed himself between the two men, his back to Guyon, his formidable blue glare for the other man. 'Sir Walter, you forget yourself,' he said coldly.

'I forget nothing!' de Lacey spat, but lowered his blade to wipe it on the corpse before ramming it back in his scabbard and turned on his heel to examine the stolen horse, running his hands down its fine long legs to check for signs of lameness.

Guyon compressed his lips and swallowed bile, the rapid rise and fall of his chest and the hard pulse at his throat a display of the fury he was striving to control.

De Lacey straddled the black, looped his remount's reins to the cantle and, after one final, glittering glance at Guyon, rode over to where Pembroke waited.

Guyon watched his retreating back with slitted eyes and, breathing out, slowly unclenched his fingers from the hilt of his sword.

Chester bent beside the dead man and picked up the bow. 'You were drawn here to be killed, you realize that lad?'

Guyon laughed harshly. 'Oh, I suspected it back in the keep and realised it the moment we caught up with them. A man so anxious to retrieve his horse would hardly lag to wait for us. Did you see the way he blocked my path to make of me a sitting target for this poor greedy wretch?'

'It was all arranged last night,' de Bec said, leading over Rhuddem and Miles's grey. 'I'm sure of it now. If you search his scrip, you'll probably find the cost of his betrayal.'

Chester reached to the purse that was threaded upon the huntsman's belt, unlatched the buckle and delved. The small silver coins, minted with the head of the conqueror, gleamed on his broad, fleshy palm in mute evidence of treachery. He trickled them from hand to hand, eyes following their flow and then looked up at Guyon. 'Will you take it further?'

Guyon gingerly remounted. 'How can I? Oh, I know that's proof in your hands, but it's not damning. It could as easily be claimed that Rannulf won it at dice. Besides, with this arm I have no intention of risking a trial by combat which would be the sure outcome of a public accusation. No, let it stand. Each of us . . .' He broke off and looked around at his father who had reached for his mount's bridle only to desist, hand pressed to his side. 'Are you sure you are all right?'

Miles grimaced. 'At least a couple of cracked ribs and my pride sore-wounded. In the old days I'd have taken Rannulf like a wraith from behind and him none the wiser until my dagger was at his throat. Our flesh grows old and our mind forgets.' He shook his head regretfully. 'De Lacey has come out of this coil with a halo of glory, hasn't he?'

'Shining with corruption,' Guyon agreed grimly. 'At least I know where his intentions are nailed.'

Distantly a wolf howled, the sound thin and eerie, coiled in mist like the hunting cry of the *Cwmni Annwn*.

CHAPTER 6

ALICIA FETCHED THE comfrey salve and a fresh dressing and went to Miles where he sat on the bed. He was stripped to the waist and she had just unbound the yards of swaddling bands from his injured ribs in order to treat again the nasty graze sweeping over his left side, legacy of yesterday's scrimmage.

'You and your son between you seem determined to exhaust our supplies,' she remarked to break the silence, and raised the pot of salve.

'Entirely unintentional,' he said ruefully and stroked the narrow skull of the white bitch sitting at his knee. Now that their guests had departed – some of them precipitously following the incidents of yesterday, Guyon and Judith were in the strong room examining the account rolls, Melyn tucked sleepily across the latter's shoulders, and thus Cadi was banished.

Alicia flicked him a swift blue glance. 'Hold this for me.'

He took the ointment and sniffed its green herbal aroma. 'It's only a scrape and a couple of cracked ribs. You need not go to all this trouble.'

'It could have been your life!' She dipped two fingers in the jar and began to smear the salve over his ribs. He tensed at the first, cold touch. She murmured an apology, her colour heightening. He made a disclaimer and slowly relaxed. The light touch of her fingers was soothing. He fondled the dog's ears and stared straight ahead.

'So what happens now?' She spoke quickly, the first thing that came to mind, trying to distract her thoughts from the feel of his flesh, still taut and well-muscled beneath her fingers.

Miles shrugged. 'Nothing. We keep a close watch on all future moves of Walter de Lacey and our new Montgomery kin.'

'You are not going to report the matter?' Voice and brows both rose incredulously. 'Murder and twice attempted murder?'

'And no proof. You cannot make a corpse speak. It is Guyon's word against de Lacey's with an equal number of witnesses to swear for either side.'

'But . . .'

'Oh, I like it as little as you, but our hands are tied. If it went to justice, it would end in trial by combat. You've seen Guy's arm. Every marcher lord, no matter how stained his character, is bred from the cradle to fight. The odds are too close to load them in de Lacey's favour. Perhaps I'll just stick a knife in his ribs on a dark night. My Welsh blood permits me such lapses of honour.'

'You'll do no such thing!' Alicia gasped, wiping her fingers on the edge of one of the swaddling bands, her eyes widening in terror. 'He is Arnulf's friend and de Belleme's vassal. Robert would impale you on a stake at the Shrewsbury crossroads and leave you there until your flesh rotted off it!'

He flashed her a brief, distorted smile in which there was more than an enamelling of pain. It was at moments like this that he realized the true depth of his loss. Christen had been one of four within the keep to succumb to the sweating sickness. It came, it claimed haphazardly and it moved on. Even now, two years later, the scars were scarcely healed over and inadvertently Alicia was laying them open again, bleeding to the air, reminding him of what he no longer had.

He was drawn from his introspection by the sudden awareness that she was trembling violently. 'What's the matter? I was jesting, I swear it.'

'You would not jest if you had lived beneath Maurice's

70

code of cruelty,' she said bitterly. You have not had to sit at meat with Robert de Belleme and Walter de Lacey when they have come red-handed from torturing some poor wretch out of his life and wonder if you or your daughter might be their next victim!' Her lower lip trembled and abruptly she pressed the end of the swaddling band against his ribs. 'Hold this,' she commanded, voice rough.

'Alicia . . .'

She reached around him. He felt the warmth emanating from her body and smelled the drifting scent of attar of roses. Of an impulse he let go of the bandage, slipped his arm around her waist and bent his head to kiss her.

She shuddered. He could feel the quivering of her body through tunic and undergown. Hesitation, a brink and then with a smothered sound that might have been despair her lips parted beneath his and her arms circled his neck, the bandage falling to the floor at their feet.

As impulse gave way to a deeper need, Miles forgot that he had been going to give her detailed reassurances about himself, Guyon and Robert de Belleme, forgot everything but the quickening beat of his blood responding to the feel and taste of the woman in his arms.

Alicia gave a soft, whimpered gasp and pushed her hips forward, obeying his hand as he pressed it down over the curve of her buttocks. He unwound her braids and threaded his fingers through their black masses. She could feel him hard and ready, but he did not appear to be in any rush, taking his time to kiss her face and throat and ear lobes before claiming her lips again. He ran one hand lightly up her rib-cage, found the soft curve of her breast and teased her nipple until it budded and hardened beneath his gently moving thumb and she moaned low in her throat.

'Alicia, tell your maid to make sure we are not disturbed,' he muttered hoarsely against her temple.

Dimly, through a haze of sensual delight, she heard his words. It took a moment for them to reach her brain, but when they did their effect was as immediate as a deluge of frozen water. The thought of Agnes listening outside while she coupled with a man she but vaguely knew, the thought of instructing the woman with her hair all unbound and her lips swollen by his kisses, the memory of a time almost seventeen years ago when she had done just that ... The images coagulated to lose the fluidity of the moment and fill her with self-disgust. She removed her arms from around his neck, averted her mouth from his kiss and pushed away from him.

'I am not a whore,' she said flatly.

'What?' He sought her blindly for a moment and then his eyes opened and slowly refocused. 'Alicia ...'

'If you want a woman to tumble, there are plenty of serving girls accustomed to Maurice's ways who would relieve your need.' Gathering her hair, she began clumsily to rebraid it.

In silence Miles cursed himself for a fool. It had been a mistake to mention the maid, for it had roused her from a drifting sensual trance to consider a sordid detail, albeit one that would have safeguarded their privacy. Had he just continued to kiss and caress her, they would have been merrily abed by now.

'I don't want another woman, I want you,' he objected, taking a step towards her. She took several steps back.

'You would make a whore of me in my own household before my servants and vassals!'

'Don't be ridiculous!' he snapped, eyes beginning to glint. 'Why do you think I told you to speak to your maid?'

'What would you have me say to her?'

'Anything. That we wished to discuss a private matter concerned with the wedding or dowry.'

'With my hair all unbound?'

Miles turned away with an oath and scraped his fingers through his hair. 'You led me to believe you were willing ... more than willing.'

72

Colour scorched her face and throat. She worked frantically at her braids, lower lip trembling. There was no answer to that, for she had indeed been eager to couple with him until brought abruptly to common sense. Her nerve endings still tingled. 'You took advantage!' she accused, gulping back a sob.

'Yes,' he said cuttingly. 'Blame me, because you dare not blame yourself!'

Alicia began to cry then, deep-rooted sobs that shook her whole body and threatened to tear it apart.

'Oh, Christ on the cross!' Miles swore with exasperated anxiety and started towards her, not knowing whether he intended to berate or comfort.

Cadi whined and flagged her tail. Guyon swished through the curtain, a roll of parchment in his hand, his grim expression changing on the instant to comical, slack-jawed amazement. 'I'm sorry, I did not realize . . .'

'There is nothing to realize!' Alicia responded through her tears and, gathering her skirts, pushed blindly past him and out of the room.

Guyon gaped at the curtain as it fell, then back at his sire.

'Do not ask me,' Miles groaned, subsiding onto the bed and putting his head in his hands. 'I seem to be making one mistake after another. Where's Judith?'

'Ensuring the cooks know what they are about.' He scrutinized his father, wondering precisely how to interpret the scene he had just encountered. A small, reddish-purple mark was flowering on Miles's collarbone and the front of Alicia's gown had been smothered in green unguent.

'Are you any good at binding cracked ribs?' Miles handed him the length of swaddling, his expression wry, but giving nothing away. Guyon took the linen from him and set about the task. The recent Welsh campaign had given him plenty of opportunity to practise such skills.

'What's this?' Miles unrolled the parchment and squinted at it. His eyes had grown long-sighted with age and, although literate, it was hardly one of his foremost skills.

'The amount owed to Robert de Belleme for the stone and craftsmen to build this place.'

'The what?'

'According to that document, de Belleme lent Maurice a thousand marks to purchase men and materials. There are still four hundred owing and, knowing de Belleme, I doubt he will waive the sum as a wedding gift to his niece. In fact, it gives him the excuse he needs to claim Ravenstow if I cannot pay. With Maurice it did not matter, a convenient hold on his loyalty, but there is no profit to be had from me except in full payment, and he knows it.'

'Can you raise the silver?'

Guyon finished banding the linen around Miles's chest and secured it. 'Probably, but it will be no small inconvenience and will leave my new vassals considerably poorer than when they swore me homage.'

'Providing of course that they are willing to pay in the first place.'

Guyon smiled thinly. 'They are obliged by custom to render a relief on Judith's marriage and I will have that from them at the oath-taking tomorrow before they leave.'

Miles glanced uneasily at Guyon. He did not doubt his son's ability to wring the relief from his vassals, nor his ability to hold them loyal to their oaths of fealty. What did disturb him was the glint of devilry lurking dangerously beneath the surface of Guyon's thoughtful expression. He had seen that look before, usually preceding some act of rash lunacy. 'Guyon, what are you plotting?' he demanded sharply.

'Nought, as yet. I'm a newly married man, or had you forgotten? Speaking of which, you have a very pretty lover's bruise on your throat.'

There was a warning behind the flippancy. He was being pointedly told to mind his own business and for a moment resentment flared. He flicked his son a hard stare. Guyon's own eyes returning the look were a soft, luminous brown, edged with silky, thick lashes. They masked a will as flexible

74

and strong as a willow wand. You might bend it, but the moment you let go it sprang back to its original way of growing. It was useless to argue.

Miles dropped his regard to the parchment still in his hand and sighed heavily. 'As I said, I seem to be making mistakes hand over fist.'

CHAPTER 7

THE SKY WAS the colour of a wild harebell, its infinity interrupted by brilliant small flocks of clouds scudding west into Wales, and the occasional wind-tossed bird striving to control the direction of its flight.

Judith clicked her tongue to the sedate brown gelding and he increased his pace, ears flickering. The wind gusted playfully at their backs. Her cloak flapped. Her veil attempted to fly away. She released the reins to feel for the pins that held it in place and pulled them out, exposing her thick, tawny braids. It was a mark of her confidence astride a horse and her swift ability to learn new skills that she felt sufficiently secure to trust to balance while she performed her toilet.

Before her as they crossed the heathland between Guyon's holdings of Oxley and Ledworth, rode Guyon's shield-bearer, Eric Godricson and six serjeants, with a like number behind. An attack by the Welsh or other hostile factions was unlikely but it was still better to be safe than sorry, particularly with Guyon absent raising revenues among his other honours.

Judith stared at the dark trees beyond the heathland without really seeing their stark outlines, her thoughts drifting over the ten weeks that had elapsed since her precipitous marriage.

The oaths of fealty sworn two days after the boar hunt had for the most part been sincere, with the odd protest at the steepness of the marriage relief. Guyon had dealt smoothly with complaint. He had the silver tongue of a courtier and a merchant's shrewd acumen – men smiled and agreed with him, then scratched their heads and wondered how they had been manoeuvred into parting with their coin when they had intended fiercely to resist.

The incident with de Lacey and Arnulf de Montgomery had sunk out of sight like a rotten log into a quagmire. Guyon's arm had healed cleanly to leave a thin, pink scar. He seldom spoke of the boar hunt although occasionally, in repose, his expression gave her cause to wonder at his thoughts.

Arnulf de Montgomery was busy in south Wales. De Lacey was sitting on his lands like a disgruntled heron on a nest − God alone knew what he was hatching. Ralph of Thorneyford was ailing with pains in the chest, brought on by a severe winter cold from which he had not properly recovered. The harsh weather of January and February had also prevented Robert de Belleme from travelling further up the march than the seat of his new earldom, where an array of defences were being constructed beneath his critical architect's eye . . . And defences cost money.

Judith was aware of Guyon's edginess. He was as tense as a hunting cat, prowling and alert. For the most part, he kept it to himself, although occasionally he was wont to snap. The first time she had recoiled, awaiting the slap that was sure to follow, but he had lowered his gaze to the account rolls over which he was poring, trimmed his quill and continued to work. After a while, when her frightened silence had registered, he had set down his pen, considered her for a moment, obviously summoning up a reserve of patience, apologised briefly and told her to go away. Since then, she had learned to recognise the warning signs and instead of attempting to be sociable would go and attend to her duties elsewhere in the keep, leaving him well alone.

A month ago, when the weather had eased enough to make travelling possible, they had moved down the march to Guyon's mainholding of Ledworth, recently inherited from his uncle who had died in battle during the ill-fated summer campaign in north Wales.

The keep was imposing, built upon a high crag to dominate the growing town below and the drover's roads leading from these middle borders into the heart of Wales. It was also, despite its recent construction, musty, dirty and cold. The former lord had neglected the domestic side of keep matters when his wife had died. The seneschal's wife was elderly and crippled by stiff hips and the maids had taken advantage of her infirmity to do much as they pleased, which was precisely nothing.

Three weeks of purgative chaos had ensued as Alicia and Judith set the worst of the rot to rights so that at least the place was habitable. Alicia in particular had thrown herself into the exercise, chivvying the maids remorselessly, addressing them all piecemeal as sluts and husseys, her tongue as abrasive as the brushes and lye with which she made them scour the dairy floor and slabs.

Judith was concerned, for the shrewish woman with whom she shared the bower was not her gentle mother. The bouts of feverish activity spoke of panic or despair. Once she had come across Alicia choking back tears in Ledworth's private chapel and begging whispered forgiveness. Forgiveness for what? Her mother was more sinned against than sinning, her confessions to the priest usually of oversights and peccadillos, nothing that would stain the soul with such grief.

Judith guided her mount with her knees and frowned, trying to remember when she had first noticed the change in her mother's manner. A couple of days after the wedding it would have been. Alicia had retired to her own chamber with a megrim and stayed there for a full two days, refusing all ministrations save those of Agnes and had emerged on the third day a full hour too late to wish Guyon's father Godspeed on his road home. Miles, as she recalled had been rather distressed at her absence and Agnes's firm declaration that her mistress was still asleep and, having been so poorly, was best not roused.

'Riders to the rear!' cried one of her escort, interrupting her train of thought.

Eric frowned. It was not the direction from which he expected his lord to come, although he was indeed expected soon. He rubbed the side of his nose. 'Best play safe,' he decided. 'If it be lord Guyon, he'll take no offence at our caution. If it be another, we owe them no excuses. Are you up to a gallop, my lady?'

Judith, her heart beginning to thump, raised her shoulders in a nonchalant shrug. 'If this nag is, then yes,' she responded and gathered up the reins.

The serjeant who had first cried the warning circled away behind them to discover the identity of their pursuers. They quickened their pace. A distance of about nine furlongs separated them from the safety of the keep, but much of that route was uphill.

Judith's gelding started to flag. She dug her heels into his sides and heard him wheeze.

'It's Robert de Belleme!' yelled the serjeant, his voice indistinct but explicit with panic.

'Blood of Christ!' cursed Eric, assailed himself by that same emotion. The Welsh, fair enough, he could deal with them, having been trained since youth in that particular way of warfare. Small rebellions and insurgencies, they too were little problem. The savage cunning of the most dangerous man in the realm, an earl of high magnitude, was a different matter entirely and it was with the cold-sick sweat of relief and terror that he saw they were going to make it into the safety of the keep with only moments to spare.

What did one do, he wondered? Permit the wolf into the fold, or deny him and watch him open his mouth to swallow Ledworth in its entirety? Within or without, neither prospect held forth much hope.

The drawbridge was down over the moat. The wet winter and spring had raised the level of the water table and instead of the noisome sludge that usually offended the nose on crossing the ditch, there was a glistening moat of sky-blue water. The hooves drummed on the planks. Judith glimpsed the glittering wind-stirred ruffles. She flung a look over her shoulder but the wind whipped her braids across her face and all she saw between the errant tawny strands were the heaving horses behind her and the solid mailed protection of her escort.

Robert de Belleme. Oh God, what were they to do?

Her mount stumbled as they rode beneath the portcullis and into the ward. She pulled him up, his ribs heaving like bellows, his legs trembling, spent and, without waiting for aid to dismount, kicked her feet from the stirrups and slid herself over his side to the ground.

The last man pounded over the bridge at a hard gallop. The guards on duty began winching the bridge the moment he clattered onto it. The portcullis closed its black-fanged mouth. Ledworth snarled granite defiance at one of the most powerful men in northern Europe.

Eric spat and crossed himself as they heard the drawbridge thud flush with the outer wall. 'It is called burning your bridges,' he said grimly. 'Do you go inside, my lady, and join your mother.'

Judith gnawed her lip. Her smooth brow puckered. She laid her arm upon Eric's leather sleeve. 'Wait,' she said. 'If we deny him entry we offer him unpardonable insult and he never allows a slight to remain swallowed for long.'

'But mistress . . .'

'I was prey to be snatched when I was outside the keep, but within he must preserve the civilities. I know why he is here. Lord Guyon has been expecting him all winter.'

Eric looked unhappily at the chequerboard squares of light between the spars of the portcullis and the security of the solid oak planks beyond. Faintly from without there came a hail. 'My lady, I am reluctant to admit him. Lord Guyon would string me from the highest tree on the demesne if ill should come of this.'

'Let me worry about lord Guyon,' she replied with more than a spark of bravado. 'How many men does my uncle have with him . . . Thierry?'

The young serjeant cleared his throat. The sure command in lady Judith's voice sat quite at odds with her waifish appearance. 'About thirty at a rough guess, m'lady,' he replied and fiddled with the hilt of his sword, eyes shifting from her to the barred drawbridge.

'Then admit my uncle and his five most senior companions,' she commanded Eric. 'You will take custody of their weapons and put the guards on full alert. Have a messenger ride out and find lord Guyon, one of his Welshmen by preference; they have the stealth to go unseen.'

Eric spread his hands. 'What if the seigneur de Belleme refuses to disgorge his weapons and abandon his men outside?'

'He won't refuse,' she said with grim surety. 'Balk them awhile until I am fittingly dressed to receive them.'

'But my lady . . .'

She was gone, lifting her skirts to reveal her ankles as she ran, her plaits dishevelled and snaking to the movement of her spine. Eric closed his eyes and swallowed, braced himself and set about giving commands that he was not at all sure he should be obeying.

Alicia de Montgomery gaped at her daughter in disbelief as she seized a comb and began to mend her hair. She had retained her honey-coloured undergown and discarded her riding dress in favour of a tunic of dark gold wool lavishly banded with embroidery in two shades of green.

'You have done what?' Alicia whispered, clutching her throat as if a noose was already tightening there. 'Are you mad? You might as well open the chicken run and let the fox run amok inside!'

'Mama, I am not mad. I would as lief not grant him entry, but on this occasion, at least, he means us no harm.'

'It is not experience of years that has gained you such foresight!' her mother said acidly. 'Jesu, when I remember what that whoreson did to your father!'

'I thought they were fond kin and allies,' Judith answered in a preoccupied manner, fingers working with nimble haste.

'He quenched any spark of decency that might have lurked forgotten in Maurice's soul with his silver tongue and his foul corruptions,' Alicia said bitterly. She sighed and looked at Judith with a mingling of sacrifice and exasperation. 'I suppose I will have to go down and face him now that you have been so foolish as to grant him entry.'

A spark of resentment flared in Judith's agate eyes. 'It is my responsibility, mama,' she said quietly. 'Besides, he does not know me, and it will be easier than you greeting him with hatred when I can plead the ignorance of youth.' She turned back to her toilet, clipping the ends of her braids with bronze fillets and smoothing her gown.

Alicia stared at her daughter. The change from child to woman had accelerated rapidly since her marriage to Guyon. There was command in her voice, the same authority that made men perform her father's bidding, or else back off with frightened eyes. She had his way of looking, too. An open, fearless stare, locking will with will. Alicia was strongly aware of an instinct to protect, to shield her only child against the wickedness of the world, and had to struggle to control it.

'Be careful, my beloved,' she warned. 'Snakes bite slyly.'

'And cats have claws,' Judith retorted tossing her head, then belied her self-assurance by turning to her mother and hugging her fiercely.

Alicia felt her cling and returned the embrace full measure. It was all that she could do.

Robert de Belleme, Earl of Shrewsbury, lord of Montgomery, eldest son of the notorious Mabel Talvas who had been murdered for her own sadistic cruelties, ranged his gaze over the construction of Ledworth's great hall and considered how to go about the matter of besieging the keep. Not that it was anything personal – yet – merely a constructive and pleasant pastime while he awaited his hostess, and one never knew when such ruminations might be called upon to bear fruit.

The eyes viewing the thick cross wall were without expression and almost without colour. A pale, beautiful, glassy grey, they sat either side of a strong, autocratic nose and beneath straight-slashed black brows. He was thirty-eight years old, looked little more than twenty-five. Some men in their ignorance said that he had sold his soul to the devil in exchange for the earthly trinkets of youth and power. Others, more knowledgeable, said that he had no soul at all. Robert de Belleme did not give a damn what anyone thought, contemptuous to the core of all his fellow men.

He tapped his whip against his leg and eyed with scornful, cold amusement the scuttling, insectile avoidance of the servants, their sidelong stares and limbs poised to leap aside if he should uncoil to strike. It was sweet to see their terror which was, of course, totally justified.

A girl crossed the length of the hall and came towards the fire where he and his companions stood warming themselves, Walter de Lacey among them. Her pace was confident, her head carried high, her eyes making direct contact with his. It was such a contrast to the twittering fear he so usually encountered that his interest sharpened and he narrowed his eyes to appraise her.

'I am sorry we kept you waiting, my lord, but the times cause us to err on the side of caution,' Judith said in a low, sweet voice and dipped him a deep curtsey.

He looked down on the bent amber braids and the long, fine-boned hands clutching the folds of her gown. 'Indeed, it is difficult to judge enemy from friend,' he concurred with a thin-lipped smile and cupped her chin to raise her face to his scrutiny.

There was nought of his half-brother to be seen. Her broad brow, cheekbones and softly curved lips belonged to Alicia, but the fine, narrow nose, slightly cleft stubborn chin and strange, grey opal eyes were completely individual.

'It was a pity your marriage took place while I was occupied elsewhere. I would have liked to attend.' He lifted her to her feet. She was as slender as a willow wand, thin almost, with scarcely a figure to mention. He raked her length with emotionless pale eyes. If FitzMiles had got a child on her, it did not yet show. Probably as poor a breeder as her dam which was a pity. If the lord of Ravenstow were suddenly to die, the widow's lands would revert to the crown. Not that he foresaw any particular problem in wheedling them out of Rufus's pocket and into his own, but if FitzMiles were to die with a babe in the cradle, then the estates of both parents would devolve upon the head of that one small being and the wardenship of such wealth would be power indeed to whomsoever owned it. Still, there were more ways than one to milk a cow.

He circled Judith's wrist in a grip of steel and drew her to her feet. 'Your husband should be here to take care of a prize so valuable,' he remarked caressively. 'Is he always so careless?'

Walter de Lacey sniggered. Judith was reminded of her mother's panic-stricken remark about the fox in the chicken run. Her mouth grew dry, her stomach jinked queasily but she permitted no fear to show on her face, only blank innocence. 'He had business elsewhere, my lord. I would not presume to question him ... Do you care to wait?' She signalled to a servant who crept forward with a flagon and cups.

Robert de Belleme released her wrist and lounged his buttocks against a low table behind. 'Playing at chatelaine,' he mocked as she waved the terrified creature away and served him and his men herself. 'How old are you my dear?'

'Sixteen, my lord.'

'And sweet as a medlar ripe on a tree.' He rotated the cup in his fingers to examine the interlaced English design. 'Tell me Judith, does your lord hope for an heir before the anniversary of your marriage?'

Colour scorched her face and throat, the brilliant flush clashing with the rich tawny hair springing from her brow. 'If God wills it, my lord,' she managed, feeling as though the pale eyes had stripped her down to the truth.

'And if your husband can restrain himself from the company of his Welsh paramour and other lights o' love,' de Lacey sneered nastily.

Judith set the flagon carefully down. Anjou wine was too expensive to be flung, she reminded herself, and it was her best flagon. 'I do not interfere in my lord's private business,' she said stonily. Her look flashed over de Lacey and quickly down before her revulsion betrayed her. 'He treats me well, and I thank God for it.'

De Belleme smiled, seeing steel beneath the douce façade, and anger. 'I have yet to meet a woman who is not taken in by Guyon's charm,' he said lightly.

'Or a man for that matter!' guffawed de Lacey. 'It is not every bride can count the King as her rival for his body!'

'Shall I instruct the cooks to make a feast, or is this just a passing visit to express your joy upon my marriage?' Judith's voice was choked as she fought with her fury.

A side-slung glance showed de Lacey the Saxon oaf who professed himself captain of the guard, moving to intercept, his square jaw jutting like granite.

De Belleme shrugged. 'I have to be in Shrewsbury tonight. There is a business matter to be discussed with your husband, but it can wait and in the meantime I have brought you a belated wedding gift.' He stood straight and half-turned to pat the stitched bundle lying on the table behind him. De Lacey, a sudden sly grin on his face, presented his overlord with a sharp dagger to slit the threads.

Shaking inside like a junket, outwardly composed, Judith watched him apply the blade. The strands parted in staccato hard bursts of sound and the skins spilled out onto the table, glossy, supple, jet-black against the coarse woven linen of their coverings.

'Norwegian sables to grace your gowns . . . or your bed,' he said with an expansive sweep of his beringed hand and delved to present her with one of the glowing furs.

The sable still possessed its face and feet. Judith swallowed her aversion – the thing looked as though it had been squashed in a siege – and thanked him. It was a very costly gift, fit to grace the robes of a queen.

Her uncle dismissed her gratitude. 'It is nothing,' he said, and meant it. In the fullness of time he expected them to return to his keeping and all they had cost him was a little joyful exertion of his sword arm. 'Is your lady mother here with you?'

'Yes, my lord. She pleads your indulgence. She has a head cold.'

'I have that effect on her.' Smiling, he caressed the blade of the knife he still held as if stroking the body of a mistress.

Judith shivered, suddenly very thankful that the majority of her uncle's men were outside the keep.

'Are you afraid of me, Judith?' he asked pleasantly, admiring his reflection in the mirror-bright steel.

'Has she cause to be?' Guyon's voice was soft, cat-footed at his entrance.

De Belleme spun, the speed of his movement betraying his surprise. For all his height and breadth, Guyon FitzMiles moved like a wraith. It was a trait that irritated the Earl intensely, for God alone knew what the man was capable of overhearing in his stealth.

'Christ's blood no!' he laughed, tossing the dagger back to de Lacey whose face was pasty. 'But you know how reputations travel.'

Guyon's eyes fell to the sables puddling the board. His fine nostrils flared and his luminous gaze lifted, suddenly hard, to nail de Belleme's. 'I know the very roads,' he answered in that same, soft voice and unpinned his cloak. 'I have granted your men a corner of the bailey. They may have their weapons when they leave.'

The thin, sarcastic mouth quirked. Guyon tossed his cloak onto the table and rested one haunch on the wood. 'Is this a social visit to congratulate us upon our marriage, my lord, or do you have other fish to fry?'

'Your hospitality dazzles me, nephew,' said de Belleme dryly.

'Yours would blind,' Guyon retorted. 'I wonder what you would have done had you caught up with my wife before the drawbridge?' His eyes flashed to de Lacey and burned there for a moment, before returning to de Belleme.

'Nothing improper, I assure you.'

'By whose code?' Guyon snarled.

'My uncle has brought us a wedding gift of these fine sables,' Judith said quickly, aware that if Guyon had been a cat, his fur would now be standing on edge in a stiff ridge down his spine. They could not afford a rift with the Earl of Shrewsbury and Guyon, more than she, was obviously struggling with his courtesy.

There was a moment's silence. The balance teetered. Judith held her eyes on Guyon's and pleaded silently. She stepped forward and took hold of his right arm in a proprietory fashion as a bride might do, but in actual fact to prevent him groping for his sword. The muscles beneath the mesh of mail and linen gambeson were like iron; taut and shuddering with rigid effort, and his eyes were a blazing brown. She was holding a leashed leopard that at any moment would spring to its own destruction.

Frantically she stood on tip-toe to kiss his tight lips, trying to break the terrible concentration.

Through a fog of rage Guyon became aware of her desperation and the spark of sanity that had prevented him from leaping at de Belleme's throat kindled to a steadier flame. He dropped his focus to her upturned face and filled his vision with her shining honesty instead of the glass-grey contemptuous challenge of his uncle-by-marriage.

'I would set your worth even higher than sables, *cath fach*,' he said with the strained travesty of a smile as he slipped his arm around her waist and lightly kissed her cheek, knowing that she had fetched him away from the edge of a very dangerous precipice.

Judith could still feel the tension cording his muscles, but he had himself under control. His hands were open, not bunched into fists.

'As it happens,' said de Belleme pleasantly, as if unaware of the corked pressure of Guyon's hostility, 'I do have other fish to fry, nothing too important. Indeed I am embarrassed to make mention of it.'

Guyon doubted that the lord of Shrewsbury had ever been embarrassed in his life. He lifted a brow and looked enquiringly blank, pretending not to see de Lacey's lounging smirk. Beside him Judith was still, but he saw her jaw clench and knew that she was as aware as himself of what was coming next.

'*Cariad*, go and bestow your wedding gift safely and organise some fitting repast for our guests,' he murmured to her.

Judith looked at him sharply. He released himself from her grip and ran one finger lightly down her freckled nose and smiled. A charming, light dismissal, but a dismissal nevertheless. His gaze flickered to the sables and then quickly away.

Judith curtsied, she could do little else, and excused herself.

'You were saying?' Guyon folded his arms.

'It is a small matter of some silver owed to me by my late brother Maurice for the building of Ravenstow . . .' said the Earl of Shrewsbury and he smiled like an executioner.

Judith smoothed one of the sables beneath her palm, staring down at the glowing fur without really seeing her action or feeling the luxury beneath her caress.

The midday meal had been somewhat more elaborate than their usual custom of bread and cheese and watered wine, the flustered cook having organized additions of roasted pigeons, mutton in pastry coffins, salted herrings seethed in milk and sprinkled with almonds and small honey cakes, crusty with chopped nuts and dried fruit.

Judith did not know if it was fare fit for an earl, but it was the best she could provide at such short notice. Certainly her uncle had not complained. Indeed, he had settled to the meal with a hearty appetite which was more than could be said for her husband, who had attacked the wine as voraciously as others attacked the food, seeming set to drink himself beneath the table in as short a time as possible. Barely a morsel of food had passed his lips and every time his cup neared the dregs he would signal the lad serving to replenish it to the brim. He had begun to slur his words and his voice had grown over-loud.

Robert de Belleme had watched Guyon's disintegration with a contemptuous slitted eye and a cool little smile playing about the corners of his fastidious mouth. No more than a cupful had flowed over his own tongue which remained mellifluous and precise, a bladed organ sheathed in gentle satis-faction.

Judith's tentative plea to her husband had met with a snarl to mind her distaff and a half-raised fist. It was at this juncture that she had begged leave to retire, having no desire to bear the humiliation of a public beating. She could remember only too well how it had gone with her father in the past. He would drink. Someone would make a remark that he did not like and the blows would fall, cutting if he happened to be wearing rings.

Steeped in misery, she sat waiting now for she knew not what and wondered what had happened in the strongroom to drive Guyon over the brink like this.

Her uncle was owed a large sum of money. Guyon had been thoughtful about that for some time, deeply thoughtful and busy, but certainly not depressed. She knew that he enjoyed the taste of good wine, but in three months of marriage she had yet to see him merry, let alone drunk. It was beyond her to fathom the reason for such deviation and her fear was all the more potent for her lack of understanding.

There was a sound outside the door. Melyn, coiled in a warm ball upon the bed, popped her head erect and uttered the soft greeting miaow she reserved solely for Judith and Guyon. Judith dropped the sables and hastened to the door, unbarring it to admit Eric and one of the serjeants bearing Guyon's upright weight between them. Stinking of hippocras, he swayed on the threshold.

'Traitors!' he bellowed for all and sundry to hear, taking a wild swipe at Eric and almost overbalancing as he staggered into the room. 'I'm shtill shober enough to shee my gueshts on the road . . . Lemme go!'

Protesting loudly, he was manhandled to the bed. Judith watched him, her fingers at her throat, her whole body tensed to avoid if need be, terrifying memories of her father flooding her mind.

Eric glanced at her and gave her of all things a wink and a smile. 'Don't you worry mistress, he'll sober up quicker than you think,' he said comfortingly and, with his grinning companion in tow, left her alone with her dread.

Melyn leaped onto Guyon's wine-drenched chest and kneaded the spoiled cloth with splayed, pristine pink claws. Guyon scooped her up and, depositing her on the coverlet, sat up.

'God help me,' he grimaced, reaching for his tunic hem and pulling the garment over his head. 'I stink like the morning after in a Rouen brothel!' He slung the richly embroidered silk across the room and followed it with his shirt.

Still standing near the door, Judith's eyes were as round as those of a landed trout. 'You're not drunk!' she discovered.

'Sober as a stone, *cath fach*,' he declared and moved purposefully to his clothing chest.

Sunlight rayed obliquely through an arrow slit and bathed the sleek feline play of his muscles as he sought. It picked out the scar from the boar hunt on his arm and the marks of stitches neatly made. It sheened with gold his thick, crow's wing hair.

'But why?' she enquired in bewilderment. 'Why did you want us all to believe that you were sodden drunk?'

'You did not have to act your responses and they were more convincing than ever you could have feigned. Your uncle as well as most of the keep think that I have drowned in hippocras my despair at losing so much silver into his wanton care.'

'But I saw how much you swallowed. Your back teeth must be awash!'

Guyon flashed her a grin. 'A gut full of red-dyed water, and just enough hippocras to reek my clothes and skin. It was Eric's lad serving at table, did you notice?' He took a shirt and an overtunic of coarse, patchily dyed linen, devoid of all embellishment, and threw them on the bed. Melyn extracted herself with a growl, claws flashing to add another line of burrs to its already ragged appearance.

'But in God's name why? Why would you want my uncle to believe that you are a swiller?' Judith moved away from the door and picked up the wine-soaked tunic and shirt to put them on the chest beside the sables.

Guyon, in the act of stripping his chausses, glanced at her from beneath his brows. 'He has my silver. I am a distraught weak reed and, as far as anyone knows, saving a precious few, I shall wallow abed in a drunken stupor for the next full day at least.'

'What are you planning?' Judith said, looking frightened again. 'And why are you dressing yourself in those disgusting rags?'

'An exercise in stealth, *cath fach*. The less you know, the better.'

Her eyes flashed. 'I am not stupid!'

'No,' he agreed and raised his head to appraise her gravely. 'You are too clever by half. And do not scowl at me like that. I meant it as a compliment. It is very hard to deceive you on any matter for long.'

'Such as your Welsh paramour and other lights o' love!' she snapped and then pressed her hands to her mouth, wondering in horror what on earth had made her quote de Lacey at him like an accusation.

His gaze held hers steadily. 'If I have been over the border of late, it is for reasons other than the pursuit of pleasure.'

Judith dropped her lids. The heat of a blush warmed her face. 'I was being foolish,' she said stiffly. 'I am sorry, my lord.'

From the set of her mouth he doubted the latter was true, but for the nonce had neither the time nor inclination to unravel what was eating at her.

Judith picked up one of the sables and rubbed the cool fur against her hot cheek. 'Why were you so angry when you first arrived, my lord?' she asked, as association brought sudden remembrance.

Guyon latched the buckle of his belt and for a moment frowned as though he was not going to answer. But then he shrugged and spoke. 'I passed a pack train two days ago, heading for Shrewsbury. The merchant, Huw ap Sior was a likeable man. I've traded with him before now, my father too. If he had a fault, it was that he could talk the hind leg off a donkey and he was heedless of danger where he thought there might be gain . . . They found his body in a ditch this morning, choked by the binding of his own chausses and his limbs carved off, and of course not a sign of his goods. I believe that the sheriff is blaming Huw's servant for the deed because the lad has vanished into thin air and, being in de Belleme's pay, he's not going to look further than the easiest scapegoat.' He drew a hard breath to steady his rising revulsion and anger.

'Huw knew that there were men of high import in Shrewsbury at the moment. He was taking his pack of silks and Norwegian sables there to sell . . . only the poor stupid sod never arrived . . . Look at the canvas in which your bride-gift is wrapped. Do you think that those brown stains are merely blotches of mud from the road?'

Judith swallowed and flicked her gaze sidelong to the pack and its tell-tale pied markings, 'No Guyon,' she whispered hoarsely. 'It is not true.'

'All right, *cath fach*, it is not true,' he said flatly and turned from her to pull on a rough sheepskin jerkin and brown woollen capuchon. 'It is my imagination playing tricks.'

Shuddering, Judith dropped the sable back among its light-silvered companions and pressed the back of her wrist to her mouth, feeling sick. Tight-lipped, Guyon continued to make his preparations. After a moment he straightened, alerted by a faint sound from behind. Her breath was shaking free from her throat in small, effortful gasps as she fought to stifle her sobs. It was on his lips to snarl at her that grief came cheaply, but he remembered in time, reminded by the white, pinched horror in her face that for all her cleverness she was still a child.

He swore beneath his breath and went to take her in his arms. She gripped his jerkin, struggling for control, the smell of sheepskin pungent in her nostrils, the beat of his heart steady against her hidden face, his voice flowing softly over her, gentling her as he might have gentled an unbroken horse, the words in flawless, fluid Welsh.

Gradually beneath the soothing movement of his hands and the coaxing of his voice, Judith calmed. 'My mother was right,' she gulped with loathing. 'Snakes do bite slyly.'

'Unless you pin them behind the neck and draw their fangs,' Guyon said softly.

He was still speaking Welsh. Her head jerked up, her wet lashes wide. 'Guyon, I do not know what is in your mind save that it be more than dangerous. In God's name, have a care to yourself!'

'You worry too much,' he retorted with an indulgent smile and kissed her cheek. She moved her head. For an instant their lips met, hers soft, pink and unpractised; his gentle without the slightest hint of possession or demand, and he was the first to disengage from the embrace.

'As far as everyone else in this keep is concerned, I am confined here in a drunken stupor. I trust you to keep up the pretence for a day at least.'

'When will you be back, my lord?'

'By moonlight I hope.' He drew up the hood of the capuchon and laced it tightly. His face disappeared into brown shadow. '*Da bach chwi cariad*,' he said, and tugged her tawny braid and slipped silently out of the room. She stared at the door he had just closed, then went over and dropped the bar and, sitting down beside the bundle of sables, to keep herself from fruitless worry, set her mind upon more practical paths, such as what to do with this gift culled from murder.

To keep the sables was impossible. She could scarcely bear to look at them. The sight of the bloodstains upon the bindings curdled her stomach. Burn them? That was waste upon waste. Throw them back in her uncle's face? No. Guyon would have done that had it been feasible. Give them away? She steepled her fingers, interlaced them and rested her chin upon them. Return them to where they belonged. A little enquiry should secure the knowledge.

She fetched ink and quill and parchment and, reseating herself on the bed, Melyn curled at her side, began carefully to write.

CHAPTER 8

THE EARL OF SHREWSBURY lounged easily in the high, gilded saddle, his legs loosely straight, heels crowned by gilded prick spurs, supple kidskin boots reaching elegantly to mid-calf and laced by tasselled green thongs.

His face wore an expression of invidious, scornful satisfaction. The cruel mouth and pale eyes smiled. His sword rode lightly in its scabbard, his left hand relaxed upon the curved rock crystal pommel.

Behind him, sweet on the ear, the pony bells jingled, the sturdy clevelands laden with the Earl's travelling accoutrements. Flanked by two guards, another pony bore its complacent load of scarred brown leather sacks, fat with jinking promise.

Four hundred sweet silver marks. Guyon FitzMiles had been sufficiently wise to pay up. The only thing that had surprised de Belleme was the bridegroom's ability to pay in full, although he suspected that the effort had nigh on beggared the young man.

Magnanimous in victory, he had offered to take two hundred marks now and leave the balance until the Michaelmas rents had been paid, and for his pains had been told on a swallowed snarl where to put his largesse. A solicitous suggestion that FitzMiles could sell his mother-in-law to cut his losses had for a moment held them on the edge of an exciting precipice. He had felt his sword arm tingling with anticipation and de Lacey had begun to reach for his dagger, but FitzMiles, holding hard to the control he was later to lose in wine, had stalked from the strong room, crashing his fist into the door as he went.

Such was the folly of youth. De Belleme smiled, remembering the young man swilling his wine like a street drunkard, the loose-limbed grace growing clumsy, the cultured accent slurring, the eyes becoming slack-lidden and glazed beneath. It was what he had half-expected. On more than one occasion at court, FitzMiles had roistered away the entire night with Prince Henry, drinking himself beneath the table to the accompaniment of lute and tabor and dancing girls. Lack of moral fibre was of no consequence to the earl; it was the lack of self-discipline that gave him cause to be scornful. A man should always know what he was about, but then FitzMiles was not a man but a part-Welsh barbarian, deserving of all that came his way.

The bleating of sheep roused him from contemplation of a ripe future to the more immediate, startled contemplation of the road before his eyes. A woolly cloud as enormous as a grey-bellied rolling white thunderhead stretched in baaing, smelly munificence as far as the eye could see.

His horse lashed out with its hindlegs as de Lacey's mount, brought up short, collided with its rump. De Lacey swore and wrenched at his bridle.

'God's eyes!' snarled de Belleme, his complacence deflated. 'Get these stinking sheep out of my way!'

His words were smothered in a chorus of mournful bleating as the sheep advanced and closed around the troop. His destrier began to plunge in earnest, unnerved by the seething ovine sea. The pack ponies kicked. Cursing, his men attempted to control them and their own mounts and draw their weapons at one and the same time.

Beside him, Walter de Lacey swung his sword at a sheep, but before the blade reached the beast, he turned his wrist in shocked response to the nocked arrow aimed directly at his heart. A range of less than ten yards made death a certainty.

There were men among the sheep, rising to their feet, their

tunics wrong side out affording them a sheepskin camouflage, unseen until it was too late. Welshmen, dark and slender, with short swords at their hips and the deadly wild elm longbows in their hands.

'*Yr cledd*,' said the nearest Welshman gruffly, jerking his nocked bow at de Lacey's sword. The baron's mouth tightened. For a moment the blade gleamed in his hand as he turned it, contemplating folly and then, as the Welshman adjusted his line of sight, he spat and threw it down among the sheep.

'You'll die for this,' he said thickly.

Without vocal reply, the Welshman gestured him and his overlord down from their horses and they had no option but to comply.

Robert de Belleme was not afraid. It was an emotion he seldom experienced even in the teeth of death, but his fury at being trapped and helpless to extricate himself, surrounded as he was by bumping, bleating sheep, raged so hot that it threatened to burn the eyeballs from his head.

His hands were lashed behind his back. A black hood was forced down over his head and tied there, clogging his sight. Barbarian, mellifluous Welsh jostled his muffled hearing. De Lacey's invective was cut off by the sound of a dull blow and then retching. Someone laughed. The rage stuck in his gullet and almost choked him. His breath was hot inside the rough black cloth. Small coarse hairs of it clung to his lips and tongue. He writhed and struggled and felt the bonds saw weals into his wrists.

Guyon lowered the nocked bow, his eyes sparkling with laughter. His mouth quivered as he controlled the impulse to howl his triumph aloud. Commands flickered in Welsh. Fresh pack ponies were brought and the loads transferred. Sheep, destriers and former pack ponies began their escorted journey deep into the wilds of Powys where, except by Welshmen, they would not soon be found.

Guyon murmured something to one of his companions,

tone warm with joyful malice as he looked down on the two men, bound like caterpillars in a web, and straddled the mount that Eric had brought him.

The words were lost upon his victims, but not the rich delight with which they were spoken and, had de Belleme not seen with his own eyes Guyon FitzMiles sliding beneath the trestle, mazy with drink and had not his assailant been so obviously Welsh, he would have known immediately at whose feet to lay the blame.

As it was, he lay in the road, struggling within his cocoon, hearing the curses of men similarly encapsulated fighting to win free. Horses circled and plunged around him. The Welsh tossed banter cheerfully hither and yon in dips and swoops of sing-song language, haranguing each other and their victims alike and then, like autumnal swallows, they were gone. A lazy hoof kicked his side as the last horse departed and involuntarily he arched at the sudden buffet of pain.

The wind soughed. Silence descended. It began to rain.

CHAPTER 9

RHOSYN LISTENED TO the rain as an eddy of wind drove it against the hafod shutters. A spring squall. In between, the stars would peek through the scudding fierce clouds in pin-prick points of diamond-white light.

The fire, banked for the night, gave off a low, comfortable glow, eyes of red jewel warmth winking beneath the aromatic logs of the diseased pear tree that Twm had cut down last week.

Rhys and Eluned were newly abed. She could hear their conspiratorial whispers behind the bed curtains. Her son had turned eleven last week and thought himself very much the man. Indeed, he had complained at having to share his sleeping place with a mere girl. Her lips curved. The innocence of youth was still in his eyes. The time would come when he would gladly share his blanket with a 'mere girl' and for purposes other than sleep.

At fourteen, in Wales, he could claim his manhood. She would be thirty then, Eluned ten and this new babe, if it survived the early months, would be rising from helpless infancy into sturdy childhood.

She picked up her sewing, took a few half-hearted stitches and, with an irritated cluck, put it down again. The rushlight was too poor for this kind of delicate work and her mind was restless tonight, fluttering purposelessly like a moth at a candle flame. The baby turned in her womb, busily flexing new, delicate limbs. She felt the thrust and flicker with a protective hand. With almost four months of carrying left before the birth, she had not as yet burgeoned into ungainly discomfort. Her ripening body was a flower unfolding, full of mysteries and she was lost in the wonder of it.

The old dog sitting with its moist nose at her knee suddenly growled deep in its chest and stiffened. Rhosyn stood up to face the door, one hand reaching for Gelert's collar, the other for the rake that Twm had earlier been using on the floor rushes.

It was Twm's voice she heard outside now, gruff and questioning. A horse snorted. A man replied with amusement, the tone deeper than her servant's and edged with a foreign inflection to the Welsh she would have known anywhere. She fondled the dog and bade him lie and, dropping the rake, flew to the door and unbarred it to the night.

'Guyon!' she cried and flung herself into his arms. Twm arched a knowing resigned brow and, completely ignored, dismissed himself to his bed. Rhosyn withdrew from the hard clasp of Guyon's arms and drew him inside the hafod. Gelert whined and thumped his brindle tail on the rushes. She reset the bar and came once more into the circle of his arms.

'You smell of sheep,' she said against his mouth.

He nuzzled her cheek with a stubbly jaw. 'What kind of greeting is that for a man who has ridden hard for your sake?'

'Not for your own?' Rhosyn queried pertly, her eyes laughing, as green and gold as moss agates. 'You are overblown with vanity indeed.'

Her dark hair spilled down over his hands in a fine, cool cloak. Her breasts were ripe and warm against his chest. Within her belly the child kicked.

'How goes it with you?' he asked softly, his face suddenly all tenderness and concern.

Rhosyn gave a little shrug. 'I'm not sick any more, indeed, I've an appetite like a bacon pig. When I start to waddle like one, I will curse you and a certain hot, harvest night . . . Have you come alo . . .' She stopped. Guyon lifted his head from contemplation of her glowing skin and brilliant eyes just in time to be bowled over, or nearly so, by the two children.

They were like puppies, gambolling and clamouring; Rhys's new-found manhood had flown out of the window to leave only the excited child. Guyon bore with it very well, riding out the first storm with wry, rueful humour, curbed behind a half-turned head as their mother calmed them with dire threats and a voice suddenly grown as sharp as the flick of a lash.

Subdued, but not defeated, Eluned went to fetch him something to drink and Rhys sat down before the banked fire, hugging his knees, a compact boy wearing a darkling scowl on his strong, economical features.

'How long will you stay?' he demanded suddenly, slanting Guyon a glance from eyes as black as midnight tarns.

'Rhys!' his mother reprimanded more sharply than she had intended. It was a question that she herself had to the fore of her mind but dared not ask.

Guyon waved aside her anger with a grin. 'Do not take on so, *cariad*. I am accustomed to it by now. If he was not so obviously a boy, I would think it was my wife sitting at my feet. She has that way with her too.'

There was a queer little silence. Rhys's question was just the crust of the loaf, one of a thousand questions Rhosyn longed to ask him, but would not do so in the presence of the children and for the sake of her own pride.

'A few hours only, Rhys,' Guyon said into the calm eye of the storm. 'I have dared to pull the devil's tail and I must be in my own bed ere dawn lest he scorch me with his pitchfork.' He smiled at Eluned and took the mead she offered him. It was strong and sweet and as honey-golden as the fragrant harvest evening on which the unborn child had been conceived.

Rhys looked blank for a moment and then his quick mind took in the implications of the rough Welsh garb and coupled it with his knowledge that Guyon had skills most Normans did not. Something clandestine had been afoot and lord Guyon did not intend the blame lying at his door. Eluned, younger and impressionable to tales, took his words at face value and regarded him wide-eyed, a thrill running down her spine.

'And precisely where is your own bed?' Rhosyn asked, setting a platter of bread and cheese before him and thinking with a slight hint of bitterness that they were like courtiers, feting him with adulation.

Guyon gave her one of his quicksilver glances. 'Ledworth,' he answered and did not elaborate. Instead, he tossed something to Rhys.

The boy caught it deftly and transferred it to his lap. It was a leather sheath, lined with raw wool to hold in place the knife it contained and keep it naturally oiled with lanolin. The knife itself was almost a weapon. Eight inches long with a whetted blade gleaming as bright as fish scales against the blue herringbone pattern welding that fanned from its centre. The hilt was carved from a narwhal tooth, its surface flowing with the movement of bears and seals and thrusting ice caps.

'I know it is a month after Candlemas, but I had not forgotten your year day,' Guyon said as Rhys examined the knife with speechless delight.

Rhosyn eyed the gift with mixed feelings. Childhood was almost behind the boy and the knife was a symbol of the man too soon to emerge. 'You should not,' she said to Guyon, a little frown marring the smoothness of her brow.

'Scold,' he answered lightly and drew Eluned round into the circle of his arms. 'And I had not forgotten that it is your own year day come Easter and, since I am unlikely to be here, I have brought your gift early. Guess which hand.'

Delighted, Eluned played the game with him and he teased her, brown closed knuckles outstretched, his sleight of hand eluding her. At length she pounced on him, giggling and he conceded defeat, begging abjectly for mercy and gave her a small leather wallet containing a necklace of linked dainty daisies also carved from ivory.

Eluned flung her arms around Guyon's neck and delivered

him a smacking kiss, causing him to laugh. 'The surest way to a woman's heart,' he chuckled as he fastened the gold clasp around Eluned's slender throat.

'You buy us all,' Rhosyn agreed and, blinking, turned away to mend the fire. Guyon watched her over the child's tumbled black hair.

'That is not true, *cariad*,' he challenged softly. 'I have never had the price of you and I doubt I ever will.'

Rhosyn savagely poked the logs. 'You have always had the pretty words to cozen what you cannot buy!' she retorted. 'Rhys, Eluned, it is long past time you were asleep. Go on, get to your beds now!'

'But mam . . .!'

Her eyes kindled wrathfully, her hands set upon her hips, fingers tapping there.

Guyon lifted his brow at her tone, shot her a speculative look and squeezed his warm, rebellious armful. 'Do as your mother tells you, *anwylyd*,' he said gently. 'I think she wants a private word with me. We owe her that grace at least.'

Eluned pouted, unconvinced. Rhys stood up, the knife in his hand, his expression a mingling of childhood and maturity as selfishness warred with duty. After a long hesitation, the latter dominated. He thanked Guyon most properly for the knife, kissed his mother on the cheek and crossed the hall to withdraw behind the bed curtain.

'It's not fair!' Eluned complained.

'Life never is, my love,' said Rhosyn coming to hug her daughter. 'You'll learn it again and again as you grow older. Now say goodnight and be off with you.'

The child sighed heavily but did as she was bid. Her grip around Guyon's neck almost throttled him out of breath. 'I wish you could stay,' she said with heartfelt wistfulness, her lips warm on his cheek.

'So do I, *anwylyd*,' Guyon replied and meant it.

When they were alone, Rhosyn again unnecessarily mended the fire, her back to him. The silence stretched taut and the old dog whined. After a moment when she could bear it no longer, she threw down the poker and spun round to face him, her words almost a cry. 'Why have you come?'

'I thought you would be pleased to see me,' Guyon said neutrally.

Rhosyn drew breath to snap that he thought wrong, but changed her mind before the words were spoken. 'I am too pleased. You disrupt our lives. You come with your gifts and your ensorcelments, you beguile us into adoration and then you leave. I cannot bear it!'

'You have it in your power to change that,' he answered gently. 'You are welcome to make your home at Oxley.'

'A pretty caged bird to sing at your pleasure!' she flung, turning back to the fire.

'I did not come here to quarrel, *cariad*. Nor do I intend to leave upon one. We know each other better than that. If I have rubbed salt into a wound then I am sorry. You never gave me cause to believe that it ran any deeper than a mutual pleasuring.'

Rhosyn bit her lip and dug her nails into her palms, striving for the control to smile lightly and say that yes, he was right, it had not run any deeper. She felt his hand lightly on her shoulder turning her to face him. 'If the mountain will not come to Mohammed, then Mohammed must come to the mountain,' he said with teasing humour, eyes wandering to her belly. 'I needed to know how you fared.'

'Well now you do,' Rhosyn retorted coolly and would have drawn away except that now he held her fast and kissed her averted temple, the corner of her eye, her cheek and her mouth, refusing to release her and, indeed, her struggles were only half-hearted and soon ceased.

'I am foolish, Guyon,' she murmured, her arms collaring his neck as she faced him, a tremulous smile curving the mouth that he bent to kiss. 'I see the moon in a pool and I am disappointed when my hand despoils the illusion instead of grasping the reality. Be welcome for whatever time you choose to stay.'

Their embrace deepened, warm and sweet and poignant, desire sweeping but hard-held by the presence of the children a thin curtain away and, in Guyon, by a reluctance to cause . Rhosyn a deeper wound than she had already suffered.

He broke away first, his breathing ragged, and prowled to sit at the fire. His body protested at the discipline. It had been a long time since he had lain with a woman and his hunger was sharp. Sharp, but not uncontrollable. Whatever his detractors said, sexual liaisons were not to Guyon an immediate necessity of life. Given the leisure, the right circumstances and a willing partner, he enjoyed indulging his senses. Being as now he possessed only the latter, he drew several deep, slow breaths and made his mind busy with other thoughts.

'Where is your father?'

Rhosyn sat down beside him, just out of touching distance and picked up her distaff. Her fingers were trembling. She concentrated on the raw wool until the hot weakness should leave her limbs. 'Gone to Bristol. We expect him home tomorrow or the day after. I worry about him Guy. He is not well. He gets pains in his chest and Rhys is too young as yet to take more than an apprentice's responsibility.'

Guyon turned his head, eyes sharpening. 'The pack routes are no place for a woman,' he warned.

She did not answer, but the line of her mouth grew mulish and she gave all her attention diligently to the distaff.

'Rhosyn, so help me, if I hear you have stirred from your hearth to go trekking about the borders in a drover's cart, I will carry you off to Oxley myself and lock you up like a caged bird, in truth!'

'You have not the right!'

'I have every right. You carry my child. I will not see you dead in a ditch like Huw ap Sior!'

'I won't . . . What did you say?' Her fingers ceased their nimble twirling. Her eyes opened upon him, wide with shock. 'Huw, dead?'

'At the hand of Robert de Belleme and his gutter sweepings.

Huw's pack load of sables was brought to myself and Judith as a blood-smirched wedding gift.' Grimly, sparing her nothing, he gave her the details.

'He was my father's best friend,' she whispered jerkily when he had done. 'They were boys together . . . *oh Duw*!'

Their bodies closed again of a necessity as Guyon grabbed hold of her, afraid that she was going to faint. She leaned her cheek against his jerkin, her eyes closed, sick to the soul with grief and fear and shock.

'Promise me, *cariad*,' he murmured, stroking her hair, his voice as soft as silk, hard as steel.

She made a little movement against his chest. Her fingers gripped on his arms.

'Promise me.'

'What good is an oath given under duress?' Rhosyn replied shakily. 'I could give you my word and it would be worthless. Welsh oaths always are.' She uttered a desolate small laugh.

'Rhosyn . . .'

She pushed gently away from him and, having wiped her eyes, poured herself a cup of mead. 'I might be fickle Guy, but I am not about to step deliberately within de Belleme's ring of fire. I will swear you this much honestly; that I will not stir from here until after the child is born and only then by necessity. And I will send to you for an escort.'

Guyon studied her through narrowed lids but did not seek to persuade her further. He had her concessions in his hand and was not about to jeopardise them with bitterness and anger.

'All right, *cariad*,' he said quietly. '*A bryn gig a bryn esgyrn*. I do not suppose I would care so much were you not so cursedly independent.' He sat down beside the fire and picked up the mead that Eluned had poured for him.

Rhosyn stared at him across the firelit space that separated them. With his Welsh clothing and dark complexion he might have been of her own race and class and no barrier but the fire's glow between them. It was a bitter-sweet illusion.

Merchant's daughter and marcher lord, already married for the sake of convenience and dynasty. He looked tired, she thought. The shadows beneath his eyes were not all the result of the dull light.

'Does your wife know your whereabouts, Guy?'

He took a swallow of the mead, swirled its golden surface and then looked at her and, surprisingly, there was rueful amusement in his eyes. 'She may have a suspicion,' he admitted. 'And for sure, if I am not over the drawbridge come dawn, I'll have to deal with a hellcat . . . and not for the reason I can see on your face.' The amusement became a wry chuckle. He drank the remainder of the mead and did not offer to elucidate.

Rhosyn swallowed the temptation to ask. If Guyon was on this side of the border after dark and dressed in native garments and murmuring about scorching the devil's tail, then it was best she knew nothing at all. 'What is she like?'

'I think she would surprise you,' he answered, putting down the cup to fondle the cold thrust of Gelert's nose at his thigh. 'God knows, she certainly surprised me . . . and continues to do so.'

'Is she pretty, Guy?'

A curious, casually spoken woman's question with tension lurking beneath the surface.

'Not as you are pretty, *cariad*, but striking in her way I suppose, or she will be when she grows into her bones. She's a child Rhos, man-shy and half-wild.'

Rhosyn knelt at the hearth, her face bathed in red light. She had thought about him at the time of his marriage, imagined him abed with his unwanted young Norman bride and wondered if the skills of the bedchamber and sweet grass meadow had stood him in good stead then.

'No,' he said softly into the small silence of her thoughts. 'I have not bedded her. She has the frightened eyes of a lass half her age. She knows nothing of men except what her father was and her uncle is.'

Rhosyn turned her neat head in surprise.

'Even if she opened to me for the sake of duty, it would be little less than rape. She is as flat as a kipper before and behind and the crown of her head scarce reaches to my armpit.'

'*Duw*, Guyon!'

'Wishing you had not asked?' he said with a mocking smile, then shook his head. 'The match is not entirely a disaster. Judith has abilities beyond most young women of her station.'

Rhosyn lifted her brows. Guyon laughed, this time with genuine mirth. 'It is not given to every wench to be able to handle a dagger, or hone it to perfection on a whetstone. She has a wicked sense of humour, too. I would not put it past her to grease a slope for the joy of seeing someone slide down it – probably me. I do not believe I shall grow bored – if I live. One of my neighbours at least would dearly love to dance on my grave and rule in my stead and Robert de Belleme merely bides his time and, fool that I am, it offends my sensibilities to murder the pair of them in stealth as they would do to me without a qualm of conscience.'

Rhosyn considered him. He had spoken lightly, but his eyes above the shadows were veiled and the fine mouth was set in a straight grim line, and she realized how trivial her own complaints would seem when set against his various burdens. Crossing the space between them, she laid her hand on his shoulder and her cheek to his in a wordless embrace, her black hair spilling down over his rough jerkin and capuchon.

His own hand reached to grip hers, long-fingered, blade-bruised and graceful. She wished suddenly that the child she carried should inherit those hands.

They sat like that while the silence of the night settled around them. Rain thudded against the hafod walls, rhythmic and heavy. Guyon closed his eyes, meaning only to rest them for a moment and instead fell asleep.

Rhosyn gently, stealthily, disengaged her hand from his and stared at him, vulnerable and long-limbed, his jaw blue-stubbled, his eyes blue-circled and swallowed the lump in her throat, remembering the time she had first seen him.

She had been a bride of fifteen then, with her new husband proud at her side, indulgently buying her trinkets in Hereford. He had been a coltish nineteen, awkward with his limbs, still filling them out and possessed of melting, long-lashed brown eyes that stood quite at odds with the firmly held mouth and arrogant jaw. He had not noticed her then, nor yet in the times that she visited Milnham with her husband and her father. Not until four years ago when, widowed, she had personally bargained with him over the price of wool clip. Those eyes of his, so tender and innocent, had almost been her downfall. She had believed that innocence until she realised belatedly that she was being ruthlessly manoeuvred into a corner from which the only extrication was agreement to his price. *Yr llewpart du*, they called him – the black leopard – and, like a cat, there were honed claws beneath the velvet and the tuned instincts of a soft-padding hunter.

She had not let him catch her; not then, nor when she went to his bed, and especially not now. She rubbed her sleeve over her damp eyes and gave a small, self-deprecatory smile, her practical merchant's mind beginning to surface from the maelstrom of emotion in which it had been bogged down. She took his cloak and spread it across a stool to dry and prepared a small, stoppered bottle of mead, her movements brisk but silent. In an hour she would wake him and he would go, and their meshed worlds would slide apart like two sword blades gliding off each other in a hissing spangle of sparks. *Yr cath yn yr tywllwch fy anwylyd.*

She sat down again when all was done and took up her distaff, and listened with pleasure to the slow, even rhythm of his breathing while she wondered idly what had brought him over the border in so clandestine a fashion.

Twenty miles away and some hours later, wondering was also the preoccupation of another who waited, vacillating

109

between terror and rage at Guyon's continued absence. Judith's nerves were raw. The very touch of a thought agitated them to agony.

It was almost dawn. A glimpse through the arrowslit repeated several times this last hour had revealed the sinking stars and a milky glimmer to the east. Her stomach felt as if a thousand butterflies fluttered there and the words that scalded her lips as she peered out on the imminent morning were burning with fury and filled with guilt lest she was cursing a dead man to hell for his tardiness. The thought of him staring sightless into the dawn, his body sword-cloven caused her to whirl from the arrowslit with a gasp, her hands over her eyes.

Eric and the others had ridden in through the postern shortly before midnight. She would not have known of it had not Melyn yowled to be let out, thus disturbing her from a light, restless sleep. The arrowslit which looked out on the postern had revealed the stealthy entry of the men and ponies. She had expected Guyon then, but he had not come. The ponies had disappeared promptly like beasts of the Wild Hunt into the hollow hills and when she had let Melyn out and gone down to Eric, he had been taciturn and evasive and not best pleased to see her. Lord Guyon had business in Wales. He would be back soon enough. He advised that she retire.

Judith knew that when she recovered her equilibrium she would be thoroughly chagrined at her furious loss of temper, but for the nonce, like a drunkard, she just did not care. Eric had recoiled from the lash of her tongue, eyes popping. When Guyon returned, she intended to do more than just make him recoil. He told her nothing, left her to worry, treated her like a child who did not have the skill to understand.

'Nor shall I,' she said through clenched teeth as she flounced away from the arrowslit and began to dress, 'if he does not give me the chance!'

She had just pulled on her stockings and shift and was scrabbling about on all fours, half beneath the bed, searching for a wayward shoe, when Guyon entered the room on cat-silent feet.

'*Bore da, cath fach*,' he declared in his impeccable Welsh, a grin on his face at the sight of her upturned wriggling posterior.

The wriggling ceased. For a long moment she was still and then, backing out, turned to face him, her complexion flushed with chagrin and anger and the effect of gravity.

'Strange moonlight,' she said sarcastically, her eyebrows linked across her brow. 'I have been sick with worry! Eric rode in before midnight matins. Guyon, where have you been?'

'I went to see Rhosyn and I fell asleep,' he replied matter-of-factly and came further into the room to sit on a stool and begin unthonging his boots.

'You went to see Rhosyn?' she repeated and swallowed the urge to hurl her newly found shoe at him. 'Have you changed your mind?'

'About what? Fetch me a drink, there's a good lass.'

Judith dropped the shoe and turned away, her back as rigid as a lance, her voice choked with the effort of controlling her rage. 'You said that you had no mistress.'

Guyon flashed her a glance from beneath his wind-dishevelled hair. 'I don't. Huw ap Sior was a close friend of her family. I took her the news of his death and a warning to be on guard. I am sorry if you are vexed, but expect apology for nought else.'

'Vexed is not the word!' Judith retorted, pouring wine into a cup with a shaking hand. 'I could kill you myself!'

'No doubt . . . Pass me those clothes over there.'

'Those?' She swung to him, lids widening. 'But Guyon, they stink!'

'I know.' He grimaced, took the wine she offered, drank a mouthful and then set it down. 'Spike it will you?' he said. 'With white poppy.'

'What for?'

'To make me sufficiently difficult to rouse when Robert de Belleme hails at our drawbridge.'

'And why should he do that?' Judith challenged. She had a strong inkling as to the reply having had plenty of time to think during the long watches of the night while her absent husband enjoyed another woman's company without thought for his terrified wife, but she wanted to hear the reply from his own lips, not be treated like an imbecile who would give the game away if possessed of knowledge.

Carefully he stood up, aware that he had made a mistake. A child he had thought, a child with an amusing precocious wit, her domestic skills to be admired, her company refreshing but unessential to the fabric of his life. Obviously with her the thing went much deeper, her sense of wounded pride and possession a tangible thing, beating upon him in the silence following her last flung question.

'He might think that I was involved in a Welsh raid upon him and his men that took place on the Shrewsbury road yestereve,' he answered calmly. 'I did not tell you before in case we failed. At least you could truthfully have claimed your innocence.'

'And what good would that do?' Judith retorted, not particularly impressed. 'You know what my uncle does to "innocents".' Her mouth tightened, but it was because he had been ensconced at another woman's hearth, perhaps even in her arms, while she paced the floor here at Ledworth in a cold sweat of terror for his life.

'Look,' he said a trifle wearily, 'I do not expect you to go into the kitchen details of how you make a particular dish, but I will praise it or otherwise when it comes to table, and it is the same with certain of my doings. I told you what was needful.'

'What you thought was needful.'

Guyon swallowed and cast around for a fresh reserve of patience. A day of pretence and fencing with men he loathed, a night of clandestine work, an hour's sleep in a hard chair and some chancey riding over rough terrain in the pitch dark made it very difficult to find. 'Judith, don't push me,' he said softly.

A trickle of cold ran down her spine. The gentle tone was far more frightening than a bellow to mind her own business and a raised fist. She turned abruptly away and began to prepare a draught of the poppy syrup.

Guyon continued to strip. 'What about the rest of the keep?' he asked after a moment. 'What do they think?'

She looked round at him, her expression impassive, her eyes blank. 'Some of them believe that it is good for you to release your tension in a surfeit of drink, all young men do it. Others say that they always knew you were wild and incontinent. Mama is desperate for my safety. Papa used to beat us both when he was in his cups . . . He split my lip once . . . Mama cannot act to save her life. I dare not tell her the truth.'

'Pot calling the cauldron black,' he snorted with brusque amusement. 'You accuse me and then do the same to your mother!'

Judith drew breath for a hot retort that it was not the same at all, but prudence gritted her teeth on the words. Do not push me he had said and she had no way of knowing how close to the edge he actually was.

'I am sorry that your mother should be deceived in me, but there is no help for it. So much depends on de Belleme believing my innocence, or at least being unable to refute it,' Guyon added and came forward to take the cup from her fingers, tipped up her stubborn chin on his free hand and kissed her gently. 'Trust me, *cath fach*.'

His lips were as subtle as silk, his beard stubble prickly on her tender skin. Something stirred and uncoiled itself along Judith's nerve endings, and, disturbed, she drew quickly away from him. 'Will you tell me how you retrieved the silver?'

Guyon eyed her narrowly but could read very little in her expression, so carefully was she guarding it. His own fault, he supposed, for warning her off. It was just that he was tired and unsure that he could cope with whatever she would throw at him in her hurt and anger. One contrary woman a night was enough on any man's trencher.

He looked down into the wine and swirled it thoughtfully around. 'It was worth every drop of this foul brew,' he said after a moment and took a gulp so that the heavy sweetness would not cloy his palate. And then, beginning to laugh, he told her precisely what they had done.

Foul-tempered, his insouciance flown out of the window, Robert de Belleme demanded hoarsely to see the lord of Ledworth.

'He's still abed, m'lord,' Eric answered staunchly, broad Saxon bones concealing all qualms. 'It'll be the devil of a job to rouse him.'

'Do it!' snarled de Belleme, 'or I'll flay your hide and use it for a saddle cloth!'

Given another man, the speech would merely have been picturesque. Being as it was the Earl of Shrewsbury who spoke, Eric knew the threat was not idle.

'If you will wait a moment my lord . . .'

'Make haste, peasant!' growled Walter de Lacey from his place at the Earl's left shoulder and he wiped his hand across his bruised mouth.

Eric bowed low, mouth tightening under cover of the full brown moustache, and left the two men at the fire, a wine flaggon close to hand.

It was late morning, the servants bustling. The smell of new bread wafted past the men's dust-caked nostrils as a maid laid out the dais table.

'Returning for hospitality so soon, my lords?'

De Belleme whirled, raw-eyed and sleep-riven to regard the cold blue glance of his former sister-in-law, Alicia de Montgomery. A bitch in blue sarcenet with a milky collar of pearls at her still surprisingly young throat.

'Recovered entirely from yesterday's malady I see,' he answered with mock pleasantry, continuing to look her up and down. 'You are remarkably well-dressed for a drudge.'

'You should take a gazing-glass to yourself,' Alicia retorted, the pearls jumping hard on her collarbone. 'What can we offer you to be on your way this time?'

His right hand flashed out to grip her wrist and tighten over the knobs of bone. It was so sudden and so painful that involuntarily she cried out. A servant with a pitcher in his hand hesitated. De Belleme flashed him a red-rimmed glare that sent the man scuttling for cover.

'You always were a clapper-tongued clever bitch!' he hissed at her. 'My brother was a fool not to silence your jabber with the blade of his knife!'

'It runs in your family,' she retorted, struggling in his grip, feeling as if her bones were about to give way beneath the grinding pressure. On his own wrist, the weals burned by the cords of his humiliation were a raw, blistered red.

'Where was Guyon FitzMiles last night?' he demanded, his face so close that she could see the small open pores pin-pricking his high-bridged nose and feel the flecks of spittle on her face as spat the words at her.

'Blind-drunk in his bed!' she gasped. 'My lord, you are breaking my arm!'

'And so I will if you do not tell me the truth, you whore!'

It was no idle threat and Alicia knew it. The pain was making her feel sick. One slight twist and her bones would snap like dry twigs. 'It is the truth. You saw him carried away yourself!'

De Lacey muttered a warning from the side of his mouth and the earl flung her several paces away from him with a routier's oath.

Gasping, tears of pain and fury in her eyes, Alicia glared loathing at him.

De Belleme returned the look with contempt and an unspoken threat and turned away to view the man staggering across the hall, supported on one side by the captain of the guard and on the other by his anxious wife.

De Lacey swore in dismayed surprise. The earl stared blankly at Guyon who was stained and rumpled, ungroomed, still stinking of wine and completely without coordination.

'Whatever you want,' Guyon enunciated slowly, his tongue stumbling round the words, his eyes owlishly squinting and unfocused; 'I pray you be quick before I am most vilely sick all over your boots.' He swayed alarmingly. Eric grimly propped him up. Judith bit her lip and looked tearfully concerned, clinging to her husband's wine-soiled sleeve.

De Belleme gazed round at the circle of hostile faces. 'We were attacked on the road, pillaged, tied up and left for the wolves,' he bit out. 'I thought you might know something.'

Silence. Guyon's sluggish lids half-lifted. 'Lost your silver too?' he said with a slow smile. It almost became a laugh but the movement of his shoulders brought on a sudden bout of nausea and he folded retching against his wife and his bodyguard.

Judith looked across at the enraged men. 'I am sorry to hear of your misfortune,' she said doucely. 'Is there anything we can do? Horses? Food? Are there wounded among you?'

Impotent, beaten, Robert de Belleme stared into the topaz-quartz cat's eyes with all their innocence and Eve-like deception and then he flicked his gaze to the huddled man at her feet, the feline grace snuffed like a candle flame, lank black hair grazing the rushes.

'Pray,' he snarled. 'Pray very hard that you are innocent.' He swung on his heel, spurs jingling, de Lacey dogging his footsteps, a sneer on his lips. Alicia flinched away and crossed herself.

'Oh God,' Guyon groaned, half-raising his head. 'You wretched girl, I ought to kill you before you kill me.'

'Perhaps I put too large a measure of the drug in your wine, but at least your display was convicing,' Judith answered judiciously. 'Do you feel sick, or are you able to stand?'

Alicia, about to set her foot where angels feared to tread, once more found herself a baffled outsider to the understanding that existed between Judith and the green-faced man now gingerly rising to his feet.

'You'll be all right by this evening,' Judith consoled him and gestured one of the household knights to help him back to bed.

'Hecate,' he muttered, but managed a wan smile over his shoulder.

'I do not suppose you are going to explain any of this to me?' Alicia asked, a line of exasperation between her brows.

'No mama,' Judith agreed and smiled that gentle, secretive smile that was all her father's legacy.

CHAPTER 10

THE SHADOWS OF the June evening had begun to lengthen. The sunlight was as golden as cider, but the wind that cut across the marches and ruffled the slate feathers of the peregrine on its eyrie was edged with cold.

Guyon stood upon Ravenstow's wall walk and appreciatively inhaled the clean, meadow-scented air. Below, the hall was hazy, redolent with the smell of smoked herrings and eels that had been the main dish of the evening meal, it being Friday. A lingering aftermath of the deception practised upon de Belleme – a punishment and a penance – was the delicacy of his stomach where such items as smoked fish were concerned.

Cadi thumped her tail, eyes cocked adoringly, alert to move if he should, but he remained staring out over the demesne. The water meadows gave way to the peasant's strips sown with oats and pease, green-blowing in the wind that chased a contrast of shadows and oblique amber sunlight over the land. A harsh land, filled with the dangers of sudden Welsh raids and the slinking shaggy shadows of grey winter wolves.

As the summer advanced, the Welsh had grown bold in their raiding. A flock of sheep here, a bull there, a woman in one of Guyon's border hamlets. He had, of course, retaliated. An eye for an eye. Everyone knew the rules ... except Robert de Belleme who rampaged up and down his earldom like Grendel of the marsh, destroying and torturing. Doggedly the Welsh retreated into the hills where he could not follow, taking everything with them and letting their flimsy hafods burn. Reconstruction took only a matter of days and de

Belleme was too great a lord to occupy his entire summer chasing ephemeral shadows through wet Welsh woods. He left that to his vassals, men such as Walter de Lacey and Ralph of Thorneyford.

The latter had died last mouth during one such foray into Wales. He and his men had been ambushed and, while fighting his way out, he had suffered a seizure and fallen dead from his horse. Guyon and Judith had attended the funeral as a mark of respect but, circumstances and the other mourners being what they were, had not remained much beyond the ceremony.

Guyon had dealt efficiently with the raids on his own lands and kept a jaundiced, watchful eye on de Lacey's savage attempts to do the same. He did the rounds of his vassals and castellans, holding manor courts, advising, solving, replacing and recruiting, granting, denying, his finger firmly on the pulse.

He began to move slowly along the wall walk. Cadi leaped to her feet, shook herself and followed, nose grazing his heels. A young guard saluted him. Guyon paused a moment to speak, remembering from long training the man's name and family circumstances. It was a little effort that never failed to repay more than double its expenditure in willingness and loyalty.

The guard paused in mid-reply to Guyon's query and saluted again, this time flushing scarlet to the tips of his ears.

Guyon swung round to find his wife, pink and breathless from her climb, strands of hair escaping her tawny braids and blowing free in the stiffening breeze. The guard's blush he attributed to the fact that women seldom came aloft and certainly not as informally as this. It never occurred to him that the young man might find Judith attractive to look upon.

'I've found her!' Judith panted, clutching Guyon's arm, her eyes as bright as two polished serpentines. 'She was in one of the bailey storesheds nestled down among a heap of fleeces.'

He slipped his arm absently around her waist and kissed her cheek. 'I told you she would not have gone far,' he said with a slightly superior air.

Judith stiffened. 'You groaned the words at me from the bed because you wanted to be left in peace to sleep,' she said tartly. 'You could not have cared less!'

'Well, not at the time,' he conceded with a grin. 'But I knew she was bound to turn up. I've never known a beast with a life so charmed.'

'She's taken a lover. The same one that sired her last lot of offspring. A great black mannerless leopard of a tom that lives wild on the slope!'

Guyon smiled and leaned upon the limewashed sandstone to watch the clouds ride the wind in sweeps of feathery flamingo pink. 'Well, it is spring after all,' he said with amusement.

Judith felt the colour warm her face. He had been very patient with her thus far, his embraces light and fraternal, teasingly affectionate without so much as an edge of desire. Her stomach no longer lurched sickeningly when they retired of a night. She knew that she was not about to be raped. Once, unconsciously he had reached an arm across her naked, flat body and murmured a name into her hair, his lips nuzzling her nape and her blood had prickled, moved by something alien and unsettling that flushed her loins with moist heat. Afraid, she had tossed vigorously and coughed and the pattern of his breathing had broken, he had removed his arm with a wry, half-waking apology and rolled over away from her.

The time would come, she knew, when she would have to know his flesh. He was his father's sole heir, the duty pressing upon him to beget more branches on the tree than Miles had done.

'If I was barren would you divorce me?' she asked curiously.

He left the merlon and walked onwards until they could

120

overlook the river and its bustle of traffic at the toll as boats
sought to moor before nightfall. He looked over his shoulder
at her, expression sparkling with laughter. 'Come now *cath
fach*, where else would I find a wife capable of besting me at
dagger play?'

'I do not suppose it would matter if she bore you half a
dozen sons.'

'Kind of you to offer,' he rejoindered, cheerfully misconstruing her words. 'I have the patience to wait on your ripening
lust.' She pinched him. He yelped and then suddenly craned
forward and slitted his gaze the better to view the distance.
'Behave yourself, graceless wench!' he reproved, slapping her
rump. 'Can't you see we have visitors?'

Judith came to his side and stood on tip-toe. Below them, a
long barge had just nudged into its mooring and the crew
were making her secure.

'Your father!' she exclaimed as Miles stepped onto the
wharf.

'Cat among the pigeons,' Guyon murmured with interested
humour.

'Who is that with him? Jesu, she's beautiful!' Judith bobbed
against her husband. A stray tawny wisp of her hair cobweb-
bed his face.

'My half-sister, Emma. If you remember, she could not
attend our nuptials because she was in London.'

'Those girls with her are your nieces?'

'Christen, Celie, and Marian,' he agreed, looking wryly
amused.

Judith regarded the group for a moment. The older
woman, even from this distance, was obviously lovely and
rich. The white fur lining of her cloak gleamed like silk on
snow as it caught the sunlight and her braided hair was the
precise colour of a horse-chestnut new-hulled from its case.
The girls too were elegantly robed and visibly scrubbed and
shining. Delicately bred, gentle young ladies.

Dismayed, Judith clamped her lower lip between her teeth,

aware that she was wearing her oldest gown and that it was rough with Melyn's moulting fur. Her hair was unkempt, her kirtle dirty and there was nothing prepared to make them a fitting welcome.

'What am I going to do?' she gasped.

Guyon turned, looked her up and down from the bird's nest crown of her head to the scuffed toes of her leather slippers and grinned. 'And yet you can face down Robert de Belleme with never a qualm.' He lifted her chin on his forefinger and kissed her nose before whirling her about to face the stairs down. 'Em's all right, she won't eat you.'

'She might if there's nought else on her trencher,' Judith responded wryly.

'Em's got a heart of gold beneath the steel. She'll fold you to her breast like a waif and stray and I will be the one to receive the scolding. She still thinks of me as a brat of six filching griddle cakes from the bakehouse door and putting headless mice on her trencher.'

Momentarily diverted, Judith flashed him a glance compounded of horror and amusement. 'And things have changed?' she said saucily and ducked adroitly beneath his playful cuff.

'Headless cats now,' he retorted and hugged her.

They had reached the bottom of the stairs. 'I am very fortunate,' Judith said on a sudden, blushing impulse. 'And very grateful. Guyon I . . .'

'Do not set your worth too cheaply, *cath fach*,' he interrupted easily and tugged her braid in an affectionate gesture with which she was now thoroughly familiar.

'Your wife is contrary to my expectations, Guy,' murmured Emma, reaching manicured white fingers to the chased stem of her cup.

Guyon smiled faintly and stretched out his legs to lounge more comfortably in his chair on the dais. 'Why, what did you expect?' He followed her gaze to the fire and the four girls who crouched there, heads close, intent over a game of knuckle bones. Christen possessed her mother's chestnut-red colouring. The two younger girls were plain brown like their absent father. Judith's hair sparkled the bronze-blond of a young vixen's pelt against the contrasting darkness of the other three. Christen said something. Judith capped it wittily and her laughter rang.

Emma sipped the wine. 'Well she's certainly not a Montgomery to look upon. I can see her mother's bones, but where on earth did she get those eyes and that hair?'

'From her grandam perhaps?' Guyon said disinterestedly. 'Maurice was only a bastard son of the house. By all accounts his mother was a Danish widow out of York.'

'Yes, perhaps. I thought she would be slight and dark . . . and less of a child. At sixteen I was extremely conscious of my appearance and how to use it on men to gain my own ends.'

'Oh, Judith has her ways and means,' he said easily. 'And if I ever had a yen for women who primped and preened, I lost it swiftly enough at court. The difference between those harpies and Judith is the difference between dross and pure gold. No insult to yourself intended, Em. You use your talents with subtlety.'

'Thank you,' Emma retorted archly. 'I'll treasure the compliment.'

'Christen does not appear to have inherited your discretion,' he added casually as the chestnut head lifted from the game and a long-lashed glance was slanted at one of the youngest knights in the hall.

Emma sighed heavily. 'You have noticed it too? There is a devil in her, Guy and it will destroy her unless it can be contained.'

'She is scarcely yet fourteen,' he said quietly, all humour flown.

'And older than Eve.'

'And part of the reason you were summoned to London and are here now instead of with Robert at court?'

She gave him a sidelong look. She had forgotten how sharp his perception could be. 'The cities are foul and full of disease in summer and it is time I paid some attention to my dower lands. I suspect the steward has been using my absence to line his own pockets.'

Guyon looked thoughtfully at his niece. Pert and pretty with strongly marked red eyebrows and a bone structure beyond her years. There was no malice in the child, he thought, rather an unthinking precociousness. 'You have decided to remove her from the vices of the court, you mean.'

'It seemed a sound idea at the time,' Emma said bleakly. 'To send her to housekeep for her father while my duty kept me here in the marches after mama died. The girls see so little of him that I thought it would be of benefit to them both.'

Guyon grunted. 'You see little enough of him yourself.'

Emma shrugged. 'It is not given that every match should scorch the soul. We are content, Guy.'

'Have you spoken to Richard about her?'

'He says the sooner we mate her the better, but I do not know. Perhaps she is merely playing at what she sees the court trollops do and, because she is pretty and men respond, she does it the more, never knowing how close to the fire her fingers are. Then again, my mother was a Rouen whore. Perhaps it runs in the blood. I truly do not know, Guy.'

He was silent for a time. A serving lad replenished his cup and moved on. Cadi stirred restlessly at his feet.

'You were right to bring her away,' he said at length, his gaze considering the circle of girls. 'Christen has always been swayed by the actions of those around her. Do you remember when she was nine and wanted to become a nun because one of the maids took the veil?'

A faint, pained smile twitched Emma's lips. 'And last year the crusade,' she said. 'I caught her sewing a cross on her best cloak, her belongings packed in a travelling bundle and vowing to see Jerusalem or die.'

124

'So what she requires is a spell of gentle domestic harmony with myself and Judith for examples?' Emma flicked at his straight-faced eyes, laughing. Guyon flicked her a look. 'I thought you had serious doubts concerning my state of grace?'

'Oh that was just irritation at the weakness of all men,' she said impatiently. 'I know why you act the rutting stag at court and you and Rhosyn have long had a private understanding. You handle Christen better than any of us. She might listen to you . . . and she might listen to your Judith. There is not so much difference in age and they appear to like each other.'

'It depends upon what you want her to learn in lieu of coquetry,' Guyon chuckled, thinking of Judith's repertoire of dubious skills. He rose to his feet and, still smiling, left the high table. Emma followed him.

His father and Eric were locked in mortal combat over a game of nine men's morris beside the hearth and neither paid any attention to Cadi's inquisitive nosings.

Guyon nodded towards his father. 'Have you noticed any difference in papa these last few weeks, Em?'

'Not really. Perhaps a little quieter, but you know how he broods. Before we set out, he spent a long time kneeling at mama's tomb and then complained that his knees were stiff. Why do you ask?' Her voice sharpened. 'Is there something wrong?'

'No, nothing,' he soothed, a hand on her arm. 'Mere filial concern. What he needs is another wife . . . or a mistress.'

Emma scowled at him. 'You don't seriously mean that, Guy.'

'Why not?'

'Would you welcome another woman in mama's place – a stepmother?'

'You are deluding yourself if you think he has lived like a monk since her death,' he snorted.

'I know he has taken casual women for comfort and pleasure!' Emma said with asperity, 'But they were in no wise partners for life.'

'That's what I mean, Em. He needs something more. Mama was his anchor and he is in danger of going adrift without one.' Having gained the information he sought and not wishing Emma to pursue the matter, he attempted to distract her attention. 'What colours do you think for a new tapestry on that wall?'

She narrowed her eyes, quite aware of his ploy, for the question was a feminine one designed to draw forth her enthusiasm. 'We heard that Robert de Belleme had beggared your coffers of all but dust,' she said tartly. 'Was the rumour wrong?'

'What do you think?' he answered sunnily and, leaving her, he went to play knucklebones with his wife and nieces.

Guyon ceased examining the delectable golden mare and stared at his father with round-eyed interest. 'What did you say?'

The Alfred lantern swung in a breeze and shadows lumbered clumsily up the stable walls. The mare was a gift for Judith, the furtiveness of this night visit to the stable because she was to be a surprise.

'Only that Rannulf Flambard has officially been granted the bishopric of Durham as payment for his tireless endeavours,' said Miles, his face studiously blank.

'God preserve the devil when *he* gets to hell.' Guyon's mouth twitched. 'What's he going to do, strip the church from within and give it all to Rufus?'

'Oh, of a certainty, weasling little runt.'

The mare lipped Guyon's tunic. He scratched her beneath the chin. 'But shrewd and clever with it. At least if he's snatching food from the mouths of monks, he's not snatching it from us,' he conceded with a shrug.

Rannulf Flambard, a common cleric, had risen by his own diligent efforts from obscurity to the ranks of the most highly powered men in the land. He had become indispensable to Rufus and a menace to every single member of the barony; a

126

tax collector with a herculean grip on men's financial affairs and the ability to tighten that grip and squeeze his victims dry.

Guyon thoroughly disliked the man, rather for his attitude than from any squeamish qualms concerning his lowly birth or task of crown revenue raiser. Indeed, with a numerical talent of his own, he had the good sense to respect Flambard's extraordinary skills and step warily around them.

'Of course,' Miles added sarcastically as Guyon admired the mare's conformation, 'Flambard is not the only hazard to our coffers. The Welsh take their tithe of silver too.'

Guyon eyed his father nonchalantly across the mare's satin withers. 'I thought you might have heard about de Belleme's misfortune,' he said with a hint of regret in his voice.

'And yours too?'

Guyon smiled. He could not dissemble with his sire who knew him too well and saw too clearly. Silence was by far the better line of defence.

'Have a care, Guyon. Step very softly around the Earl of Shrewsbury. His rages are all the more deadly for being silent and the remains of his victims are not a pretty sight. And he is stronger than ever now. Did you know that he has paid Rufus another relief to take Roger de Bully's lands?'

The flippancy vanished, replaced by startled attention. 'No, I didn't.'

'Blythe and Tickhill straight down the devil's throat. He's likely to be short of coin and temper. Don't try any more clever tricks like that last one . . . You know what I mean.'

'So if he wants to eat the world, I just stand aside and let him?'

'You don't fling your gage in his teeth!'

'I haven't. A trip rope across his path perhaps, in revenge for a parcel of bloody sables.'

Miles scraped his fingers through his hair and gritted his teeth, reminding himself that Guyon was almost thirty years old and the mould too firmly set to be broken or altered by an exasperated lecture.

'Just be careful, that's all.'

'Meek as a virgin,' Guyon answered lightly.

'Just don't get deflowered,' Miles said acidly. 'I'm going to bed.'

The lightness left Guyon's face. 'Chance would be a fine thing,' he said to the horse and followed his father.

CHAPTER 11

JUDITH GASPED AND wriggled round in the bed, squinting through her lids as the brightness of daylight flooded into the room. The covers were wrenched aside, leaving her nought for modesty but a cloak of tawny hair.

'On your feet you lazy baggage, or are you going to sleep until noon?'

She sat up, glowering.

Guyon laughed. 'You'll miss a surprise if you do.'

She rubbed her eyes and regarded him blearily. He was wearing a short hunting tunic of green plaid and thick linen chausses, his hose bound with leather cross-garters. She had not heard him wake and dress, but then he could be as soft-footed as Melyn when he chose.

'What kind of surprise?'

'The kind that will not wait forever.' He hooked his thumbs in his belt and studied her. Her hair spilled down. A freckled white shoulder gleamed through the untidy tresses and a small, apple-sized rosy-tipped breast. Flank and leg were lithe and long, her mother's gift and not displeasing.

Suddenly nervous, she lowered her eyes, a pink flush staining her throat and face. Abruptly he turned away to her clothing pole and, selecting garments, tossed them on the bed.

'I'll send in Agnes. Don't be too long, *cath fach*.'

His tone was teasing, his face wearing its customary light smile and her momentary qualm dissolved into an impudent grimace as he reached the door.

Most of the household was still asleep and, as Judith indignantly discovered on entering the hall, it was not long after dawn. A yawning boy was arranging the side trestles for the serving of bread and curd cheese and small beer. Guyon was leaning on the edge of the dais, deep in conversation with the steward and the reeve, Cadi as usual appended to his side.

The two standing men bowed. She smiled a greeting to the steward. To the reeve she spoke. He had not long been appointed to the position – a young man with small children, well able to cope with the task of mediating between the lord and his tenants, but still finding his feet.

Guyon listened to her warm queries after the health of the man's family with whose every name and circumstance she was familiar and was once more amazed at her scope.

'I didn't know his aunt Winifred suffered from gout,' he chuckled as he led her out of the forebuilding and into the early morning bustle of the bailey.

'She doesn't,' Judith said, regarding him with grave clarity. 'She just likes their attention. There's nothing wrong with the cantankerous old bag. I could think of several effective if drastic remedies to cure her condition. Cutting out her tongue, for one.'

'Judith!' he spluttered.

'It is the truth and only you to hear it. Why should I lie?'

Guyon shook his head, unable to think of a response or reprimand because in essence she was right, and held to an amused silence as he led her into the stables.

A lanky youth of about Judith's own age was forking soiled straw into the yard. Hens pecked and scratched near his feet. Balls of yellow fluff twinkled hither and yon, imitating in miniature the actions of their parents, miraculously avoiding the lad's stout brogans and the sweeps of the fork.

'Good morning, Hob,' Judith greeted him warmly. He turned a dusky campion-pink and mumbled and louted like an idiot.

'What's the surprise, Guy?' She smiled up at him as she had smiled at Hob, quite unaware of what it did to her face.

'You are, constantly, *cath fach*,' he replied, somewhat warily and then in English to the boy, 'Where's your father?'

'Just coming, m'lord. He's walking her round to stop her getting cold.'

'Who?' asked Judith.

Guyon took her arm and turned to face his head groom who appeared around the edge of the building with a harnessed mare following doucely behind.

'Guyon?' She twisted to look up at him and then back at the delicately stepping jennet.

'I thought it was time you had a more mettlesome mount than that old bay nag you've adopted. Her name's Euraidd. She's four years old and from the stud herd down at Ashdyke.'

Judith stared at the vision filling her eyes and it swung its convex Spanish head to return the compliment out of limpid, long-lashed black eyes. Euraidd – golden. A mare the colour of the sun. Darker dappled rings like gold coins shimmered on the silken haunches and contour of shoulder and belly. Her mane and tail were a flossy, butter-blonde, the former braided with tassels of scarlet teased silk. The harness, like the horse, was Spanish and expensive.

'She's beautiful!' Judith gasped, more than a little awestruck at the worth and magnificence of the dainty-legged mare. 'Are you sure that you want me to have her?'

'That's a very silly question!' he grinned. 'How else do you expect to keep up with me when we go riding? That bay bag of bones might as well have been standing still the other day.'

'He ran his heart out for me when we were fleeing Earl Robert,' she defended, but stepped forward to stroke the soft tawny nose. The mare had a white star between her eyes and two small trails of stardust dribbled beneath. She lipped Judith's fingers, seeking a titbit and the groom obligingly produced a wrinkled apple.

The undergroom emerged from the stables with Guyon's grey saddled up and ready.

131

'Care to try her paces?' Guyon cupped his hands.

'You should not make such an open display of your wealth,' she reproved, faintly troubled even in the midst of her joy.

'My father has one of the best stud herds in the land. Even impoverished as I am, I still have access to good horseflesh. Besides, ungrateful wench, you should know not to look a gift horse in the mouth.'

Judith made an agonised face at the literal pun and set her foot into the bowl of his linked fingers.

They rode far and wide over Ravenstow's demesne. The mare's gait was like silk, her muscles flowing like water beneath a cloth of golden satin. Her mouth was sensitive to Judith's slightest touch on the reins. She moved effortlessly from walk to pacing trot, to canter and back to a walk and Judith felt not so much as a jolt as she changed step.

Guyon considered Judith's seat in the saddle with a critical eye and discovered that, as with all skills, she had mastered this one in a very short space of time.

'My mother used to hate riding horseback,' he reminisced as they rode at length side by side for home. 'For my father's sake she bore it, but it was a sacrilegious waste of good horseflesh. The best in England and she appreciated it not one whit.'

Judith looked down at the golden power heaving beneath her. There was exhilaration in riding its smooth crest, a tingling of triumph in the knowledge of mastery.

'He misses her, doesn't he?' she said thoughtfully to the mare's flickering neat ears.

'My mother was the light of his life,' he said, not without a trace of pain in his own voice. 'They fought on occasion fit to bring down the keep around our ears, but I remember the love. She would have given him her lifeblood in a cup to drink if he so asked, and vice versa.'

Judith gnawed her lip unable to contemplate such a depth of feeling and trust. Her own parents had spent their time damning each other's souls into the pit of hell. Slaps, blows, ill-treatment, degradation, cruelty. She knew only too well the nature of marriage . . or thought she knew. She looked through her lashes at her husband's arrogant darkness and tried to imagine cutting her own veins at his command. No, she thought. I would take up a knife and defend myself to the last bitter drop of blood.

Hard on that thought followed a wave of guilt. He had been so good to her, tolerating her whims, handling her with patience and good humour, gifting her richly, not least with this beautiful horse. She liked him well enough, knew that she had been more fortunate than her mother as a heifer in the ring, but it was too great a trust to give her soul into another's squandering.

'You are very quiet, *cath fach*,' he commented, sensing the tension behind the closed lips.

Judith half-smiled and tossed her head. 'Foolish thoughts,' she laughed, mouth twisting. 'Not worth a penny for their time. Does she gallop, is it safe to give her free rein?' And without waiting for his reply she used her hands and heels to command the mare into a sudden spectacular burst of acceleration. Guyon muttered a startled oath beneath his breath and spurred Arian in pursuit across the meadow.

Geese scattered honking from beneath the flying hooves. The swineherd, out with the keep's pigs, shaded his eyes against the slant of the sun and watched the horses hurtle past. Ground-nesting plovers broke cover and took hasty wing. A blackbird chipped at them from a stump.

The golden mare flew lightly over the ground like a faery beast from out of the hollow hills, her tail rippling behind like combed flax.

Inch by inch the grey gained on her, his stride that slight bit longer, but it was a slow process. The weight he carried was greater and the mare was determined to keep her head in front. He reached her shoulders, his neck outstretched, his shoulders and hindquarters working like pistons and slowly his nose began to draw level with hers.

Judith glanced round, her braids whipping her face, her agate eyes blazing with exhilaration and met Guyon's laughter, white-edged with triumph.

'Oh no!' she cried, laughing back at him. 'Not this time my lord!' And as they pounded on towards the edge of the meadow, she leaned as far forward as the saddle would permit, gripping like a monkey, the reins clutched hard on Euraidd's neck. From somewhere the mare found an extra thrust of speed and, aided by Judith's forward weight, once more pulled ahead of the stallion to reach the marshy end of the meadow a length ahead.

Mud splattered up around the mare's forelegs and dappled her glowing coat with brown splotches and freckles as Judith breathlessly wound her down to a halt and hung over her braided mane, laughing with delight.

Guyon reined round beside her, drawing the stallion's head hard into the wide grey chest. Strings of foam globbed and spattered. The stallion's hooves danced. He was less equable than his master over the matter of being beaten.

'That was wonderful!' Judith gasped, her eyes shining like two coins, her face flushed and vibrant.

'And you are a madwoman!' he answered, half angry, half amused. 'What if you had fallen off?'

'I would have broken my neck, but I didn't and it was wonderful. And if you are going to scowl at me like that, I'd rather ride on my own anyway!'

'*Coegen!*' he chuckled despite himself.

'*Gwrach!*' she retorted, poking out her tongue.

Guyon's eyebrows shot up. It was the first time anyone had called him an old woman!

Before he could think of a suitable retort, Judith clicked her tongue to the mare and shook the reins, urging her across the stream and towards home. At a safe distance, she looked over her shoulder to where he sat staring after her and grinned impishly.

Guyon steadied his hold on the bridle. A hot pulse

throbbed between his legs and he was possessed of a rash impulse to ride after her and cool the irritation where it would do him the most good . . . and her the least. She is a child, he reiterated to himself. It has been too long an abstinence, that is all. After a moment, the impulse and its source subsided. He walked the stallion meekly in her wake while he consolidated his hold on things rational.

At the keep they had visitors. Tethered in the bailey were a dozen sturdy pack ponies tended by an equally sturdy black-haired boy. He was loosening the pack of the foremost pony and speaking to a dour, frowning, middle-aged companion who was unloading what looked like bales of Flanders cloth.

The boy lifted his gaze and met Guyon's dismounting scrutiny and, unlatching the last buckle, spoke a quick word to the servant and came across the ward to greet them. Judith looked curiously at the lad as he approached to stand smiling before them. He was as solid and stocky as a young oak tree and darkly Welsh, his eyes onyx-black and extravagantly fringed. His wide-planted stance exuded the confidence of a man, the flicker of his lids the uncertainty of boyhood.

'I'm here with my grandfather,' he said in rapid Welsh. 'We've brought cloth to trade for salt and we need new ponies and grandfather has other business besides.'

The grooms took the two mud-smirched horses.

'How fares your mother?'

'She had a baby girl two days since,' Rhys said, gaze darting to Judith, obviously wondering how much Welsh she understood. 'She is well and so is the baby . . . Eluned is jealous.'

Before Guyon could compose himself to reply, Madoc himself strode out of the forebuilding and clapped a brown, knotty hand on Rhys's shoulder.

'Rapscallion! I thought you'd have finished unloading by now!' he declared, but his hazel eyes were laughing and his tone was indulgent. 'God's greeting, lord Guyon. I see that you've had the good tidings. A fine, healthy babe and blessed

135

with your grandsire's red hair and, to judge from the sound of her lungs, his temper too!' He chuckled, clearly pleased. Rhosyn's liaison with Guyon FitzMiles and the resulting child were useful bonds to future profit, no matter that his daughter should stubbornly deny it.

Judith opened her mouth to speak, but changed her mind and clammed it tight shut instead, not trusting herself.

Smiling, but with something uncertain behind that smile, Guyon invited the merchant into the hall to drink to the infant's health and discuss the business he had brought with him upon the back of a dozen ponies. Belatedly, he remembered to introduce Madoc and Rhys to his wife.

Master Madoc made the proper responses in impeccable Norman French and concealed his curiosity and surprise behind deep-set lowered lids. The girl who tepidly smiled her own impeccable duty was not the fey, frightened thing that Rhosyn had led him to expect. Her agate eyes were cool, her voice clear and firm. Slender, yes, with barely a curve to her name, but possessed of a certain gauche grace and also a certain coldness of manner and, from the quick look she had tossed at Guyon as they entered the forebuilding, it did not take much of his merchant's shrewdness to guess the cause.

At first he and Guyon discussed the merits of the new downland rams that had been introduced to Guyon's herds and the effect they would have on the quality of future wool clips.

'It will make your fleeces whiter and increase the length of the staple. The Flanders looms are crying out for good quality wool. If God grants me my health, I should be crossing the sea after harvest.'

'Rhosyn said that you had been unwell.'

Madoc shrugged. 'I lack breath occasionally and my chest gripes, but the bouts are infrequent, usually when I've done more than I should, or the weather grows too cold. A few more years and Rhys will be old enough to shoulder much of the burden.' He smiled at his grandson, who smiled in return as he plied his meat with a fine, ivory-hilted blue steel dagger.

Madoc applied himself to his own meal for a while, then turned his shrewd gaze upon Guyon's young wife who had been rather silent throughout the previous conversation 'My lady, if you permit, there is a matter I would like to discuss with you.'

Judith inclined her head. 'Master Madoc?'

'I believe you wrote a letter to the widow of Huw ap Sior, offering to her the sables that had come by underhand means into your possession. She has asked me to act for her in this business and gratefully accepts your generosity.'

'It is nought of generosity, it is her rightful due,' Judith said with a grimace. She had put the sables away at the bottom of a chest, wrapped in fresh canvas and had discarded the blood-stained original coverings on the back of the fire. Even to think of them made her shudder.

Guyon looked at her with surprise and approval. He had not asked her what she had done with the furs, merely assumed that their disappearance marked their disposal.

Madoc too studied her and wondered if she knew her own power. Probably not, she was still very young and her eyes were innocent of all guile. One day she would be formidable. A black leopard and his golden mate. He smiled at the whimsy.

'You will need an escort,' Guyon said. 'Sables these days are worth their weight in blood.'

'Is Rhys yours too?' Judith enquired a trifle acidly when they were alone in their bedchamber.

Madoc and his grandson were asleep on bracken pallets in the hall among the other casual guests, travellers seeking a night's hospitality.

Guyon scratched the sensitive spot just behind Melyn's pricked ginger ears. The cat purred and kneaded his tunic with ecstatic spread paws. 'No,' he said, giving his attention to the cat.

'You look very much alike.'

137

'Colouring mainly. His father was black of hair and eye. You're not the first to assume my paternity. I wish it were true. He's a fine lad.'

'You have a daughter of his mother's blood,' she said, watching him through her lids.

Guyon's fingers stilled in the cat's thick cream and bronze fur. 'Not one who will know me as more than a shadow,' he said carefully.

'Why did you not tell me about the child before?'

'Where would have been the point? It is not as though she is going to be raised beneath my roof. Rhosyn will give her a Welsh name and bring her up to be Welsh.'

'And you have no say in the matter?' she asked incredulously.

Melyn leaped from his knee and lay down to wash beside the hearth. 'What should I do?' he demanded testily. 'Snatch her from her mother's arms and bring her to Ravenstow and salve my pain at the expense of Rhosyn's hatred and a blood feud with the Welsh?' He rose and, going to the flagon, jerkily poured himself a cup of wine. 'My say has been said. I once asked Rhosyn to stay with me and she refused. I could no more constrain her to live with me or give up the child, than I could bear one of those caged birds in my bedchamber.'

'Will you go to her tomorrow?'

He looked at Judith over the rim of the cup. Her expression was guarded, her face milk-pale, the stubborn chin lifted as if to face a challenge.

'Probably.'

Judith clenched her hands into claws and fought a completely new and unsettling emotion that left her wanting to do nothing more than shriek like a harpy that she was not going to stand for him riding off into the arms of another woman, and longing to claw out that woman's eyes and call her whore.

Frightened, she turned away and busied herself unlocking

the chest that contained the sables. True to his word, Guyon had not taken a maidservant or mistress into his bed, or if he had, it had been discreetly elsewhere without insult or humiliation to herself. Having lived beneath the cruelty of her father's code, she should have been grateful and was both confused and chagrined to find herself so annoyed by his one small weakness. Desperately she scrabbled in the chest.

'Why ask me if you do not want to know?' Guyon said and crouched beside her to put his arm lightly across her shoulders. 'I have known Rhosyn for many years and her father since I was your own age. You cannot expect me to sever those ties.'

The package of sables came into her hands. She lifted them and turned. 'I do not, my lord.' She gave him one swift look before lowering her lids. 'It is just that you pat me on the head and give me presents and laugh when I amuse you, but I wonder if you ever see me as more than just a child with whom you are saddled.' She put the furs on top of the chest and stood up. So did he, a frown between his eyes.

Her lids were still lowered. After a moment, he tilted her chin on his forefinger and kissed her gently. 'Come, *cath fach*, look at me.'

Her lashes flickered up to reveal the shine of tears in her eyes. She pushed herself away from him. 'Don't patronize me!' she said from between gritted teeth.

Guyon let his hands fall to his sides and drew a slow breath. Then, carefully, he let it out. 'How should I treat you?' he asked, a certain baffled exasperation in his voice. 'You are not a woman, you are not a child. You waver over the line between the two like a drunkard. You laugh and play knucklebones with my nieces and skip around the keep hoyden-wild. You tease me like an experienced coquette, but were I to take up the offer in your smile you'd bolt in terror. In God's name Judith, make up your mind!' He swallowed down the wine and picked up the flagon.

Her gaze widened. 'Where are you going?' she said breathlessly.

139

'To think,' he said with a twisted smile. 'Don't wait up on me.'

The curtain dropped behind him. Melyn stretched in a leisurely fashion, eyed her mistress from golden agate slits and padded to sit expectantly at her feet. Judith scooped her up, buried her cheek in the thick, soft fur and refused to cry.

Actually, Guyon did very little thinking, for he took his flagon to the guardroom, sat down, propped his feet on the trestle and was soon thoroughly absorbed in the convivial, vulgar gossip of his soldiers. It was a long time since he had spent an evening thus and, besides relishing the salty, masculine conversation, he was able to bring himself abreast of current marcher gossip.

Walbert of Seisdon's wife was pregnant yet again. One of the mills at Elford had a broken grindstone. The remains of a butchered deer had been found in the woods on Ravenstow's border with Wales. Robert de Belleme had brought a grey Flemish stallion to run with his native mares. Robert de Belleme had offered the widow of Ralph of Thorneyford in marriage to Walter de Lacey.

Guyon's face emerged abruptly from the depths of his cup. 'What?'

' 'Tis quite true, m'lord. My sister's married to a Thorneyford man and is a seamstress up at the keep. Regular upset it has caused, I can tell you.'

Guyon wiped his mouth and removed his feet from the trestle. 'You are telling me that Walter de Lacey is to marry Mabel of Thorneyford?' he demanded.

'Aye m'lord. Not common knowledge yet, but it soon will be.'

'Imagine waking up wi' that in bed beside you.'

'De Lacey won't be too impressed himself!' quipped the joker in their ranks. Somebody groaned.

De Bec leaned over to refill Guyon's cup. 'Thorneyford's a rich estate,' he said. 'Mabel's dowry was huge and sir Ralph a regular nip-cheese.'

Guyon rolled him a look that said far more than words and drank. 'Do you think he'll invite me to the wedding?'

'More likely the funeral,' grunted de Bec. 'Mabel's not likely to outlive her second husband.'

Guyon dabbled his fingers in a puddle of wine. The main-holding of Thorneyford lay on Ravenstow's south-west border, separated from Wales by a deep, defensive ditch. There were other keeps in the honour too, forming part of the fortifications ringing Shrewsbury and, coupled with what de Lacey already possessed, it would make him a baron of some considerable standing along the middle marches and increase threefold the threat he posed to Guyon's interests.

One step forward and two steps back, Guyon thought, staring at the spilled, bloody wine. 'You'd better tighten up on the patrols,' he said to de Bec. 'I don't want him cutting his new-found teeth on my borders.'

'You reckon he would, m'lord?'

'Depends on how much backing he gets from de Belleme and how good a grievance he can find to start a war. Knowing our respective overlords, I do not suppose an excuse will be long in presenting itself.' Grimly, he held out his cup to be refilled. 'Do you think de Lacey will celebrate his nuptials with a boar hunt?'

His voice was light and brittle. Prudently, de Bec forbore to answer.

CHAPTER 12

JUDITH STARED INTO the Saracen hand mirror and found nothing that pleased. Her eyes were dark-circled for want of sleep and her complexion was pallid, bedevilled here and there by blemishes. Her women's courses which for the past two years had been an erratic, seldom-seen inconvenience seemed to have settled down into less than welcome four-weekly visitations of cramp and messy discomfort. That it was supposedly Eve's curse and thoroughly sanctioned by the church was no comfort, as was the kind of information imparted by Christen, her fourteen-year-old niece-by-marriage – that they would cease as soon as she conceived.

'I should have been a man!' Judith said rebelliously.

'They don't live as long,' Christen pointed out. 'And they are easy enough to handle once you have learned the knack.'

'If you had known my father, you would not say that.' Judith picked up an ivory comb and drew it down through her hair. 'His remedy for everything was a bellyful of wine and the thrashing of the nearest scapegoat. Has your father ever beaten you?'

'Sometimes,' Christen answered with a light, dismissive shrug.

'Until you bled from his rings?'

Christen made a swift gesture. 'That was your father. Guyon's not like that and his needs are transparent if you know where to look.'

'Indeed?' Judith arched her brow, wishing the precocious child would leave her alone. Her thoughts skimmed back

142

over the last few hours. Guyon had come late to bed, smelling strongly of drink and had fallen asleep the moment he lay down with never a word in her direction. Probably he assumed she was already asleep and she had done nothing to contradict that assumption, afraid of what he might do in his cups.

The morning saw him in possession of a splitting headache, a rolling gut and numerous responsibilities to organize. The cramps in her stomach had made her feel sluggish and sick. They had scarcely exchanged a word. Neither of them had the time or inclination to be civil and his kiss on her cheek before he mounted up and left had been a matter of form. He had looked through her to the waiting grey and the train of pack ponies and had omitted to tug her braid as was his usual wont. *Don't patronize me.* Perhaps she had brought it on herself. Perhaps last night he had thought and decided how he should treat her. She blinked very hard.

'Where then do I look?' she challenged the other girl.

Christen eyed her thoughtfully. 'Guyon likes to hunt,' she said after a pause. 'Women who are easy just bore him. You must twist and turn and evade and, even if he catches you, refuse to give in.'

Judith's wayward eyebrows rose higher.

'And of course,' Christen added knowledgeably, her gaze flickering sideways to the bed. 'There is always that particular method of persuasion as long as you are subtle.'

'You know all this from experience?' Judith asked with more than a hint of bad temper.

Christen laughed. 'Of course not! I had it from Alais de Clare. She used to be his main solace at court until her husband found out.'

'I see,' said Judith, tight-lipped.

'No you don't,' Christen giggled. 'Her husband wanted her to sweeten Prince Henry, not waste her time on a minor fish like Guyon . . . only she preferred Guy's looks and got waylaid, so to speak.'

'And she told you, his niece, all about it?' Judith said scathingly.

Christen blushed beneath the ripe scorn in Judith's voice. 'It wasn't like that,' she said uncomfortably.

'If Guyon offered me to another man by way of a bribe, I'd make hell seem cold by comparison!' Judith snapped, eyes flashing. 'God help me, I'd kill them both before I'd be sold like a slab of meat!' And then she clamped her bottom lip in her teeth, remembering that being sold like a slab of meat on a block was precisely the manner of her marriage.

'But you love Guy and Alais's husband is fat and getting old and . . .'

'Do not be so sure about the love!' Judith bit out.

Christen stared at her with round eyes. 'I do not think Guyon really wanted Alais,' she said anxiously, afraid that she had roused Judith's jealousy and that it would cause trouble for Guyon. 'It was just that her timing was impeccable. The King was chasing him and Guy literally had his back to the wall. He would not have looked at Alais otherwise.'

Judith compressed her lips. She did not think there was any malice in Christen. She meant well enough, but her perception was a trifle clouded. She narrowed her eyes thoughtfully. There were, however, lessons to be learned here, both from Christen and this Alais de Clare who had been bartered by her husband for the favour of a prince. Subtle persuasion. The use of her body as weapon and defence. It had not occurred to her to think in those terms before and, now that it did, she required leisure to think. Another skill to be learned. She slanted a look at Christen, some of her irritation waning. The girl was only just fourteen, but already she had a ready command of the art that Judith was suddenly aware of lacking.

Subtlety. The chestnut eyebrows were plucked, but only to remove the straggling hairs and the well defined, strong lines went unaffected. Her hair was plaited in one shining, heavy braid threaded with gold ribbon and her gown was of a flattering holly-green wool, moulded tightly as a glove to her slender body and embellished only by a girdle of engraved bronze links. She looked exquisite and with very little effort and Judith knew how those blue-green eyes could angle across the hall, hiding a wealth of promise and refusal behind the downswept lashes.

Judith eyed her own self in the mirror and grimaced, making the damage worse. It was not an area that she had previously dared consider, but perhaps in the light of last night's conversation, she ought to do so. Did she want to attract Guyon's notice in that sense? That was something else to be pondered at leisure rather than panicking in his presence.

He was susceptible to the persuasions of the bed. She coloured and, over her shoulder, looked at the object with disfavour, wondering how one acquired such skills. Through practice she supposed, and shuddered at the thought, remembering two of the keep dogs copulating in the hall and the bawdy shouts of the men egging them on. She knew all the words for what male and female did together, precious few of them mentioned in the bible, and was reluctant to join the circus. If only she could see the thing as power, not a humiliating subjugation.

Christen was watching her in the prolonged silence with a frightened curiosity.

Judith met her eyes in the mirror. 'Perhaps you are right,' she conceded, frowning. 'Honesty may be the best policy, but a crust slips down better if it is spread with honey first . . . I think I have a great deal to learn.' She laid the mirror down and stood up. 'For the nonce, I've got to instruct the cook and see about employing a new seamstress and I need to check the spice cabinet and fabric chests. Master Madoc promised to fulfil any commissions I had for him . . . and then,' she added, drawing a deep breath, 'I will consider the matter of subtlety.'

Christen smiled in return without knowing why and decided in future to keep her mouth firmly closed.

★

In her own chamber, Alicia shook out the drab-coloured widow's gown. A packet of dried lavender and rose leaves fell from its folds along with severe evidence of moths. She clicked her tongue and tossed the garment on the bed.

'Not takin' it, m'lady?' enquired Agnes, reaching to inspect the damage.

Alicia shook her head and regarded the half-packed trunk behind her. She had gowns enough for a life of retirement upon her dower lands, indeed too many. She doubted that the rose silk she had worn for her daughter's wedding would ever see service again, unless of course they buried her in it.

Her estates, although wealthy, were a backwater when compared to the border violence of her former husband's holdings. At least she could be alone with her indecent hunger. What did you do if you were starving and a meal you could not have kept following you around, begging you to eat it? You either went mad or you fled as fast as your horse would carry you.

'What about this belt, m'lady. Shall I put . . .?' Agnes stopped and bobbed a curtsey, her expression going blank.

Alicia whirled, her heart thumping like a battle drum at the base of her throat.

Miles studied the travelling chests, open to reveal their neatly packed contents – clothes and cups and vials and combs and embroidery. His eyes ranged the strewed bed and the bare clothing pole, then returned to Alicia and nailed her.

'If it is on account of me,' he said, 'there is no need. I am leaving tomorrow.'

Alicia shook her head, too choked by panic to speak.

Miles flicked a look at Agnes. 'I need to talk to you,' he said and then, as her eyes answered, flying wide and stricken, 'you may tie me up if you wish.' The words were spoken lightly, but there was little humour in them.

Alicia carefully folded the veil she had been holding and, after a hesitation, drew a deep breath and gestured Agnes to leave. The maid's mouth tucked itself thinly away, but she

146

dropped a curtsey and retreated beyond the thick arras curtain.

Miles sat down on the bed and picked up the veil that Alicia had just so painstakingly folded. 'Last time we were alone I acted like a green youth in rut,' he said. 'It was the action of impulse. I'm sorry.'

No response, save a bitten lip and fingers clenched to show the whiteness of bone.

'Alicia, look at me.'

Wearily she raised her lids. Her eyes were the colour of a peregrine's plumage – dark and fierce . . . and vulnerable.

'Do you think that it has gone unnoticed? For the sake of our children, we must come at least to a truce.'

'Why do you think I am going to my dower lands?' she replied.

'Because you are afraid?' he suggested.

Her mouth twisted. 'Not for the reasons you think.'

Miles unfolded the veil. It was made of fragile gauze, the embroidery edging it skilfully worked in gold thread. 'You will miss her,' he said gently.

'She has her own life to live and will the sooner grow into a woman without me for a leaning post. In time it is I who would become the child. Indeed, it has begun already. She shuts me out from her thoughts and she is very strong willed.'

'Not a whit like her father, is she?' he mused.

There was a hesitation that made him look up. Alicia's face was the unhealthy colour of raw pastry. Then she rallied herself, smiled and drew a shaky breath. 'I wouldn't say that.' She turned her face into the shadows. 'There are many similarities.'

Something rang false. Memory searched and pieced disjointed fragments. A lock gently clicked. A cog was fitted and turned another cog and aroused a carillon of understanding. 'Who is he?' he asked quietly.

He heard the clatter of her rosary beads against her skirt,

147

saw the silent vibration of her shoulders. 'That is my own affair,' she answered huskily.

'And mine too when it will touch the blood of my grandchildren.' He stood up and went to her and turned her shuddering form to face him.

'And if I say a baseborn groom or a passing pedlar?' she challenged defiantly.

'If that were true, you'd not have denied me the day of the boar hunt,' he reasoned, moving his fingertips along the taut edge of her jaw.

Alicia shook beneath his light touch, knowing what she risked if she told him the truth.

'Does he still live?'

'Yes.'

'Does he know?'

'Probably not,' she lifted her shoulders. 'To him it was a night of pleasure, a comfort along the road to be forgotten in the dawn.'

'And to you?' he asked, watching her with checked tension.

'Expedient. When your heifer fails, get a different bull to service her.' She laughed at some private bitterness.

Miles let her go and, folding his arms, frowned.

'Not pretty is it?' she said. 'I cuckolded my husband in his own keep and deceived him with my lover's child.' And then, 'You see too much my lord, or perhaps I have just grown careless of late.'

'I see too much,' he said, smiling painfully, 'because I want you.'

'You don't even know me,' she said faintly.

'Well enough to see too clearly,' he retorted, studying her, trying to decide from the set of her face the approach he should take. 'And I've known you for a long time, ever since you were Judith's age and defying your father's will. And in the years since then, I've watched you from a distance grow and change.'

'And wanted me?' she challenged, blue eyes hostile.

Miles saw the trap yawning at his feet and skirted it deftly. 'I had Christen,' he said. 'There was no space in me to want another woman. You know that.'

Some of the hostility left her face, but she remained strongly cautious.

Miles shrugged. 'It is two years since I lost her. Sometimes it seems as close as yesterday. Sometimes the loneliness rides me so hard that I think I will go mad. I have taken women to my bed so that I do not have to sleep alone, but there is no lasting solace in that. What I need is another wife and, if I can get a dispensation, your consent.'

Alicia stared at him, dumbfounded. 'It is impossible!' she said huskily.

'The dispensation or your consent? Rannulf Flambard will perform any miracle for the right amount of gold and I will not take no for an answer from you . . . not without excellent reasons.'

Alicia sat down. Her knees were gelatinous. 'I could give you them,' she said shakily.

Miles persisted. For every protest that she made, he had an answer ready, a reasonable solution. He made a nonsense of her fears . . . all but one. She told him the name of Judith's father.

Miles drew breath, held it, stared at her in dawning amazement, and very slowly exhaled. She saw his mind make that final, vital connection, saw his eyes flicker.

'Yes,' she said harshly. 'He was fourteen years old and I was twenty-eight, and in one night he taught me everything that Maurice did not have the imagination to know.'

'Sweet Jesu and his mother,' Miles swore softly, staring at her as if she had suddenly grown two heads while he tried to assimilate what she had just told him.

She watched his face, waiting for the revulsion, but it did not come. It was a blank mask behind which any thought could have lurked. She covered her face and turned away.

149

After a moment, Miles mustered his wits. She was trembling so hard that he thought her flesh would shiver free of her bones. He laid a firm hand on her shoulder. 'It makes no difference to me,' he said quietly. 'It is in the past and, knowing him, even at fourteen, he was no innocent to be seduced unless he so wished.'

Alicia swallowed, remembering how it had been. She with a plan half-formed, afraid to dare and he with his mind already made up.

'So you will marry me?'

Alicia removed her hands tentatively from her face and looked at him. 'How can you say it makes no difference? I set out deliberately to cheat my husband. I bedded with a boy whose voice had barely broken, I . . .'

'You flay yourself with guilt,' he said, capturing her hands in his. 'I do not doubt you. The Welsh have a saying: *Oer yw'r cariad a ddiffydd ar un chwa o wynt.* Cold is the love that is put out by one gust of wind. I have taken women to my bed for the comfort and the pleasure they offer, never out of forced desperation. I account your sin the lesser.'

Alicia's mouth twitched into a tremulous smile. 'You are very persistent, my lord.'

'It is the Welsh blood,' he agreed cheerfully.

She shook her head and sniffed. The meal, it seemed, was about to devour her. 'I cannot give you an answer. I am so confused that I do not know my head from my heels.'

He put out his hand as if to touch her, but let it drop again to his side, aware of how much was at stake. It was like stalking a deer. Softly, slowly and no sudden moves. 'Perhaps you should remove to your dower lands,' he said thoughtfully. 'It will give you time to think.'

Alicia stepped away from his disturbing proximity. It was obvious that his own mind was made up. She had shown him the black secret lurking at the bottom of her soul and he had dismissed it as of no consequence, still valuing her enough to offer her marriage. It was the first time she had felt her worth to be above that of a mere chattel. A pity it was thirty years too late.

'I hazard you do not often lose an argument,' she said eyeing him warily.

'It depends on the subject,' he said with a disarming smile that played havoc with her stomach. 'I could escort you home if you wish it. I have business with Hugh of Chester. He needs a strong warhorse to carry his bulk, but I could take you when I return, say in four days' time'

'And if I say no?' Her tone was sharp, for she received the distinct impression that she was being manipulated in the direction he desired her to go.

'I'll have to think of something else, won't I?' he replied, still smiling.

CHAPTER 13

I T WAS FORTUNATE for Guyon that the journey into Wales proved uneventful, for he felt as though his brains had swollen to twice their size and were thumping the cage of his skull in a vigorous attempt to escape. His lids were weighted with lead, his tongue as thick and furred as a lump of moss and his body, not surprisingly, was extremely sluggish of function. It was a long, long time since he had fallen victim to an overindulgence of English ale. Mixed with red Anjou it was lethal and, since quitting the court, he had held to sobriety and his capacity to drink had thus diminished.

It occurred to him that he had not been very considerate of Judith, but her sulky, mulish expression, the frown between her eyes as he mounted up to ride out and his own physical discomfort had not lent him the inclination to tug her braid or smile and bear with her. The guilt and the knowledge that he would have to make amends and somehow smooth out their differences of opinion when he returned, only caused his head to pound more viciously and his stomach to churn like a dyer's vat.

By the time they had reached the hafod it had been full noon, the sun shimmering the mail to fish scales of light, dazzling the eye. Madoc, in his russet fustian with coney trim was as red as a brick and sweating like a hog on a spit, his breath coming in rapid whistles from between blue lips.

Guyon tethered Arian to a post in the yard and then, his skull feeling as though it would split asunder, removed his helm, pushed down his coif and followed Madoc into the hafod.

Eluned ran to her grandfather and embraced him with a

kind of desperate enthusiasm then tossing back her silky black hair saw Guyon and went to him. 'Mam's had the baby,' she announced. Her eyes, bright hazel like Rhosyn's, were anxious. 'It's a girl.' She clung tightly to his arm.

'I know, *anwylyd*,' he said, kissing the top of her head.

The midwife paused ladling a cup of broth into a wooden bowl and looked at Guyon. 'Birth went easy enough,' she said to him with a curt nod. 'Babe's small, but she'll thrive.' Her bright, hedgehog eyes were frankly curious. Madoc's daughter had never made any secret of her liaison with the marcher lord, or the direction of her child's siring.

'May I see them?' he asked in Welsh, his tone deferential, for one did not trifle with the great respect in which these women were held. It was often upon their skill that the life of a mother and child depended.

'Take this in to her, lord,' she said, holding out the cup of broth. 'Bear in mind that she is tired.'

Eluned made to follow, but her grandfather caught her back and asked her to find him a drink. The midwife studied him for a moment and then, muttering under her breath, sought among her herbs for one that would ease his breathing.

On soft feet, Guyon pushed aside the hides that screened Rhosyn's bed from the world and put down the bowl of broth on the coffer beside it. His movement stirred the warm air and Rhosyn raised her lids. For a moment she thought she was dreaming or, worse, that she had contracted the deadly childbed fever and was hallucinating. Her eyes widened in a split second of terror and then she rallied herself. The illusion was travel-worn and sweat-streaked and altogether too life-like. It was watching her with dark, pensive eyes as if it did not know how it would be received. She sat up and softly spoke his name.

'*Cariadferch,*' he said, taking her hand and kneeling beside her.

She saw that he wore his link-mail, the rivets glistening a sullen grey in the dim light. The marcher guise. His business over the border this time was official.

'I am glad you have come,' she said and was at once annoyed by the betraying wobble in her voice.

'Did you doubt that I would?'

'There was no obligation on you to do so.'

'No obligation?'

She watched his eyes leave her face and go to the wooden crib at the bedside and the tiny, swaddled scrap of life it contained and she bit her lip, afraid, knowing that she did not have the strength to fight him if he chose to make of his daughter a battleground.

Oblivous, the baby slept, a down of red–gold hair crowning a tiny, crumpled face that was still marked by its strenuous passage into the world.

'There will always be an obligation, *cariad*.'

'Guy . . .'

'Nay,' he murmured, touching the baby's fledging fiery fuzz before turning to look at her, eyes full of pain. 'I am as leashed to your bidding as that hound out there . . . Just don't kick me out of the door without giving me a chance. Does the little one have a name?'

Rhosyn shook her head.

'Permit me?'

'I . . . I do not know.'

He took her hand. 'Why do I receive the impression that you do not trust me, *anwylyd*?'

She looked him straight in his beautiful, melting brown eyes. 'Probably because I don't. Naming is a kind of possession for life.'

'And what else am I ever likely to have of her, Rhos? A distant glimpse from a tower top. A snatched meeting here and there. From babe to child to woman in the blink of an eye. She is yours. Not without some pain I accept that, but at least grant me the grace of her naming.'

'Your way with words has always been your deadliest weapon.' Rhosyn accused, shaking her head, her eyes brilliant with unshed tears, but there was also a smile of sorts on her lips. 'Very well then. I grant you that grace . . . Do not abuse it.'

'No Hegelinas or Aiglentines,' he agreed incorrigibly, but kissed her tenderly, almost but not quite with reverence, before he went again to the cradle to look down on his sleeping daughter.

'Have you told your wife?' Rhosyn enquired and wiped her eyes on her shift.

His face was in profile. Not a feature flickered to show that he had heard. 'Judith knows,' he said flatly.

'And is not best pleased?'

He rubbed his aching forehead. 'She's developing a sense of possession,' he said guardedly. 'And sometimes it is uncomfortable.'

'I read her letter to Huw's wife. It was not the writing of a child,' Rhosyn said thoughtfully. 'Children grow up, especially at that age. It may be that suddenly you have a woman on your hands.'

His mouth moved into what might have been the beginning of a wry smile. 'It would still be rape,' he said laconically. 'Not that much of a woman.'

Rhosyn eyed him, not quite so sure. The handwriting had been firm and well-formed and through the obvious shock and revulsion at de Belleme's deed had run a maturity of style that spoke very little of the child. If I was her, Rhosyn thought, I'd certainly resent another woman's grip on his affections. He had not been so wrong when he compared himself to old Gelert. Like a dog, Guyon gave unstintingly of his loyalty, even when it was unwise to do so.

'Bear it in mind,' she said softly and then was silent to drink her broth before it went cold.

'Heulwen,' he said after a time. 'What do you think?'

She put down the cup, looking surprised. 'Heulwen?'

'I promised no Norman monstrosities.'

'I thought you would choose Christen for your mother.'

'I already have a flighty niece to bear that name. No, let

her be called for my Welsh grandmother, Heulwen uerch Owain. Besides, she has the colouring to suit the name.'

Rhosyn cocked her head, considered, and then slowly smiled. 'Yes,' she said softly, 'I approve, Guy. I approve very much.'

And then the midwife had appeared to shoo him out of the room and Madoc had been waiting to usher him to the table, still short of wind but a better colour and full of self-satisfied *bonhomie*, and Eluned had clamoured for his attention. He had given it with half a mind and smiled at Madoc with another portion, locking away what was left until it could be reviewed without tearing the fabric of his soul. *Heulwen*. Sunshine. Clouds across his vision.

That had been yesterday. Now they were on the road home and would have been at Ravenstow's gates by compline had not Arian cast a shoe and begun to limp. The fine weather had broken up at noon, the innocent, fluffy clouds of early morning uniting into a seething, grey-edged mass. Like a canker the grey had eaten inwards until the entire sky was swallowed to charcoal. And then it had begun steadily to rain.

'Best rest up for the night, my lord,' said Eric, nodding at the horizon where the grey was swollen ripely purple with unshed water. 'There's a village not far and there's bound to be a farrier.'

Guyon blinked through the rain, his lashes spiked together. Droplets trembled and dripped from the rim of his hood. The ground beneath his feet was a brown tapestry of mud and puddles and his boots and chausses had long since become saturated and, despite the fact of summer, he felt chilled to the bone. Beyond the lush June-green of the trees and against the lowering sky, a church tower reared gold stone through the lancing grey rain. Further away, dominating its knoll, crouched the yellow keep of Thorneyford like a beast asleep, or pretending to be asleep.

'You reckon it safe?' Guyon said wryly to his captain and slid the wet reins through his fingers, eyes slitted against the rain.

'No, we'll bide at the ale house if they have one while the farrier sees to Arian, then we'll be on our way. Thorneyford's hospitality is about as chancey as its new lord, and I'd rather ride whole into Ravenstow than carved into joints and stuffed into my saddlebags.'

Eric grimaced. The Chester road at night in this roke was not a heartening prospect, but his lord was right. They were too close to Thorneyford for comfort and Walter de Lacey, if he discovered their proximity, would certainly not balk at murder.

The village proved sufficiently substantial to own not only a smithy, but a good-sized ale house and while Arian was shod Guyon and his men repaired to the latter to fortify themselves for the damp miles remaining.

Inside, the floor of the main room was covered in a thick layer of rushes upon which were set two well-scrubbed long trestles. Rush dips had been kindled against the murk of the drizzle and a fire burned cleanly in the hearth. The ale-wife was a florid, handsome woman of middle years whose voice bore a strong, Gwynedd lilt. Her husband, bluffly Saxon by contrast, sent their son outside to tend the horses.

The only other customers were a young couple seated unobtrusively in the darkest corner of the room, quietly attending their meal. The girl raised her head at their entrance and stared at the armed men with wide, frightened eyes. She had the fragile bones and delicate gauzy colouring of a wild, faery thing. Her husband was a plain, wide-shouldered young man, somewhere between twenty and Guyon's own age. He looked warily round at the newcomers and put his left hand protectively on top of the girl's. His right stayed loose, dangling close to the long poniard at his belt.

Guyon, after one startled glance at the girl's luminous beauty, ignored the couple and sat down. Water dripped from his garments and soaked into the rushes. Eric gingerly eased himself down beside his lord and rubbed his aching knees.

The woman brought them bowls of mutton stew, fairly fresh wheaten loaves and pitchers of cider and ale, her manner deferential but briskly efficient. 'Foul night to be travelling, m'lord,' she addressed Guyon. 'You can bed down here if you've a mind to stay.'

He thanked her and shook his head. 'You've a new lord over at Thorneyford and I'd as lief not encounter him.'

'Worse for business than the plague!' complained the landlord, adding a bowl of honey cakes to the table. 'Started already it has and sir Ralph barely in his grave. I know he could be a bastard, but he was so mean that it was good for business. Folks would come here rather than claim a night of hospitality up at the keep, what with him and mad Mabel for hosts.'

'Now folks don't come at all,' his wife sniffed. 'Or if they do, they're like yourselves, here and gone for fear of lord Walter and his routiers.' She hitched her bosom and stalked away.

Guyon and Eric exchanged glances. The couple in the corner finished eating and went outside into the deluge, the man's arm curved around the girl's narrow shoulders.

One of Guyon's men uttered a low, appreciative whistle. 'Pretty lass,' he said, looking wistfully out of the door.

'Her father's one of the serfs bound to Thorneyford,' the landlord volunteered, helping himself to a mug of cider, weather eye cocked for the reappearance of his wife. 'The lad's a huntsman up at the keep, or he was. Had an argument wi' the new lord and didn't see fit to stay beyond packing his belongings. A proud 'un, young Brand, and his wife's a rare beauty as you all saw. Sir Ralph was never one for the women. Too old and not enough steel in his sword to bother getting it out of the scabbard, but sir Walter . . .' He paused for effect and a gulp of cider and wiped his hand across his mouth. 'Nothing in skirts is safe from his pursuit and he don't like it done normal either.'

'I know,' Guyon said quietly, remembering last summer's

Welsh campaign and the pitiful victims, some no older than ten or eleven years, thrust used from de Lacey's tent in the cold, dew-decked dawn.

'Best gamekeeper he'd got, that young man. New lord's an idiot if you ask me, to throw away talent like that for lust. Mind you, I can see why he was tempted. I'd . . .' He stopped, hastily put down the mug at Eric's arm and sprang away from the trestle, pretending bustle as his wife returned, her mouth puckered, but certainly not for a kiss.

Eric chuckled into his moustache. Guyon pushed his bowl aside and finished his ale, hiding in the tankard what Eric could more easily hide in his bristles. 'I'm away to the smithy,' he announced, biting his lip to keep a straight face as their host grimaced like a goblin behind his wife's back. 'He should have finished Arian by now.'

'I'll come with you,' said Eric. 'There's safety in numbers in this neck of the woods.'

Guyon threw him an amused look, saw that his captain was grimly serious, and stopped smiling.

'We're in need of a huntsman at Ravenstow,' he said thoughtfully as they crossed the street, deserted in the rainy evening. 'I haven't properly replaced Rannulf yet. Perhaps I should go after the lad and offer him employment.' He flickered a mischievous glance at the barrel-chested Saxon, waiting, and was not disappointed.

'You are courting danger if you do, my lord,' Eric warned. 'You heard what the landlord said. It's a brew of disaster if I ever saw one. Sir Walter won't let them go, you know that. Don't you think you've chanced enough just lately?'

'And not so much as a boar in sight,' Guyon teased as they reached the smithy.

Eric quickly inhaled to remonstrate, but stopped before the damage was done. Having been Guyon's personal bodyguard for fifteen years, he was all too aware that his lord could be a devil incarnate when the mood was upon him, witness that escapade with the sheep and the silver. Arguing with him

159

only made him all the more determined to follow his course; hold to silence and sense might just prevail.

Guyon tilted a glance along his shoulder at Eric, almost laughing to see his poor captain choking on words he was longing to utter. 'Surely I am not so unamenable to reason,' he jested and picked up Arian's forehoof to examine the new shoe.

'My lord, you know you are not,' Eric said, not in the least mollified.

The stallion's coat steamed gently as it dried in the heat from the forge, the dapple reddened to a ruddy, flickering roan. Guyon put down the hoof and, with a nod to the farrier, paid him the quarter penny fee. In the act of biting the coin the man stopped, his gaze darting into the gathering twilight.

Eric swung round, right hand going to his hilt. Hand on the bridle, Guyon stiffened. Hooves thudded the dirt road and harnesses jingled. A man swore bawdily in Flemish and a woman cried out. Guyon spoke quickly to the farrier and, taking the reins, led Arian out of the enclosure and into the village street. At the market cross twenty yards away a group of mounted, mailed mercenaries had surrounded the young couple from the ale house and were refusing to let them pass.

'I'm a free man,' Guyon heard the young huntsman say hotly in accented French. 'You've no right to bar my path.'

'Go on then, you're free!' laughed one of the men, teeth flashing. 'We've no quarrel with you that your little wife won't be able to mend. Lord's rights. She's a serf and lord Walter wants her back.'

'On her back!' corrected someone with a snigger.

'She's no serf. I've got lord Ralph's charter to prove it! Freed her when we were wed, so he did!' The young man held out a copper document tube. The foremost Fleming snatched it from him, drew forth the parchment it contained, tore it in half and in half again and threw it down among the trampling hooves.

'No proof,' he said, snarling a smile and suddenly a blade sparkled. The girl screamed as a Fleming groped for her bridle. Her husband felt for the dagger at his belt, but subsided in mid-motion to duck beneath the murderous sweep of the drawn sword.

'Let them pass,' commanded Guyon, his own sword free and confidently held, his knees commanding Arian to thrust forward between the couple and their tormentors.

The Fleming measured Guyon and the older man behind. Two of them to their nine and only the foremost mounted, but the grey was solidly boned, the man astride exuded the confidence of ability and they were probably not alone. 'Don't meddle in what ain't your business,' he growled.

'Sound advice,' Guyon retorted. 'Apply it to yourselves and let them pass.' A flickering glance revealed that the mercenaries were spreading out to encircle himself and Eric. Strained ears caught the sound of a shout from the tavern end of the street.

The Fleming wasted no more time on words, but lunged at Guyon whose arm was jarred to the shoulder as he warded the vicious blow, not on the safety of his shield, but upon the blade of his own sword. Bluish-white the sparks glanced off, and he realised grimly that his assailant was left-handed. A man was taught from the cradle to crouch behind the shield worn on his left arm, to let it take the blows and to counter-strike with his sword in his right. Sword to sword was a nightmare. You parried and risked snapping the blade, or you missed the parry and you died.

Behind him, Eric gasped as a blow caught him beneath his guard, splitting his mail but not cutting through the thick quilting of his gambeson. The girl was crying. Someone snatched the dagger from her husband's hand and pinioned his struggling arms like a coney prepared for the table.

Guyon thrust his shield against a sword blow on his left and felt the blade score and slide off the toughened limewood. With his knees he commanded the stallion to pivot and lunge against the mount of the left-handed Fleming, their leader, and brought his sword across, unexpectedly hard and low. It almost worked, but the mercenary was too experienced and at the last moment intercepted the move with a slicing sidelong slash. Guyon twisted and parried. Pain seared his thigh as the Fleming's blade bit flesh. He locked his wrist against the pommel, sweeping the other sword sideways, changed his grip, and slashed. The Fleming grunted, lost his grip on the reins, and hunched over his saddle tree, blood gushing through a rent in his hauberk.

Guyon swung Arian. The ball of a morning star grazed his hair. He slammed his shield into the backswing, kneed Arian forward, and was rewarded by the shriek of someone unexpectedly unhorsed.

'Oxley!'

Guyon heard with relief the rallying cry of his own men.

'*A moi!*' he bellowed, hacking about him. Arian lashed out, and another horse neighed high and shrill with pain. The mercenary leader fell from his saddle, hit the churned mud, shuddered and was still. His second looked around, saw that they were now outnumbered and, with panic in his voice, yelled the command to retreat.

A rearguard attempt to bring their captives away with them was aborted as Guyon spurred Arian between the girl's mount and that of the Fleming tugging on her bridle. The sword chopped downwards, cleaving leather, flesh and bone. The mercenary shrieked as three of his fingers were trampled in the mud beneath the grey's dancing hooves. Guyon grasped the severed ends of rein and pulled her gelding hard about. One of his men took the bridle from him and passed her through to safety.

Her husband had thrown himself sideways from his own saddle and rolled to his feet, winded and bruised but otherwise unharmed, his hands still lashed behind his back.

Guyon turned Arian around. The horse was bleeding freely from several slashes on his neck and forequarters and was jittery, still spoiling for battle, so that Guyon was forced to stay in the saddle. There was blood running down his leg. It would have to wait. The way matters stood, it was unwise to linger here longer than was necessary. Undoubtedly reinforcements would be summoned from Thorneyford and set on their trail.

The young man had been cut free of his bonds and was entwined now with his wife. Guyon sidled Arian towards them, but did not move in too close, for the stallion was quite likely to attack. The man raised his head, murmured something to his wife and left her to squelch over to Guyon.

'Watch him, lad, he'll brain you if you come too close.'

The young man smiled, his sombre countenance lightening to reveal why women might find him attractive. 'I know my way around horses, my lord,' he said confidently, and stood stock still so that Arian could become used to his presence without seeing him as a threat. 'There is no way we can thank you enough, my lord. We are deeply in your debt. Indeed, we owe you our lives.'

Guyon smiled bleakly. 'Walter de Lacey is no bosom brother of mine. You owe me nothing. It was a pleasure. I'd advise you to be on your way as soon as you can. He tends to nurture grudges.'

'You don't need to tell me that!' the young man snorted. 'I'm a free man and I'll not work for the likes of him. Old Sir Ralph was mean and sour, but he'd not lay about him with a whip for the pure pleasure of it, nor take a girl to his bed if she were not willing!'

Guyon shifted his gaze to the delicate blonde girl watching them anxiously through the rain. Probably she was about Judith's age but looked no more than a nervous twelve, just the kind that de Lacey enjoyed.

'She's not a serf, my lord,' he said with quiet dignity. 'I swear it on my soul.'

'He has a fetish for other men's wives and girls who are not yet women,' Guyon said with distaste. 'You'd best pick up

163

the pieces of your charter and have a scribe make a copy. You may well need it. Where are you and your wife bound?'

'I have relatives in Chester, my lord. They will take us in while I find work. I thought I would seek employment with Earl Hugh.'

'There is work nearer to hand at Ravenstow if you desire it. I've been a huntsman short since last winter.'

The young man considered him from beneath a tumble of springy brown curls, eyes wary and thoughtful. Guyon FitzMiles was a huntsman short because sir Walter had almost beheaded the man in a fit of fury during a hunt to honour the marriage of Ravenstow's heiress, or so the rumour went. Something about the theft of a horse and a broken boar spear.

'Make up your mind as we ride,' Guyon offered, turning Arian towards the ale house. 'Ravenstow is on your road anyway and you would do well to take advantage of an armed escort off Thorneyford lands. If you decide against staying, I can always recommend you to Earl Hugh. He's a personal friend of mine.'

'Thank you, my lord,' Brand said, gratitude mingled with the gravity of caution. Knowing what rumour whispered about FitzMiles and women, he was relieved to see that Guyon did not acknowledge Elflin above a brief nod as he passed her. Escaping one master with his mind between his legs for another of the same ilk was not what he intended, even if that man had saved his life.

He went to pick up the pieces of his parchment from the mud.

CHAPTER 14

JUDITH CEASED COMBING her hair and regarded her mother across the space that separated them. 'I thought you might,' she said without surprise.

It was not quite the response that Alicia had expected of her announcement that she was going to her dower lands as soon as Guyon's father returned from his business with Hugh of Chester to escort her there. She had come to her daughter's room prepared for tears and pleading and was completely thrown by Judith's aplomb.

'I do not want you to think that I am discontented here with you and Guyon, but you have your own life to live . . . and I have mine.' She gnawed her lip and wondered if she should test that aplomb by telling her daughter what else she intended besides.

Judith put down the comb and went to her mother and wordlessly hugged her. They were much of a height now, almost eye to eye, for Judith had grown since the early spring and had put some not unpleasing flesh on her bones.

Alicia returned the embrace. 'Of course, I will visit you often and you will know where to find me should the need arise,' she said, feeling guilty, but then guilt was nothing new and about to be consolidated.

'You will always be welcome, you know that!' Judith answered, kissing her. 'But why do you speak as if you intend your stay to be permanent?'

'Because I do.'

Judith lifted her head from Alicia's shoulder, her agate eyes roundly anxious. 'Is there something wrong? Something that myself or Guyon can do?'

Alicia stroked Judith's shining tawny hair. 'Understand when the time comes,' she said pensively, 'and do not judge me too harshly.'

'Mama?' Judith looked up at her, beginning to feel worried. Her mother's eyes would not hold her own and her lids were red-rimmed as they so often were these days.

Beside the fire, Melyn arched in leisurely feline fashion and stalked past the two women to the door, her head cocked expectantly. Alicia sniffed and gained control of her precarious emotions. *Mother and child.* She could sense the reversal.

Judith had stiffened, her eyes on the cat and the door, her tension palpable.

'What's the matter?' Alicia said.

The curtain parted and Guyon stepped into the room, or rather a drowned travesty.

'Mother of God!' exclaimed Alicia.

Water dripped from every visible portion of him and puddled the skins spread atop the rushes on the floor. His walk was far from its customary lithe prowl as he squelched to the fire. Indeed, he was limping badly.

'What's wrong with your leg?' Judith demanded, hastening to his side.

He unfastened his sodden cloak and handed it to her. 'A sword arm that was too slow,' he answered wearily.

'You were attacked?' she asked sharply, her eyes flicking his soaked chausses and the rain-washed streaks of blood channelling down them.

'Clever girl.' His tone was sarcastic. 'Have you any wine?'

Alicia made herself scarce, pausing at the door to exchange a wry look with her daughter. Guyon's temper appeared as chancey as tonight's foul weather.

Judith fetched the flagon and a small vial of aqua vitae and two cups. 'Do you want a bath?' she asked cautiously.

'Does it look like it?' he snorted. 'God's death, we nearly

166

drowned at Elmford. The horses were in the river belly-deep and the current was full of calf-licks.' He took the wine from her and swallowed it down, coughing a little on the strength of the aqua vitae. His face was grey except for two flushed points of colour highlighting his cheekbones.

She put her cup down, fetched a linen towel and knelt to unbuckle his swordbelt. 'What happened?'

The weight slid from his hips into her hands and he sighed with relief. The garnets set in the pommel of his sword glowed dully like drops of dried blood. Flatly he told her of their encounter with the Flemings, its reasons and its likely consequences.

'It is true then. I thought it was just rumour that de Lacey was going to marry Mabel,' she murmured, as she disposed of the belt and returned to help him off with the hauberk. 'Mama says that she's not really mad. Her mouth's deformed and what she says comes out as gibberish unless you know her well.'

'I doubt it will trouble her new husband for long,' Guyon said and put down his cup so that she could draw the hauberk over his head.

Judith frowned, for he was shivering violently. Her knuckles touched his throat as she drew the garment over his head. His skin was cold and clammy to the touch. 'I'd better look at your leg,' she said and began to unlace his gambeson.

'The tavern-keeper's wife bound it for me,' he said with a shrug. 'Let be, Judith. I'm so tired I could fall asleep on my feet. The last thing I need is you poking at me with your tortures and nostrums.'

'Nevertheless you will drink what I give you,' she answered authoritatively and threw him a stern look from beneath her brows.

The faintest twist of humour twitched his lips. 'Oh God,' he said. 'What have I ever done to deserve this?'

'You married me,' she retorted, her own lips curving for an instant from their severity before she took the wet gambeson from him and the clinging damp linen shirt he wore beneath it.

Guyon eyed her, vision throbbing to the lead weight pressing down on top of his head, sensing a change in her, but unable to fathom what or where. She returned with a sheepskin bed covering and flung it around his shoulders and turned away to mix him a brew composed of poppy and feverfew in wine.

'So I did,' he said softly and bent to remove his boots. The room swam around him. The needles of pain inside his skull coalesced into one deep-plunging dagger. He reached to brace himself against the clothing chest and missed.

Judith spun round and with a cry of consternation ran to him. There was a brighter red stain spreading on his chausses and his breath was coming in harsh, effortful gasps. He was on his knees. She knelt down and unlaced his chausses.

'Lie down,' she commanded him.

'I don't . . .'

'Lie down!' she snarled and none too gently pushed him. He subsided as though she had struck him with a mace and not the flat of her hand.

Efficiently she stripped him, her lips tightening at sight of the ineptly bound linen strip, newly wet and red. 'How long have you been riding with this?'

'Five . . . six hours,' he muttered from between clenched teeth.

'You fool!' she said contemptuously and left him to fetch a wad of clean linen which she folded into a pad and pressed hard to the leaking edges of the wound.

'No choice, not with Walter de Lacey and his *Cwmni Annwn* howling for my blood.'

'It looks like they got it!' she said acidly. 'And perhaps your life with it.'

'I've taken worse.' He tried to smile and failed.

'I doubt it,' she said repressively, leaning on the pad. 'You've lost more blood than a stuck pig, to look at you.'

'I knew it would come back to boars in the end,' he said and lapsed into semi-consciousness.

Judith almost panicked and fled to fetch her mother. Almost, but not quite. There was nothing Alicia could do that she could not and he was her charge. 'So much for subtlety,' she said shakily, looking down at her wet, bloodied bedrobe and smeared hands and, seeing that the pulse of blood had eased up, left him to fetch the powdered comfrey root and fresh bandages and sent her maid Helgund for a bowl of mouldy bread.

Returning to him, she shook the comfrey root into the wound, wondering with a touch of suppressed hysterical humour how the fair Alais de Clare would have coped with such a situation. And the humour died as she wondered how the fair Rhosyn uerch Madoc, mother of his child, would have dealt with it.

The maid came back with the bread and was dismissed. Judith braided her hair and pinned it out of the way and set to work with needle and thread. The Fleming's sword had caught his inner thigh where the hauberk was slit to allow for riding and no mail to protect his flesh. It was not a long wound, but it had pierced deep and, had it been two inches higher, she would not have needed to worry about the matter of subtlety, and neither would he. Indeed, as she worked, the hysterical urge to giggle almost overcame her again, for kneeling between his legs she had a very intimate eyeful of what had previously so terrified her. Not so daunting now for the simple reason that she had the control. If she wanted, she could leave him to bleed to death. It was a sobering thought. She swallowed her sense of the ridiculous and attended single-mindedly to her purpose.

Having dressed the main wound as best she could, for it was in a difficult position to bind properly, she examined him for signs of other injury.

Surprisingly, for a man so dark, he was not hirsute, just a ridge of dark hair running from the centre of his breastbone down into the thick bush at his groin and she was able to scrutinize his flesh closely. It was something she had never done before, preferring to dwell in deliberate ignorance and he, sensing her fear and awkwardness, had seldom stripped naked in front of her.

It had never occurred to her to think of his body as being attractive. A source of pain and brutalization, so her previous experience said. Now, almost in wonder, she traced with light fingers a thin white line scoring one muscular pectoral and one higher up, just grazing his jaw bone.

Guyon groaned and opened his eyes. Judith sucked a sharp breath between her teeth and quickly withdrew her hand.

'*Cath fach,*' he said weakly and found a smile from some-where and this time his tone was not patronizing. 'How bad is it?'

She could see the pulse racing in his throat and the sweat sheening its hollow. 'Bad enough. You've lost so much blood that there's scarcely a drop left in your body and you're quite likely to develop wound fever. There were flakes of rust in the cut. I've packed it with mouldy bread, but it's hard to bind. I can't move you for fear that you'll open it again. You are going to be uncomfortable for no small time . . . if you live . . . and no, I am not japing with you. You had best prepare your soul.'

'What kind of comfort is that?' he said, tried to laugh and desisted, eyes squeezing closed.

Judith used the moment to scrub her face with her sleeve, refusing to be seen in tears. 'The only kind you'll get from me!' she retorted bravely. 'And don't go to sleep. You've got to drink this first.'

He lifted his lids, then with an effort widened them at the sight of the stone pitcher full to the brim and the cup she was filling from its bounty.

'All of it,' she said with a certain satisfaction.

'God's death, you evil wench. Robert de Belleme does not have sole monopoly on torture after all. What is it?'

'Boiled water, a sprinkling of salt and three spoonfuls of honey. It is to make up for the blood you've lost.'

'I'll be sick,' he said faintly.

Judith propped him up on a bolster and pillows fetched from the bed and rammed the cup under his nose. 'Drink it!' she commanded in a voice of steel that gave no indication of the fact that her knees had turned to jelly.

Something like surprise flickered across his pallor as he looked at her. 'I'm not worth it, *cath fach*,' he said huskily.

'You are when I think of the alternative,' she answered, and lowered her lids over the betraying tears.

As Judith had predicted, the wound fever struck and sent his temperature soaring out of bounds and with it his grip on reality. Steadfastly she did what she could to bring the fever down, Alicia giving her aid and relief between times.

During one of his lucid periods they moved him to the bed and Judith forced him to drink ox-blood broth in an effort to give his body the strength to fight back. He was promptly sick and she went away and wept in a corner, then returned and gave him more of the salt and honey water.

Once, his eyes glittering like black glass, he looked through her and spoke in Welsh as if holding a conversation. '*It would still be rape. Not that much of a woman.*' And another time, '*She's developing a sense of possession and it's becoming uncomfortable.*'

Bouts of raving showed her facets of his life that he had previously hidden from her. His relationship with Rhosyn, twisting like the current of the Wye, bitter-sweet as aloes and honey. Once he laughed and called her Alais and made a suggestion that both flustered her and filled her with curiosity. She had not known that such a position was possible. During an occasional lucid spell, he would recognize her for her own self. *Cath fach*, he would say and smile ruefully at his own febrile weakness. If she had ever desired revenge for his treating her like a child, she had it now and the taste of it was sour as vinegar.

171

After the second night, his condition worsened. Miles rode in at dawn to find his eldest granddaughter gulping tears and clinging to her mother for comfort and the priest bending over the fever-pared bones of his son, administering the last rites. Judith, colourless as an alabaster tomb effigy, stood opposite Father Jerome, her hands clenched upon the cloth with which she had been wiping Guyon down in a vain attempt to lower the raging of his blood.

Miles came to the bed and gazed down upon his son's fight for life as he had gazed down on Christen two years since. Guyon's hair was lank with sweat, his cheekbones like blades with blue hollows beneath.

Miles looked at Judith. She returned the look fearlessly with eyes that were full of fear. It had gone beyond what she could do for him. In God's hands his life now lay and the odds against his recovery not favourable. Beyond the moment she dared not think. Life went on, she knew it all too well.

Miles stood a moment longer and then, unable to bear it, turned and strode from the room. Judith put down the cloth and hastened after him and found him leaning against the rope-patterned pillar of the cross wall's arch, his fist tight white on the stone work, his eyes staring blankly at nothing.

'I have done what I can,' she said, setting her hand on his shoulder. 'He may yet improve, only at this stage it can happen so quickly . . . his heart might give out.'

Miles closed his eyes, opened them again to pain and faced her. 'How did it happen?'

She told him. 'Eric won't be using his arm for some little time. I have scarcely spoken to the girl or her husband, but he came to me himself to say that they owed Guyon their lives and their gratitude. I need not tell you that at the moment it is no compensation.'

'No,' Miles agreed bleakly.

Judith bowed her head and returned to her vigil.

Two hours later, de Bec came grim-faced to tell her that Walter de Lacey was waiting in the outer ward.

She put down the mortar in which she had been grinding herbs. 'And what could he possibly want?' she said sarcastically as she made sure that Guyon was as comfortable as his condition allowed, and bade Helgund stay close by him.

De Bec lifted his craggy owl's brows at her. 'Mistress, when he saw our new huntsman, he didn't know whether to leap for glee or fall into apoplexy.'

'What a pity he couldn't decide,' Judith said viciously.

De Bec cleared his throat. His young mistress had hardly stopped to eat, let alone rest since lord Guyon had taken ill of the wound fever and it was beginning to show. In this kind of mood she was lethal and the man to have best dealt with her was in a raving fever at the gates of death. He took a deep breath. 'From what I have heard, you had best bring the lass up here out of sight until sir Walter's gone.'

Judith eyed him narrowly for a moment, considered, nodded and sharply bade one of the maids fetch Elflin of Thorneyford to her chamber.

The girl duly arrived from her duties in the kitchens. There was a smut of flour on her cheek and her deep, hyssop-blue eyes were as huge as candle saucers and filled with terror.

'Oh m'lady, please don't send me back to him, for the love of God, I beg you. I'll kill myself, I swear I will!'

Judith looked down on the bent flaxen head, the clenched small hands that were as finely boned as a child's. 'Get up,' she said neutrally. 'Do you think that I would give you up to that scum when my lord has perhaps sacrificed his life that you should go free?'

The girl stood up and bobbed a wobbly obeisance.

'You say you would kill yourself?' Judith said coldly. 'You would do better to take a knife to the tryst and put it through his black heart.' Her voice seethed on the last words. She eyed the girl with contempt. 'Elflin, is it not?'

'Yes, m'lady.' Her voice quavered, thin and reedy with fear.

'Well then Elflin, stiffen your spine and stop snivelling.

173

There is no room for a wet fish in my household. He won't have you, I promise. Now, do you take up that distaff over there and that basket of carded wool and work awhile. Ask Helgund if you should be in any doubt.'

Elflin squeaked assent and bobbed another curtsey.

Milk and water thought Judith impatiently, then checked herself, recalling her own fear of the unknown during the early days of her marriage to Guyon and remembering too, with a guilty pang, his patience and good humour during that time. If she was not afraid now, it was because of him. Besides, she thought as she left the room, this new girl had been a serf until her marriage, the property of the lord of Thorneyford to deal with as he chose. No surprise then that she was nervous of authority.

In the hall, Walter de Lacey was standing before the hearth. FitzWarren the steward had furnished him with a cup of wine and she saw with a sinking heart that he was deep in conversation with Father Jerome, who had about as much guile as a newborn lamb. From the smirk on de Lacey's face as he watched her come forward, it was obvious that he knew and delighted in the news of Guyon's grave illness.

Stifling the urge to be rude until given grounds, Judith made a stilted, traditional speech of welcome.

De Lacey's smile was supercilious. He looked at his nails. 'I am sorry to hear that your husband is so grievously wounded, but the fault is his own. He should not have meddled in my affairs on my lands.'

Father Jerome frowned at him. 'My lord, as I understand matters, he came to the aid of innocent travellers being wrongly molested.'

'A jumped up gamekeeper and a runaway serf?' De Lacey's laugh was caustic. 'Guyon FitzMiles prevented my men from carrying out their lawful duty. Indeed, I am sorely tempted to seek compensation from him for the death of my captain.'

'Your former gamekeeper is a free man to sell his services

174

where he desires and his wife is no more a serf than I am,' Judith said, looking at him with repugnance.

'I have the charter to prove it,' agreed Father Jerome. 'And two copies. Lord Guyon bid me write them before he grew too ill to be lucid.'

'Any scribe can forge a charter for the right fee!' sneered de Lacey.

Father Jerome's scalp turned pink. 'There are witnesses enough – just about the whole of Thorneyford. It was a popular wedding and you'll not disprove the charter's validity, my lord, even ripped to pieces and besmirched by hoofprints.'

'So you refuse to turn them over to me?' De Lacey tilted his gaze to Judith. She was very pale, her sandy freckles the only colour in her face, but she met his yellow lupine eyes coldly, with complete conviction.

'It gives me the greatest satisfaction to deny you both them and your compensation,' she said through her teeth. 'I suggest that you drink your wine and leave.'

His lids narrowed. 'I do not think that with your husband on his deathbed you can afford to annoy me, *doucette*,' he said softly. 'After all, who knows where these lands will be bestowed next and my wife is growing old and not in the best of health. I expect soon to be bereaved.'

'Rot in hell!' she hissed.

He smiled at her, his teeth white and crowding his thin-lipped mouth. 'There'll be more pleasure in taming you than that bag of bones I've got at the moment. My compensation is already assured.'

Father Jerome made a shocked exclamation.

'If you want to be a gelding, that's your own choice,' she retorted, her fingers itching to draw her eating knife from her belt and do the deed here and now. She swallowed hard and forced herself to discipline. 'I think we have nothing to trade but threats and insults. Excuse me if I do not see you on your road. My husband needs me.'

He raised his cup to her in a silent, mocking salute and

looked her insolently up and down as if she was already a piece of his property.

In the bedchamber, Judith collapsed shuddering beside the hearth, so cold that her teeth were chattering together and her hands were like two blocks of marble. The maid, Helgund, a sensible woman, fetched a sheepskin from the foot of the bed, set it around her mistress's shaking shoulders and hunted out the flask of aqua vitae.

Judith choked on the strong liquor. 'I'm all right,' she reassured the maid, finding a wan smile from somewhere. 'Lord Miles will need to know. Have you seen him?'

'Not recently, m'lady. He did not come here while you were gone.'

'My lady, he was talking to your mother in the hall before lord Walter came,' Elflin offered timidly from her corner where she sat deftly spinning the wool, her manual dexterity far in advance of her mental. 'But they had gone when you summoned me to your chamber.'

'I'll try his room in a moment,' Judith said and, finishing the aqua vitae, cast off the sheepskin and went to look at Guyon.

He was sleeping deeply and his temperature, although still raised was, she fancied, not as high as it had been, or perhaps it was just wishful thinking. She turned round and saw the dainty Saxon girl watching her with a wide-eyed mingling of expectancy and fear.

'Sir Walter has gone,' Judith said. 'I think it will be safe for you to seek your husband now.'

'Thank you, my lady!' Elflin quickly put down her work, pale face radiant as a candle flame and, bobbing a deep curtsey, departed the room at a near run.

'What it is to be young and eager,' smiled Helgund tolerantly, addressing Judith as if she were a staid matron beyond love's first sweet violence.

'Yes,' Judith agreed flatly and smoothed the coverlet. 'What it is.' Her chin quivered. She stiffened it and stood erect. 'I must find lord Miles and tell him what has happened. Let me know if there is any change.'

'Yes m'lady.' Helgund looked at her curiously.

Judith left the room almost as swiftly as Elflin had done, got half way down the stairs, stifled the familiar panicky instinct to run and continued at a more sedate pace across the great hall and up the stairs to the small chamber that was her father-in-law's when he visited.

She could hear the murmur of voices as she approached, one deep and hesitant, the other higher, softer, a woman's. Then the voices ceased. At the curtain, Judith hesitated, warned by some sixth sense that to clear her throat and just walk into the room would be very unwise.

Cautiously she drew aside the merest fold of material and peered within to assess whether she should go or stay. Being set into the thickness of the wall, the room was tiny with space only for a bed, a small clothing pole and a brazier for use against the chill of the solid amber stone. And before the brazier, blocking it from view, her mother stood locked in Miles's embrace, her blue gown melding into the dark green of his tunic and chausses, his hands lean and brown against the snowiness of her wimple. Her mother's arms were locked around his neck and they were kissing as, only yesterday in the hall, she had seen Elflin and Brand kissing.

Judith dropped the curtain, stepped away and wondered why she had not realized it long ago. There had been enough beads to make a necklace if one had the eyesight to pick them up. The swings of her mother's moods, the looks and counter-looks cast across the hall, met and avoided. What had her mother said? *Understand when the time comes and do not judge me too harshly*. No more harshly than Alicia had judged herself, she thought and wondered if Guyon, less naïve than herself, had known.

At the foot of the stairs, she encountered the lady Emma about to ascend and quickly blocked her way.

Emma's vivid eyes sharpened.

'I should not bother him until later,' Judith said, her voice slightly constricted. 'He is otherwise occupied.'

Emma searched Judith's face for meaning. The girl looked dreadful. Pale as a ghost, her eyes blue-circled for want of sleep and full of shadows. 'With a woman?' she asked.

Judith hesitated. 'Yes.'

Emma shook her head. 'That always was his source of oblivion,' she sighed, turning with Judith to go back down to the hall. 'He's not much use at getting drunk and he's too slightly built to go out and pick a fight. I've known him ride a horse half to death, but a woman by preference is his usual form of solace. At first after my stepmother died there was scarcely a night when he slept alone . . . God knows some of the sluts and trulls Guy and I had to tolerate in the early days!'

Judith coloured. 'He is with my mother,' she said quietly, 'and they still have all their clothes on.'

Emma's eyes rounded. She stopped and turned. 'Your mother?' The thought seemed to have blocked her brain.

Judith stared her out. Emma drew a long breath between her perfect white teeth and let it out again slowly. 'Well then, I am sorry if my words gave offence but in the past it has been true.'

'The past is not now,' Judith said, not quite keeping the coldness from her tone. For all that Emma was Guyon's sister and he professed her to own a heart of gold, Judith was hard-pressed to find it beneath the various layers of steel and ice.

Emma bit her lip. She and Judith were never going to be more than tepidly cordial. Their natures had too many similarities, subtle shades apart and, within this keep, like two stones in close proximity on a riverbed, they had begun to grate against each other. Emma began to think with new longing of her dower estates and how, when Guyon's crisis was resolved one way or the other, she would go there with her daughters.

Christen seemed to be cured of her affliction to flirt. No

more was '*Alais says*' the bane of their lives. In part she knew it was due to the seriousness of Guyon's condition. That, in itself, was sufficient to put meaningless frivolity in its true perspective, but part was also due to Judith's steadying influence. Guyon's wife might laugh and play childish games with her nieces, might have a puckish sense of humour and an impudent tongue, but attracting men appeared scarcely to interest her. Nor did she wish to gossip about them to the detriment of all else and her domestic skills were more than competent, as were her knowledge of healing and sickbed nursing. Christen, receiving an indifferent or bored response to most of her tattle, had steadied her own giddy attitude and begun to think a little for herself. What profit there was in that had yet to be seen.

More profit than I have had pray God, thought Emma wryly as she followed Judith into the main bedchamber.

CHAPTER 15

A WEEK CAME AND went. So did the priest. Twice. Guyon wavered on the narrow brink between life and death, teetered and stepped back from the edge. Another week passed. There was a terrific thunderstorm. Three sheep in the bailey were struck by lightning and one of the storesheds caught fire. The sheriff came calling, found Brand's charter to be valid and left again. Guyon's temperature descended to normal. He recognized those who stood at his bedside and spoke to them, but he was as weak and dependent as a newborn kitten and even the effort of speech left him exhausted.

In August they received the news that Jerusalem had fallen to the crusaders. The people of the town held a great bonfire and rejoiced for two days. Guyon got out of bed for the first time, walked three paces and collapsed with vertigo and lack of coordination. Judith made him swallow iron filings in wine and more of the disgusting ox-blood broth and gave him a stick to help him walk.

Emma and her daughters left to go first to Emma's dower lands and then back to court. At the end of the month, Alicia departed for her own dower lands with Miles for escort, her leave-taking of Judith somewhat tearful, but there was a new kind of peace behind the emotion and Judith did not begrudge the cause of it, only hoped that it would last.

By late September the wound in Guyon's thigh had healed to a livid pink scar that he would bear for the rest of his life, but, precluding such disasters as her Montgomery uncles and

Walter de Lacey, the latter was not now measured in terms of hours and minutes.

At the moment, Robert de Belleme was in Normandy conducting a private war against a neighbour who had offended him and was not expected back in England this side of spring. Walter de Lacey had been occupied in a localized but savage war against the Welsh, persuading them to stay on their own side of the border and leave his herds alone. The patrols went out from Ravenstow, but their own borders, due to the vigilance of Eric and de Bec, remained relatively secure.

Outside, the wind was playfully gusting a carnival of brown and yellow dead leaves against the keep walls. Pigs on the edge of the forest rooted for acorns, or snuffled among the windfall apples in the garths of the cottages. In the fields, men were digging in the stubble and preparing the land for its winter lying and the women and children were out gathering the blown-down dead twigs and branches for kindling in the long dark months ahead.

In the main bedchamber, Guyon closed his eyes and buried his head on his forearms, lulled by the soothing motion of Judith's strong fingers on his back, massaging stiff muscles with aromatic oil of bay. It had been his first time on a horse since his illness. He had discovered that although his recently healed tissue protested, he was not overly uncomfortable and had thus spent longer in the saddle than he should. 'Learning to ride before you can walk,' Judith had said with exasperation.

Peevish with exhaustion, he had snapped at her that he knew his own limits.

'Then why overstep them?' she had smartly retorted with a toss of her head and left him to struggle upstairs on his own.

She had been right of course – as usual. He stirred beneath her touch as she found a strain and thought that he owed her his life. Without her knowledge of simples and her care in the early days, he would have died. In between, she had faced down and seen off Walter de Lacey and, with the aid of his father and the keep's official machinery, had run the demesne with commendable efficiency.

One of the maids murmured something and Judith replied softly. A slight shift of his head and a lazily lifted lid showed him Brand's wife Elflin for whose sake he had almost got himself killed. Strikingly beautiful in a strange, ethereal way, her bones bearing the fragile delicacy of frost on glass. Brand, he remembered, had been holding Rhuddem's bridle this morning, a smile of welcome on his taciturn features. They had decided to remain awhile, he said. Judith had confirmed that Brand was indeed a skilled huntsman, quick, willing and conscientious. The girl, Judith had brought upstairs to train. Kitchen work was too heavy for her and her beauty was the kind to cause trouble among the general melee of servants who visited the kitchens, or had been recently finding cause to do so. Here, within Judith's immediate governance, she was safe.

Guyon's thoughts drifted drowsily. Judith's hands worked lower over the small of his back. She paused for a moment, and then there was the cold touch of the herbal oil and the slow, undulating motion of her firm, gentle fingers.

Long abstinence, the slow pressure of her hands above and the mattress below, made it inevitable that his body should react in a way that he was quite unable to control. Heat flooded his loins and burgeoned.

Judith felt the change in him. Quite suddenly, beneath her kneading palms, the fluid muscles were rigid with tension.

'Are you all right, my lord? Did I hurt you?' Anxiously she leaned over him. The ends of her braids tickled his back. Her movement released a waft of gillyflower from her garments, spicy and warm.

'No,' Guyon muttered, voice choked. 'No, you did not hurt me, but I think it would be best if you made an end.'

'I was nearly finished anyway,' she said with a shrug, thinking that he wished to be left to sleep. 'Do you turn over and I will anoint your leg.'

A strained, horrified silence. Judith began to feel frightened.

'Guyon, what's wrong?'

He closed his eyes and clenched his teeth, willing the offending member to subside. It did nothing so charitable. The feel of her breasts, warm and round against his back as she leaned over him in consternation, was only making matters worse. Fuel to a fire that could be so easily sent raging out of control.

After a moment, he raised his head from his buried arms and said with agonized amusement: 'What's wrong, *cath fach*, is that the condition I'm in won't do either of us the least bit of good if I give it free rein now.'

'What condition?' she asked, looking blank.

'Oh God, Judith, just give me the ointment and get out!'

'But your thigh, it needs . . .' Her voice trailed off and her agate eyes grew as wide as goblet rims as belatedly she made the connection and with a gasp sprang away from him, her face flaming. Picking up the jar of oil, she thrust it down beside him and fled the room in a state of utter panic.

Guyon looked at the little pot by his head and, with a groan, buried his face again in his forearms.

It was impossible to run down the sharply twisting narrow stone steps when hampered by a full pleated undergown and thick woollen tunic. As Judith slowed her pace, the racing of her mind began to subside as well. Scarlet chagrin washed her face anew. She had been a fool to panic. More than ever now he would think of her as a child. Wherein lay the point of washing her hair in herb-scented water and perfuming the points of her body, tempting fate, only to flee in terror the moment that fate appeared briefly on the horizon?

And if I had stayed, she thought and gave a small shudder, half fear, half something else. Snatching hot chestnuts from the fire. Was the prize worth the pain? And if I go back . . .

Poised at the foot of the stairs, her dilemma was resolved for her by FitzWarren stooping to inform her that the lord of Chester was here and asking hospitality overnight for himself and his retinue.

'I have found accommodation for most of his men, but the cook says that we do not have enough bread and no oven space to bake more with all the new preparations he will have to make.'

'There's an oven in the town, use that,' she said, her present problem abandoned for one of literally far greater dimensions. Where in the name of Holy Mary were they going to lodge Earl Hugh? The great bedchamber it would have to be, and Guyon could have his father's tiny wall chamber. She would make do with the maids in her mother's room on a straw pallet. Mentally clucking her irritation, she sent one of the girls scurrying aloft with the news and went forward wreathed in smiles to greet the lord of Chester.

He was even more huge and solid than she remembered and the kiss of peace he stooped to bestow on her cheek was as warm and gluey as a pot of melted pig's trotters. 'Well well!' he chuckled in his husky, brown voice, looking her up and down and quite misconstruing the breathless pink flush on her cheeks for something less innocent, 'I see that marriage is suiting you!'

Judith's colour darkened and the Earl gave a phlegmy chuckle of delight, and then proceeded to view with approval the way she mastered her embarrassment and with commendable efficiency set about making him comfortable. 'I remember when you were a little pig-tailed maid at your mother's knee,' he grinned, as she drew him to the fire and bade a servant take his cloak. 'Mind you, it also reminds me that I was still slim enough then to chase women for the fun of it!' He patted his enormous paunch ruefully.

'Don't believe a word,' Guyon said behind her, setting his hand lightly on her shoulder and giving it a gentle squeeze. 'He's still frighteningly fast when he chooses.'

'Faster than you, so I hear,' said Earl Hugh, the blue, flesh-lapped eyes disconcertingly shrewd.

'I was rash and I paid for it.'

Chester grunted. 'Not for the first time. Watch him,

wench. He'll run rings round you both and you'll end up tangled in knots.'

Judith's laugh was more than wry. 'Do you think I do not know it!'

Guyon tugged her braid. She risked a glance at him. His face was a little fine-drawn with tiredness, but his expression was light enough and there seemed no change in his usual manner. Involuntarily her eyes went lower and colour flamed her face anew. His mouth twitched. What did she expect to see – a flaunting, rampant erection?

'Do not be too sure of the outcome, Hugh,' he grinned. 'She makes an awesome gaoler.' He led the earl towards the small solar behind the dais. Judith excused herself to consult with the cook and see if she could get the carpenter to strengthen the guest's chair so that it would not collapse beneath the strain of so great a weight, as it had almost done during his last visit at their wedding.

'You have been very busy making yourself enemies since Mon,' Chester remarked, hunching his powerful shoulders. He wore a collar of rough cut emeralds, and on his broad thumb a ring set with an enormous cabuchon ruby.

'Have I?' Guyon eased himself down onto a padded stool.

The earl considered him. He had come to know Guyon fairly well during last summer's difficult Welsh campaign. A competent leader of men and an excellent scout with an innate knowledge of the workings of the Welsh mind. If he had failings, they were composed of a slightly unpredictable wild streak, probably due to the Welsh blood and a disturbing inclination to go his own way if not minutely scrutinized and checked. 'You know damned well you have!' he growled. 'Hardly Robert de Belleme's favourite nephew, are you? He has some very nasty suspicions concerning your involvement in a raid on the Shrewsbury road back in the spring.'

'Nothing he can prove.'

Earl Hugh lifted a flagon from the cupboard against which he leaned and examined the intricate crystal and lapiz Byzantine workmanship. 'Maybe, but when has lack of proof ever stopped Montgomery from pursuing his intended victim?'

'I might as well be impaled for a sheep as a lamb,' Guyon said and smiled with private amusement, remembering the flock of sheep and the incredulity on the Earl of Shrewsbury's handsome, narrow face.

'It is no game, Guy,' Chester said quietly.

'Did I say that it was?'

The Earl's eyebrows lifted towards his greasy thatch of thinning auburn hair. 'Don't be obtuse with me!' he warned. 'I'm not a woman to be deceived by the twists of your tongue.'

Guyon propped his leg on a foot stool. 'All right, I admit it was foolhardy to risk de Belleme's rage, but at the time I was raging myself. Since then I've been a model of propriety.'

'Excluding this recent escapade?' enquired the Earl, pointing the flagon at Guyon's leg. 'Antagonizing the new lord of Thorneyford with a display of mad bravado?'

Guyon snorted. 'Yes, look at me. Do you think I fight odds of nine to two because I enjoy flirting with death and rousing a wasp's nest of trouble? Bad fortune, nothing more. If Arian had not cast a shoe, I'd not have been anywhere near that village.'

Chester put the flagon down on the cupboard. Guyon's lids were heavy, but it was not all the aftermath of fever. Part of it was concealment. He cleared his throat and said conversationally, 'I was in Shrewsbury before de Belleme left for Normandy. A pedlar with more mouth than sense brought in the news that you had survived your wound. Needless to say the poor wretch is dead for his pains, although it wasn't de Belleme's hospitality that got the better of him this time.'

'No?' Guyon affected indifference.

'The lord of Thorneyford was there in the hall and not best pleased to say the least. It was a blessing for the pedlar. The knife slipped and gave him a clean death.' He pursed his small, cherubic lips. 'He wants Ravenstow, Guy . . . and Judith.'

Guyon snorted with humourless amusement. 'Tell me something I do not know. He's had a dagger at my back ever since my wedding.'

'I won't share my boundaries with such a one as him if I can help it. No control over himself, for a start. Half a brain and too much cunning, and he slobbers over de Belleme's boots like a hound with the slavers.' He gave a breathy laugh. 'The Welsh nibbling me one side and him the other. It behoves me to keep you alive and in a state of grace!'

'Is that why you're here?' Guyon raised his lids to reveal luminous amusement. 'To protect me from the worst part of my own nature?'

Chester shook his head. Guyon's tongue could be as maddening as a gnat to a bull on a summer day but, if so, his perception was equally sharp. 'To make sure you know how close to the fire your fingers are!' he retorted.

'You sound like my father!' Guyon laughed.

'Is he not wise?'

'Oh, very.'

Chester's restless fat fingers toyed with the fortune in emeralds chained upon his breast. Guyon's face was impassive. He had heard several drifting rumours in Shrewsbury concerning Miles and Maurice de Montgomery's widow. Well, and why not? She was well-preserved and her dower lands, although not vast, were pleasant and fertile. A man could find it in him to plough both with ease. Perhaps it would be entertaining to pay Miles a visit in the near future and see about the purchase of another horse . . .

'I know how close to the fire I am,' Guyon said into the earl's ruminative silence. 'But uncle Robert will have his eyes on a broader arena than mine now that Jerusalem has fallen into Christian hands. I hazard that for the nonce he'll leave my demise to the hands of fate and expendable tools such as Walter de Lacey.'

Chester spat on an emerald and polished it on his furred sleeve. The King's older brother, Robert Curthose, had pawned the Duchy of Normandy to Rufus in exchange for the necessary silver to go on crusade and departed forthwith. The Christian force had been successful and, barring mishap to Robert's cast-iron frame, a few more months would likely see his return and an ensuing broil of trouble. Rufus was not going to smile sweetly and hand over the Duchy like a joint on a trencher.

'De Belleme will thrust his sword where it will cause the most mischief,' Guyon continued. 'I'll wager you five marks to a penny that the moment Robert sets foot on Norman soil, the Earl of Shrewsbury will hare to his side and offer him all assistance. You know what he thinks of Rufus.'

'So do you,' Chester pointed out dryly.

'But I have held my oath to him, have I not? Therein lies the difference. De Belleme doesn't give a pot of piss for his own fealty. I can see it coming as clearly as a thunderstorm over Ledworth ridge. Brother Robert returns from the Holy Wars mantled in glory and demands the return of his earldom. Rufus throws one of his famous tantrums and refuses. De Belleme joins the side that is most advantageous to himself and merry havoc holds sway. All we need then is for the Welsh to come hotfoot over the border aflame with raiding fever and it'll be worse than a drunken brawl at Smithfield fair! It won't matter about me because everyone's fingers will be in the fire then.'

The white bitch at Guyon's feet raised her head and nuzzled his hand. Chester absently admired her narrow-loined conformation while he considered Guyon's words. Most of the content had already occurred to himself and doubtless half the other barons in the country. Stormy water lay ahead and those with sense were battening down to weather it, or else seeking a new harbour, as in the case of the powerful de Clare family who were quietly cultivating the third brother.

'And Prince Henry?' he said. 'What about Prince Henry?'

'What about him?' Guyon rubbed his thigh. 'He'll watch us all burn for a while, toss the occasional twig on the fire and, when he's had enough, he'll either douse it or walk away, whichever suits his purpose most. Probably he'll side with Rufus. He wants him to get him Edith of Scotland for a bride and he wants Rufus to name him the heir.'

'You know a great deal for a man who's been on his sickbed since before harvest time,' Chester remarked a trifle warily.

Guyon lifted one nonchalant shoulder. 'My brother-in-law writes letters to his wife, my sister and she shows them to me to relieve the boredom.'

'Your brother-in . . . Ah yes,' said the earl. 'He assists the chamberlain, doesn't he?'

'Something like that. We all have our ways and means. Speaking of which, is there a purpose behind your visit, or is it truly just social to comfort my convalescence?'

'That depends upon how sick you still are,' Chester cocked a glance at the propped leg.

Guyon shook his head and laughed. 'Sick only of being wrapped in swaddling. If I so much as sneeze, Judith appears at my side with some noxious potion or other.'

'She's a young wife, eager to show off her skills,' Chester said, momentarily diverted. 'Considering the life she led before her marriage, you ought to be grateful she's not spiked your wine with monkshood.'

Guyon's laughter deepened and seamed his eye corners. 'You don't know the half of it, Hugh. Monkshood is far too swift a revenge!'

Chester rubbed his beaky nose and looked a question.

Guyon sobered. 'I owe her my life,' he admitted. 'And more than twice over.'

'She's a fine-looking girl with a sound head on her shoulders. You are luckier than most.'

Guyon clasped his hands behind his head. Fine looking? Well, yes, perhaps she was growing that way as her body filled into womanhood and he would not deny her intelligence; but as to his being luckier than most? He thought back to her reaction in the bedchamber, the look of terror in her eyes, the way she had run as if from rape.

For close on a year now he had held himself in check. The first months it had been easy for she was still so obviously a child, but time had blurred the division between girl and woman. He was aware of his own physical hunger and the fact that it could not be appeased. Whatever the change in her body, it was obvious that she was not mentally prepared to accept his flesh ... might never be. Monkshood was indeed too swift for revenge.

'What did you want to talk about?' he asked abruptly and brought his hands down.

Chester darted his brows at the sharpness of Guyon's tone which was quite at odds with the amusement of a moment since. 'Where your land borders mine, up on *Llyn Moel* ridge, there is a blind spot between the hills, and the Welsh ride down the valley to raid. A keep is needed and the best site is within your bounds. When you see it, I think you will agree.'

'Within my expense as well?' Guyon asked. 'I know the place you mean. Lord Gruffydd's men came through the gap this spring and carried off some of our herds.'

'I am sure we can come to an amicable agreement,' Chester said with his deceptive, benign smile.

'It might be possible,' Guyon fenced, knowing that look of old. Hugh D'Avrenches was no man's fool when it came to arguing prices and what he did not know the canny officials he kept around him did.

Chester's smile became a rich chuckle and his eyebrows flashed swiftly up and down. 'I thought we could ride out tomorrow, your health and your wife permitting. There are some fine hunting grounds up there on my side, too. I've recently built a lodge.'

'I may be able to escape for a few days,' Guyon answered cautiously. 'Providing that your quarry is not boar.' His eyes went to the door. 'I don't hunt them for pleasure.'

'Does anyone?' Chester said, taking his meaning immediately, and changed his expression to one of beaming welcome as Judith entered the room followed by a maid bearing a flagon and cups.

190

CHAPTER 16

London
Whitsuntide 1100

HE CRY OF a boatman floated up from the river. Judith set her sewing aside and went to the casement. Blossom was drifting down from the apple trees in the garth, as green-tinted through the glass as the bright feathers of the popinjay regarding her beadily from its perch. Being momentarily high in the King's favour, Emma's husband could afford to waste silver on such rare frivolities as green glass windows and exotic foreign birds.

She and Guyon were in London to attend the Whitsuntide gathering of the court, held this year at the newly completed Palace of Westminster designed by Rannulf Flambard, who took men's money and spent it in the name of the crown. The city was crowded, as packed to bursting as a thrifty housewife's jar of salted beans, and only the highest magnates in the land were granted sleeping space within Westminster and its immediate environs. The rest had to manage as best they could. Conveniently for them, Richard, Guyon's brother-in-law, owned a house on the Strand but a few minutes' walk from the new palace and was able, with a bit of a squeeze and a great deal of organizing from Emma, to house Judith and Guyon and their immediate servants for the length of their sojourn. They were uncomfortable and cramped, but more fortunate than most . . . fortunate being a relative term, she thought and scowled over her shoulder at the bed in the corner of the curtain-partitioned room.

It was Richard and Emma's and they had insisted on

giving it up to herself and Guyon during their stay. A kindness that was a cruelty in disguise. Last night Guyon had sat up until the early hours talking to Richard and used the excuse of not disturbing her and the other sleepers across whose pallets he must step in order to reach his own bed as a reason to roll himself in his cloak among the other men in the hall.

Judith leaned her head against the wall and folded her arms, her eyes troubled. Ever since that incident in the bedchamber at Ravenstow, when his body had reacted to her touch and she had run from him in terror, he had taken pains to avoid the physical contacts of their relationship.

The morning after Earl Hugh's arrival, he had ridden out with him to inspect the proposed site of the new keep. Judith, her mind and emotions in turmoil, had not been so foolish as to try and stop him. Indeed, when he told her of his intentions, after one brief, involuntary denial, she had listened quietly to his calm reasoning and to Earl Hugh's jovial bluster and agreed with them that they must go, had even found a smile from somewhere and the will to be interested in what they intended.

In the morning she had served them both the stirrup cup and wished them good fortune with a smile on her lips, and when Guyon had leaned over Arian's neck to tug her braid she had suffered it with humour and dammed behind clenched teeth the scream that rose in her throat. It was only for a week at most that they would be gone, only a week she told herself, but it might as well have been a lifetime. She had sobbed furious, bitter tears into her pillow for what was lost. Her hawk had flown. The mastery was no longer hers. She had lost it the moment she ran from him in panic, her hands slick with aromatic oil and the cold sweat of terror.

In the event, it had been a full ten days before he returned, looking positively refreshed for his freedom. His skin had worn an outdoor glow and his manner had been ebullient as he discussed the plans for the intended new keep. It was literally a stone's throw from the Welsh border. *Caermoel*, the place was called in Welsh, meaning fortress upon a crag, and there were ruins upon its crest to show where an earlier civilization had once built its own defences. There were merlins nesting on the lichened rock face and wolf pugs in the mud of the river crossing at its sheer, boulder-tumbled face. To the west, the hills of Gwynedd were a purple dragon-back in the distance. To the east lay the fertile Chester plain.

A price had yet to be haggled and the costings worked out, but both men professed themselves content that the project should commence by the early spring. So much Judith had heard from Guyon, his manner enthusiastic, nothing concealed. In a roundabout way, as it went from guardroom to hall servants to her personal maids, she also heard that Earl Hugh not only kept an excellent table at his hunting lodge, but also provided a comprehensive list of other creature comforts for the benefit of his guests. Apparently the girl had been well endowed and willing and Guyon's enthusiasm as boundless as that which he displayed when discussing the proposed new keep.

At first Judith had been hurt and jealous, but these emotions had been replaced by self-irritation and a certain wry acceptance. At least he had not sought his relief with Rhosyn. She did not think she could have borne that. As of now, the remedy she knew lay in her own hands could she but bear to reach out and grasp it, thorns and all. He still called her *cath fach* and pulled her braid, but he was more wary of touching her now. Fewer hugs and kisses. Sometimes he would look at her in a way that made her insides melt with nervous fear and on those occasions his eyes were not on her face.

He lingered more with his men. Some nights he did not come to bed at all. He spent much of his time away, some of it genuine, concerned with the new keep and maintenance of those he already held, some of it an excuse to avoid. The easy cameraderie of the early days was gone. The thread that bound them was taut, whining with tension and stretched a little further each day. And if it snapped . . .

Stifled by her thoughts, Judith opened the casement and looked out. The apple blossom, prematurely detached by a boisterous breeze, drifted in pink-tinted snow across her vision. The sound of laughter silvered her ears and she saw that a boat was being manoeuvred into the steps at the foot of the garden, a private river boat with protective bright canopy and furs piled within against the nip of the spring breeze.

The source of the laughter was an exceptionally pretty young woman in a rich, variegated catskin cloak. She was seated on the nearside of the canopy and leaning intimately into Guyon's shoulder, her braid the colour of new butter against his own dark cloak and his blown ink-black hair. He laughed too and the woman leaned further to kiss him playfully on the lips as he rose to leave the boat. Richard, his brother-in-law, followed him, chuckling a remark and receiving a jesting slap from the woman in punishment. The last to leave was an elegant, slender young man who bent with polished courtesy to kiss the beringed white hand offered to him.

'That's Prince Henry's private craft,' Christen said, nudging her way in to lean beside Judith and watch the boat steer out into the swift, grey current of the river. 'He still sees Alais on occasion.'

'That is Alais de Clare?' Judith narrowed her eyes, but the blonde figure was too far away now to be freshly appraised.

'Oh, there's no cause for concern,' Christen said blithely. 'She flirts from habit and Guy was never really that interested.'

'I'm not concerned,' Judith said with far more nonchalance than she actually felt. 'Who else was there with Guyon and Richard?'

Christen coloured rosily and smoothed her already immaculate gown. 'That was Simon de Vere, one of papa's assistants. He's heir to a manor just outside the city, but papa thinks he will rise to much higher things in the King's service.' So much higher that he was hoping for a match between Simon and his eldest daughter. Christen was amenable to the idea, for Simon was nineteen years old, likely to be rich and already an accomplished courtier.

Outside, masculine voices were raised in jovial, bantering conversation and Christen hastened to open the door to them, almost tripping over Cadi who was determined to be first.

Richard strode into the room laughing and wiping his eyes at some joke and tossed his cloak casually onto a chest, Emma being absent among the stalls of the Chepe with her maid and not there to take him to task.

The popinjay screeched at the men and bobbed on its perch. 'You ought to get one, Guy, they're good company when your wife's not around.' Richard grinned, as Guyon paused beside the perch to eye dubiously. 'Mind you, so is Alais de Clare, eh?'

'Not much to choose between the two,' Guyon answered neutrally as he walked around the bird. 'But I rather fancy that Alais bears more resemblance to a coney than a popinjay.'

Robert guffawed and turned to take the wine that his daughter brought for him.

Guyon looked round at Judith where she still stood at the open window, her own expression censorious. 'Where's your cloak, *cath fach?*'

'*Cath fach?*' Richard looked round, still laughing. Familiar with Latin, French and Flemish and even a smattering of Anglo-Saxon, he was totally nonplussed by the Welsh that his wife's marcher relatives used so freely.

'Kitten,' Guyon translated in the same, neutral tone. 'She might look sweet, but don't try picking her up unless you want to be scratched.'

'A coney, a popinjay or a kitten,' Richard mused. 'Which would you rather?'

'A kitten any day,' Guyon said, smiling across at his wife. 'They know how to fend for themselves.'

She looked at him and then away, crossly aware that she was blushing. 'Why do I need my cloak?'

'Simon's grandfather has a house this end of the Holborne road and he's renting breathing space if we want it.'

Judith glanced around the room. Christen and Simon had drawn aside and were talking in stilted formal fashion, painfully aware of Richard's approving, amused paternal scrutiny. Tonight there would be straw pallets laid out over every portion of floor space and not even the privacy to piss in the chamber pot without alerting half the household to the event. Besides, she and Emma were only tepidly tolerant of each other and the crowded proximity in which they were forced to dwell was straining that tolerance to the limit. She nodded to Guyon and went to pick up her cloak from the foot of the bed.

'Get your cloak, Chris,' Guyon said across the room to his niece. 'You might as well come too. Simon's grandfather won't object. He enjoys company.'

'He'd be delighted,' Simon confirmed, his face alight with that particular emotion before he turned a pensive look in Richard's direction. 'With your permission, sir?'

'Dare I trust you for a chaperone, Guy?' Richard enquired, lifting a sardonic brow. 'Emma will have me chopped into gobbets and fed to that damned bird if anything untoward happens.'

'Papa!' cried Christen indignantly, as if his concern had not, at one time, been warranted.

'I will have every respect for Christen, sir,' said Simon, smothering in stilted courtesy his desire to laugh.

Guyon considered minutely the bright ludicrous bird upon its perch. 'Does it eat meat, anyway?' he asked with spurious gravity.

Christen hit him.

Simon's grandfather was a garrulous white-haired old man of seventy, delighted to greet company. He teased Simon unmercifully about Christen, pumped him and Guyon for court scandal, sucking his gums with relish over the juicier bits and making acid remarks about the brains and breeding of the people involved. He gave them wine and honey cakes. The tables board came out and a set of dice and counters. He invited Christen to play and swivelled a jaundiced eye to Guyon.

'I heard about you from the Prince last time he was here. "Never play tables with anyone from Flambard's household, or with Guyon FitzMiles," he said. "They'll strip you naked in less time than it took you to dress in the first place!"'

'That's untrue!' Guyon protested, laughing. 'I'd leave you a loincloth for decency at least!'

The old man dismissed him with a disgusted wave. 'Nay, but you're not as pretty to look at across a trestle as your niece here and I've a close interest in her, being as she's likely to be future family. Take your wife above and show her the rooms awhile.'

Simon, not about to miss the opportunity to study Christen's pure, dainty profile, drew up a stool so that he could watch her as she played.

Judith and Guyon went outside and climbed the wooden outer staircase to the two rooms above.

'What did he mean about the Prince?' Judith asked as Guyon opened the outer door and drew aside a heavy curtain.

'Oh, Henry occasionally stays here, or he used to before the new palace was finished. Sometimes he games with old Walter to humour him.'

Judith examined the room with renewed interest. The walls were plastered and illuminated with seasonal scenes – hunting, plouging, reaping, women dancing at a feast, a man catching fish. The colours were rich and vibrant. There was a brazier in the room and a small *prie dieu* and in a niche in the wall stood a small alabaster statue of the virgin. There were chairs, a handsomely carved chest and a long trestle table.

'He used to hold meetings here sometimes,' Guyon said, glancing round at the familiarity. 'That mark on the table is where he used to prop his feet with his spurs still on.'

'Dicing, wenching and carousing?' she said archly.

'Not often. There are places on the Southwark side for that kind of sin,' Guyon said incorrigibly and followed her through the second curtain into the slightly smaller bedchamber.

'Where's the bed?' she asked. 'Or do we sleep on these skins on the floor?'

Guyon drew breath, but released it silently, the obvious reply unspoken, for Judith's spine was rigid. 'Henry's had it transferred to Westminster I expect, but I daresay we can find one from somewhere.'

'One?' Judith looked over her shoulder at him.

'Whatever,' he answered as if he did not care.

Judith examined the rest of the room. The windows, like Richard's, were glazed and the walls as in the first room were plastered and illuminated. The floor was thickly strewn with rushes and crushed lavender and there was a heap of pelts in one corner that were obviously bed coverings. One bed . . . her thoughts raced around in a circle and tripped over each other. She looked down at a second tables board set upon a cloth-covered trestle and nervously moved one of the polished jet counters.

'We can remain with Richard and Emma if you'd prefer,' he said, picking up one of the other counters, tossing it in the air and catching it on the back of his hand as if he was playing knuckle bones.

She shook her head, eyes stubbornly lowered, fingers toying desperately with the smooth, cold lump of jet whose twin was lodged in the pit of her stomach. 'You have seen how cramped we are. Emma will not thank us if we refuse and it would be a discourtesy to Simon and his grandfather.'

Guyon considered her with slightly narrowed eyes. She was shaking to the swift beat of her heart and he saw her struggle and swallow. He set his counter down and tilted her

198

face up on his fingertips. Judith raised her lids, feeling hot and weak and frightened, and wished desperately that they had stayed downstairs.

'That is their preference, not yours,' he said gently.

'It is mine too,' Judith said, not having sufficient bravery to be a coward and stood her ground as he traced the line of her jaw with his fingertip until he reached her ear, skirted it and feathered it down her throat. Her scalp prickled.

'Stop fighting it, Judith,' he pleaded softly. 'There is nothing to fear. I won't hurt you. You know that, or you should by now.'

A chill ran down her spine and shuddered her body. The finger became a hand that slipped slowly down to her waist, curved there and drew her lightly against him. He brushed her temple with his lips, her cheekbone and jaw, slanting to seek her ear lobe beneath her braid and nibble it gently. Involuntarily Judith gasped and arched at the sensation.

He nuzzled the sensitive hollow behind her ear, kissed her throat, returned to her face, his lips light and butterfly travelling the same path again to return to her ear lobe. He held her loosely, not compelling her to the embrace, stroking her as he might stroke Cadi or Melyn, soothing her while enticing her to want more.

At length, he moved his other hand from her back and slowly took it up the side of her rib cage to the small, neat outer swell of her breast. Softly he touched her lips with his own, applying no demand, then moved on, kissing her chin, trailing the tip of his tongue over her throat.

Hesitantly Judith began to respond. One hand came up tentatively to rest on his belt, the other, palm flat, smoothed the dark wool tunic on his back. She moved closer. His hand tightened slightly at her waist and he extended his thumb across her breast to rub the soft peak of her nipple. It budded and hardened at his touch and Judith, totally surprised by the spark of sensation that flashed from nipple to loins, gave a small convulsive shudder.

Guyon forced himself to a patience he was far from feeling. His body, responding to instinct and abstention, was eager for release. It had been a long time since Earl Hugh's hunting lodge, but Judith was so mistrustful and afraid that one step too soon or too clumsy and he would lose all the ground he had thus far gained. Besides, a hasty coupling on the floor with one ear cocked for a tread on the stairs was hardly the best method of initiating a frightened virgin and, while it might satisfy his current appetite, it would do nothing for his abiding need.

Keep it within the bounds of control, he told himself and fought a losing battle to hold onto that control as Judith moulded herself closer still, pressing upon the thickened length of his shaft.

Judith's lips parted beneath the gentle, urging insistence of his own. It was not like the time when Walter de Lacey had groped her in Ravenstow's great hall on her wedding day. There was no violence or desire to devour in Guyon's kiss, or in his stroking fingers. What he was doing was far more insidious and subtle, a slow process of arousing her senses rather than seeking immediately to satisfy his own. She knew he could do it if he chose, for she could feel him iron hard against her belly and it was an act that could be accomplished in a matter of seconds. As a child she had seen her father shut the bed curtains in her face and behind their flimsy barrier take her mother in as little time as it took to gulp down a cup of wine. Guyon was choosing to wait and prolong. She had not known that such a thing was possible.

She felt as if she was drowning, the rock to which she clung slipping her slowly and treacherously beneath the flowing warm waves. Her breasts tingled. Her loins were moist and aching, her whole body a boneless supple mass of manipulated nerve endings.

Downstairs there was a shout of laughter from the old man and loud exclamations from his two young companions. The spell shattered. Judith leaped like a doe and Guyon's arms involuntarily tightened to hold her. Judith struggled and tore free, her eyes huge and wide and frightened, a sob catching in her throat.

Guyon slowly let his hands fall to his sides. He was breathing hard, as if he had just run up a tower in full mail. 'You see what happens when you stir a banked fire,' he said ruefully. 'I've been wanting to do that for a long time.'

Judith gulped. She could not stop shaking. He was melting her with that burning brown stare. Their relationship was paused on the brink of another plane and it terrified her. Snatching hot chestnuts from the fire indeed! Licking her lips as if she could still taste his kiss, she took several more paces away from his frightening proximity.

Guyon paced to the window, braced his forearms on the thick wooden ledge and looked down at his hands gripping the dusty edge while his blood cooled and subsided. He had seen the fear and rejection in her eyes and did not know how to deal with it aside from schooling himself to further patience. There were remedies of course, none of them satisfactory. There was no pleasure in drinking water when it was wine you wanted.

Judith hastily sleeved her eyes as Simon walked into the room, grinning broadly, a half-eaten apple in his hand. Christen had just defeated his grandfather in a move that was as much a surprise to herself as it had been to the old man. 'Is it all right?' he asked, nodding around the room and taking another bite of the fruit. 'Don't worry about the bed. Grandfather says that he knows where he can get hold of one.'

His back turned. Guyon muttered something at his spread hands and then laughed without humour.

'It belongs to the Abbess of St Anne's,' Simon added, brow cocking curiously. 'It's got a feather mattress and silk hangings and everything else. It was part of her dowry, but the Bishop says she has to give it up . . . What's wrong, Guy, have I said something funny?'

'No,' Guyon said, turning round. 'It's not funny at all. Do I have to say Grace before I get in?'

'Depends on what you have in mind,' Simon said. 'For what we are about to receive and all that.' He smiled round at Judith. She turned pink and looked as if she might burst into tears and, choking an excuse, gathered her skirts and hurried from the room.

'I didn't think that she would take offence. I'm sorry,' Simon said, staring at the still moving curtain with a perplexed frown on his face.

'How many Hail Marys does it take to work a miracle?' Guyon asked and wearily left the window. At the tables board he stopped and overturned it.

CHAPTER 17

J UDITH LIFTED THE GOBLET. It was made of swirled green chalcedony, delicately carved in the English style. The wine within was sweet-sharp and cold from the well in which it had been chilled prior to being brought to table.

The King's new hall of Westminster blazed with rich colour, the walls painted in a bold, angular design that glowed red and blue, gold and shadowed matt black. Banners sparred the walls in primary pagan colours. Candles flamed and dripped, cream and gold, reflecting the napery on the long trestles. The high barony of England glowed like a mobile, flowing tapestry.

Judith sipped her wine and watched the weaving men and women – her uncle Arnulf, lord of Pembroke, as objectionable and ugly as ever; her maternal uncle William Breteuil was with him and they were talking amiably enough, although the frequent flicker of their eyes betrayed their mistrust. Her most notorious relative, Robert de Belleme, was not here at this gathering, preferring to hold his own court in Arundel prior to taking ship for Normandy, but Arnulf, among others, was his informant as to what transpired at court during his absence.

Further down the room Gilbert de Clare, lord of Tunbridge, was deep in conversation with his brother Roger and Robert FitzHamon of Gloucester who had been at her wedding. Guyon himself stood on the edge of the group that included them, having just arrived from the direction of the garderobe – tall and lithe, resplendent in a gown of garnet-red Flemish cloth embroidered with thread of gold. The tunic, unlike those worn at thigh or knee-length for the rigours of everyday life in the marches, fell to the shins and the intricately pleated bleached undergown was even longer, sweeping the ankles. He was a lord of some importance and at court, if nowhere else, had perforce to dress as one, even down to the heavy rings encumbering his fingers.

A man on his way from the hall paused in the act of pinning his cloak to speak with the group of men. Prince Henry. She had seen him sitting on the high dais beside the King his brother. He was of middling height and girth with a shock of soot-black straight hair and unprepossessing narrow features. Guyon replied to something the Prince said and Henry laughed aloud. The plain features lit up, became attractively mischievous and he thumped Guyon's shoulder and walked on. Guyon bowed, then straightened to glance across at her. Caught in the act of her own scrutiny, Judith blushed hotly and quickly attended her wine. A youth refilled her cup to the brim and passed on down the board with the flagon.

She drank in deep gulps until her panic had subsided. She could not forget the delightful but frightening sensations aroused in herself by the skilful play of his hands upon her instincts. The body as a weapon. It was a two-edged sword and she had yet to learn how to handle it. What was it the Welsh said? *Arfer yw mam pob meistrolaeth.* Practice is the mother of mastery. Guyon had a vastly unfair advantage and he knew it. It was there in every look he had given her since that afternoon. He had not touched her again. He did not need to. The tension between them was a palpable entity crackling the air. The eye sufficed, speaking all that the tongue avoided and the body subdued.

Some tumblers leaped before the trestle, their costumes parti-coloured and sewn with bells. One of them between gyrations juggled with six flashing knives, catching them expertly by the hilt.

204

'Enjoying the experience?' Hugh of Chester said in her ear.

Judith jumped and looked around at him. He was opulent in blue silk, loose cut for comfort over his great belly. Roped gold winked across the width of his breast and there was a huge round Welsh brooch pinned to one shoulder.

'I am glad to have come, my lord,' she said with a smile, 'but I think I prefer the clean air of the marches to that of the city.'

An elderly man at the Earl's shoulder was staring at her with frank, almost startled curiosity. Chester introduced him as sir Hubert de Caen, a veteran of Hastings and aide of the late King William. Judith smiled and responded politely.

'Ravenstow's wife?' he murmured, taking Guyon's place at the trestle. 'Forgive me for asking, but surely you are related to the Conqueror?'

'Well yes,' said Judith, looking doubtful, wondering at his intention. 'My grandfather and King William were cousins.'

He looked disappointed. 'The tie is no closer than that?'

'I'm afraid not.' She glanced up at Earl Hugh who shrugged his flesh-padded shoulders and surreptitiously tapped his head.

'It is curious,' pursued sir Hubert. 'You are the living image of Arlette of Falais, the old King's mother. She had freckles too you know and hair of your colour in her youth and that same way of looking.'

'I am sorry to disappoint you, but the lady Arlette is no part of my bloodline. My grandfather was related through the male line.'

'Remarkable,' sir Hubert murmured, shaking his head and he rose stiffly to his feet.

The juggler nearly missed one of the knives but swooped and recovered. On the dais, Rufus roared with laughter at a joke. Hugh of Chester moved on with his companion. Judith drank her wine, looked for Guyon and choked on it when she noticed that Alais de Clare had accosted him against one of the stone arches supporting the roof of the hall. A blue and gold banner drifted in the haze above their heads. Alais had her arm linked proprietorily through his, her face upturned and dazzling. He dipped his head to listen to what she was saying. She giggled and flashed a glance around and then stood on slippered tip-toe to whisper in his ear, her hand going boldly down between them.

Judith sat in stupefied amazement watching her do it and the wine bubbles in her blood exploded into rage. She jerked to her feet, shivering the surface of the remaining drink in her cup, walked around the startled juggler and stalked over to her husband and the pouting, shameless courtesan.

Taking hold of his free arm, she stood on tip-toe in mimicry of Alais, but instead of whispering she bit him hard. Guyon jerked with a stifled yelp. Judith stood flat. 'Just thank Christ I chose your ear,' she said and looked across him at the startled and somewhat apprehensive older woman. 'You must be Alais,' she said dulcetly. 'I have heard much about you, indeed too much, so I won't waste any more of my time or yours, or *my* husband's,' and, in guardroom Anglo-Saxon purloined from childhood escapades, her voice low and honeyed with venom, she told Alais de Clare precisely what she could do.

Guyon spluttered. Alais just gaped at Judith in horrified astonishment. Judith, taking her rival's rooted shock for defiance, whipped her eating knife from her belt to threaten the long, white throat. Guyon seized her wrist and bore it down in a grip of steel.

'It is best if I go, Guy,' Alais cooed in a pillow-soft voice and patted his arm. 'You can give me your reply later.' Ignoring Judith's dagger-bright stare, indeed ignoring Judith altogether, she left him to intercept, with a ready smile, a young knight attached to Chester's household.

'What in hell's name do you think you are doing?' Guyon hissed at her, wrestling the knife from her grasp. She fought him furiously before conceding the victory to his greater strength. 'You're a marcher baroness, not a fish wife and the sooner you remember that the better!'

'And she's a high-bred gutter whore!' Judith spat in return, pert breasts heaving. 'I suppose you have organized to bed with her!'

'You've hardly grounds for complaint, have you?' he retorted.

For a moment they glared at each other, the air between them charged high with tension. And then Guyon released his breath on a hard sigh. 'I wasn't making a liaison behind your back,' he said and tugged her silk-twined braid. 'Jesu God, don't you think I have enough trouble controlling the woman I've got without noosing myself to a feather-brain like Alais de Clare?' He grimaced and rubbed his bitten ear.

Judith lowered her lids and looked down at her soft gilded shoes. The impetus of the wine was beginning to wear off. She felt foolish and a little sick. 'But I thought . . . Christen said that you and she used to . . .'

Guyon snorted. 'Once, twice, no more. I was too drunk the first time and too desperate the second to make better provision and Alais was so pleased with herself that she made the whole court a party to her conquest until her husband clapped his hand over her mouth and pushed her at Henry. He's very partial to brainless blondes.'

'And you are not?' she challenged, raising her head.

'I have a marked preference for tawny-haired vixens,' he murmured and slipped his arm around her narrow waist, drawing her close to his side. Judith gulped.

On the dais, William Rufus laughed again and clapped a brawny arm across the shoulder of the slender young man seated next to him. He was dark-haired and dark-eyed with a mouth like a freshly bitten strawberry.

'His latest toy,' Guyon said with a wry mouth. 'He's called Ernoul and comes from Toulouse. No wonder Henry chose to leave. It's fortunate that Anselm of Canterbury isn't here, he'd have a stroke.'

'Who's the priest on the dais with him, then?' Judith asked and shifted her hip from the intimate sidelong pressure of his thigh.

207

Guyon pretended not to notice. 'Rannulf Flambard, bishop of Durham. He wouldn't flinch if Rufus led a goat in here and held a black mass before his very eyes, providing there was money in it of course.' He roved his gaze around the feast. Chester's young knight had his arm at Alais's waist and was looking across at him, laughing. 'Flambard designed this hall. Rufus says it's too big for a room and too small for a great hall, but that's just his nature.'

'As is Ernoul?'

'As is Ernoul,' he confirmed with distaste and tried not to think of how it felt to have the King's arm draped heavily across the back of your neck, or to feel his breath hot on your cheek and know that any moment you were going to be sick. Probably Ernoul didn't mind. Probably Ernoul was going to get paid a lot of money.

Judith shuddered. The royal court was twice as dangerous and barbaric as life in the marches. As in nature, the bright colours were a warning not to touch. She too knew how to stalk and snarl in all that jungle of colour, but inwardly it made her nervous. When everyone was a predator, someone was bound to get eaten.

The evening continued. Yet another course of the interminable feast was brought in. Things disguised as other things, stuffed and gilded and caparisoned in mimicry of the great gathering they were intended to feed. The wine changed from cold, sharp Anjou to a cloying French red. The dishes ran the gamut of the head cooks heat-sweated imagination. Decorated roast meats served with spicy perfumed sauces, pies filled with fruit and chopped meat and one full of tiny live birds that flew amok and twittered around the hall, soiling the new hangings in their panic. The King sent to the mews for his sparrowhawks.

Musicians played with varying degrees of skill. A jester told some bawdy jokes. A sword swallower amazed the gullible. The knife juggler attempted a refinement that did not quite work and was carried off bleeding like a stuck pig.

Rufus did the rounds of his vassals, full of a bluff, jovial *bonhomie*, the force of it hinting at the choleric temper that lay so close behind.

The King was a squat, compact barrel of a man with a thrusting, sanguine face and short, powerful limbs. None of the Conqueror's sons were able to boast their sire's inches, although all of them possessed his breadth and inclination towards middle-aged corpulence.

Florid and strutting as the barnyard cockerel he so resembled, Rufus chucked Judith beneath the chin as though she were a kitchen maid. 'So,' he grinned, exposing greyish crowded teeth, 'this is Maurice FitzRoger's wench, eh?'

'My liege,' Judith murmured and lowered her lids. His fingers were as thick and clammy as raw sausages, but instead of being limp they gripped powerfully, pinching her flesh.

'Skinny little thing, isn't she?' Rufus mused to Guyon as if Judith was deaf. 'No sign of a belly on her yet either?'

'I'm in no hurry, sire,' Guyon responded with a lazy smile. 'A flat furrow's easier to plough than one with a slope.'

Rufus let out a great guffaw of laughter and his variegated grey-brown eyes disappeared into puffy slits. His sense of humour was crude and boisterous and it was the kind of remark that he wholeheartedly appreciated.

Judith lifted her taut jaw off his fingers, feeling like a market beast on a block. Rufus opened his eyes and she looked back at him, her stare direct and cool.

'God's blood!' he chuckled softly. 'I remember my grandam Arlette giving me that look when she was wrath.'

It was the second time that evening that she had been compared to the dead Countess of Conteville and it disturbed her not a little. 'Probably you deserved it,' she said.

A momentary silence. The *bonhomie* slipped a little. 'You've a saucy tongue,' he remarked sharply.

'It's the teeth you have to watch,' Guyon grinned, touching his bitten ear and kicked her hard beneath the trestle.

Rufus chose suddenly to laugh. 'I can see that!' he said.

'Speaking of which, Hugh d'Avrenches told me a good one just now: *"If you were a knight, you'd not have done that." "If you were a lady, you'd not speak with your mouth full!"* '

Guyon snorted and laughed. Judith looked blank as Rufus chortled. 'I thought that, knowing Alais de Clare, you'd appreciate it. Meet us tomorrow at Clerkenwell if you list to hunt. I've a new Norway hawk I want to fly.' Slapping Guyon's shoulder, Rufus moved on to accost another victim.

'Christ, are you trying to get me exiled?' Guyon demanded, scraping his fingers through his hair.

Judith drained her goblet. 'I am not a lump of meat on a trencher to be poked and prodded and discussed intimately as if I have neither ears nor feelings!' she snapped.

Guyon shrugged. 'Rufus is like that. I'm afraid it's just another thorn in the rotting rose of the court.'

'I did not understand his joke.'

Guyon crumbled a piece of bread and watched the action of the ring-bedecked fingers, a pained smile curving his lips. Judith's fear of the normal sexual act between man and woman was already so strong that he was not about to begin explaining the various paths of deviation that might be pursued. 'It is probably best that you did not. It was very crude.'

Judith narrowed her eyes at him. Her thinking processes were by now badly impaired by the wine and it was a struggle to remember how to control her limbs let alone set about cajoling Guyon into explaining what he did not wish to explain, or solve it for herself. She smiled hazily at the servant who refilled her goblet and raised it to her lips. 'Rufus still fancies you, doesn't he?' she said instead, her consonants slurred.

'Fancies is as far as he will get.' Guyon quirked his brow at her. If she had been less than sober before, she was now well and truly on her way to being sodden drunk. It was seldom that she took more than two cups of wine at the evening meal and frequently they were more than half water. Tonight, he had lost count of the quantity she had swallowed.

210

He wondered if she was nervous of such an important gathering, although it was not in her nature to soothe herself with drink. The occasional stiff swig of usquebaugh or ginevra when the going was not just grim but dire, was her only concession to the vice. He had a strong suspicion that the opulent bed manoeuvred that evening into the bedchamber of the house they had rented on the Holborne road was the main reason for her attitude now. Terrified of what the night held in store, she was taking the advice of many a mother to her daughter on a wedding eve and drinking herself insensible.

He thought back to her reaction that afternoon, the tentative response, the kindling of a timid flame that had just begun to grow in heat and brightness when they were disturbed. He had not dreamed the desire; it had been there but fettered beneath Christ knew how many layers of fear and aversion and wariness and he did not know if he had the fortitude or skill to strip those layers down to the pleasure.

'Judith, no more,' he said compassionately, staying her hand as she reached to her cup.

'Why not?' she protested. 'I'm enjoying it now. It was hob ... hobbir ... horrible at first, but you get used to it don't you ... like a lot of things?'

'When you're drunk,' he agreed wryly.

'Who's drunk?' she demanded in a loud voice. Heads turned. Fortunately, at that juncture the King chose to leave the hall and amid the etiquette of rising and reseating, Guyon succeeded in calming his belligerent wife to a muttering simmer. That mood did not last long. The wine had reacted upon her blood to produce aggression. Now it reacted against the contents of her stomach and she began to feel very sick indeed. When Guyon drew her to her feet she lurched against him, her balance awry, her hand to her mouth and, by a stupendous effort of hazed will, prevented herself from vomiting where she stood.

Guyon took one look at her green face and propelled her out of the hall and into the cool, blossom-scented starlit night

211

where she was violently sick, shuddering against his support.

'Sorry,' she gulped weakly.

'I can see that,' he said with exasperation. 'Why in hell's name did you do it?' and already knew the bitter answer.

After it was over, he swung her up in his arms and took her lolling and semi-conscious to where Eric waited with Rhuddem and Euraidd.

'She won't want her head in the morning, my lord,' he whistled with the familiarity that came of having known Guyon since he was a swaddled scrap in lady Christen's arms.

'She doesn't want it now,' Guyon answered wryly. 'And certainly not her stomach.'

'Poor lass,' said Eric sympathetically, recalling many a night of his own mis-spent youth. 'You'll not be needing the mare then.'

'No.' Guyon gave Judith to his captain while he mounted Rhuddem, then reached to take her up before him. 'God's bones,' he muttered, trying to settle her so that she would not give him a dead arm on the ride home. 'You'd think to look at her that she weighed less than a feather.'

Incapable of helping him, Judith merely groaned and flopped against him like a dead doe.

Helgund unbarred the door to him and exclaimed in horror at the sight of Judith's wan face.

'Too much Anjou,' he said, sweeping past her to the spacious, vulgar scarlet-bedecked bed and depositing her there.

Clucking like a mother hen, Helgund leaned over her mistress. Judith's eyelids fluttered but did not open. Another maid goggled around the curtain, received a sharp command from Helgund and disappeared again.

'I'll sleep below with sir Walter,' Guyon said, aware that he was now redundant but oddly reluctant to leave. Judith looked so vulnerable, her hands pale and long-fingered against the cover of stitched beaver skins, her profile pure and softly severe. He knew how her nose would wrinkle when she laughed and that one of her teeth was chipped where she had fallen down the dais steps as a child. He knew that her waist was slender and her breasts as round and resiliently soft as the breasts of the white doves in Oxley's cote. She had also quite deliberately drunk herself into a stupor rather than share the intimacy of this bed with him.

Helgund arranged the cover and looked around at him, her broad Nordic face creased with concern. 'My lady has been very unsettled of late,' she ventured.

'I know, Helgund.' The same could be said of himself he thought and for parallel reasons. He looked thoughtfully at the maid. She was Agnes's replacement, owned a position of some considerable trust and as a result knew most of what did, or rather did not transpire between himself and Judith, and must also be aware of the undercurrents and tensions that existed as a result.

Helgund returned his scrutiny beneath the deference of half-lowered lids. Shafted in moonlight, the night candle culling twinkles of gold from the chains of his cloak fastening, she could feel him waiting, muscles tense and mind-leashed. 'She is like a vixen confronting food in a trap, m'lord. She wants the meat, but dare not attempt to snatch it for fear of paying the price.'

His brows twitched together. 'Am I the meat or the price?' he enquired.

'Both m'lord. She fears lest she become reduced to the status of bitch or brood mare, or cast off wife. It is rumoured at court that you prefer the chase to the kill.'

Guyon's brows locked. Helgund swallowed but continued doggedly. 'It is not her fault, m'lord. If you had seen what lord Maurice did to her lady mother in front of us all, and mistress Judith no more than a mite of three years old. Said he would fill her belly with enough seed to plant a dozen children and dragged her to the bed there and then before us all and used her like a whore ... Happened more than once too and sometimes he was in too much of a hurry to draw

213

the hangings. We protected the child as best we could but . . .' Helgund drew a shaken breath and fell silent beneath the onslaught of his stare, her innards threatening to dissolve and trickle out like water.

'All right, Helgund,' he said, voice frighteningly quiet to belie the fury she had just seen flicker in his eyes. 'Thank you for telling me. I can see the precise kind of caltrops thrown in my path now. Before I just kept treading on them. Go back to your bed now. I'll seek mine in a moment.'

Relieved, icy with cold sweat, Helgund curtseyed and scurried away from his disturbing presence.

Guyon drew a deep breath and controlled his anger. Maurice de Montgomery was already dead. It was no use wishing to throttle him. The Welsh had got there first.

'Well, *cath fach*,' he said softly, brushing a stray wisp of tawny hair away from her eyelids and the thick, downswept bronze lashes, 'how do I avoid these caltrops of yours?'

He knew that she was not indifferent and that the times when her guard was down, he would have sold his soul to keep her that way. The times when her guard was up, she was impossible and feinting through her defences was as difficult as hacking down a ten foot thick briar hedge.

Never once of her own accord had she offered him a sign of affection or endearment. Jealousy, yes, but that was an emotion born of insecurity and mistrust. The moves were all his and straining the bounds of her acceptance. Today she had stepped beyond the limit. Tonight she was blind drunk. So what else was left? He shied from the thought and the pain.

'*Nos da, cath fach*,' he murmured softly, tugged her braid and, head down, quietly left the room.

CHAPTER 18

O N THE CREST of the hill, Guyon reined Rhuddem
to a halt and shielded his eyes to watch the goshawk
assault the air on dark, swift pinions, gaining height
against the hot blue sky before stooping like a wind-ruffled
stone upon the desperate, rolling flight of a round-bodied
partridge.

Prince Henry, triumphant owner, fisted the cool morning
air as the partridge tumbled over in a puff of feathers and was
borne in victory to earth beneath the goshawk's black scimitar
talons. The falconer and a huntsman ran towards the two
birds, one to be retrieved in proud prowess to Henry's wrist,
the other to be added to the mound of soft bodies already
culled that morning. The King's Norway hawk was a skilled
killer too.

Henry stroked the breast of his own bird where she perched,
dark wings folded and deftly replaced the leather hood over
the seeking fierce golden eyes. Then he looked at Guyon.

'I hear that your wife made quite an impression last night,'
he remarked laconically, a grin curling into existence.

'She is not accustomed to quite so much wine, my lord,'
Guyon excused and eased himself in the saddle. His back was
aching as a result of sleeping on a lumpy, makeshift pallet
within range of a sly draught.

Henry grinned. 'No, no, I didn't mean that business with
Alais, although I wish I had been there. I meant her resemblance to my grandmother, Arlette. Old Hubert couldn't believe
his eyes, thought he'd seen a ghost and Rufus remarked on it
this morning at mass . . . and he told me an appalling joke.'

Guyon lifted his stiff shoulders. 'As far as I know, the only blood she shares with your family is that of her maternal grandsire, and, even then, the Countess of Conteville is not of that line.'

'Maurice FitzRoger's girl, isn't she?' Henry looked thoughtful. 'How old is she now, Guy?'

'She was born in the November of 'eighty-three, my lord.' Guyon squinted against the sun at the prince whose look had suddenly grown secretive, the way it sometimes did after he had been closeted with Gilbert and Roger de Clare. Still waters ran deeper than anyone could fathom.

'Any wench of seventeen who looks like my grandmother deserves closer examination,' Henry said, still stroking his hawk, dark-grey eyes intent upon the action of his fingers.

'Angling for an invitation?' Guyon jested with the familiarity of long acquaintance and the occasional deeper friendship.

'How did you guess? Anyway, I used to rent the house. You cannot refuse. Is tonight all right? After the hunt?'

Guyon's gaze flickered and sharpened, for Henry's interest was perhaps a little too keen for comfort.

'I did wonder,' Henry said softly to the bird, 'but she never sent word. Perhaps it was just as well.'

'My lord?'

Henry recalled himself. Guyon's face was blank, but not his eyes. 'God's blood, Guy, stop thinking wild thoughts!' he laughed. 'With a face like yours, is it likely that I'd be able to seduce your wife before your eyes, or even behind your back! I want to meet her, no more than that. Look, Rufus has started a hare!' He turned to the falconer, gave him care of the goshawk and clapped spurs to his courser's sides.

Guyon followed more slowly, aware of a niggling doubt at the back of his mind. Henry could lie the hindleg off an ass if expediency demanded, his face as innocent as May sunshine. Guyon did not believe that he was lying now, but he was sure that something was being concealed from his view. The problem with a devious man like Henry was knowing precisely what.

Judith would need to know that they had guests. He had looked in on her this dawn before departing to hunt and found her huddled beneath the pelts in a heavy, drugged sleep. He knew the symptoms and how dreadful she would feel on awakening. Renewed nausea, a tight, swollen drum where her head should be, a raging thirst and probably, the way she had been last night, an impaired sense of balance. Hardly the best equipment with which to organize food and entertainment for a prince of the realm who was coming to visit her because she resembled his grandmother. In her present state Judith would doubtless give a commendable imitation of the said lady risen untimely from her crypt.

He muttered an oath beneath his breath, bent a scowl upon Henry's fast disappearing back and, calling Eric to him, sent him off with a message.

Judith woke late in the morning with all the vile after effects that Guyon had predicted and a few more besides. Half an hour voiding in the garderobe made her swear a miserable oath that she would never again drink the seemingly innocuous wines of Anjou, whose potency was so wickedly concealed. She had meant to drink only enough to dull the edge of her fear and instead she had swallowed her way into hell. Of the night before she remembered nothing except being ill.

Weakly, green-faced, she directed Helgund to mix a valerian posset to ease her rolling stomach and skull. Of course it tasted disgusting and, fighting the urge to retch because by now her stomach was so sore, she retired again to bed to let the herb do its work. She had been there perhaps an hour when Eric rode in with his message, half a dozen limp partridges over his saddle bow.

For another half hour panic ensued. Judith, her headache aggravated to a megrim of titanic proportions, presided over a household that resembled a disorganized corner of hell. At the end of that time, her tenacious common sense reasserted itself. This had once been Prince Henry's house. Well and good, let the Prince's machinery do what had to be done. Mustering her wits and taking another dose of valerian in honeyed milk, she tidied her hair, put on a clean overgown and went below to visit sir Walter and explain her predicament.

By noontide, the kitchen shed was bustling, the cook in receipt of the recipes for Henry's favourite dishes and two servants sent off to the markets to fetch whatever was not available on the premises. A minstrel had been engaged, Helgund and Elflin were busy with brooms and beeswax polish and Judith had retired to the sinful luxury of a hot tub, the water scented with attar of roses, in order to compose herself for the coming ordeal.

Her gaze on the bed as she soaked, ignoring Helgund's dire warning that all the goodness would come out of her body, she wondered how she had been brought home last night and where Guyon had elected to sleep, for there had been no imprint in the bed beside her. Probably below with sir Walter. A memory came to her, hazy and thick as wine dregs in a goblet. Alais de Clare had been whispering in Guyon's ear and pressing herself against him. Perhaps he had shared a feather mattress last night, and not for the purposes of sleep.

The water rippled as she grabbed for the soap dish, thoroughly disconcerted to find herself violently jealous. Alais de Clare would give Guyon what he wanted without balking or complaint, as would many other of the women who frequented the court. She had seen the way they looked at him ... and at her, the amused patronizing hostility, their thoughts naked in their eyes as they wondered how long she would hold him faithful.

She looked down at her body, shimmering white beneath the water, and then at the sinewy freckled forearm and wrist resting on the edge of the tub. Bruises braceleted the latter. The image of a knife and a struggle came vaguely into her mind and slipped away again as she concentrated on the main problem. She did not have Alais's natural advantages of a

218

lovely face and ripe, lascivious curves, nor her amoral aptitude for coupling, but she probably had at least as much imagination if shown the right direction and she had always been quick to learn. The only problem was overcoming the nervous fear of pain and subjugation, of being held down and used as a mere object and receptacle with no private identity. She knew that it was foolish, that Guyon would not treat her thus, but knowing did not prevent the thought from occurring, or the shuddering reaction. It was no light thing to step off the edge of a precipice into a void with only ingrained fear and a tenuous, recent trust for company.

Her mind plodded a fruitless circle. She cursed with soft vehemence and called for Helgund to bring her a towel.

Henry sniffed appreciatively as they passed the bakehouse door. Rich, savoury scents wafted to his nostrils and also the sound of the cook paddling the spit boy's behind for failing to turn the spit at the crucial moment.

Simon's grandfather hobbled out to greet the hunting party, wrinkled face wreathed in smiles. Henry stopped to speak with him. Guyon cast a suspicious look over his shoulder at the industry within the bakehouse, then back at sir Walter, who winked at him.

'Resourceful lass you've got there' he chuckled as Guyon followed Henry up the stairs.

Helgund and Elflin stood to one side, their working gowns covered by fresh, snowy aprons, their hair tidied beneath pristine wimples. Henry turned from their nervous obeiances before their bobbing up and down made him sea-sick and was welcomed within by Judith.

She was very slender; he could have spanned her waist with his mount's noseband. Her breasts were high and small, her flanks long and lithe and her voice clear and low. The years fell away and for a moment it was a different woman who welcomed him into a different room, a woman with crowswing braids and tilted violet eyes. Judith of Ravenstow had the tilted eyes, but they were grey-hazel, not violet and her hair was a warm sandy-bronze, bordering on red.

'I hope I have not put you to any trouble, lady Judith,' he said with a smile as he raised her to her feet. It was a meaningless civility. Henry had long ceased to care about putting people out in order to have his own way.

Judith made a sincere sounding disclaimer and, taking his cloak, gave it to Helgund. Guyon handed his own directly to the maid while looking his wife up and down. 'I'm glad to see you are better,' he said. She was wearing a plain cream undertunic and a long-sleeved gown of russet silk, the exact chestnut shade of Rhuddem's hide. Gold Byzantine earrings swung from her lobes and a girdle of gold links and shaved, polished amber oblongs snugly hugged her waist. Her face was smooth and calm, as enigmatic as Melyn's, and bore no trace of the previous evening's excesses.

'Patched up and surviving on valerian,' she said, twitching him a smile. 'I've still got a raging headache for my sins, but thank you for the warning. At least I have had the time to prepare.'

'More than time,' he murmured, tugging one of her braids and glancing round at the white linen cloth upon the trestle, the fine cups and flagon, the tall wax candles, delicately tinted and surrounded by fresh flowers and greenery.

Judith smiled her secretive smile and Guyon's fingers left her braid as though one of her gold fillets had scorched him and his gaze flickered between herself and Henry.

'Dear God,' he said softly.

'What's the matter?'

Guyon shook his head and mutely went past her into the room. Henry paid Judith a compliment concerning her domestic abilities. Guyon snapped his fingers at one of sir Walter's servants drafted in for the evening. The man hastened to pour wine. Guyon watched him without seeing his practised actions, absorbing the shock of what he had just seen and deciding that it was patently impossible. Henry was only thirty-two now.

He thought of himself at fourteen. An undiscovered mystery then. Fumblings in dark corners, snatched kisses and giggles, pleading persuasion, his mother's sharp eye upon the younger maids. The dry throat, the anticipation, the blinding flash finished too quickly to be savoured until familiarity lent refinement and control. And Henry at fourteen? Henry at fourteen had already possessed the sexual assurance and technique that came of long acquaintance with the act.

'Penny for your thoughts, Guy?' Hugh of Chester nudged him.

'You'd need more than that,' he said with smile that was not a smile and, taking his wine, went to join Henry.

Hugh d'Avrenches frowned, but after a moment shrugged and followed him.

The evening progressed and so did Guyon's doubts. The similarities were infinitesimal, mainly in the smile and the tilt of the head and fleetingly seen, but the prince's attitude gave them credence. He was acting on two levels. On the superficial topmost, he was the charming, genial guest, fluent of phrase and gesture; on the second, with which only his intimates were familiar, he was studying Judith, drawing her out, examining her piece by little piece, using both his eyes and his expert sleight of mouth. Warmed by his subtle attention, Judith responded as all women responded to Henry, opening like a tightly cored rose to the warmth of the sun.

Towards the end of the evening when the men were relaxed with food and wine, the conversation was pleasantly upon the merits of Irish hounds for coursing deer and the minstrel was softly plucking out the notes of *Stella Maris* on his lute, one of Henry's messengers arrived and was shown upstairs.

Henry, drawn from indolent comfort, listened to the kneeling man, his features impassive, but the wine in his hand rippled and trembled and an ugly dusky flush came up beneath the stubble edging his jaw and corded throat.

His older brother Robert, sauntering glory-clad home from

his crusade, had paused in Sicily to take to his bosom a wealthy young bride, one Sybil of Conversano, daughter of an Apulian count with strong Norman ties. The name did not really matter, nor the rank, but the girl's considerable wealth would enable him to buy back his pawned duchy from Rufus and the marriage itself made the prospect of Robert's heir an imminent possibility. Henry's proximity to the crown was suddenly seen distantly across a smoky hall instead of glittering above his cupped hands.

The messenger finished. Silence descended. No-one looked at anyone else. And then Gilbert de Clare muttered something at his boots and Henry flicked him a sharp glance and warningly shook his head. 'A toast,' he said in a light, brittle voice and raised his cup. 'To my brother and his bride, may they find safe harbour.'

Cups clinked. The toast was mumblingly repeated.

'What will you do now?' Earl Hugh folded his hands comfortably over his paunch, body slack, eyes as sharp as shards of blue glass.

Henry pursed his lips. A look flashed between himself and Gilbert de Clare. 'Rufus won't make me his heir,' he said softly, 'and Robert's got the hammer and anvil to beget his own brood now. I suppose I needs must follow the example of my father.'

Chester waved a hovering gnat away from his face. 'If it's civil war you're suggesting, count me out,' he said, tone still comfortable. 'Got enough problems with the Welsh warring over who inherits what without looking down this end for trouble.'

'Civil war?' Henry opened his innocent grey eyes. 'Nay, who would back me?'

'You have friends, sire,' said Roger de Clare, voice low but full of fierce meaning.

'It's not friends I need, but opportunity and the right kind of backing . . . Would you give it to me, Guy?' There was bitter mischief in his eyes.

'A feudal oath is sacred unto death, my lord,' Guyon said quietly after a moment. 'It might cause me pain, but I'd shut my keeps to you.'

'Precisely,' Henry twisted a smile. 'Excellent building material were it but mine. Can I offer you no inducements?'

Their eyes met and held. 'Not even if you were related, my lord,' Guyon said deliberately.

Henry stretched like a cat and his smile deepened. 'I thought not. But supposing it came to a choice between myself and Robert? What then?'

'Then I hope I would make the right choice,' Guyon said, refusing to be drawn.

'Where does your father fit into all this?' enquired Earl Hugh politely.

'No-one handed him his meat on a platter, so he went out and shot his own deer.'

Judith decided that this conversation had sailed quite far enough into murky waters and deliberately let her cup slip from her fingers. Exclaiming in distress, she set about collecting the glittering green expensive fragments and accidentally caught the fingerbowl with the trailing end of her sleeve, tipping it over into Henry's lap.

The prince dragged his breath over his larynx in a glottal sound of shock and then was rendered silent. Earl Hugh gave a great bellow of laughter, slapped his hand down on the table and drove a dagger of glass straight into his palm. Blood spurted. The bellow became a howl of pain. Judith grabbed a napkin from the table and sought to staunch the wound but, in her flustered haste, knocked over a candlestick and set fire to Gilbert de Clare's elegant furred sleeve.

Guyon, his eyes hilarious, snatched the flagon and doused their guest with a great deal of enthusiasm and a very poor aim for a man who was so skilled a warrior. Gilbert's lyme hound snarled and tried to bite Guyon's ankle and was kicked across the room to fetch up howling against the wall. Pandemonium reigned. *Stella Maris* faltered, twanged and stopped.

223

The minstrel sidled out of the room, de Clare's abused dog snarling at his heels. Judith flapped around the room like a headless chicken, creating more chaos than she was clearing up but at last, Chester's wound thoroughly, if clumsily, staunched with the napkin, she looked around at the wreckage with brimming eyes, then covered her face with her hands, muffling little sounds into them, her shoulders shaking.

Guyon flicked a look at his wife, spluttered and quickly bent to retrieve a dish from the floor while he mustered his control. 'I suggest, madam, that you go and find some fresh garments for my lord prince,' he said in a choked voice, his face suffused.

Judith squeaked and fled. Gilbert de Clare saw an embarrassed husband struggling manfully to control his rage at the shortcomings of his foolish wife. Hugh of Chester in contrast saw a man striving to contain his mirth and banishing its giggling catalyst from his presence until he should be capable of controlling himself. He also saw why it had been done and, looking down at the wad of embroidered linen screwed ineptly round his cut and knowing how her competent medical skill had saved Guyon's life, concluded that Judith of Ravenstow would take some holding if she ever decided to take the bit between her teeth.

Judith re-emerged, biting her lower lip, her shoulders still displaying a disturbing tendency to tremble as she handed Henry tunic and chausses. Henry quirked his brows, not quite as befooled as his bland expression suggested.

'Do not fret yourself, lady Judith,' he said magnanimously. 'Accidents will happen.'

Gilbert de Clare coughed and, after a quick glance at Henry, pretended great interest in the rushes strewn on the floor. Henry ignored him and changed into the garments. He and Guyon were of a similar breadth, but whereas Guyon measured around two yards in height, Henry fell a full six inches short of that mark and the chausses had to be extensively bound with cross garters to take up the surplus material. Consequently, the evening ended in laughter and a deal of good-humoured jesting.

Henry swung to horse in the torchlit courtyard, his face open and smiling, black hair tumbling in an unruly shock over his broad forehead, grey eyes shining with the remnants of a good joke. 'You are most fortunate in your wife, Guy,' he observed, glancing over his shoulder to where she stood silhouetted in the doorway out of reach of the high-stepping coursers. His tunic reached almost to his fingertips in the new style of the court women and the chausses, even with the bindings, were appallingly wrinkled.

'I know, my lord,' Guyon answered warily. 'Although as you have seen, most of her ploys have a sting in their tail.'

Henry chuckled. 'To be expected when she is under the sign of the scorpion,' he said.

Guyon looked up sharply.

Henry leaned down over his saddle bow and said impishly, 'Remember me to Alicia when you next see her. Tell her I approve.'

The horse jibbed and lunged forward. Guyon stepped back and watched the glossy bay, a stallion from his father's herd, trot out of the yard. Gilbert de Clare followed on his patchy, raw-boned roan, his brother in tow, and then came Earl Hugh and the bodyguard.

'What was all that double talk about being related?' the earl asked, stubbled chins wobbling.

'Nothing,' said Guyon, uncomfortably aware that Hugh d'Avrenches missed precious little. 'A private joke. I am not sure that I understand it myself. What's more to the point, Hugh, is Henry's closeness to the de Clare's. There was a deal of double talk there, too.'

'Keep your nose out, Guy. Judith was right to drop that cup when she did. What the eye does not see and the ear does not hear cannot be a source of grief in time to come.'

'Oh yes,' Guyon said a trifle bitterly. 'I am an expert in the art of diplomacy.'

'Well then, don't fall foul of the de Clare's. They bid fair to be as powerful as the Montgomery line one day, and one day soon at that. Hunting tomorrow? I'll see you there.'

Guyon watched him leave, a frown locking his brows, then went across to the stables to check a slight sprain upon Rhuddem's off hind which might give trouble if he were to hunt the horse tomorrow.

Upstairs, Helgund bustled around the bedchamber, lighting the night candle, folding and tidying, setting matters to rights. Judith slowly removed the gold fillets that clasped the ends of her braids and unwound her hair. Helgund helped her unlace the tight-fitting overgown and, after Judith had drawn it off, hung it tidily on the clothing pole and fetched her mistress an ivory comb.

Judith eyed herself thoughtfully in the polished steel mirror. Sharp-boned and solemn, her reflection wavered back at her. The evening had not passed without incident, but at least a potential disaster had been avoided. A pity that the prince possessed a sharper vision than Gilbert and Roger de Clare, who both obviously saw her as a muddle-headed juvenile. She had the impression that Henry had been amused because he was already several steps ahead of her and could afford to laugh. It was not a comfortable thought, but then neither were the other ones that jostled her brain for space and recognition.

Slowly she combed the kinks from her hair until it hung in a glowing, fiery fan to her thighs and tried to coax her tense muscles to relax. In a quiet voice she thanked Helgund and bade her go to bed. The maid curtseyed and left. A soft silence descended and was infiltrated by the sounds of the spring night. Judith sat in the stillness and stared at her image and fiddled with the drawstring of her shift.

When Guyon finally came up to the room, having reassured himself as to Rhuddem's well-being, he found Judith sitting on the bed buffing her nails, the candle light making a golden halo behind her head. She looked up and gave him a strained smile and, rising, padded barefoot across the room to pour him wine.

He took it from her, his expression blankly preoccupied, drank, looked at the delicate glass and seemed to come to his senses, for suddenly his eyes refocused and he concentrated all the force of his stare upon her face.

'What's the matter?' she asked. 'Why are you looking at me like that?'

It was there. You could see it when you knew. The expressions, the occasional mannerisms, the way her hair sprang from her brow. 'Nothing,' he said flatly, wondering if his father knew. Perhaps. If it became common scandal the results would be disastrous. She was not Maurice of Ravenstow's daughter, therefore the barony was not hers by right of birth but belonged instead to her Montgomery uncles – Robert de Belleme, Arnulf and Roger. He suddenly felt very cold.

'Guy?' Feeling frightened, Judith touched his arm and, when he did not move, his brow also. It was clammy and his olive complexion was positively yellow. He started at her touch and looked at her, but as if she was a complete stranger he had never seen before.

'What's wrong? Has Prince Henry taken offence at me? Did he realize that I . . . ?'

'Prince Henry?' He gave a humourless small laugh. 'Prince Henry will take no offence. How could he?' Oh no, it was very much to his advantage. The halter, yoke and hobble of blood. He stared down at the cup in his hand, set it down and paced restlessly to the shutters. The catch was loose and he pushed them open. The scent of hawthorn was thick and sweet. He could see the blossom gleaming softly white in the garth. A breeze ruffled his hair and eddied one of the wall hangings.

'Is it something so terrible that you cannot tell me?' Judith asked at his elbow. 'Do we face ruin?'

Guyon gathered his speculating, reeling wits and after a

moment turned to face her. 'I cannot tell you, love,' he murmured. 'Call it a political secret if you will, or just plain discretion. It is a confidence I think I would rather die than break.' He kissed her freckled forehead and tugged a burnished strand of her hair.

Judith frowned. Henry had told him something in the courtyard, of that she was sure and could only hope that it was not along the same lines that she had earlier curtailed with her deliberate clumsiness. 'It is not a wise hold to have over a man of power,' she said doubtfully.

He stepped away from her proximity where the scent of the hawthorn had been replaced by the more dangerous beguilement of gilly and roses. 'Henry intended me to know. He deliberately turned a vague suspicion into a certainty.'

'Is it very important that you say nothing to anyone, even to me?'

He went to his wine, drank it and glanced over the cup's rim to where she stood, the thrust of her breasts outlined by the yellow gilding of the night candle. 'Especially not to you, *cath fach*,' he said and, putting down the goblet, went towards the curtain.

'Where are you going?'

'Below to Walter. There's a pallet made up in an alcove for me and it's getting late.' He picked up his cloak.

'But the bed . . .' She gestured around, her heart thumping in her throat. 'It's big enough.'

'Not for us both,' he refuted with certainty.

'Yes it is . . . ' She drew a deep breath, her eyes enormous.

Guyon looked at her frightened bravery and his heart turned over. 'When I made contract, *cath fach*, I did not want you. Now I do. If it were lust, it would not matter, I'd slake it elsewhere. Being as it isn't, I'll sleep downstairs.'

Judith gulped but the lump in her throat did not go away.

'*Nos da, fy anwylyd,*' he said to her with a wry smile and, cloak over his shoulder, snapped his fingers at Cadi.

She waited until he had almost reached the curtain, struggling and struggling until at last she forced her voice beyond the choking lump of fear.

'Guyon!' she croaked, holding out her hand. He turned. She cleared her throat. 'Before you go, can you do this for me? I've dismissed Helgund and it seems a shame to waken her for a mere knotted lace.'

Guyon hesitated for a moment, then put the cloak down. She padded over to him and showed him the tangled drawstring on her shift.

'I'm not a lady's maid,' he growled, stooping over the knot. 'Perhaps you should rouse Helgund, or just sleep in it.'

'I would be too hot and I have run poor Helgund off her feet all day. Let her sleep.'

He turned her to the light the better to see what he was doing and began to realize that the task was impossible. Even the maid's skill would have been unable to undo the knot, so tightly was it pulled. The fact that his fingers, usually so clever and deft, were serving him with about as much dexterity as a platter of sausages, did not help matters either, nor the fact that the scent of gilly was drowning him in its spicy waves as it rose from the warmth between her breasts and her hair kept tangling with his efforts.

Impatiently he reached to the sheath at his hip and drew his knife. 'I'll have to cut it. How in hell's name did you snarl it up like this, Judith?'

The blade tugged against the material, jerking her against him. She did not resist the pull, but flowed towards him. The blade was newly oiled and sharpened and sliced cleanly through the knot and the shift dropped to cling precariously to her shoulder edges, held up by the merest whim of fate.

Guyon swallowed, his throat dry, aware that if he did not pick up his cloak and leave, he was going to do something very stupid. 'In God's name, Judith,' he said hoarsely, 'do you think that I am made of stone?'

She raised her eyes to his. They were round and afraid and

full of a stout determination. 'Show me,' she commanded and set her arms around his neck, craning on tip-toe. 'I want to know.'

The shift fell from her body, leaving her slender and naked, pressed to his length. Guyon closed his eyes, fighting the urge to throw her down flat beneath him and take her there and then. That was pure lust as he had said, not love. Besides, if the best wine was served, you drank it slowly, savouring it on the palate, not swilling it down your gullet in one fast gulp. Very difficult when you were dying of thirst.

'Hadn't you better sheathe that blade?' she said against his jaw.

The wheel had come full circle. He remembered Rhosyn saying that to him, twined in his arms, only her voice had been ripe with amused experience and Judith's was innocent, devoid of innuendo. The message, however, was the same. He put up the knife. She buried her face in his neck. Gently he held her away so that he could look at her.

'Well, *cath fach*,' he said quietly. 'I am not sure that this is the right moment, coming to it cold like this and so intent of purpose.'

'Guyon I . . .'

He put his finger to her lips, took her icy hand in his and led her to the bed and sat her down upon it, then he sought around the room, found her bedrobe and gave it to her. 'Put it on,' he said gently. 'You're too much of a temptation without it.'

Tears filled Judith's eyes, but she did as he bid in order to bring some control to her limbs. 'You say you are not sure,' she sniffed. 'But I am. I've had time enough to think and if I have any more, I will go mad, I swear I will. I feel like an ox on a treadmill and there's only one way to end it!'

Guyon shook his head, torn by several emotions at once — doubt and desire and reluctance and need. 'I do not even know if I can show you,' he said. *I do not know the limit of my control.*

230

Judith blushed and smoothed a crease in the coverlet. 'It doesn't have to be cold,' she offered timidly. 'We have all night.'

He laughed and looked away. 'You have a blind faith in me, do you not?' he said grimly.

'What else is there?'

An oath trickled softly from between his lips. Folding his arms, he sat down on the bed and considered her darkly for no small time.

Judith cast round for something to say that would sway the balance or lighten the difficult weight of his stare. The silk coverlet was cool to her touch and as red as blood. She remembered where it had come from. 'You haven't said Grace yet,' she reminded him, forcing her mouth to smile.

Guyon let out his breath on a heavy sigh. 'I haven't said any Hail Marys either,' he replied, but after a moment's hesitation unfolded his arms to curve one around her shoulders and draw her within the dim red shadows of the hangings.

At first, stricken by the enormity of what she had done, Judith did not respond except to shiver rigidly against him, her breathing swift and shallow with fear. He held her, stroked her gently as he might have stroked Melyn or Cadi, spoke to her of trivia, whatever came into his mind, making of his words a soothing, murmurous flow.

Slowly, Judith calmed and started to relax, allowing langorous, pleasant sensations to filter through the numbness of the barriers that held her imprisoned. The rigidity left her body, and the feeling of cold. She snuggled against him, her arm reaching up around his neck. He brushed his lips over her temple and cheek and the corner of her mouth, twisted his head slightly to trail small, nibbling kisses along her jaw until he reached her ear lobe, paused there to play and then sucked the small, tender hollow behind.

Judith gasped and pressed closer, a strange emotion twisting in the pit of her belly. Hesitantly she nuzzled his throat where the tunic parted and moved her arm a little further so that her hand touched not cloth, but the bristles of cut hair at his nape. His hand stopped at her waist and tightened and the feeling tingled in her belly again and flashed down to her loins. She tasted his skin.

When he first slipped his hand inside her bedrobe she stiffened, more with surprise than fear, but Guyon stopped immediately and made as if to withdraw. She dug her fingers fiercely into his nape, drawing him down and lifted her face. 'Show me,' she said again, eyes narrow with concentration. 'I want to know.'

He studied her doubtfully and she returned him a look that was at one and the same time wanton and innocent and full of a strange, wild tension, and then she broke the gaze and leaned into his body. Her lips touched the hollow between his collar bones and her tongue flickered out. Guyon drew a sharp breath and pulled her close, seeking her mouth with his own. Hesitant at first, Judith quickly mastered the skill and pushed herself forward with a soft, impatient sound, lips clinging and yielding sweetly.

He ran his hand up her side, lightly brushed the small curve of her breast, sought inwards with his thumb and feathered it over her aureola and nipple. Judith broke the kiss to cry out at the intensity of the sensation and surged against him, craving, but as yet ignorant of precisely what.

Applying gentle pressure to her waist with his free hand, he drew her down and over until she was lying on top of him, her hair tumbling around and curtaining them both, and he caressed its shining thickness. 'You have the advantage, *cath fach*,' he said softly. 'Do with me what you will.'

Judith tossed back the errant strands and considered him, her swift breathing no longer a mark of panic, but of increasing arousal. The fingers of his other hand were still describing lazy circles around and upon her nipple, sending warm chills through her body and, pressed to his length, she could feel him thick and hard across her hip and belly, could feel too with considerably more discomfort, the cold pressure of his belt buckle and knife hilt against her abdomen. 'Do you mean that?' she asked and sat up to regard him through slitted, wicked eyes, beginning to feel drunk again, this time on power. Slowly, she reached towards the hilt of his knife and was gratified to see his look flicker with consternation and feel his body tense as she trailed her fingers lightly over the grip.

'Within reason,' he qualified, eyes dubious.

Her lips curved mischievously, but she left the knife and moved her hand across to his belt buckle instead and began slowly unlatching it, her eyes never leaving his face.

He arched so that she could slide the belt from beneath him and drop it with a slithering clink onto the floor. The heat of his erection pressed up between her straddled thighs but, strangely, it was no longer a threat. She rubbed herself teasingly upon him and heard the breath catch in his throat, watched the expression of pleasure-pain cross his face and her own sensations heightened with the knowledge that she was able to affect him thus.

He drew her back down, lips replacing his fingers which busied themselves in sliding the bedrobe down from her shoulders. Judith cried out at the sharper intensity of feeling and wriggled upon him, seeking to ease the core of trembling, sensitive pressure that existed between her thighs.

'Wait,' Guyon said breathlessly and shifted her off him so that he could sit up and pull his tunic over his head and then his shirt. Judith flickered appreciative eyes over his chest and shoulders, the muscles developed by a lifetime of war and practising for war and occasionally marred in white and recent pink by its results. They were face to face. Guyon circled her waist and drew her against him, flesh to flesh, fingers lacing her hair and running over her scented skin. He buried his lips in her throat, the white valley between her breasts, found the cord of her bedrobe and gently tugged it undone, pulled her down upon him again, his hands cupping her neat, round buttocks, squeezing her against him.

Judith purred and rubbed herself upon him like a cat. She kissed his throat and chest, twisted her head to follow the line of hair that ran from the centre of his breastbone and over the ridges of his flat belly, her breasts lightly grazing his flesh. He groaned softly and tightened his hold on her and Judith felt her excitement growing as the knowledge of power triumphantly redoubled. She sought the drawstring of his chausses, continuing to nibble the line of hair as it descended. A fuse to a barrel of burning pitch.

Suddenly he gasped and banded his arms around her and rolled her hard beneath him. 'Jesu!' he exclaimed hoarsely against her mouth. 'What need have I to show you anything?'

Judith had cried out at his lightning pounce. Now she shuddered beneath him. The rippling twinges of desire radiating from her loins faltered, for there was the hint of savagery and lust in his voice, the threat of what he might do, and she did not know how to deal with it. 'You're hurting me!' she sobbed, going rigid in his arms.

Guyon stopped and braced his weight on his elbows to look down at her and drew a deep, shuddering breath, let it out again slowly while he mastered himself. 'Judith, I'm sorry,' he muttered, brushing a wisp of hair from her face. 'It is only that I did not expect you to learn quite so quickly. You outpaced me.'

She sniffed and swallowed, rubbed the back of her hand across her eyes and looked at him warily.

'I wouldn't hurt you for the world, you know that.' He bent his head to kiss her wet lids and then tenderly her mouth, playing with her, stroking, nuzzling and nibbling until her tension subsided and her body once more began to undulate against his own.

'Trust me,' he murmured, leaving her mouth to press small kisses over her throat, then delicately brushed lower, deliberately tickling. 'Trust me, Judith?' Laughter edged his muffled voice.

'No!' she cried, wriggling. 'Stop it, Guy . . . don't. Laughing herself, she struck out at him. He trapped her fingers, kissed them one by one until they unclenched, then turned them over, tongued her palm and nibbled his way up her arm, along her shoulder to her throat and back to reclaim her mouth. Slowly, lightly as a drifting feather, his fingertips trailed over the mount of her bronze pubic hair.

'Trust me?' he repeated against her lips.

'No,' Judith whispered, twining her arms around his neck and arching her hips as the liquid flickerings with their beckoning, elusive promise began again.

Guyon fondled her gently now, stroking her body, the sensitive zones in particular; the tips of her breasts, her inner thighs, the small bud within her cleft. Judith writhed and cried out, striving towards his teasing, knowledgeable fingers. Her thighs slackened and parted. She pushed against his hand and arched.

Swift as a lance thrust in battle, Guyon pierced her body and held her there, his hips pressed down flat, unmoving. Her parted flesh settled around him. 'Judith, look at me,' he said gently.

She opened her eyes which had been squeezed closed against the sudden thrust of pain. It had diminished now, but the feeling of him fully within her was strange. The dreaded intrusion was accomplished and, although not stricken, she was disturbed and uncomfortable.

'Have I changed?'

She searched his face. His eyes were open and shining in the dim candle glow, his expression tender. She could see the gleam and trickle of sweat on his chest and feel the trembling of more than hard-held restraint.

'No, my lord,' she said and, smiling, touched his face and shifted her hips to ease the pressure. The movement pressed him deeper within and involuntarily her muscles tightened around him. A keener sensation arced across her loins and was gone. Seeking its source, she pushed against him in a movement older than time. Guyon's head went back, his eyes closed and his breath emerged in a drawn out groan. She moved again, her own pleasure sharpened by the knowledge of his and, conceding her the battle, he started to thrust in slow counterpoint.

It was like the first time she had galloped Euraidd – wild and exhilarating and a terrifying, delightful risk. The pace increased by steady degrees and so did the imperative needs of her body. She gasped and dug her nails into his shoulders, sought his mouth, demanding with her own, clung to him dizzied, her only thought to hold onto something solid as the world began to tremble and dissolve. And then she did not think at all. She cried his name, unaware that she did so, as her body totally submerged her mind, shattering the barriers to storm-tossed flotsam.

Guyon seized her hips and held her still, panting at her to stop, his forehead thrust into the curve of her neck, but Judith did not heed him and struggled against the restraint, desperate to regain the friction where she needed it.

'Judith, I cannot . . .'

Her nails clawed him with sudden urgency and she arched her spine and thrust down hard on him. He felt the small convulsions ripple along the length of his shaft and, with a gasp of relief, surrendered his own control to the exquisite pulses of climax.

Slowly Judith became aware of his weight on her, no longer taken on his elbows, of his harsh breathing and of his body pressed hard against and within her own. The pleasure still flickered in dying twinges, promising renewal. She slid her hands over the sweat-damp ridges of his rib-cage and shoulder blades and moved a little beneath him, made uncomfortable by his weight.

Guyon sighed and murmured something inarticulate, and rubbed his lips over her throat. Then he raised his head and looked her in the eyes.

'You are squashing me,' she complained breathlessly and stifled the urge to giggle as his face fell.

236

'Did I hurt you? I thought . . .' He narrowed his eyes, considering her. The clawing of her nails could be misconstrued, perhaps even the muffled cries, but not the tremors of her inner flesh. 'Wanton!' he pronounced, rolling over and drawing her with him. 'I shall not call you *cath fach* again. *Cath wyllt*, perhaps!'

Judith moved sinuously upon him. 'It is better than getting drunk,' she admitted, giggling openly now. 'Just.'

'Remind me to ask you in the middle next time, not afterwards,' he said drily.

'Next time! You mean we have to do all this again?' She widened her eyes in mock horror. 'Where's the nettle salve?'

'For my back you mean? You must have clawed it to shreds!'

'You should not be so clumsy,' she retorted swiftly, poking out her tongue and then using its tip to flick over his throat, her hips surging playfully.

Guyon laughed. 'Then I needs must practise,' he said and caught her down to him.

Judith awoke to the noise of a herd of sheep being driven down the road on their way into the city and the sharp whistle of the shepherd commanding his dogs. They were sounds with which she had grown up and it brought to her now the image of the marches greening lushly into summer and filled her with an impotent longing to be out of the city and home.

There was a warm weight across her body – Guyon's arm, the fingers in relaxed possession of the curve of her breast. He was still sleeping deeply, sprawled upon his stomach, and had not moved since their last pre-dawn bout of love-making. Her mouth twitched. It was her fault, she knew. She had told him that it was better than getting drunk. Well, indeed it was but, just like wine, it could become addictive.

So great had been her fear of the sexual act through residue of witnessing her mother's degradation at the hands of her violent, contemptuous father, that her own survival of the deed, indeed her enjoyment and satisfaction, had led her to prove to herself again and again that it was no illusion. It was not. The last time, Guyon had asked her, groaning, if she was trying to kill him. Her gaze flickered over his lean, sleep-abandoned body. Coaxed and cajoled, he had become aroused, but it had taken him a long, long time and it had been wonderful. There was a low, dull ache in the small of her back and her body was langorous with content. It was certainly a better aftermath than a drink megrim.

She heard Sir Walter speak to the shepherd and make a fuss of one of the dogs. Secure, and reluctant to break her mood of drowsy contentment, she snuggled back down into Guyon's embrace and closed her eyes.

When Guyon finally roused sufficiently to lift his lids, the morning was high and hot, first mass long over and the hunters long gone on their quest. Sunlight slanted dustily through a warped gap in the shutters and shot the red silk bed hangings to the colour of flame. The night candle was burned to a puddle of congealed wax. He knew how it felt. He flicked a wary glance at the sleeping innocence beside him . . . Innocence! Good Christ, Rhosyn and even the inimitable Alais de Clare were mere novices compared to the supple, oblivious girl in his bed this morning. How many times was it? Four at least. If there were more beyond that, they were without his knowledge. Rape. She had feared rape. He stifled a chuckle at the irony.

Gently he touched a tendril of her hair and looked at her curled form, remembering when she had cowered from him, a half-grown starveling with terror-filled eyes. They had come a long way since then, not always along the same road, but converging here at a new crossroads. The Conqueror's granddaughter with the Viking blood of Duke Rollo and the common tanners of Falaise mingling in her veins.

In the light of what he had realized last night, he pondered her immediate parentage, wondering what had driven Alicia to mate with a boy of half her age and twice her experience. Probably he would never know and there were good reasons for keeping such knowledge a private isolation, not least the needs of this vulnerable wanton at his side.

As if aware of his musing regard, Judith stretched and opened her eyes, and yawned at him.

'*Bore da, cath wyllt,*' he greeted her and kissed her lightly on the lips.

'You missed the hunt,' she said with a sleepy smile.

'No I didn't,' he contradicted with a grin. 'I just had no inkling that I was the quarry.' Judith blushed. 'No matter, I can think of better ways to spend the day than aiming a bow at a driven deer or whatever. Besides, I'd rather not straddle a horse today.'

Her blush deepened and extended to include her throat and shoulders. 'Are you angry with me about last night, Guy?'

'Which part?' he teased. 'Where you froze Henry's manhood in the finger bowl, or when you drained mine to a husk?'

Judith bit her lip. Against her scarlet chagrin, her eyes were brilliant, almost topaz. 'It was like drinking that yellow wine, I did not want to stop,' she excused, hanging her head. 'Guyon, I'm sorry.'

'Drunk two nights in a row!' he chaffed her. 'What am I to do with you? No, don't tell me, I haven't the strength. Just don't ask me to show you anything ever again, even if you are desperate to know!'

Judith fisted him in the ribs and he yelped. 'I think it was the relief at discovering how easy it was.'

'Easy!' he contradicted. 'God's life, it nearly killed me!' And then, looking at her rosy, flustered face, 'But if you were content, it was worth it. I have no objection to dying like that, unless it be four times a night!'

She slanted him a quick glance through her lashes. 'At least there will be nought left of you for Alais de Clare,' she observed with a return of her accustomed tartness and, sitting up, shook back her hair. The sunlight shafted across one shoulder, gilding it and lit her eyes with small, sparkling glints of mica.

'I don't want Alais de Clare,' Guyon answered lazily and stretched. 'Why settle for dross when you can have gold?'

Judith looked along her sun-streaked shoulder at him. His eyes were heavy and the marks of her nails were here and there inscribed on his skin. 'I am dreaming,' she said pensively. 'One day I am going to wake up alone and cold and realize I have been the dupe of illusion.'

'What has happened to last night's blind faith?' He tugged a strand of her hair. 'Isn't it enough now?'

'It's not that, Guy,' she answered, frowning. 'It is the opposite. I have too much. It isn't true.'

'Never satisfied, are you?' He put his arm around her. 'What do you want me to do? Cut my other wrist for you as well and swear an undying oath?'

Judith shook her head, refusing to be cozened. 'It is I who have bled this time,' she said softly, turning back the covers to look down on the dried blood smearing the insides of her thighs and the sheet.

'Trust me?' He kissed her shoulder. 'Trust me, Judith?'

She could feel his lips smiling there in remembrance. Her own trembled slightly. 'Did Rhosyn trust you?'

He had not been expecting it. She felt his lips pause and then leave her skin. He sat up and pushed his hands through his hair and muttered something beneath his breath. 'You know where to kick, don't you?' he said.

Judith lowered her lids and toyed with the bedclothes. Guyon took his hands from his hair, linked them around his upraised knees and looked at her carefully. 'Rhosyn was not prepared to trust me,' he said after a moment. 'We were never committed in that kind of way. It would have been too dangerous and Rhosyn saw it, even if I did not.'

Judith regarded him sombrely. 'Guyon, I cannot give you my soul.'

'Nor would I want it,' he said quietly. 'It is too private a thing to give into another's possession. Keep it whole, *cath fach*. I understand more than you think.'

Judith blinked at him and impatiently scrubbed her forearm across her eyes. Outside she heard Elflin speak to Helgund and the sound of ale or milk being poured into a container. By the door Cadi whined. Judith put her arms around Guyon and kissed him as if the kiss itself was a talisman. 'I do believe that you could wheedle your way through a thorn thicket,' she sniffed.

He returned the embrace and then drew away to begin finding some garments from the scattered creased heaps on the floor. 'What do you think I'm doing now?' he said with a wry smile. 'You are the thorniest thicket I've ever encountered.' He paused dressing to lean over the bed and kiss her warmly on lips and white long throat. 'And the sweetest rose.'

'And you cannot grasp one without risking the other,' she agreed gravely, trying to put all dark qualms behind her while her own words rang like a prophecy in her head.

Guyon stood up, finished buckling his belt and headed towards the door. 'I'll send in Helgund,' he said and paused in fondling Cadi's thrusting head to stoop and pick up her discarded shift with its knife-slashed lacing. 'You did this apurpose, didn't you?' He tossed the garment towards her onto the bed.

Judith leaned back against the bolster and smiled exactly like her father.

CHAPTER 19

August 1100

THUNDER RUMBLED IN the distance where the sky hung in purple billows like mulched grapes. Upon the wall walk, Judith narrowed her eyes to study that distance. Lightning zig-zagged. The trees were brilliantly green and the stone of the merlon against which she leaned was a rich, warm gold. Most of Caermoel's defences were still timber, but the curtain wall of double thickness sandstone was almost completed, as was the gatehouse containing the portcullis and winding gear.

The messenger had ridden in an hour ago while the sun still shone, bearing the news that Guyon would be here before nightfall and that the retaliation for the recent Welsh raid had been successful. She had set herself to make all ready in the way of food, warmth and comfort and had then hastened up here to look out for his return.

It had been five days since the young men in their hot blood had ventured through the gap to steal cattle and corn from the wealth of the plain beyond. Five days since the alarm had been raised, and Guyon had quickly gathered his immediate troops and ridden out in pursuit of a fine dairy herd, three Flemish mares with foals at foot belonging to him and the contents of one of Earl Hugh's grain barns.

She looked down as Melyn twined an erect tail around her skirts and mewed plaintively before clawing her way aloft onto her shoulder to settle there, oblivious to the storm that was blowing in from the south.

A cry from the far side of the wall walk caused her to strain her eyes in that direction and then, her heart thudding ridiculously in her breast, to smile and spin towards the bailey steps.

The edge of the storm hit as the men dismounted. The thunder snarled across the sky, displaying jagged fangs of white-gold lightning. Several cows bellowed and balked as they were penned in a corner of the ward until ownership could be decided. A groom was taking custody of the three mares and their foals and a belligerently spirited Welsh pony stallion that was lashing out indiscriminately with wicked, small hooves.

Guyon turned from speaking to his groom and saw Judith running towards him, her face alight with welcome. She moved unaffectedly, like a man, but her gown moulded itself to her slender curves, marking her all woman. The time-wrought changes of her mind and body never ceased to amaze him. A year ago she would have greeted him gravely and stood just out of his reach as if anticipating a blow. Six months ago they would have avoided each other with eyes downcast to conceal hunger and tense fear. Now, laughing, she flung herself into his arms and drew his head down and kissed him. Melyn, jolted from her perch, gave a feline growl of displeasure, leaped vertically from Judith's back and stalked off in the direction of the living quarters.

'It is only five days!' Guyon chuckled, delighted at the warmth of the greeting. 'What will you do when it has to be forty?'

Judith relinquished her grip and blushed, aware of the amused glances of his men. 'I shall take a lover,' she riposted smartly. 'There's a tub prepared and food at the ready. How did you fare?'

Guyon followed her, ducking his head and increasing his pace as the rain began to cut down. 'We took back what was ours and also a little of what was theirs. You know the rules of border warfare. They won't come raiding again . . . not for a while at least.'

'Unless they come *en masse*,' Judith pointed out as they entered the wooden building in the bailey that was their private living quarters while around them the walls and towers went up. 'Could we withstand a full Welsh assault, not just the prickings of their hot-blooded young men?'

'Probably, but it's not a notion I want to test just yet. Has all been quiet here?'

'Mostly. Madoc came two days ago with Rhys and a distant relative from Bristol who's helping him with the business. They brought that new ram you asked Madoc to get. He says that Heulwen's walking now and chattering nineteen to the dozen and that she's already strewing the road with broken hearts. I think he wanted to remind you of the bond.'

'I hardly need reminding of that,' he said, half under his breath. 'Did he mention Rhosyn?'

'Only that she was well and sent you her duty. If there was more, he probably thought it unwise to confide it to me.'

'How could there be more?' Guyon teased, squeezing her waist. 'You leave me neither the energy nor the inclination to play games with other women. What's this?' He moved the polished agate weight and picked up the letter from the trestle.

'From my mother,' Judith said, going to pour hot wine. 'She asks when we are going to leave our eyrie and make her a visit.'

Guyon took the wine and kissed her hand. 'Somewhere between Michaelmas and Martinmas,' he replied, expression thoughtful as he drank. 'I want a word with her anyway.'

'What about, Guy?'

He tossed the parchment down and finished the wine. 'Nothing. A minor detail concerned with your inheritance.'

Judith's lips tightened in response to his casual tone and the open, blank innocence of his eyes. The reality was upon her, warm and secure as a duck down mantle, but now and again she pondered the difference between belief and blindfold.

244

Guyon was dissembling with her. She knew that look by now and also the method. A smattering of sugared truth and eyes warmly guileless to conceal what he wished to conceal.

Dutifully she unbuckled his swordbelt but her hands were jerky. Guyon looked at her mulishly set lips. His own mouth curved and then straightened. It was not really funny, for he had no defence save to tell her the truth and the shock of that would probably do far greater harm than the withholding. If he had not been so road and battle-weary, he would never have permitted his tongue the mistake of speaking an absent thought aloud.

'What kind of minor detail?' Judith challenged, stepping away from him, the belt in her hands, sword and dagger still attached.

Guyon busied himself removing his garments. He was not wearing the customary Norman war gear of mail hauberk and gambeson, but hunting clothes topped by a sleeveless sheepskin jerkin. When in Wales it was wisest to do as the Welsh did. It was impossible to cross a swiftly flowing torrent and pursue winding, scant paths if weighted down by armour and slowed by supply trains which were vulnerable to attack.

'The kind that is your mother's private business. If she wants to tell you, then well and good,' he answered more evenly than he felt, wondering how to extricate himself before the thing got out of hand.

'I am surprised that your brain does not burst with all the little matters you cannot confide to me for fear of breaking your oath!' she snapped.

'So am I.' Guyon gave her a wry look. 'Judith, I don't want to quarrel.'

'That is up to you,' she said coldly and turned from laying his swordbelt aside, hazel eyes glinting with anger, then stopped and gasped aloud at sight of the clotted red line diagonalling his chest. 'Holy Mother!' she cried and ran to get her basket of medicines.

Guyon drew breath to say that it was only a scratch and the Welshman who had given it to him was in much worse case, but quickly thought the better of it and, closing his mouth, contrived to look as wan and limp as rude health and a summer tan would permit. Extrication was within his grasp. Unresisting, he let her lead him to the bed and push him down.

'How did you get this?'

He looked at her through his lashes and saw the terror in her eyes and felt a faint flicker of guilt for his deceit. Last time he had come to her wounded he had almost died and the memory had obviously left its taint of fear. 'The raid leader didn't want to relinquish his gains and he was faster than I thought. He's gone to Chester as a hostage – if he does not die of his wounds on the way.'

'Why not bring him here?'

'I don't want to encourage Welsh hoards to come visiting, not even to parley, until the defences have grown a little, and I haven't the time to . . . ouch!'

'Lie still then. You are lucky it is so shallow. Some comfrey and marigold salve should suffice. Are you hurt anywhere else?'

'Yes.' He closed his eyes as though faint.

'Where?' Anxiously she leaned over him.

Fast as a trap closing, his hands circled her waist and pulled her down on top of him. 'Where only you can ease me,' he murmured, subduing her retort against his lips.

Judith struggled briefly in order to satisfy her conscience, but without any real enthusiasm and, in a moment, with a soft sound of capitulation, yielded herself up to the pleasure. Three months of intensive, inventive tuition had taught her the refinements of this new and delightful skill and how to use it to its best purpose. How to provoke and tease and taunt him to the brink and then hold him there suffering, until she herself could bear it no longer and took them both over the edge.

Of course, she reminded herself hazily, it was a double-edged weapon and Guyon was expertly adept, as demonstrated by the dextrous manner in which he had just divested her of clothing. Frequently he gave her the control, knowing that it heightened her pleasure, but if he chose to take the initiative, as now, he was quite capable of subduing her mind in a welter of pure, fierce instinct, shocking in its intensity. He is trying to make me forget, she thought, narrowing her eyes even while she ran her fingers over the smooth, muscular contours of his back. And, Mother of God, he is almost succeeding. The acrid smell of horse and sweat sharpened her hunger, as did the nibbling play of his stubble-surrounded mouth on hers and the feel of his hands seeking down over her belly.

'Guy, what about the bath?' she asked somewhat breathlessly and at the same time arched her hips to receive him.

'It can wait,' he muttered. 'I can't,' and he sheathed himself in hot, clinging silk, pausing for a long moment to savour the sensation before easing deeper into its dewy core.

Lightning zig-zagged and dazzled and the rain beat down, thudding the ground like the footsteps of an army running. In the bailey, Simon de Vere swung from the saddle of his trembling, near-spent horse. He had been in the saddle for such a long time that his legs at first refused to support him and the groom had to help him up from the mud as he fell.

'Lord Guyon is, er . . . busy,' said de Bec to the young man as he was helped, limping, into the hall. 'Best sit down and recover yourself awhile first. We've not long ridden in ourselves.'

'He won't be too busy to hear these tidings,' Simon said, pushing his fingers through his rain-sleek hair and wiping a drip from the end of his nose. 'The King is dead, slain in the New Forest and Prince Henry's claimed the crown. I've half-killed my horse getting here.'

De Bec's bushy brows shot into his silver fringe. 'God have mercy,' he said, automatically crossing himself. 'Here, sit

247

down closest the fire. You, wench, bring food and drink for sir Simon and tell mistress Helgund to fetch my lord and lady.'

Judith arched, a cry locked in her throat, her nails scoring Guyon's back, oblivious of everything but the slow, hard thrusts of his body taking them both to release. As the peak of the life force blended them together, through the pleasure-pain of the contractions, she heard him gasping against her ear that he loved her and almost gave way to the impulse of the moment and cried that she loved him too. Almost, but not quite. Before she could damn herself by uttering the words, she sought his mouth and silenced her lips against his own, her body clinging like a limpet to a rock, washed by the last tidal ripples of pleasure. Her flesh tensed to hold him as he shifted his weight and moved away, but still she did not speak.

Guyon sleepily nuzzled her throat and shoulder, aware of her reticence, but not unduly bothered by it. These things took time and there was time enough. Her actions spoke all that her voice did not.

Judith looked at him sidelong through her lashes, the sweat drying on her body. Outside the thunder rumbled and the lightning blinked against a gap in the shutters. 'I've just remembered,' she said. 'When Madoc came, he told me something else too. Apparently, Mabel of Thorneyford's breeding.'

Guyon's lids had been closing. They flew open again and he raised himself on one elbow to stare at her. 'Impossible! She's ninety if she's a day, Judith!'

She laughed at the horrified incredulity of his expression. 'Not quite. She's only a few years older than mama. Eight and forty or some such. Oh, I know it's old to catch for a babe, but not impossible.'

'And I thought Walter de Lacey was a coward,' Guyon murmured facetiously, but a frown forked his brow. He wondered what would happen if the same God's grace was granted to Alicia. Even if she and his father did obtain a dispensation to marry, it would be the devil's own work to sort out the resulting blood ties.

'I suppose it is all in his favour,' Judith added, stretching sinuously and rolled on her stomach to plant a playful kiss on his subsiding erection. 'If she carries the babe successfully then he gets an heir out of her; if she dies, then he's free to look elsewhere and because he is rich, he will be able to pick and choose. He cannot lose.'

There was a soft knock on the door and Helgund's voice came impassively from without. 'My lord, my lady, you are sought in the hall. There is important news from Winchester.'

Guyon groaned and swore. Judith scrambled from the bed and in flustered haste snatched up her bedrobe and belted it on. 'Can't it wait?' she snapped, feeling like a serving wench caught coupling in the straw.

'It is Simon de Vere, my lady. He says that the King is dead.'

'What?' Judith stared round at Guyon. He swore again and reached for his discarded clothes.

'Sir Michel sent me to fetch you both, my lady. I do not know any more.'

'All right Helgund. Thank you.'

Silence fell. Judith abandoned both bath and bedrobe to find her shift. 'If Rufus is dead, who is King in his place?'

'Who do you think?' Guyon snapped because it was such an obvious question. 'You'd better have one of the lads scour my hauberk because I'm going to need it.' He stood still long enough for her to smear his wound with salve, then dragged on his shirt and tunic, tugged one of her combs through his hair and strode muttering from the room. Judith stared after him, her eyes narrowed, hot words filling her mouth. They cooled unspoken. He had been tired when he rode in and wounded, and the energy expended just now between the sheets had further drained his resources. Small wonder if his mood was sour when instead of sleep he received a summons to grave news. She sighed heavily, dropped her hands, and called for Helgund to help her dress.

'An accident,' said Simon, whom Richard had sent from Winchester on the morning of the funeral. 'A hunting accident last Thursday evening. Walter Tirel shot at a deer and missed and hit the King in the chest. He died instantly. Prince Henry was with the hunting party, but not near the scene of the death. He rode straight to Winchester and secured the treasury. He's to be crowned in London by the bishop. He claims the right of porphyrogeniture over Robert.' Simon knuckled his bloodshot eyes. 'He expects your feudal oath as soon as you may.'

Guyon pressed his own eyes with the heels of his hands. It was too late to set out tonight, but arrangements would have to be made for the following dawn and riders sent on ahead to organize their nightly stops. From Caermoel to London was a good six to seven days' ride, more if the weather continued dire, and not to be undertaken without prior provision.

'Myself and Richard must have been the last to see him alive, except for the hunting party,' Simon added into the silence, compelled to speak by renewed ripples of shock. 'I still cannot believe it. If only he had stayed abed and not taken up de Clare's suggestion to hunt, he might yet be alive.'

'Gilbert of Tunbridge?' asked Judith.

'Aye, and his brother. The King had been plagued by a queasy gut, the reason he didn't want to hunt in the morning, but he was fully recovered by nones. After the dinner hour, de Clare said he would not mind clearing his head by riding out to see what he could bring down and it seems to me that he was not talking of deer and that his head had never been clearer in his life.' Simon clenched his jaw and jerkily attacked his trencher. Rufus had had his failings, but he had never found him a hard taskmaster and Richard had been moved openly to tears at the news of his untimely death.

'Are you saying he was murdered?' de Bec asked sharply.

'I'm not saying anything.' Simon looked sidelong at his companions. 'Tirel has fled the country squawking his innocence like a dust trail. He says he was nowhere near the King, that it was not his arrow.'

'And the de Clares are his brothers-by-marriage.' Judith's voice was as colourless as her face.

'I suppose the inquest will decide the truth of the matter,' de Bec said, stretching out his legs until his heels pressed Cadi's white rump.

'What inquest?' Simon demanded sourly. 'Henry's not holding one.'

Guyon paused eating to stare at Simon, then continued to chew, but slowly, as if ruminating. 'Who else went out to hunt, Si?'

'Rannulf des Aix en Louvent, your lady's uncle William Breteuil, Gilbert de Laigle and William de Monfichet.' Simon shook his head. 'He must have been mad. He might as well have ridden out with a pack of wolves. They didn't even stop to bring his body back to the lodge in decency, but rode straight for the treasury at Winchester. It was left to me and Richard to take charge of the body from the back of a charcoal burner's cart and compose it decently for the return to Winchester. It's wrong, I . . .' He gulped convulsively and clenched his fist on the trestle. 'Anyway, Henry's claimed the crown and you'd best be quick about swearing your allegiance. He hasn't stopped since the arrow was loosed.'

Judith rose from the board, her eyes blank and, without excuse or explanation, drifted away from the men like a sleepwalker. No-one took much notice. A sidelong flicker of surprise from Guyon, but his mind was occupied with Simon's budget of news and its implications and what now had to be done. The Welsh situation was fairly stable for the nonce and could be left to cook awhile unattended and Henry, whatever the blots on his soul, had the makings of a strong monarch. Besides, with the private connections of bloodline, Guyon

251

knew that providing he did nothing wildly asinine or treacherous, he was guaranteed the royal favour ... for as long as Henry remained King.

'There'll be a flaming barrel of pitch when Robert Curthose gets to hear of this,' he bleakly understated and rubbed his hands slowly together, feeling the hard bands of skin across right and left palm where he had recently grasped sword and shield.

'And de Belleme will be delighted to light torches from it as he did in 'seventy-seven,' said de Bec.

'Oh yes. We will need to work very hard indeed to make sure that Henry keeps his crown, no matter the manner of his obtaining it. Curthose has about as much control over Robert de Belleme as a wrung chicken has control of its limbs. You've seen what he's done in Normandy. God forbid that he should get to wreak his worst on our lands too.'

'Want me to increase the patrol on our boundary with Thorneyford? It's been very quiet there of late.'

'It won't harm, but don't stretch the patrols too thinly elsewhere to compensate.' Guyon shoved his trencher aside and called for a scribe to be brought so that he could issue news of the changes to his vassals.

Judith picked up Guyon's swordbelt and examined the strip of buckskin without really seeing its embossed golden leopards or the elaborate twists of gold wire decorating the buckle, or indeed the article itself. The sword lay sheathed on the bed. She had had one of the boys clean and oil it, for it had seen recent hard use against the Welsh. The sharpening of the two edges she left to Guyon's auspices. She could have done it herself, she was perfectly capable, but the feel of it in her hands would have frightened her with suggestions of what she should do with it.

Carefully she sat down on the bed and stared at the rumpled sheets, remembering a warm spring night and the laughter of high born men feasting in a candle-lit room, drinking out of green glass cups; feasting with murder on their minds. The Prince and the de Clare brothers had all been members of the fatal hunting party and Walter Tirel was married to Gilbert and Roger's sister.

Malwood, the royal hunting lodge, was only sixteen miles from Winchester, the seat of the treasury. Tirel had fled, all eyes flickering in his direction instead of looking at those men left behind. And Guyon knew, and had known since that May evening. She remembered him coming to her in the bedchamber when their guests had gone, his face waxen, his eyes preoccupied and when she had questioned him, he had balked the answer. What had he said? A confidence he would rather die than break, especially to her. And if he knew, then he was implicated. He had long been a companion of Henry's and his apathy for Rufus was no secret.

Judith bit her lip. The disarrayed sheets reminded her all too clearly of that first night, only now the memory was not tender, but obscene. He had come from plotting a man's death and lain with her. It was a violation. She felt sick and wished suddenly that the bathtub was still in the room so that she could scrub herself free of his touch, the very thought of his touch. His seed was deep within her body. She put her hand to her mouth, striving not to retch.

Guyon came into the room, stretching and yawning. 'I could sleep for a week,' he complained as he dropped the curtain, 'But I suppose a few hours will have to suffice. I never realized that Richard was so fond of Rufus. Then again, it's probably his position at court he fears to lose.' He picked up the scabbard, examined it absently and held out his hand for the swordbelt. She dropped it on the bed and, rubbing her arms as if frozen to the bone, turned her back on him.

Guyon cocked her a look from beneath his brows and busied himself with fastening the thongs. 'We're stopping at Ravenstow tomorrow noon. It's safer if we escort you there on our way south. I do not think that the Welsh will attack

Caermoel, but you never know how this news will affect them. I've already spoken to Elflin and Helgund about the packing.'

Judith did not speak because she could not trust herself to do so. Guyon put down the belt, scrutiny sharpening, for neither of his remarks had been granted a reply and he had not seen her stand like that, clutching herself protectively, since the early days of their marriage.

'Judith?' he questioned softly.

The night candle flung lumbering shadows at the walls. Melyn leaped at a moth, caught it deftly in a flashing paw and bore it triumphantly away to a corner to devour.

'It can't be helped. I'll come home as soon as I can,' he added and then, aware that without saying anything she had put him on the guilty defensive, he tightened his mouth and began to remove his garments.

'Don't flatter yourself!' she snarled. 'Stay as long as you choose!'

Guyon pulled off his shirt, swearing as the linen caught the rough line of the dagger scratch on his chest. He wondered briefly if it was near her time of month again. Her tongue was apt to be sharper then and her moods liable to swing without warning. After a moment when she remained aloof, contained within herself, he relented and tried again, coming up behind her and setting his hand on her shoulder. 'Judith, love, what's wrong? Tell me.'

She shrugged away from him, fighting nausea and flung round to face him. 'Rufus was murdered, wasn't he?' she challenged him, chin thrusting hard.

Guyon shrugged, expression slightly puzzled. 'Probably.'

'Oh, do not play the innocent with me Guyon, you knew what was going to happen!' she spat.

'Don't be preposterous!' He reached for her. She avoided him. 'I haven't been near the King or the court for a full three months and Henry knows that whatever the de Clare's would do for him, I certainly would not!'

'No? You had reason to dislike Rufus and you have long associations with Henry.'

'Oh Christ, Judith, what do you take me for?' he growled with tired exasperation. 'I might not have liked Rufus or approved of his private habits, but that is hardly a reason to plot his death or barter my honour.'

'Then tell me what Prince Henry told you when he dined with us at Whitsuntide,' she challenged.

She saw it; the quick flicker of his lids, the bunching of muscle beneath the exquisitely chiselled cheekbones before his face went blank and his eyes opened wide and dark and fathomless as moorland peat pools. 'He told me nothing,' he said tonelessly.

'Liar!' she flung at him. 'It was less than three months ago. Do you think that I am so besotted by your charm that it makes me lose my memory? You said there was something you could not tell me, a political secret, a confidence you would rather die than break and you were shaken by it. There was cold sweat on your brow.'

'That was nothing to do with Rufus's death.'

'What was it then?' Her mouth twisted in a sarcastic smile. 'After all, nothing can be much more damning than plotting a King's death.'

The wide innocence grew bleak. 'I will not tell you, Judith. It is not my place and perhaps it would do more damage than it would resolve.'

She gave him a look compounded of triumph and defeat. 'I thought you would have an answer,' she said scornfully.

He seized her shoulders and shook them. 'Judith, I swear to you on my soul . . . on my mother's soul, that whatever was plotted against Rufus, I had no part in it. I have no defence except my word. Those that would absolve me, I will not speak. It would only shift burdens and guilts to shoulders less able to bear them.'

'You're hurting me,' she said dully.

He swore and relaxed his grip, but only to soften it to an

embrace and draw her against him. 'Judith, what do I do if you won't trust me?'

She stood quivering within his arms, torn between doubt and doubt. Shield or blindfold, she dreaded to make the decision. He was adept with words, fashioning them to his needs, could convince her black was white if only given the opportunity. 'What do I do if you betray that trust?' she responded and slid her hand over the fine black hairs of his braced forearm, denuded by the ridge of scar tissue where the boar had tushed him, and on up to the smooth curve of his bicep. 'Prove me wrong.'

Emotion flickered the edge of his mask. 'How?' he asked hopelessly. 'If I fulfil your trust I break another.'

She looked at him without relenting. 'And which is more important?'

He left her and sat down on the bed and dug his hands through his hair. 'I don't know. Neither. The edge is so finely balanced that I dare not tip the scale. All I can swear to you again is that I was not involved in any plot to murder Rufus.' He looked across at her where she stood braced as if waiting to receive a blow and let out his breath on a slightly impatient sigh. 'Now, it's late, are you going to come to bed, or stand there glaring at me all night?' He held out his hand.

She looked at his outstretched graceful fingers, knew how they would feel gliding over her body, trailing fever in their wake, knew how they looked holding reins or a sword, knew their tensile strength and of what they were capable.

'Neither,' she said, and walked out of the room.

CHAPTER 20

R HOSYN LOOKED AT the rowed jars of salted beans on the trestle, product of a long morning's work, then down with misgiving at her reddened hands. They were gritty with ground salt and the tiny cuts incurred while slicing the beans now stung and burned most painfully.

'All done?' queried Heulwen, beaming up at her. Rhosyn smiled and lifted her youngest daughter to sit on the trestle. Heulwen was a chubby bundle of energetic health with a bright crop of red-gold curls and huge aquamarine eyes, the legacy of her Norman great-grandfather so Madoc, who had known him, had said. The legacy of her Norman father was her ability to cozen warm approval and adulation from smitten members of the opposite sex. Rhosyn had not seen Guyon since immediately after Heulwen's birth. Messages passed with Madoc. The trading bond remained strong, but the gossamer ties that had bound herself and Guyon for four years had dissolved into the wind, saving this one warm, living, finespun thread.

'All done,' she confirmed and, straddling the infant on her hip, left the kitchen quarters and set off across the small, withy-enclosed compound, towards the hall. After ten strides she stopped short as if she had been struck with an ox-mallet.

Eluned was jumping up and down at Guyon's stirrup and his chestnut courser was sidling restlessly and rolling a white eye. Beyond, she saw Eric and the men of the guard. Guyon leaned over the high pommel, one gauntleted hand on his thigh, the other drawn tight on the reins and spoke to

Eluned. She tossed her head mutinously, but after a moment stepped aside from the horse. He spoke again and smiled and Rhosyn's heart began to thud and flutter. As if it did not matter, as if she had only seen him last week, she went forward with a cordial greeting on her lips.

Guyon dismounted and took hold of Rhuddem's cheek-strap. Rhosyn saw that his clothes were powdered with dust and that the points of his cheekbones and the bridge of his nose had caught the burn of the late summer sun. 'May we claim the hospitality of a drink?' he asked. 'And water for the horses?'

'You know that you are welcome whenever you choose to come,' she responded and felt her face grow warm beneath his stare. The luminous brown gaze flickered to Heulwen, who struggled against her mother's confining arms.

'I did not know,' he murmured, giving Rhuddem to one of his men. 'It has been a long time and so much water has flowed beneath our bridges. Where's Madoc?'

'Away with Rhys and my second cousin Prys to Bristol, but we expect him home any day now. Did you especially want to see him?'

'We need wine and I want him to get a couple of Flemish mares for me. I want a bit more bone in my bloodstock. Is Madoc all right?'

'He works too hard, but I might as well try butting down a stone wall with my head as try to stop him. His breath whistles in his throat and he gets a pain in his arm, but he won't give up.' She turned to lead him into the hafod. 'I hear that he spoke to your wife recently.'

'Yes.'

Rhosyn did not miss the lack of inflection and looked at him curiously. Her father said that lady Judith had been glowing with the contentment of being well-loved and secure. Guyon had not come here in over a year. She had begun to assume he would not come again and that the contentment must be mutual.

'You are growing tall, *cariad*,' Guyon said to Eluned as he seated himself and, staring, she looked down on him, hazel eyes serious. The ivory flower necklace he had given her lay pale and glossy against the dark wool of her gown. 'And pretty as your mother.'

'Am I prettier than your wife?' she challenged him.

'Is an apple prettier than a pear?' he countered and drew her down to him, lightly kissing her cheek, his eyes meeting Rhosyn's troubled stare over the child's narrow shoulder. 'No-one can answer that, *cariad*.'

'Not even you?' Rhosyn mocked with bitter sarcasm before calling one of the serving women. 'Do you want my father to call by?'

'No, I've instructions for him here.' Guyon produced a roll of parchment and took the cup of mead that was given to him. 'Payment in raw wool as usual, unless I hear otherwise.'

She nodded briskly. Their eyes met again, examining, searching. Heulwen, released from her mother's grasp, wobbled towards him, lost her balance and plonked down squarely on her bottom. Undeterred, she struggled up again, grasping Guyon's cross-garter for support.

'*Da*,' she said, and smiled disarmingly at him. It was the Welsh word for father.

'She says that to everyone,' Rhosyn muttered quickly, her colour high.

Guyon looked from the engaging fire-haired child to her mother who was biting her lip and obviously struggling to retain her equanimity in his presence. It had been a mistake to come, he thought, born of his own pain, and he stirred restlessly as if he would rise and leave.

Rhosyn was on her feet before he could make the thought a fact. 'I want to show you something,' she said with forced brightness. 'Can you spare a moment?'

He looked slightly taken aback. 'Of course.'

'Eluned, look after Heulwen for me.'

Eluned pulled a face but was not so foolish as to refuse.

Guyon raised a brow as she led him into her private

259

chamber, but forbore to utter the ambiguous remark that came first to his tongue. Things had changed since then. Whether or not for the better, he no longer knew. Rhosyn selected a key from the bunch upon the iron ring at her waist and looked over her shoulder at him. 'We hear that you are pushing into north Wales now. A new keep no less.'

'To protect the border against lord Gruffydd's raiding. It's no use breeding good raw wool only to have it disappear into the mountains.'

'I sometimes think that you Normans would eat the world if you could.'

'A nibble here and there,' he answered, refusing to be drawn, for there was no heart in him to argue. 'What did you want to show me?'

She stooped and unlocked a stout oak coffer and withdrew from its depths a bolt of fabric. 'What do you think of this? My father bought it in Flanders on the last trip, from an Italian merchant who owed him a favour.'

The cloth flowed onto the bed. It held the rich amber and russet tones of autumn leaves and where the light was trapped by the pile, it shimmered like a sunlit pool. To the touch it was soft and thick and springy, like sun-warmed moss or cat's fur. Having never set eyes on the like before and being thoroughly curious, Guyon sat down on the bed and sought to discover everything that Rhosyn knew.

'So all this is done with shears,' he murmured, smoothing the pile.

She looked at his slender fingers on the nap of the cloth. Heulwen's were chubby little stars, formless as yet. 'It is a detailed skill and not many have it. My father thought of selling it in Winchester at the next court gathering.'

'Next court gathering's in London in November,' Guyon said. 'What price for a Flemish ell of this stuff?'

Her green-gold eyes met his melting brown ones and locked. His crinkled at the corners. She suggested a sum. He laughed and responded with an amount much lower.

'What's happening in November?'

'King Henry's marriage to Edith of Scotland. Judith suits autumn colours.'

'Your new King is to wed?'

'It's been under negotiation for a while, since before Rufus died. I think that they have only met once or twice. Still, that's more than me and Judith had.'

Rhosyn gave him a considering look. 'Is she still a child, Guy?'

'Neither child nor virgin, but as vulnerable as blown glass.' His brow furrowed. 'God knows Rhos, I think I have her and then she eludes me with a twist of her mind and we are back where we started.'

'I know what you mean,' she said with a pained smile and then named another sum a little lower.

His brow cleared. 'I can get two ells of silk damask for that price!'

'But then silk damask is not so rare.'

'And you are priceless.' He glinted her a look from between half-closed thick lashes and made another bid. She snapped a response. He pretended to ponder before answering.

Rhosyn began folding the bolt back upon itself.

'I'm not even sure that I want it,' he added softly. 'Judith will probably think I am offering it to her as a sweetener. We quarrelled before I left and I had no defence except my word and that, apparently, is not good enough.'

Rhosyn straightened and stared at him. He looked quickly down, but not quickly enough and was caught. 'And is it a sweetener?' she asked coldly. 'Are you buying because you cannot have for the asking?'

'No, I don't think so.' He gnawed his lip. 'The King's marriage will throw her into the royal circle. Henry's new Queen will be feted by the wives and daughters of the English barons and Judith will need to dress according to her rank. It is a practical luxury, I suppose.' And then his expression lightened and his eyes sparkled with devilry. 'And since Judith will be wearing it at court among all those other envious rich men's wives who will nag their husbands to death for a gown of the same, it behoves you to be generous in your dealings with me!'

Despite herself, Rhosyn was forced to laugh. 'Guyon, you wretch!' she exclaimed, slapping him.

He grinned at her. Her heart melted but she did not show it. 'All right, I'll meet you halfway.'

'As ever,' he said gravely, mouth twitching and stood up.

She had forgotten how tall he was and the mail he wore made him seem twice the breadth that she knew his rangy frame to possess. Her starved body drooled. Her mind, cold and clear, checked it sharply and prevented her making a fool of herself. Her time was past. Out in the hall she could hear his men and Heulwen's crow of laughter. She moved towards the sounds of sanity.

'Robert de Belleme is back in the marches,' he warned her, catching her arm as he followed her out. 'Alert your father if he does not already know. He's in a savage humour. Henry's much harder to handle than Rufus was and he'll take it out on those least able to defend themselves. Have a care to yourself and the children and remember what I said about an escort if you should need to travel.'

'How could I forget when you keep ramming it down my throat?' she said, rolling her eyes heavenwards. 'Guyon, I am not a half-wit.'

He squeezed her waist gently. 'No *cariad*, but I am.' He gave a self-deprecatory wry smile and thought of Judith.

CHAPTER 21

London
November 1100

ALICIA MUTTERED AN oath beneath her breath as she inadvertently stabbed herself with the embroidery needle for the third time in as many minutes and bade Agnes light the candles. Then she looked across the brazier towards her daughter where she sat, shoulder pressed into the wall, unseeing eyes on the fading grey, rain-spattered light that came through the thick, flawed window glass.

It had not escaped Alicia's notice that her daughter and Guyon were barely on speaking terms these days. Judith behaved as if she loathed the sight of him, would not even let him near enough to lay a hand on her shoulder and refused if possible to make eye contact. Sometimes when he turned away, she would look at him, her eyes filled with bewilderment and the pain of a mortal wound. Alicia's only conclusion thus far was that Guyon had consummated the marriage and that Judith had reacted badly, but it did not satisfactorily explain all the other tensions she felt roiling around them. Judith seemed to feel that she had a genuine grievance. Guyon defended himself like a man with his hands tied behind his back, desperately but without any real effectiveness. Occasionally she had seen the temper flash in his eyes and then extinguish, doused by Judith's cold contempt and his own iron-hard mastery.

Indeed, since Henry had granted Guyon an earldom on the day of his wedding to the new young queen last week,

Judith's mood had been vicious, her behaviour going beyond the bounds of reason. She had snatched the charter from Guyon and, in front of Miles and herself, had ripped it across and across and thrown it down at his feet like a challenge.

'Take it to your Welsh whore!' she had snarled at him, eyes blazing with tears. 'Do not expect me to dabble my fingers in blood!'

No wonder then that he chose to remain absent, attending upon Henry in council at Westminster. His wife, who should have been with him visiting the queen, had dully professed a headache and declined to come and now sat shivering on the window seat, staring blankly into the distance.

'Come away to the brazier, love,' entreated Alicia with a worried frown. 'If there's a draught, you'll catch a chill.'

There was a wordless shake of the turned head. Alicia carefully set the needle into the fabric, put her sewing down and crossed to the window. Close to, she saw why Judith had not answered. Her throat was jerking convulsively as she fought down the sobs that were struggling to tear their way to the surface and, in the stark, cold light, tears tracked glistening trails down her cheeks.

Alicia's own throat wrenched with pain at the sight of her daughter's suffering. Frowning with worry, she sat on the windowseat to face Judith, looked at her for a moment and then folded her in a tender, comforting embrace.

Judith shook with the desperate effort of trying not to cry, but the feel of her mother's arms enfolding her, the secure, familiar smell of the scent she used and the outflowing of love and sympathy were too much for her to fight and she gave herself up to a turbulent storm of grief. Alicia held and rocked her, soothed her with murmured words and reassurances, stroked her hair and, when the first violence had passed, drew her away to a seat near the brazier and dismissed the hovering, worried Agnes with a brief nod and a request for more charcoal.

'Now then,' she said as the curtain dropped behind the

maid. 'What is wrong between you and Guyon? Sweeting, can it not be mended? Is it a matter of pride? Another woman?'

Judith shook her head and blew her nose on the square of linen that was handed to her. 'They would be easily overcome,' she said shakily. 'No mama, it is a matter of trust. He looks me in the face and lies. I cannot bear it!'

'Most men lie at one time or another,' Alicia said ruefully. 'Are you sure you are not making a mountain out of a molehill?'

Judith lowered the linen square to her lap and wrung it into a rope. Her chin wobbled. 'I am sure. There is something he will not tell me. I have asked and asked him, but he just backs away, walks out of the room if I persist and the stupid thing is, mama, that if he did tell me, admitted to my face what I already know, I think I would die.'

'Judith, what do you mean?' Alicia looked at her sharply, beginning to feel queasy, sensing deeper water than a mere lovers' misunderstanding or jealous quarrel.

Her daughter bent her head and began to cry again and shiver. Through the tears, muffled, a little incoherent and punctuated by long hesitation, Alicia received the tale and her own stare became as desolate as Judith's had been on the rain-spattered window-pane. She put her hand to her mouth, feeling not just queasy but dreadfully sick.

'Mama, what am I going to do?' Judith wept brokenly.

Alicia stood up and moved stiffly to the flagon. It was almost empty but she splashed dregs into a cup and, ignoring the sediment, gulped it down. 'Guyon is innocent,' she said abruptly. 'The guilt is all mine. Lay the blame at my door, child, not his.'

Judith raised her head and stared across the candle shadows at her mother, an expression of utter bewilderment on her tear-streaked face.

'Yes, you do have a right to know, but not from your husband's stumbled upon knowledge.' Breathing quick and shallow, assailed by shock and dizziness, she reached for and grabbed the high back of her sewing chair. She had not believed in her wildest nightmare that it would come like this, so suddenly without time to prepare. *What am I going to say to her? Mary, mother of God, help me . . .*

'Judith . . .' Her throat closed. She swallowed hard, lifted her chin and forced out the words as if they were scalding her tongue. '. . . Judith, Maurice de Montgomery was not your father . . . I should have told you long since, but it was never the time . . . And now I fear it is too late.'

Judith stared blankly, stupidly at her struggling mother, as if she had suddenly grown two heads or sprouted wings.

Alicia put her hand to her breast and was unable to differentiate between the rapid juddering of her heart and the panic-stricken fluttering of her fingers striving to keep it within the confines of her ribs. I know it is difficult for you to understand, but if Maurice had ever found out . . .'

'Then who is?' Judith interrupted harshly, voice shuddering into an atmosphere as tense as the wild violence at the centre of a thunderstorm.

'Judith, I . . .' The hand left her side to be held out supplicating to her daughter.

Judith leaped to her feet, ignoring it. 'Who, mama?' she demanded again, lips writhed back from her teeth, expression suddenly feral.

Alicia made a small, frightened gesture. 'Henry . . . Prince Henry . . . the King.'

'That's not possible. He is only Guy's age now!' Judith spat.

'Even at fourteen he was no novice to the game,' Alicia answered wearily, knowing that this reckoning was more than she could handle. 'He knew more than a woman twelve years wed.' She hung her head for a moment, raised it again of a necessity upon the stare of her frightened, angry daughter and felt the guilt and betrayal dragging her down towards the darkness of hell.

'Why, mama, why?'

The anguish in Judith's eyes and voice seared Alicia like a brand. She bit down on her lower lip to stop herself from crying out and gripped the chair so hard that the carving was imprinted upon her skin.

'Why?' Judith asked again relentlessly and dashed a defiant sleeve across her eyes, before returning them, burning with accusation, to her mother.

'Maurice blamed me for being barren. Every month when I bled he would beat me and the times in between he used me as if we were dog and bitch . . . nay, for a bitch consents to be mounted and I was raped . . . and for nothing. Maurice had more sluts and casual whores than I can recall, but not one of them quickened unless it was with another man's seed. He was unable to beget children.'

She looked down. A faint, bitter remembering smile twisted her mouth. 'The Prince came visiting on a hunting trip. Maurice was away. I had the fading remains of a black eye and bruises on my arms and his latest whore was flouting my authority in the hall. It did not matter that Henry was so young. I was so sick of Maurice that I'd have lain down for a leprous beggar in order to get myself with child and shut his filthy mouth. We had a night and a morning and you were conceived. For a time things were better. He did not beat or abuse me lest I miscarried, but after you were born, a daughter, matters went from bad to worse. He expected me to conceive again and when I did not the beatings increased apace.'

Judith's voice cracked. 'Mama, why didn't you tell me before?' she said hoarsely.

Alicia bit her lip. 'I meant to, truly I did, but the time was never right and I knew how much you hated Maurice. At least when he beat you, you thought he had the right. I was afraid what you would reveal to him if he drove you too far.'

'And Guyon knows the truth of my begetting?'

'Not all of it,' Alicia said, watching her narrowly. Judith's expression was now unreadable, but her hands were clenched stiffly at her sides and much as she desired to cross the gulf and embrace her, the fear of rebuff was greater and held her rooted to the spot. 'Probably he has Henry's version of the event . . . I was not even sure until you spoke that Henry knew of your existence.'

'There have been remarks passed in court concerning my likeness to Arlette of Falais,' Judith said flatly as the control to understand warred with the need to strike out. Her marriage had been ripped apart by this dark secret from the past – her mother's past. She remembered the things she had flung at Guyon in her pain, she did not know if it could ever be stitched together again. The agony clutched her in an almost physical pang, like the thought of love. 'Mama . . .' She stopped and looked round.

Cadi clattered into the room and shook herself, spraying water from her close white coat. Scattered diamonds of rain winked in and out on Guyon's fur-lined cloak and his hair had begun to curl at the edges. A single soggy brown leaf clung across the top of one boot. He was clutching a roll of parchment in one hand and his expression was at first blank, then wary as he looked across at the two women and sensed the tension.

Alicia gave a soft, relieved gasp and let go of the chair and consciousness. Guyon did not quite reach her in time and her head struck the sharp side of the brazier as she fell.

Judith stood immobilized, unable to move bone or muscle or nerve. Guyon bent over Alicia and felt for the pulse in her throat. It beat there steadily enough – in rhythm with the blood welling through her dark hair. He swore and propped her senseless form against him, raising her up so that the blood would not flow so swiftly.

'Judith, for God's love, don't just stand there like a sheep, go and get your medicines . . . Run damn you, before she bleeds to death!'

The snarled urgency in his voice jerked her into movement.

She snatched up the nearest thing available to staunch the flow – her mother's painstakingly worked embroidery – thrust it at Guyon and sped to find her nostrums.

Grimly, quickly, she worked, ruining her beautiful velvet bliaut, her commands to Guyon terse and authoritative and he did as she bid him without complaint or demur at her tone. At last, finished, she sat back to regard her handiwork. It was not as neat as it might have been, for the light was poor and she had been in a hurry, but it would not matter. Alicia's hair would cover the scar.

Her mother was still unconscious and likely to be so for some while longer. Her colour, however, was reasonable, her breathing and heartbeat steady and her pupils responded to the candle flame passed in front of them. Gently, they undressed her to her shift and Guyon carried her to the huge, red-curtained bed and laid her in it. Together they looked down at her and then at each other, and slowly Judith walked into Guyon's embrace and laid her head against his chest.

'I can see why you kept it from me,' she said in a small voice. 'Guyon, I know it is inadequate, but for what it is worth I'm sorry.'

'She told you then? I was going to speak to her about it, but Henry has kept me too busy for leisure these last few days and, truth to tell, I could not bear the atmosphere in this house to stay for longer than it took to change my clothes. I felt as though a dagger was being twisted in my gut every time you looked at me . . . or didn't.'

'Guy . . .'

He looked down at her capable blood-caked fingers gripping the dark stuff of his tunic. 'Hush love, we've all made our mistakes, yes and paid for them.' He grimaced. And perhaps still were paying.

She lifted her eyes to him. 'Do you think that Henry will openly acknowledge me?'

'Christ in heaven, I hope he has more sense!' Guyon said, alarmed at the notion. 'Mischief prompted him to tell me. He likes to pull men's strings and watch them dance awhile to his tune. But if he officially recognizes you as his child, what do you think Robert de Belleme will do? Aside from the insult your mother's adultery would cast on the Montgomery blood-line, there is the matter of your birthright. You hold lands that are not legally yours. If your uncles ever discovered the truth, then we'd have a war on our hands.'

'But they wouldn't . . . not with Henry . . .'

'De Belleme is backing Robert Curthose for the crown and so are more than half the other barons. I've letters with me, rough drafts as yet, commanding out the fyrd, the common men of the shires and my own feudal levies. Henry is preparing for war with the ordinary English people as his backbone because he does not know how many of the smiling faces at his table are also smiling at Curthose. If Curthose, with de Belleme at his right hand, carries the day, then God help us!'

Judith shuddered. 'Guyon, stop frightening me!' she gasped, teeth beginning to chatter and not just because the brazier was almost out of charcoal.

'Our lives have been a misery these last three months because you thought I had lied,' he said gently and, leading her to the brazier, he bent to refuel it.

'I know,' she said in a low voice, rubbing her arms. 'And I do not really mean it. I suppose I would rather be scared to death than so miserable I want to die.'

He stood straight, dusting black powder from his hands, looking at her thoughtfully. 'So, I am innocent *cath fach*, but what of Henry? Rufus was his own brother.'

Judith considered, her eyes narrowed on some far distance. 'I do not *feel* as though Henry is my father,' she said slowly after a moment. 'I only know it is so because I have been told and even now my wits are still bemused. But I do not believe I care what Henry has plotted. Papa . . . lord Maurice I mean, committed crimes equally foul, I am sure.'

'But you cared that I might have done so?' He watched her intently, holding his breath on her answer.

'That was different.' In the light from the brazier and the candles her complexion deepened to a rosy gold. 'I don't . . . love them as I love you.' She half turned away, still fighting it even though the words were spoken. Thorns and roses. You could not have one without risking the wound of the other.

Guyon drew her back against him, within the circle of his arms, raised his hand to smooth her hair and, seeing it blood-smirched and dusty with powdered charcoal, set it instead on her shoulder and angled his head to kiss her tenderly. 'Then we have everything,' he murmured, 'and the rest does not matter.' Which was not entirely true, but appropriate to his thoughts at the time.

'M'lady, I've brought some fresh char . . .' Agnes paused on the threshold, basket clutched to her ample bosom and stared goggle-eyed at Guyon and Judith as they turned to face her. Judith's beautiful velvet bliaut was blotched and spoiled by blood, Guyon's cloak less obviously but nonetheless stained and, behind them, Alicia's form lay still on the bed, gleaming in the white shroud of her shift.

Guyon, more knowledgeable by now, moved with the necessary speed to catch her and after the first staggering weakness of sudden shock Agnes rallied herself and sat down to mop her wide pink brow on her sleeve while Guyon explained what had happened.

'Shall I fill a tub, m'lady?' Almost recovered, Agnes wallowed to her feet and went to fuss over her sleeping mistress.

Judith sighed with obvious regret. 'No, Agnes. She needs rest and quiet and all the lumbering out of the tub and the filling would make too much noise. Tomorrow perhaps. A good wash will suffice.'

The maid nodded, expression speculative. Her young mistress's face was still puffy from weeping, but she seemed to have weathered the earlier storm and was looking up at lord Guyon with her soul in her eyes.

'How long before your mother rouses, do you think?' Guyon asked.

'I don't know. Her colour is good, but she is deeply asleep and she will need watching.'

'Agnes is competent to do that? And Helgund if summoned?'

'Yes, but . . .'

'Good. Then put on your cloak.'

'But Guy, I can't go out like this and . . . oh!' She broke off to catch the garment as he threw it at her.

'Find something else to wear and bring it with you.'

She stared at him, or rather at his back, for he had turned away to rummage in his own clothing chest for a decent tunic. 'Guy, where are we going?'

'Wait and see. I've told you before about looking gift horses in the mouth.' He swung around and pinning his own cloak, advanced upon her.

'Guy?'

'Trust me?' His expression was a mingling of laughter and undercurrented tension. 'Trust me, Judith?' He set his arm around her waist and pulled her close, or as close as the bunched cloak trapped between them would allow, and kissed her in a fashion that sent Agnes bustling to a far corner of the room on the pretext of some overlooked task, her face scarlet.

'I don't know if I should,' Judith murmured, regarding him through half-slitted eyes. 'What awaits me if I do?'

'A fate worse than death?' he suggested, draping the cloak around her shoulders and fastening the pin.

She looked at him gravely. A flame flashed through her blood then settled to pulse in steady, warm flickers. Her lips curved and then parted; her eyes danced. She would think about everything later. This moment belonged to herself and Guyon alone.

'Show me,' she said, voice catching with laughter. 'I want to know.'

★

Judith was sitting beside Alicia when she woke, her fingers nimbly weaving a needle in and out of a tunic she was stitching for Guyon, her manner externally one of demure, domestic serenity. She had never been inside a Southwark bathhouse before, indeed had almost balked when she discovered their destination, but Guyon, grinning, had dragged her protesting through the doorway and the rest had been too interesting for her to want to leave.

Mention a Southwark bathhouse and most people would raise their eyebrows and utter knowing laughs, or else pucker their lips into the pursed shape of a cat's anus and shake their heads. Of course, many of the stews warranted such censure, but Guyon's particular choice, which she suspected came of long acquaintance, appeared to cater for those with the wealth to buy privacy and discretion. She had seen several people she knew from the court, two of them alone, another with a very pretty girl who was most certainly not his wife.

She and Guyon had soaked themselves clean and warm in a spacious tub and drunk yellow Anjou wine – not in any great quantity. They had played floating tables – and other less intellectual games, the kind associated with the Southwark stews and knowing laughs and pursed lips, and lent an added spice because of that very fact.

'After all,' she had teased Guyon as they were ferried back across the river by a dour, black-cloaked boatman, their breath frosting the dank, raw air. 'It is not every mother can tell her firstborn son that he was begotten in a brothel.'

'I should not think that every mother would want to tell her firstborn son such a thing,' he had answered sardonically.

Her mouth twitched. She stifled a giggle and bit off the thread and became aware that Alicia was watching her.

'Mama?' For an instant she was startled, but recovered quickly and leaned forward. 'How are you feeling?'

'As if my brains have been squashed,' Alicia said faintly and put up her hand to touch her bandage-swathed head. 'What happened?'

'You fainted and cut your head on the brazier as you fell.'

From the other room, muffled by the heavy curtain, came the reassuring sound of male voices in conversation. Alicia strove to sit up, then desisted with a gasp of pain.

Judith pressed her gently back down. 'I had to stitch the wound and quickly,' she apologized. 'It is not my neatest piece of work.'

Frowning with pain and concentration, Alicia studied her daughter. The velvet gown had gone, replaced by a neat, serviceable russet homespun. The tawny hair was woven into a single, simple thick braid and looked almost as if it were damp.

'Judith, how long have I been unconscious?'

'A few hours mama, do not fret yourself.' She placed a cool hand upon her mother's forehead.

'I seem to recall that I have cause to fret.'

Judith shook her head in wordless denial.

Alicia moistened her lips and groped through a concussion-misted mind towards what she wanted to say. 'I would have told you, truly I would. I believed in my innocence that Henry would want to do the same. I never thought that . . . is he using it to leash Guyon to his cause?'

Judith looked over her shoulder at the curtain. 'Guyon is no tame dog to trot to heel, unless it be his wish,' she said and smiled towards the sound of his voice, a conflict of pride and anxiety churning in her breast.

Her mother's voice was small and timid. 'You do not hate me then?'

'Hate you?' Judith gaped round in astonishment. 'Mama, of course not!'

Alicia's mouth trembled. Judith leaned over and impulsively hugged her. Shakily Alicia returned the embrace and then, drained, leaned back against the pillow, nauseous with pain but feeling as if a great burden had been lifted from her soul. 'I thought that you might. Or else be disgusted. Jesu knows, I have felt those things for myself many times over.'

Judith gave her mother's hand a reassuring squeeze. 'Mama, let it rest. It has caused enough grief already. You had your reasons. I think when I have had the time, I will understand them.'

'Is all well between you and Guyon now?' The anxiety flooded suddenly back into Alicia's eyes.

The dim light masked Judith's blush. 'Yes mama,' she said, voice choked as she fought with laughter. Her mother might have cuckolded her husband with a fourteen-year-old youth, but she would be horrified if she knew what her daughter had been doing not two hours since, and where.

Alicia looked doubtful. Judith had been extremely distraught and the lowered lids and muffled words could now be an attempt to stifle tears. 'Are you sure?'

'Very sure, mama.' Judith controlled herself and raised her eyes and gave her mother a dazzling smile in which there was still the hint of secret laughter. 'Miles has been twitching about outside like a cat with a severe dose of fleas. I'll send him in.' And without waiting for Alicia's yeasay, she went to the curtain.

CHAPTER 22

August 1101

GUYON LEANED HIS head against the cushioned high back of the chair, closed his eyes and within moments was asleep. It was an ability he had cultivated of a necessity since Whitsuntide. He could even doze in the saddle, although that of course was less than safe. Bred to ride from birth, he would not have fallen off, but there was always the danger of a Welsh attack or a surprise assault from one of de Belleme's vassals.

He was sorely beset. Henry was demanding men, money and supplies that Guyon was hard-pressed to find or persuade out of others; Curthose was threatening across the channel, perhaps even at sea by now; de Belleme and his wolfpack were poised to strike the moment it was politic and, just to twist the coil, Earl Hugh's corpulent body had collapsed beneath the strains imposed upon it and he was lying paralysed and close to death in a Norman monastery. His heir was a child and the Welsh were understandably gleeful. Already a few experimental raids had teased the earldom's somewhat fluid boundaries. The garrison at Caermoel had seen action twice that week.

Guyon was doing his best, but was fearful that it was not enough. Four nights ago, he had dreamed that he was tied hand and foot and drowning in a sticky, stinking lake of blood and had woken drenched, gasping and terrified to discover Cadi lying on his chest and licking his face, demanding to be let out of the room. Between relief and rage he had been unable to stop shaking and Judith had roused one of the maids and sent her for usquebaugh. It was only the edge of it. He had not dreamed so vividly since – yet. What need, when the nightmare dwelled before his naked eyes?

It had been a grim year thus far and very little light to hold at bay the yawning black cavern of de Belleme's ambition. In January, Mabel of Thorneyford had given birth to a healthy son and, against all odds, mother and child had survived the ordeal. De Lacey had used the excuse of his son's christening to host a council of war, chaired by the Earl of Shrewsbury, who smiled with his pale eyes at the King and plotted treason so openly that it was an insult. And Henry, without the support of more than half his barons, was for the nonce constrained to swallow it.

In February, Rannulf Flambard had escaped from confinement in the Tower of London and had hastened to Normandy as fast as his sandals could carry him in order to promote the cause of Robert Curthose. And Flambard was an able, persuasive prelate, capable of squeezing blood out of a stone and an excellent manager of that blood once squeezed. If Henry had been the kind of man to panic, he would have done so. As it was, he continued calmly to muster the resources and supporters he possessed into an efficient fighting unit. Efficient? Guyon had helped to train some of them, the fyrd – ordinary villagers – the backbone of the English army. They hadn't a hope in hell's chance against the men who would come at them, men who made war their profession – the *Cwmni Annwn*, the wild hunt of all Normandy and Flanders, paid to rake the heat from hell and scatter it abroad.

He remembered one hot midsummer afternoon when the King had been personally overseeing the training of his peasant-bred troops and he had suggested to Henry that he would do better to instruct them in the use of the quarterstaff and spear rather than seek to imbue them with the warrior skills that came only of instruction from birth.

277

Henry, his forelock wet, dark patches on his inner thighs where he had sweated against his saddle, had looked at Guyon sidelong and given him that familiar, enigmatic smile. 'Robert's amenable to reason,' he remarked easily. 'He doesn't really want to spill my blood and he tends to be swayed by whoever has the most persuasive tongue at the time ... particularly when they are in possession of a large, efficient army. Mutton dressed as wolf, you might say.' And he had laughed softly.

'You mean I'm sweating my guts out for a mummer's show?'

'I certainly hope so Guy, although it is hard to tell how deeply into the apple the maggot has crawled.'

How deep, how far? A yawning cavern, black and advancing to swallow the world into hell. And against it were Henry's guile and a terrible gamble on Curthose's nature.

The sound of wine splashing from flagon to goblet and the weight of Cadi's rump as she settled inconveniently across his toes, tail vibrating the floor, jolted his lids open upon his father.

'Go to bed,' Miles advised, pouring out another cup. 'Alicia remarked to me how tired you look. I know she's apt to fuss, but this time I would say she is right.'

Guyon took the goblet he was given and looked abstractedly at the design edging its rim. 'I can't. I only stopped here because it was convenient to water the horses and eat a meal without being stabbed in the back. I've got to be in Stafford by tomorrow night.'

'You will burn yourself out,' Miles warned.

Guyon arched his free hand over his eyes. 'Do you think I do not know that?' he said heavily.

'At least roll yourself in your cloak for an hour.'

Guyon took his hand away and smiled up at his father. 'Now who is fussing? I was going to do that without your urging, providing of course that I can trust you to wake me up. I've got to skirt Quatford and Bridgnorth and Shrewsbury. I'd rather not saddle-sleep in such inhospitable territory.'

Miles sat down in the chair opposite. It was Alicia's and her embroidery frame was set before it together with a small basket of embroidery silks with a padded inner lid to hold her needles. Christen had been fond of embroidery too, but her patterns had always been bolder and usually worked in wool. Staring across the frame he met her eyes, faithfully reproduced in their son.

'Is there any more news from the south?' he asked.

Guyon shook his head and dragged his feet out from beneath Cadi's weight. 'Not news, only commands. I know how a mother bird must feel feeding her chick. She rams a huge worm down a gaping beak. It vanishes and the beak gapes again. And if she does not feed the chick it will die.'

'Surely there are more resources than yours to draw upon?'

'Yes, but not in the marches. De Belleme is for Curthose; Mortimer sits on the fence and smiles; Earl Hugh is dead, or as good as and Arnulf of Pembroke is a Montgomery. Fitz-Hamon, Warwick and Bigod are bearing the brunt of the work elsewhere. Who else is there except me?' He pulled an eloquent face and drank the wine. 'It cannot go on for much longer. Did you notice the direction of the wind from the battlements? It's been blowing to our disadvantage for the past three days. If Curthose does not come now, he never will.'

'The Queen is due to be brought to bed any day now, isn't she?' Miles murmured.

'Next month. She's confined at Winchester with the treasury.' Guyon's words were bereft of inflection. 'His wife, his heir and his money. I know what I would do if I were Curthose.' He finished the wine and put the goblet down. 'Henry expects him to land near Hastings. It is both expedient and symbolic.'

Miles grunted. 'Do you think they will really fight? I was always under the impression that Curthose treated Henry as

279

his wayward baby brother – deserving of the occasional sharp slap, but never a complete crushing.'

Guyon shrugged and folded his arms. 'If Flambard and de Belleme have anything to do with it, then yes, they will fight, but as you say, they are up against Robert's nature. He has always nurtured a soft spot for Henry and he's so determined to be a *preux chevalier*, that they'll have an almighty struggle persuading him to be otherwise. But then they are very persuasive men . . .'

'Yes,' Miles said, expression revealing what the one syllable did not. He looked round the room of this solid, rectangular keep that he had built up at Ashdyke during the last thirty years. He was prepared for war because, living on the Welsh border, one was never not prepared for it, but sparring with the Welsh was not quite the same as resisting men such as Walter de Lacey and Roger Mortimer. Once, long ago, he had faced destruction at the hands of the then Earl of Hereford, Alicia's father, and had found it harrowing to the point of mental dissipation. He had mellowed since then, did not spend so much time living on his nerves, but he could feel his gut clenching now.

'Judith is coping?'

Guyon's mouth softened momentarily from its grimness. 'Better than I,' he said with a spark of humour. 'She makes a superb quartermaster and deputy. Every time I put an obstacle in her path, she floats effortlessly over it. Jesu, sometimes I am hard-pressed to stay with her, she learns so quickly. When I think of her two years ago on the day of our marriage, a gawky, frightened waif and then I look at her now, holding the reins of an earldom in her hands, not just holding but controlling, I sometimes wonder if I am dreaming. And then she looks at me and smiles and I know I am not.'

'Blood will out,' Miles said with a faint smile.

Guyon chuckled rather sourly. 'Oh yes, blood will out,' he agreed and, leaning back his head, closed his eyes again.

'She shows no sign of breeding yet?' Miles asked hesitantly. 'Alicia worries . . .'

Guyon's brows lifted over his shut lids. 'Judith's reasons can hardly be hers can they? After all, I've already proved my worth at stud, even if the outcome both times has been a daughter.'

'That's not what I meant,' Miles reproved. 'But your lands and titles are far greater than mine and Judith has royal blood in her veins.'

'And it would be a pity if no crop was sown from it to benefit,' Guyon finished for him, tone slightly nettled.

'Well it would,' Miles defended himself uncomfortably and rubbed the back of his neck. 'And it would please Alicia greatly to be blessed with grandchildren. She is afraid that the payment for her sins will be Judith's inability to conceive.'

'Complete idiocy,' Guyon murmured with contemptuous affection. 'Tell her I shall apply myself with diligence – chance permitting. I can count on the fingers of one hand the occasions we have shared a bed since Easter and most of those I was unconscious the moment my head hit the pillow. Besides, these are not safe times to bring a child into the world. I'd not damn an offspring of mine to death in Shrewsbury's dungeon. God knows, I worry enough about Rhosyn and Heulwen.'

'I saw Madoc last week,' Miles said, memory jolted by Guyon's mention of his former lover and their child.

'Did you?' His words emerged as a sleepy mumble.

'Hurrying too much as usual and full of bluster, you know Madoc. I swear his lips were as blue as blackberry juice, the fool. He had a young man with him, a distant relative from Bristol – Prys ap Adda.'

'Mmmm?'

Miles eyed his son thoughtfully. The name obviously meant nothing to him. 'A young man who talked a great deal about Rhosyn and her children. I got the impression that he'd like to be closer to Madoc than a mere distant relative . . . son-in-law, for example.'

Guyon's lids flickered open. He turned his head.

'Madoc's quite amenable,' Miles said, exploring Guyon's slightly startled expression for hints of any deeper emotion. 'He knows that his body is failing him and soon he won't be able to travel any more. Rhys is not old enough yet to take on the graver responsibilities, so it behoves him to find a willing, energetic younger man and bind him to the family.'

'Madoc always did have a need for ropes and grapnels,' Guyon said, looking for a moment faintly amused. And then his mouth slipped from its curve. 'Rhosyn has never seen herself as a rope.'

'Madoc thinks that she will consent . . . providing of course that Prys is not a complete idiot in the way he sets about convincing her. He did not seem an idiot to me.'

Guyon thought of Rhosyn and their warm, stolen moments together – the brevity of those encounters, an hour here, a half day there, scattered in disjointed fragments like pieces of a stained glass window, shattered and strewn down a path four years long. Beautiful, jewel colours that even now, when he had Judith, possessed edges sharp enough to pierce the heart. 'He won't be if she accepts him,' he said quietly, 'if the children accept him.'

'Your Heulwen included?'

Guyon's lower lids narrowed, almost as if he had flinched with pain. He drew a deep, steadying breath and controlled himself before he spoke. 'She is still a babe in arms. Belike she will cleave to him and the better so. What good would it do anyone if I raised objections?' He manoeuvred his shoulders until he was comfortable and shut his eyes again. 'Forgive me. I'm very tired.'

'No good at all,' Miles said and left him to sleep.

Guyon roused with a start to the feel of someone violently shaking his shoulder. He was so stiff that for a moment he could not move and, when he did, it was to discover that his feet were completely numb where the dog's weight had sprawled all feeling from them.

'What's the matter?' he demanded groggily, eyes still fogged with sleep. 'Is it time to go?' And then, pupils beginning to focus, 'Why are you wearing your mail?'

'Henry's messenger has just ridden in on a half-dead horse. Curthose has landed, and not at Pevensey as we all expected.'

'What? Where then?' Guyon toed Cadi off his feet, pushed himself out of the chair and, slightly unsteady of balance, began automatically to don the hauberk that Eric was holding out to him.

'Portsmouth,' Miles said grimly. 'Some English sailors were persuaded to pilot Curthose and his ships into the harbour.'

'Then the road to Winchester is open?'

'Yes.'

Guyon swore as he picked up his swordbelt and fumbled to attach the scabbard to its thongs. *The queen, the heir, the treasury.*

Alicia was hovering anxiously in the background, looking as if she might burst into tears. Guyon glanced round the room for his spurs and picked them up off an inlaid gaming board. 'Look after Cadi for me,' he said to her, 'I cannot take her with me.'

Alicia nodded distantly, but her eyes were all for Miles, devouring him. It might be the last time she ever saw him alive. Guyon flicked a look from one to the other. 'I'll meet you below,' he murmured to his father, kissed Alicia on the cheek, thought briefly of Judith and left the room, Eric clattering in his wake.

Alicia gave a small, despairing sob and cast herself into Miles's iron-meshed arms. He smoothed her glossy black braids and buried his face in the pulse beating hard in her white neck. The sword pommel intruded between them, butting up beneath her ribs. It might as well have been through her heart, blade end on.

CHAPTER 23

IF ROBERT DE BELLEME had been the kind of man to tear out his hair and swear and curse, he would have done so. Those who knew him well enough saw the overt signs of agitation with sufficient clarity to take evasive action before it was too late. Those who did not, found they had a scorpion by its venomous, dripping tail.

Now, as the troops made ready to disperse, he sat in his tent and stared blank-eyed at the rough canvas wall. A muscle ticked in his lean-fleshed cheek. His fists tightened. After a moment he glanced down at the dirty yellow colour of his clenched knuckles and gently flexed them, placing his hands palm-flat upon his thighs.

He had picked his horse, he had nurtured it, fed it from his own hand, cajoled it, coaxed it sweetly down to the water trough. It had dipped its muzzle and at the last, impossible moment had refused to drink because the water was not as crystal clear as it had imagined. By rights he should have taken his sword and hewn the beast into hound gobbets there and then.

Outside the tent, he heard Walter de Lacey and another of his vassals joking together, something about the age of the child-whore currently occupying de Lacey's tent. A red mist floated before his eyes. They were laughing about a trollop when months of careful planning and hard work were un-ravelling around them like a loom weaving backwards. He swallowed, forcing control upon himself. What should he have expected of fools? When he was sure of his temper, he rose and stalked purposefully out into the open.

'Aren't those other tents down yet?' he snarled.

'Nearly, m'lord,' a serjeant answered nervously.

He shoved him aside and snapped his fingers towards the soldier who held his stallion. De Lacey and the other man stopped laughing and exchanged wary glances. He did not even look at them, although he knew that they were part of his personal escort who were to ride with him to the signing of the peace treaty between the brothers. Peace treaty – hah! For what it was worth to Robert Curthose, he might as well use it to wipe his backside.

The horse was fetched, a prancing, lathered black. De Belleme hiked aloft and tightened the reins. Sunlight rebounded off a ring set with a chunk of amethyst.

'When you are ready, gentlemen,' he said icily, pale eyes as hard and narrow as slivers of glass.

De Lacey cleared his throat, muttered an apology and took the reins of his bay from the youth who held it.

The King and his brother were sitting side by side at a long, linen-spread trestle. Guyon, seated further down the board, watched the gonfanons flutter in the warm breeze and narrowed his eyes against the brilliance of the sun. Behind and before, two armies were amassed, one of English shire levies, commanded by the barons who had remained loyal to Henry and one of Normans and Flemings, bulked out by the vassals and retainers of such men as Robert de Belleme, Arnulf of Pembroke, and Ivo Grantmesnil.

The smell of so many bodies, the majority unwashed, was distinctly middenish, as was the language. The English were merely insulting the Normans because it was a traditional pastime. The Normans were swearing because their leader had decided to make peace with his brother when really it was crass stupidity to do so. Better by far that they fight.

Guyon and Miles had reached Winchester with their troops close on dusk of the day following the messenger's arrival, had been momentarily mistaken for the enemy and almost set upon. Cursing, Guyon had roared his name at the men on the walls, his shield flung up and furred with arrows and, after the captain of the guard had been sent for and emerged hitching his chausses and complaining that he could not even go for a piss in peace, they were admitted to spend the night there.

Curthose's army had by-passed Winchester so the captain had told them, his cynical eyes wide with disbelief. *By-passed it!* Guyon flicked a glance along the board to the bearded, stocky form of Robert Curthose. What kind of man forsook such a prize when it was his for the taking? The kind of fool who was unfit to govern, came the prompt thought.

Curthose lived in a world of chivalric unreality, a painted, pretty book of hours. It was the reason he never had any money. He was constantly frittering it away upon the panoply of war, a gilded husk. It was his misplaced sense of knightly generosity that had led him to declare he could not possibly be so much of a brute as to disturb the Queen when she was so near to her time.

Robert de Belleme, who could indeed have been so brutish and more besides without shred of a qualm, was left gnashing his teeth and mentally, if not physically, clutching his hair at Curthose's inability to maintain his sense of purpose or the anger with Henry that might have kept the fervour burning. The zeal that had lasted him through his time in the Holy Land was not even a smouldering ember of its former fire.

Those barons who had counted on being able to make Curthose fight for the English crown were now watching Henry, avoiding his eye if he watched them in return and nervously counting the cost of their mistake. Henry was not his easy-going brother to forgive and forget unless it was politically expedient to do so – and it was not. Henry's dark grey eyes emphatically said so.

They were all gathered here now, enemy and ally, on the London road at Alton, so that Henry and Curthose could hammer out their differences and make of them a smoothly polished peace treaty. De Belleme and Flambard and Grant-mesnil had advised Curthose to fight. His position was good and would never be stronger. Henry had smiled gently into his brother's myopic, childishly innocent eyes and asked why resort to bloodshed when diplomacy was by far the better way?

Curthose had been only too willing to listen to Henry's sweet-talk, which was, of course, Henry's deadliest weapon. Curthose's intention to war with Henry had considerably cooled since its first indignant eruption and, besides, he was now embarrassed for funds. Basically all he wanted was some money to cover his expenses and to go back to Normandy and let the dust settle. Henry was most amenable. All that remained to be discussed here and now was the sum Curthose would be paid annually in return for his acknowledgement of Henry's right to the crown. And what, thought Guyon, expression suitably blank, had a promise ever meant to Henry? Once Curthose was gone from English soil, so would the compulsion to pay the sum demanded. Henry gambled brilli-antly and was a superb manipulator of men, particularly when it came to members of his own family. Curthose did not even have the ability to manipulate a lump of warm clay, let alone mould it into the shape of a kingdom.

Guyon studied the assembly. Grantmesnil, de Belleme and Roger de Poitou had arrived, dark cloaks swinging, looking like a trio of warlocks, their minions swarming behind, Walter de Lacey among them. The lord of Shrewsbury was wearing some of the new velvet in a deep, blood-red colour that made him look swarthy, as did the blue beard-stubble foresting his jowls. Against all this darkness, his eyes were very pale and brightly cold and stabbed everyone that he fixed with their glare.

When the look slashed over himself, Guyon answered it calmly, shielding himself from the probing malevolence by recalling their last encounter and the gratifying sight of de Belleme and sir Walter parcelled up in the road among a herd of bleating, stinking sheep. His mouth twitched and he quickly lowered his eyes before he laughed. When he dared to look up again, the earl's gaze was stalking FitzHamon with vicious intent and Walter de Lacey was watching him instead.

Entirely without qualm this time, Guyon laughed at him.

De Lacey stiffened and his right hand twitched towards his sword, except of course that he wasn't wearing one. No man came armed to a parley. He transferred his fist to his empty belt and clamped it there until he had mastered the suicidal urge to leap over the trestle and throttle the Earl of Ravenstow with his bare hands.

Only last month de Belleme had said with smiling confidence that matters would change once Robert of Normandy had siezed the throne from his snivelling usurper of a little brother, that earldoms such as Ravenstow would be theirs for the plucking, and any widows who happened to go with them. The smiling confidence was gone now, unless it dwelt upon Henry's face viewing this bloodless, but no less lethal slaughter ground, or within the eyes of Guyon FitzMiles, glinting with unconcealed mockery.

Sweating with effort, de Lacey swallowed the hard lump in his throat and cursed the ill luck that had preserved Guyon's life through the several attempts made upon it. He built himself a wishful vision now, of his enemy impaled upon a stake in Thorneyford's bailey, writhing upon it while, before his eyes, his wife was used like the bitch she was by every last member of the guard. After a while, rage channelled into imagination, he was able to return Guyon's laughter with the snarling rictus of a grin.

The annual sum to be forfeited by Henry was set at three thousand marks. Robert appeared smilingly satisfied with the bargain. Henry's own smile was wry, but with a secretive undercurrent that Guyon well recognized. Judith looked like that when matters had not gone entirely her own way but she intended them to do so in the fullness of time. Curthose might get his payment this year and next, but as soon as

Henry's hold on his kingdom was less precarious, he would set about seeking a way to extricate himself from the agreement.

Twelve barons from each faction ratified the treaty. Guyon quilled his name beneath Warwick's cross and Meulan's thumbprint. Robert de Belleme signed with a sarcastic, defiant flourish and then spat on the grass. Henry and Robert clasped each other. Curthose's hug was ebullient and affectionate, Henry's a pale imitation. Affection in Henry was reserved for those who did not threaten his crown and even that these days was sparingly given. He was in love with the task of ruling and it left precious little room for the softer emotions.

Guyon was in the act of accepting a cup of wine and a heel of bread from his father's captain while around him the men made shrift to load the pack horses, when Henry himself approached, picking his way carefully around the campfire and assorted heaps of baggage. FitzHamon was with him, the sun reflecting off his pink, freckled scalp.

Guyon bowed, his mouth full of bread. Miles appeared from the tent, breath drawn to speak and, startled, made his own obeisance.

Guyon swallowed hastily. 'Breakfast, sire?' he asked with a touch of humour. The bread was slightly stale and the wine was warm and stuck to the palate. It was all they had left, for they were almost ready to leave.

Henry made a gesture of denial and came straight to the point. He could dissemble and meander like a mountain stream in spring if the occasion demanded, but now was not the time or need. 'I have to put a curb bit on de Belleme, his brothers and their allies,' he said tersely, 'and I need your help, Guy and yours too, Miles.'

'If it be in my power, sire,' Miles answered gracefully, eyes full of suspicion.

Guyon flickered his glance to FitzHamon whose face was unhelpfully blank. His heart sank. All he wanted to do was go home, bury his head beneath a pillow for six months, shut out the world, sleep and rediscover the pleasure of a bathtub and Judith fragrantly soft in his arms. Judith, who was Henry's daughter. 'Sire?'

'I've had the exchequer gathering evidence against Surrey and Grantmesnil since the late autumn, but I need more information on de Belleme and his brothers. There is much groundwork to be done in the marches and until I am ready to cast the noose, I do not want my prey to know how tight I intend to draw it.'

'You want us to spy for you?' This sharply from the older man.

Henry pinched the end of his blunt nose. Miles, half Welsh by birth, had been one of his father's most valued scouts, a master in the arts of reconnaissance and stealth, one of the props of the Norman army during the notorious northern campaign of 'sixty-nine. 'Not personally,' he negated with a tepid smile. 'I'd not lose either of you to one of Shrewsbury's little pastimes, but you must have contacts from the old days Miles, men you can trust.'

'To have their entrails pierced in my stead?' Miles said with quiet contempt.

'Don't be so awkward, Miles,' said FitzHamon amiably. 'Someone has to recruit the men and collate the information gleaned. Would you rather have de Belleme ravening about the borders like a mad wolf for the next thirty years?'

Miles snorted hard. 'A knife in the dark would work just as well,' he said, 'and would probably be a lot simpler to accomplish.'

Henry shook his head. 'I had thought of that myself, but it wouldn't really serve,' he said regretfully. 'If Robert de Belleme dies, then the lands go to his son, or to one of his brothers. If, on the other hand, he is stripped of his fiefs for flouting the law of the land beyond all redemption, then the estates and revenues come directly to the crown.'

'But first he has to be found in official error of the law,' Guyon murmured, beginning to understand. His mouth twisted. 'And then it will come to war.'

FitzHamon shrugged. 'You cannot make wine without treading grapes and one way or another it will still come to war in the end.'

'Blood and wine, they're both red aren't they?' Miles said neutrally, his expression blank.

'I'm sure you would rather be a treader than a grape,' Henry responded, showing his teeth in a swift grimace of what might or might not have been amusement. 'Think about it. If you decide in favour, send to me, or get a message to Beaumais in Shrewsbury. You do know him, don't you?'

'Beaumais, but he's . . .' said Miles.

Henry's smile was feline, full of satisfaction. 'Yes, he's a justicar in de Belleme's househould and he's been in my pay for the past year. You'll be working closely with him if you choose to take on this task.'

Miles swallowed and stared at Henry, the hairs prickling his scalp. Guyon, more accustomed to the devious workings of his sovereign's mind, quirked him a wry, 'should have known it' look. Henry conceded him a genuine laugh and reached up to slap his shoulder. 'Think about it,' he repeated. 'I'll talk to you later.'

'Will you do as he asks?' FitzHamon said as he made to follow Henry across the camp.

'I do not think we have a choice,' Guyon murmured. 'And there's no point in cutting off your nose to spite your face.'

'That doesn't stop him from being as much a bastard as his father was,' Miles observed with considerably less charity. 'Only William's was a matter of birth. His is a matter of nature.'

'That's why he's King and Curthose isn't,' Guyon said and went to see his destrier.

CHAPTER 24

Summer 1102

RHOSYN DREW REIN and let the leather hang slack in her capable fingers so that old Gwennol could graze the dusty roadside grass. Beyond them, pocked and rutted, the floury road cut through fields and forest and past formidable fortresses – the marcher eyries of Robert de Belleme – until it reached Shrewsbury, crouched within the protection of the Severn bend. Behind her on the drovers' road lay Wales and safety, as far as anything could be termed safe these days. Guyon had been right, Robert de Belleme and his vassals had turned the marches into hell for men who had to travel them for a living. The war in the south where King Henry sought to bring his most voracious earl to heel sent disturbing rumours scudding north. If Arundel fell to the royal forces, then the storm would burgeon here in the heart of de Belleme's honours and lightning would split the land she rode.

She considered now the left fork, moths fluttering cold velvet wings within the pit of her belly. They always did when she thought of Guyon and not just because of what had been between them once. He would be furious when he realized that she had risked crossing the border with only a drover and his market bound herd of sheep for protection.

Her father had been in Flanders when his heart had failed his driving will and he had died in a hostel on the Bruges road. Prys had sailed from Bristol to fetch his body home for burial. They would mourn and then, because time did not stand still, they would marry. Rhosyn bit her full lower lip, beginning to regret the impulse that had become a compulsion and driven her stifled from the hafod towards the beckoning colours of Ravenstow's summer fair. There were items she needed, she told herself, items for the funeral and her wedding. The item she most wanted, she could not have. Better to settle for the same thing in a serviceable day-to-day mould without the gilding and carillons. Knowing what was better and sensible did not ease the pain.

'Why have we stopped, mam?'

Rhosyn looked round at her daughter and the fine lines fanning from her eye corners deepened into a self-mocking smile. 'I am beginning to wonder if we should have come at all.'

'Too late now,' declared Twm sourly, riding up from behind, the pack ponies jinking in his wake.

'Won't Guyon be pleased to see us then?' Eluned looked anxiously at her mother and then at Heulwen cradled sleeping in Twm's broad embrace.

'Probably not,' Rhosyn admitted ruefully. 'But he may not even be there, not with the war down in the south.'

'What about his wife, will she?' asked Rhys, thinking of the wary feline girl he had met on several occasions during trading visits with his grandfather. He liked her. Beneath that wariness dwelt a sense of humour and a genuine interest in people whatever their station.

'Perhaps.' Rhosyn's fingers twitched on the reins and Gwennol raised her head and backed restively. Guyon's wife. How would she react to their presence at Ravenstow and what in God's name was she going to say to her if they met? Neither child nor virgin, Guyon had said, but as vulnerable as blown glass, and there had been an expression in his eyes that she had never seen before.

'I don't want to meet her,' Eluned muttered, hazel eyes narrowing. 'She's probably a haughty Norman bitch with long fingernails and a face like a witch!'

'That is quite enough,' Rhosyn rounded on her coldly. 'Whoever we meet and whatever happens, you will remember your manners and not disgrace my name or your grandfather's. Is that understood?'

'Yes mam.' Eluned said impatiently and scowled.

Euraidd's ears pricked in anticipation and, as the reins relaxed and the heels commanded, she moved smoothly from a walk to a controlled fluid trot. Some of the villeins paused hoeing their strips and shaded their eyes against the hard morning light to watch the Countess of Ravenstow, golden upon her golden mare, reach the crest of the hill and, with her escort quickening pace behind, begin the descent into the neatly clustered town, secure behind its Roman stone walls.

The summer market was in full cry, the booths hectic despite, or perhaps because of, the unrest and warfare swirling the country. Men had to make a living and even with the Earl absent at the siege of Arundel, the Ravenstow lands were still safer than many.

There were stalls of pies, breads and sweetmeats to tempt the hungry. Spice vendors cried their wares. One of the Ravenstow guards was having a tooth drawn, the efforts of the sweating chirugeon observed with grisly relish by a critical crowd. A performing bear lumbered in pawing, shaggy circles to the music of an off-key set of bagpipes played by a puffing man with a paunch that could have supported a cauldron. A brown-skinned girl danced, small bells tinkling on her ankle bracelets.

Livestock squealed, squawked, bleated and neighed. Women sat with baskets full of surplus home produce to barter or sell – cherries and root vegetables, butter and cheese. The potter was there with his green-glaze wares, as were the salt chandler, the cobbler, the shoesmith and the other tradesmen of the town.

Judith did her duty by the senior merchants and townspeople, pausing to speak and smile and discuss, setting their fears at rest before making her purchases. At the bronze-smith's booth, she bought a new chappe for one of Guyon's belts and a studded collar for Cadi, the bitch having deposited the last one somewhere on a ten mile stag hunt, and then she repaired to the haberdasher's stall to obtain needles and embroidery silks for the tapestry she intended to warm the solar wall.

Another woman was already there, intently scrutinizing a length of ribbon. A small child clutched her skirts and peeped up at Judith from a pair of round, bright, kingfisher-blue eyes. An older girl at the woman's other side shifted from foot to foot. Black-haired she was, and hazel-eyed, with the quick, graceful movements of a fawn. Behind Judith, de Bec muttered a startled, stifled oath.

'What's wrong?' Judith asked, half-turning. In that same moment, the boy Rhys stepped from the crowd and joined his mother and sisters at the stall. There was no mistaking the relationship. They all had variations of the same blunt nose and their hair grew to a similar pattern.

'*Heulwen, dewch yno,*' said the mother absently as her red-haired youngest one moved from the safety of her skirts towards Judith.

Judith's stomach hit the floor as the child smiled at her. She put her hand to her mouth, willing herself not to do something stupid like faint or be sick. Guyon's mistress, Guyon's daughter, here in the heartland of the earldom. Here, where she had thought she was inviolate.

What did one do? Fight? Back away like one cat sighting another? Brazen it out? Judith swallowed the bile that had risen in her throat and raised her chin a notch. She was no longer a child beset by unfocused emotions, bereft of weapons or defence. She had the knowledge now and the confidence to use it with wanton subtlety. All that this woman had were the ties of the past ... and the child. Involuntarily, Judith's hand went to her own flat belly before she crouched to the infant's level, her skirts pooling the dust. 'Heulwen,' she said with uncertainty and smiled.

Rhys turned his head, dark eyes widening. Rhosyn looked round, the ribbon twined in her neat, capable fingers, her expression first surprised, then anxious. It was a pleasant face with glossy arched brows and full-lidded autumnal eyes. Pretty, but not strikingly so and there were faint weather lines seaming her eye corners.

'I am Judith of Ravenstow, Guy's wife,' Judith introduced herself with an impassivity that gave no indication of the seething emotions beneath. 'If you have come to see him, I am afraid you will be disappointed. He's down at Arundel with the King.'

Heulwen smiled coyly at Judith and turned to her mother, pressing her face into her full, dusty skirts. Heart thumping with both apprehension and anticipation, Rhosyn stared at the woman who now rose to her feet and confronted her. Were it not for her cool statement of identity, she would never have connected the imagination to the reality. Here was a striking young woman, as slender and straight as a stalk of corn in her golden wool gown and not the slightest hint of vulnerability in her attitude.

'I am pleased to meet you,' she responded in excellent accented French marred by the crack in her voice. 'You are not as I thought.'

Gold and grey, the girdle of polished agates glowed around Judith's trim waist. Gold and grey, cool as the stones, her eyes held Rhosyn's. 'Neither are you.'

Rhosyn swallowed. 'I have not come to make of Guyon a battleground,' she said, trying to defend herself against Judith's gaze which owned the properties of winter sunlight – bright but killingly cold.

'But nevertheless you are here, and I do not think that it is because you intend buying trinkets or watching the bear dance.'

'No, there is more to it than that,' Rhosyn admitted. 'Some of it is a matter of trade. I have those spices you asked my father to obtain for you last time and I needed some

296

trimmings for a new gown . . .' She drew a shaky breath. 'My father went to Flanders last month and died there. Prys has gone to bring him home. I was hoping to ask Guyon for an escort back into Wales – he did promise me one should I need it – and I thought he should know of my father's death . . . and other things.' Her voice stalled into silence.

'Then you had best come up to the keep,' Judith said woodenly. 'There will be tallies to settle and you will need a place to sleep. I am sorry to hear about your father. We had become friends.' She wondered what she would do if Guyon came unexpectedly home now and lavished all his attention on Rhosyn and their small, engaging daughter. It was an area they had left well alone. Judith had never enquired beyond the superficial and he had seldom volunteered insights, both of them avoiding what might cause them too much pain. She saw now, too late, that they had been wrong.

The tension between the two women remained a palpable entity, although Judith relaxed her guard sufficiently to haggle prices with Rhosyn, who responded vigorously to the challenge as soon as she realized Judith's astuteness. Eluned was sulky and intractable and de Bec took her and Rhys off to the stables to show them Melyn's latest batch of kittens, before the child's rudeness became inexcusable. The two women were left alone in each other's company, except for the infant.

'Eluned has lost her father and now her grandfather,' Rhosyn sighed, 'and this new babe has not made matters any easier.' She looked tenderly down at the child curled sleepily in her lap. 'I did not mean to conceive, you know, a slip-up with the black-spurred rye. She is a tie with Guyon I could well do without.' Gently she touched the feathery whorls of red-blonde hair and smiled. 'She takes her colouring from Guyon's grandsire, Renard de Rouen. He married a Welsh girl, old lord Owain's daughter, Heulwen. My father was at their wedding, although of course he was no more than a child himself then.'

Judith was silent, not knowing what to say. Spoken in a different tone, Rhosyn's words might have been a challenge, but crooned softly like a lullaby to a drowsing infant, there was no threat but, Jesu, they stung all the same. A vision of Guyon's lithe, muscular body filled Judith's inner eye. She knew exactly how his skin would feel beneath her fingertips; the gliding, sensual promise of joy. So did Rhosyn, the child in her arms a visible, living reminder of the pleasure Guyon had taken on her body. And as yet she had no such reminder to comfort herself.

Glancing up from her sleepy daughter, Rhosyn glimpsed Judith's expression before it was masked to an icon neutrality, and her stomach lurched. Behind the cool, controlled façade there stalked a wild beast.

'Perhaps it would be better if you gave me my escort now,' she suggested with dignity.

Judith parted her lips to snarl an agreement, caught her voice in time and, hands fisted in her lap, looked away towards the space upon the solar wall where she intended the tapestry to hang. That kind of jealous anger was marring, corrosive without any offsetting benefit. Face it, she thought, force your will through it. She returned her eyes to the small, dark Welsh woman seated beside her and laid her hand on her sleeve.

'No, please stay. It is too late in the day to set out for Wales. You would not reach your home before dark. Besides, we have not concluded our business. Can you obtain some more velvet for me? The last gown was ruined in London.'

'I should imagine so. We've been swamped by demands for it since last winter, but of course you and Guyon have priority. I'll speak to Prys.' She studied Judith warily. They were navigating a deep, narrow channel and where there were not jagged rocks to be avoided, there were currents and whirlpools.

Ignorant of adult strivings, Heulwen slept, a heavy, warm weight in her mother's arms and Rhosyn was only too glad to accept Judith's invitation to leave her in the upper chamber with Helgund and Elflin.

The room was well-appointed and reasonably warm, for in addition to the braziers it also boasted a hearth. The maids whispered delightedly over the sleeping child, Helgund because she had a granddaughter of a similar age, Elflin because she was newly pregnant. Rhosyn laid her daughter in the huge bed which dwarfed the small form to the size of a doll and, after tenderly smoothing her curls, gazed around the room. There were bright tapestries hung on the walls to stay the draughts and combat the seeping coldness of the thick stone walls. The arrowslit was covered by slats of wafer-thin ox horn so that at least some daylight was permitted into the room, but rush dips still illuminated the corners and unseen things seemed to lurk there. She shivered and hugged her arms.

'Is there something wrong?' Judith enquired.

Rhosyn shook her head and smiled wanly. 'I hate these places,' she shuddered, 'no light, no air save that it be musty and tainted with damp. The walls hem me in. I never sleep well when I'm lodged in one of these keeps. I need to be free. Guy could see it, but he never understood. He loves the stones. Perhaps they grow warm under his touch as they do not under mine. It is one of the reasons I would not stay with him. In time the nightmare would have swamped the dream.' She looked round at Judith and dropped her arms to her sides. 'You are like him; content to dwell here. You do not feel the hostility. I could no more make my home in a keep than you could live rough in Wales.'

Judith took her coney-lined cloak from the clothing pole and handed Rhosyn's across the space separating them. 'Then you do not know me,' she responded with a glimmer of fierceness. 'Yes, I do enjoy the security of these walls and caring for those within their bounds, but it is not all my life and, if it was, I would go mad.'

She led her out of the room and on up the twisting

stairway to the battlements, her tread light, making nothing of the steep, winding steps. Almost defiantly, she added between breaths as they went, 'I know how to snare coney and hare and I can make a shelter from cloaks and branches. I speak a fair degree of Welsh and I can use a dagger as well as any man. When Guy goes on progress to his other holdings, I go with him and it is no hardship for me to sleep beneath a hedge or hayrick wrapped in my cloak. I need to feel the wind in my hair and the rain on my face . . . now and again anyway. Sometimes I come up here for precisely that purpose.'

Rhosyn, her calves aching, put her hands on the stone and leaned between the merlons, eyes half-slitted to counter the buffeting wind, and rested to gain her breath. A guard saluted the two women without surprise. They had become used to lady Judith's mild eccentricities. She greeted the man by name and stood beside Rhosyn, her tawny hair wisping loose of its braids.

'You have it in you to keep him,' Rhosyn said, seeing now the promise. Not just a girl who had grown into a strikingly attractive young woman, high-bred and Norman with all the domestic and social skills that a man of Guyon's status required, but a girl who beneath the cultured exterior was still only half-tame, a thing of the woods, wild for to hold. Guyon was not about to grow bored of such a complex, complementary blending of traits.

Some late swallows swooped the hyacinth air, their cries poignantly sharp, like needles darting through blue cloth. Judith looked down at her hands. 'If we are granted a life together,' she said with a hint of bitterness and stared at a white blemish on one of her nails until her eyes began to sting. 'Since last Martinmas, I have scarcely seen him. Either he is with the King, or about the King's business and the times he is home, he just eats and sleeps and his temper is foul . . . but then I suppose it has reason to be. There is no guarantee that Henry will win this war. If he fails then it

won't matter whether I have the ability to hold him or not
. . . in this life at least. De Belleme knows whose work was
behind half the charges he was summoned to answer.'

Rhosyn leaned with her and watched the swooping birds.
A trickle of fear, of foreboding, shivered down her spine.
Footsteps on your grave, as her mother had been wont to say.
'Is he in serious danger?' she asked, eyes growing anxious.

'I have never known my lord when he has not been in
serious danger,' Judith said with a reluctant smile. 'From his
own contrary nature, if nothing else. He sets out to court
trouble sometimes and I have the devil's own job to persuade
him that he should be courting me instead!'

It was spoken with humour, but it was in no wise amusing,
as Rhosyn well knew from her own painful experience.
Leopards did not make good hearth animals. They were
liable to tear out your heart.

The watch changed, spears scraping on stone, jocularities
bantered. Some sheep were driven into the bailey from the
surrounding fields for slaughter the next day. Below them,
the fair was shutting up its booths for the evening and folk
were wending their way home. Leaning over the merlon,
Judith saw the guard who had been having his tooth pulled
weaving this way and that over the drawbridge, clearly the
worse for drink. She made a mental note to check with de
Bec that he was not on guard duty that night.

'I was foolish to come,' said Rhosyn in a soft voice that
Judith had to strain to hear. 'Only I wanted . . . I wanted to
see you for myself. If I am honest, that at least was the half of
it.'

Taken aback, Judith stared at her. 'I would call it a very
dangerous indulgence,' she said quietly at last.

Rhosyn made a face. 'Do you think I have not said the
same thing to myself a hundred times over?' She gave a
self-deprecatory, sad smile. 'But it has been like a sore tooth,
nagging me and nagging me until it had to be drawn. I had
to know. Well, now I do and I am glad it is over, but that is

not the sole reason I am here.' She drew a deep breath, her eyes on the horizon towards which the sun was now angling. 'My second cousin Prys, who lives in Bristol and with whom we have strong business ties, has asked me to marry him and I have agreed.'

'Congratulations,' Judith said, too wary to put much warmth into the salutation. 'When is the wedding to be?'

'We don't know yet. Before Christmastide, I suppose. We have my father to bury and mourn first and the business to sort out.' She frowned and pressed the heel of her hand into the gritty stone. 'I've known Prys since we were children and Rhys and Eluned are fond of him . . . but it is Heulwen, you see. After all, she is Guyon's daughter and for the sake of what was between us, I felt that he should know my decision. Prys has no heirs. Perhaps in the fullness of time I shall bear him children, but he is willing to take Rhys, Eluned and Heulwen for his own and provide the girls with dowries when they come of marriageable age.'

'I do not think Guyon will stand in your way,' Judith said slowly after a pause for consideration.

'Neither do I.' Rhosyn blinked and bit her lip. '*Adeiniog pob chwant.* It has run its course, for him at least. We never had enough in common to make of it more than a dry grass fire. I wish . . .' Rhosyn shook her head and turned away, her chin wobbling.

Judith studied her. She had imagined Guyon's mistress to be dark and mysterious and beautiful with all the wiles at her fingertips. Only the first was true. The reality was a straight-forward practical woman with a generous, gentle spirit. She could see why Guyon had held onto the bond for more than four years and also why it must now be severed. And Rhosyn saw too, or else she would not be crying here beside her on the battlements as the sun began to melt on the horizon. Judith looked away and was patient, offering a mute understanding by way of comfort.

Rhosyn sniffed loudly and, wiping her eyes on her sleeve,

turned to present Judith with a watery smile. 'I am sorry, I was being foolish. Will you and Guyon come to the wedding?'

Judith looked doubtful. 'Will it not cause trouble?'

'It is not that kind of marriage, not yet anyway. Purely a business arrangement to begin. What grows from it we shall see. Prys is well aware of my past. You will be most welcome.'

'Then gladly we will come, circumstances permitting.' Judith hesitated. 'What about Heulwen? Will you tell her your past as she grows older?'

Rhosyn regarded Judith curiously, sensing a sudden renewal of tension in her attitude. 'Of course I will. As it is, her colouring will rouse remarks long before she is able to cope with them. I do not want her looking at every red-bearded Danish sailor who enters Bristol harbour and wondering if she is his get. She will have it from me, no-one else, as soon as she is old enough to understand. I would not want her to hate me.'

Judith let out the breath she had been holding. 'You are very wise,' she said shakily. 'I wish my own mother had been of your mind.' She leaned over the merlon as the drawbridge, chains clanking, was drawn up for the night. One of the men on watch shouted a cheerful insult across to the guards at the winch and was answered in kind.

'I hope that Guyon will still see her on occasion,' Rhosyn added, wondering, but not quite daring to ask, what Judith had meant by her last remark. The phrase *vulnerable as blown glass* came back to her and for a drifting instant seemed apt.

'She will always be his firstborn,' Judith said, looking round, again in complete, cool command of herself. 'It would be wrong to stop him. That far I will permit you to tread on my territory because I cannot change it, but seek further at your peril.'

Rhosyn gaped at Judith. The challenge was there in her strange, stone-coloured eyes, but a twinkle of self-mocking amusement was also present to leaven it, almost as if she stood beside herself and listened.

From the inner bailey, the dinner horn sounded and someone cheered with irony.

'Shall we go down?' Judith asked, offering her arm.

Rhosyn smiled and took it.

Rhosyn rode out the next morning onto a sun-polished road with an escort of eight serjeants and her manservant, Twm. The pony hooves echoed on the dusty drawbridge planks. She looked beyond the rise and fall of their loaded backs to where Judith stood between the bridge and portcullis, one arm shading her eyes, the other raised in farewell. Rhosyn returned the salute briefly and turned in the saddle so that, like her mount, she faced Wales.

At noon they stopped to water the horses and eat a cold repast of bread and cheese and roasted fowl. Heulwen, as usual, ate the cheese and spat out the bread and made a thorough mess. Eluned in contrast, nibbling as daintily as a deer, considered her mother for a moment, swallowed and said, 'He was forced to marry her, wasn't he mam?'

Rhosyn raised her head, concern marring her brow. Eluned had been very quiet since yestereve's sulky rudeness, a brooding kind of quiet that would not yield to cozening. 'At the outset, yes,' she answered cautiously.

'He does not love her.' Eluned fingered the ivory necklace of daisies at her throat.

Rhosyn bit her lip. The child's eyes were her own – hazel green-gold and full of pain. You grew up and learned to hide it, that was the only difference. 'You cannot say that, Eluned,' she responded softly. 'It is what you would like to be true, not truth itself. You should wish them joy in each other, not strife.'

'She's ugly!' The full lower lip was petulantly thrust out.

'Eluned!'

Heulwen choked and Rhosyn mechanically rescued the half-chewed piece of chicken wing from the back of the infant's throat, her attention all focused on her elder daughter.

'I hate her, she's a Norman slut. Guyon belongs to us, not her!'

Rhosyn's hand shot out and cracked across Eluned's cheek, imprinting it white. Eluned gasped. The men of the escort looked round from their oatcakes and ale. Eluned put her hand to her face, stared at her mother with aghast, brimming eyes as the mark of the slap began to redden and, whirling, fled beyond the startled men into the thickness of the brambles and trees.

'No mam, let her go,' Rhys said, catching Rhosyn's arm as she made to pursue. 'She's leaving a trail that even a blind man could follow. I don't think she'll go very far.'

Rhosyn subsided with a helpless little gasp. 'It is my fault,' she owned. 'I did not realize that it ran so deeply. She used to say that she was going to marry Guyon. I thought it was a child's game.'

'So did she,' Rhys observed with a dryness beyond his years.

Rhosyn reseated herself upon the spread skins to finish her meal, but her eyes kept flickering towards the trees.

Rhys considered her for a moment and then gave an adolescent sigh, heavy with impatience, and hitched his belt. 'All right mam, I'll go and find her.'

A grateful, worried smile fleeted her face. She was wondering how to go about dealing with Eluned when she returned. Diplomatic silence as if it had never happened? Detailed, careful explanations? A scolding? Sympathetic affection? Oh God, she silently cried out, wishing she had never set eyes on Guyon and, through her own widow's starved needs, seduced her way into his bed, only to find the seduction reversed.

Heulwen was rubbing her eyes and complaining querulously. Rhosyn bent her mind away from the problem of Eluned and into persuading her youngest child to take a nap beneath one of the skins.

Two greenfinches flickered across the clearing, their song a chitter of alarm. A horse snorted and, throwing up its head, nickered towards the trees, ears pricked. One of the men put down his drink and went to the restless beast.

Sounds of something crashing blindly through the undergrowth came clearly to their ears, and then a gasping cry. Rhosyn sprang to her feet, filled with a sudden lurching dread. She covered Heulwen, by now asleep, with another of the skins and dragged a nearby dead branch in front of the child, concealing her as best she could.

Swords scraped from scabbards, shields were reached for and cursingly slipped onto men's arms. One of the escort turned to give Rhosyn a command but she ignored him, transfixed by horror as she watched her son stagger towards them, hugging the trees for support, his tunic saturated with blood.

'Rhys!' she screamed and, lifting her skirts, started to run towards him. A young serjeant, Eric's brother, caught her back, expostulating.

The boy looked in the direction of her voice, but his eyes were blind, his mouth working, pouring blood. 'Mam!' he gasped frothily and then, choking, 'The *Cwmni Annwn!*'

'Rhys!' she screamed again and tore free of her captor to run stumbling, hampered by her skirts to where he had fallen face-down in the turning crisp leaves. He was dead. She could see the rents in his clothing where a blade had been plunged and the blood was hot and dark on her hands.

Bent over her son, she did not hear the horrified warning yelled by her escort, nor see the riders of the wild hunt advancing through the trees, following the trail of lifesblood to its source.

De Lacey's destrier leaned into the slope and behind him his retainers and mercenaries goaded their own mounts to keep pace. They were approaching a fork in the road where one of the traditional drovers' ways crossed the Roman road to Shrewsbury. The former traversed two of the Ravenstow holdings, threaded across the lower end of the Thorneyford estate, crossed the dyke there and the border, and continued on towards Llangollen. The pack ponies used it regularly. Wool and coal, iron, copper and lead came out of Wales. Corn, cloth and luxury goods went in.

The track as they turned onto it was potholed and scarred with a hogsback of grass down the centre between the twin valleys carved by the wheels of the drovers' wains. The bay stallion bent to snatch a mouthful of grass from the side of the track. De Lacey squirmed in the saddle. Sweat had trickled into the declivity of his buttocks and was making him sore and uncomfortable, the price a man paid for the security of a thirty-pound mail hauberk reaching from collarbone to knee, bulked and padded beneath by a thick gambeson of linen quilting.

Tonight, they would lodge at Thorneyford and begin preparing it for siege. Arundel was lost and with it their aid from Normandy and Flanders. De Belleme had pulled back to Shrewsbury. The battle for the marches was about to begin. He held out his hand for the wineskin, took it impatiently from Hakon, the captain of his guard and, withdrawing the stopper, gulped down several warm, sour mouthfuls before spitting the last one out. His stomach had been queasy all week. It had nothing to do with fear, he told himself, it was just that siege rations and lack of sleep griped a man's gut.

He thrust the stopper back into the skin and pushed it back at Hakon. His sister had lands in Normandy. De Belleme had promised him a fief there if they had to retreat beyond the channel, but he had begun to grow wary of his overlord's promises. Most of them were mere expediencies, broken in the same breath. But what else was left? He had no delusions. If he yielded up his keeps to Henry, they would be taken away from him and given elsewhere, probably to Guyon of Ravenstow or Miles FitzRenard as a reward for services rendered, for charges brought and witnesses to swear.

'I should have finished it at the boar hunt,' de Lacey said

aloud. His mount, jaws working, did not flicker its ears in response, but turned them pricked instead towards the trees bordering the road. De Lacey tensed, hand going automatically to his hilt.

'God's blood, a wench!' cried one of the knights, lips parting in a delightful, gap-toothed grin.

De Lacey looked at the child who, panting and weeping, had emerged onto the road in front of them, her blue gown and long black hair festooned with bits of twig and bramble burs, her delicate, dainty features streaked with powdered tree bark and wild emotion. He forgot the discomfort. His testicles tightened and his penis began to rise and thicken. His heart bumped erratically in the base of his throat.

'Let her be, Giles, she's mine!' he croaked, voice parched with lust. It was his particular preference, innocent, prepubescent girls, buds as yet to blossom with unsullied, tight, perfumed cores.

'Where'd she come from?'

'Let's find out, shall we?' he gave a thin, cruel smile and kicked the bay into motion.

Eluned saw them coming, the foremost horse surging powerfully, the mailed man astride wearing a snarl that would have done justice to a wolf. Sunlight sparkled on harness and armour. She saw very clearly the red diamond surrounding the boss of his shield and the decorative tassels on his knee-high boots.

She screamed and whirled to run back the way she had come, all chagrin flown in terror but, although fleet of foot, she was still only a child and hampered by her full skirt and undergown, and the trees that slowed the pursuing riders tripped her with their roots and fallen branches.

Walter de Lacey was an excellent horseman. The bay twisted and turned deftly between the trees, outflanked her and drew across her path. Eluned flashed sideways and so did the horse, bringing his rider parallel. De Lacey leaned over the saddle and hauled her up across his cantle, fingers taking purchase in her leather girdle. Eluned gasped and struggled but, face down, midriff butted by the pommel, lungs starved, there was very little she could do save wriggle like a landed fish.

De Lacey admired the taut, small curve of her buttocks, peach-round as she writhed. Caught in the mesh of her tossing hair, the ivory necklace shone glossily. He lifted it on two fingers and examined it. Simple. Expensive. The child was pleading in Welsh and her gown was a well cut Flemish cloth. Merchant he classed her, and fairly well off.

'Hakon, take her, and paws off!' he commanded his captain, and transferred his prize across. 'There's more profit to this venture, I'll hazard.'

Hakon took the girl over his saddle. She tried to bite him and he swore but, mindful of de Lacey's instruction, instead of striking her he removed his cloak and parcelled her up in it so that she was as helpless as a caterpillar in a bird's beak.

He was quite unprepared for Rhys's assault or the knife that buried itself deep in his arm, and thus dropped his bundle with an anguished howl.

'Eluned, run!' Rhys shrieked, retrieving his knife to stab again.

She was dazed from the fall, but staggered gamely to her feet and tried to do as he had commanded. Hard hands closed again around her belt and hauled her up. She was sick. Hakon, bleeding freely, wrestled the knife from Rhys's grip and used it, driving it deep into the boy's body and then thrusting him off into the thick leaf mould of the forest floor.

Rhys rolled over and scrambled up and, dazed and bleeding heavily, began to stumble away through the trees.

De Lacey smiled and deliberately held back for a few minutes, caressing Eluned's buttocks. 'It makes a change from hunting boar,' he said softly.

CHAPTER 25

SOME SHORT WHILE after Rhosyn and her escort rode out, Judith fetched her cloak and departed Ravenstow with her own escort, her destination one of Ravenstow's fiefs. The lord of the small, beholden keep at Farnden had recently died and she had promised his son, the inheritor of the holding and its military obligations, that she would attend a mass in the church there for the soul of his father before he rode out to rejoin Guyon. Also, there were the customs and rights of the new tenancy to be confirmed and the oath of fealty to be sworn.

Thomas D'Alberin was a pleasant, not particularly bright young man. Bovine of both looks and nature, he knew his feudal duties, was able to perform them stoically and well, but lacked the imagination or ambition ever to make anything more than the insignificant lord of a minor holding. That was no reason, however, to neglect him. A horseshoe nail was just as important as the horse and Judith gave him her sincere attention for the duration of the visit.

The mass was performed in the tiny Saxon church and attended by all members of the keep and the villagers of most senior authority. Alms were distributed and bread. Dinner was eaten outside in the orchard, the trestles spread beneath the lush young summer green of the trees and their hard, tight fruits. It was very pleasant and a poignant far cry from the war in the south, so much so that it brought a lump to Judith's throat and tears to her eyes, and she had to set about reassuring a worried sir Thomas that she was really all right.

About the time of nones, her business completed, she made her farewells to sir Thomas and set out for home. Eye on the dwindling height of the sun, de Bec took the short cut across the drovers' road and through the forest to reach the main track.

The day had been hot and the green forest air was thickly humid, catching earthily in the throat and nostrils as it was breathed. Judith's shift clung to her body. Beneath her veil her head itched as if it harboured a thicket of fleas. Now and then a rivulet of sweat trickled down between her breasts or tickled her spine and her thighs were chaffed by the constant rubbing of the saddle. She thought with longing of a refreshing, tepid tub, of a thin silk robe and a goblet of wine, chill from the keep well.

Such thoughts set her to bitter-sweet rememberings of a raw November night, of drinking yellow wine in a bathtub, of Guyon's eyes luminous with laughter and desire, and her longing abruptly changed direction. Heat moistened her loins. She shifted uncomfortably in the saddle and bit her lip as tears returned to prickle her lids. It had been so long since there had been the time or opportunity for such sweet, frivolous dalliance. The inclination had been swamped – or so she thought – by a combination of worry and sheer physical exhaustion. There had been odd occasions together, but snatched and unsatisfactory because there was no real enjoyment in assuaging a need that intruded inconveniently upon other needs and was tainted with fear.

Two pigeons clapped past them and a blackbird scolded. When a spotted woodpecker followed them, caakering alarm, de Bec ceased lounging at ease on her left to reach for the shield that was slung from its guige on his saddle bow. These were not birds immediately startled by their approach, but already alarmed and winging from some other, earlier disturbance. This particular band of woodland was within Guyon's

311

jurisdiction but at the north-western edge lay a boggy ditch marking the Welsh border and the standing stones on the south-western side were the boundary between Ravenstow and Thorneyford. It was for the latter reason in particular that de Bec muttered soft imprecations as he drew his sword and ordered his men to surround Judith.

A horse flickered through the trees in front of them. Both Judith and de Bec recognized the striking red sorrel immediately, for it was one of Guyon's own crossbreeds, belonging to Eric's younger brother Godric who had been in command of Rhosyn's escort. A cold hand squeezed Judith's heart, for although Godric was in the saddle, he was hunched over, clutching the pommel and did not answer to their hail. The horse, however, threw up its white-blazed head and, nickering at sight of its own kind, picked its way towards them.

De Bec leaned to grasp the reins in his gauntleted fist. 'Godric, what happened man?' he demanded, voice sharp with shock.

The young man raised his eyes but remained hunched over. 'De Lacey,' he croaked in strongly accented Anglo-French. 'Hit us out of nowhere . . . Too many of them. We never stood a chance . . . I managed to save the little lass.' He swayed dangerously, face a grey, graven mask. Against his body, tied within his cloak for security, Heulwen began to cry and push against her confines, face as flushed as her tangled fiery crown of curls.

A greying knight unfastened the child and lifted her out of Godric's cloak, then uttered an oath of consternation as he saw that she was smeared in blood from head to toe.

'Not hers, mine,' husked Godric and tumbled out of the saddle to sprawl unconscious at their feet. Judith dismounted in a flurry of skirts and bent beside the young serjeant to examine his injuries. He had taken a nasty slash to the midriff. Fortunately, as far as she could see, it had not pierced the gut, but it was still deep and it had bled a great deal. She raised her overgown and tunic and started to tear strips from her shift to make a temporary binding until he could be stitched. Two of her escort set about constructing a crude stretcher out of branches and horse blankets.

Heulwen sobbed and screamed for her mother in broken Welsh. Luckily, the guard who held her had five children of his own and was used to dealing with the fickle storms of infant temper. A borderman, he also spoke fluent Welsh and now soothed Heulwen in that language until she had calmed into the odd hiccuped sob.

Godric's eyelids flickered. Judith put her hand on his brow. 'Rest easy now,' she soothed, 'help is here.'

'Mistress, we could do nothing,' he fretted, his throat working. She held a skin to his lips and he took a jerky swallow of the warm, tannin-flavoured wine. 'De Lacey outnumbered us at least four to one. The child was asleep beneath some skins. They missed her and they left me for dead . . . Dancer bolted in the fray but he came back when I called him.' He clenched his teeth and groaned in the twisting grip of pain that Judith, without her medicines, was powerless to ease.

'How far back, son?' De Bec's tufted eyebrows drew together in a worried scowl.

'No more than a mile . . . just off the road. We had stopped to eat and they came out of the trees at us.' He closed his eyes and swallowed, mind burning with images that would leave their brand on his soul forever.

'Are they on your trail?' De Bec looked anxiously round.

'No, sir. I lay for dead and they thought me so. I heard de Lacey say that there was less gain than he had hoped and they had best be on their way . . . Thorneyford they were headed for . . . Myself and the child are the only survivors . . . The other little maid . . . Oh Christ, they took her with them!' He gasped, face taking on a greenish tinge. Judith fought down her own sick horror to lay a steadying hand back on his brow.

'Lie quiet, Godric,' she said gently and raised her head to

313

meet de Bec's grey granite stare. There was no way their own troop could pursue and the attack was more than three hours old. De Lacey would be safe within his keep by now.

'The bodies will need to be brought back to Ravenstow,' she said. The coldness of shock and fear, the knowledge of what had yet to be done, made her feel queasy and tearful, but she refused to let it show. 'We had best bring them away with us now before the wolves and foxes have their chance at them.'

De Bec looked beyond her smooth face to the fluttering of the pulse in her throat and its jerky movement as she swallowed. 'My lady, it will not be a sight to be viewed save by necessity, and Godric and the child should be got to Ravenstow as soon as possible.'

Judith considered for a moment, then nodded curtly, but with obvious relief. There was nothing to be gained by going to the scene of the slaughter herself. De Bec could note the details for Guyon and the sheriff. There would be enough trauma in washing the corpses and laying them out decently . . . and in writing this news to Guyon. What was she going to say? How was she going to face and tell him when he returned? It did not bear thinking about and yet, like the laying out, it had to be done and it was her responsibility.

The immediate reality proved far worse than Judith could ever have imagined. She stitched Godric's wound, poulticed it with mouldy bread and then dosed him with poppy syrup and left him to sleep. Heulwen kept crying for her mother and Eluned but, apart from being fractious and bewildered, seemed none the worse for her ordeal.

Judith's own ordeal began when de Bec rode in, his face the same colour as his beard and eyes, his expression so stiff that he might have been one of the ten corpses bundled in cloaks and roped like game across the backs of some pack ponies borrowed from Thomas d'Alberin. The men who rode with de Bec all wore variations of that same look on their faces and, when the bodies were brought to the chapel, Judith quickly understood why. The abomination beneath Rhosyn's cloak bore no resemblance whatsoever to the woman she had encountered yesterday. The spirit had flown and the mortal body was so horribly mutilated that it was difficult to know if it had once been human at all.

Her belly heaved. She clapped her hand to her mouth and staggered to the waste shaft where she was sick to the pit of her soul. It was not just murder, it was obscene desecration.

De Bec gently touched her elbow, wordlessly handed her a small horn cup of usquebaugh and waited until, choking and spluttering on its unaccustomed strength, she had downed it.

Shaking, Judith leaned herself against his iron-clad solidity. 'He is not a man, he is a devil!' she shuddered.

De Bec folded a mailed arm around her quivering shoulders and felt a wash of paternal protectiveness. 'Have you sent forth a messenger to lord Guyon yet?' he rumbled. 'He needs to be here.'

Judith shook her head. 'I don't know what to write,' she gulped. 'And I don't know if he is still at Arundel.'

'Tell him nought, only that he is needed swiftly. A messenger will find him sooner or later. I'll get FitzWalter to do it for you.'

Judith sniffed and he felt her stiffen against him, then pull away. 'No,' she said firmly. 'I'll do it myself. I was just being a coward.' She looked up at him and a wan smile strained her lips. 'You feel like a rock because you are one.'

De Bec's eyes actually began to sting. He blinked several times quickly. In all but name, he had regarded Judith as his daughter from the day of her birth and to see her struggle with her fears and doubts and force them down beneath her will filled him with a fierce burst of tenderness and pride. He could have crushed that indomitable slender form between his two hands – it did not seem possible that it could house such strength.

He watched her return to the horror in the chapel and

murmur to the priest, her face so pale that every freckle stood out as a deep, golden mottle, her manner composed, and knew that if he was a rock, then she was surely as resilient and strong as the best sword steel.

CHAPTER 26

GUYON SHIFTED IN the high saddle and loosened the
reins to let Arian pick his way between the trees.
The afternoon light was as golden-green as the best
French wine and as warm as new milk. Coins of sunlight and
leaf shadows scattered and sparkled among the troop of men
who rode with steady haste towards Ravenstow and prepara-
tion for war in the marches.

Arundel was theirs and de Belleme now effectively cut off
from his support abroad. Now the King intended to move
upon the chain of grim Shropshire strongholds with the
intention of clearing them out one by one and Guyon was
returning to Ravenstow to support him in that endeavour.

As they emerged from the trees onto the waste land, all
eyes were drawn to the gleaming lime-washed walls of the
huge keep dominating Ravenstow crag.

Guyon's stare upon this, the core of his earldom, was both
admiring and rueful. It was de Belleme's design and it
followed that winkling the Earl of Shrewsbury out of the
other strongholds he had also designed, but held in his own
hand, was going to prove difficult. God knew, Arundel had
been a tough enough nut to crack.

A cowherd louted to Guyon and tapped the cattle over
their mottled backs with a hazel goad to keep them moving.
His dog went wagging to investigate the horsemen and was
whistled sharply back to place. At the mill, the miller was
transferring sacks of flour onto one of the keep's oxen-drawn
wains and paused to wipe his brow and tug his forelock at the
passing soldiers, cuffing his brawny, gormless son into a

similar respect. His wife ceased beating a smock on a stone at the stream to bob a curtsey, her expression apprehensive. She groped down to the rosary at her waist and raised it to kiss the cross attached.

Guyon eyed the woman curiously and wondered anew at the speed with which news of impending war travelled. He did not believe that de Belleme would attack Ravenstow – he was too busy strengthening his own fortifications – but the Welsh were always ready to harry, loot and burn and de Belleme had several Welsh vassals who would be only too pleased to do just that, stocking their winter larders at the expense of their marcher foes.

The drawbridge was down to admit them, the yawning mouth of the gatehouse arch behind the raised teeth of the portcullis, black as the pit of hell. Guyon shook the reins, urging Arian to a trot and they emerged again into the late sunshine of the shed-crowded bailey.

A woman was feeding twigs beneath a giant outdoor cauldron, the girl beside her plucking a wrung chicken to go into the pot. She looked up at the men, nudged her companion and made the sign of the cross upon her breast. The older woman straightened her back and crossed herself too, her eyes full of pity on Guyon before she turned to stare at the forebuilding from which Judith was running.

Cadi barked and sprang joyously to greet her, tail swishing like a whip. Guyon dismounted and threw the reins to a groom. The young man said nothing but, with a look over his broad, leather shoulder at Judith, dipped his head and led the grey away to his stall.

Guyon watched his wife hurry towards him and felt a lightening of his spirit. Her hair trapped the oblique sunlight and glowed like molten bronze and her face was becomingly flushed from the effort of running down several flights of twisting stairs and across the ward.

And then she was facing him and his admiration fell away as he saw the look in her eyes and the set of her mouth.

'Rhosyn's dead,' she said without preamble. 'I have been wondering how to tell you, but there is no way to make it any easier.'

He looked at her blankly. The sun was warm on the back of his neck but suddenly he felt cold all over.

'They were attacked on our land, on the Llangollen drovers' road yestereve. I gave her the escort she requested but they were all cut down. Father Jerome is in the chapel attending to what needs to be done . . .' Her tongue tripped and stumbled because she did not know what she could say. 'Guyon, come within and I will try to tell you the rest.' She laid hold of his sleeve. 'Heulwen is safe. Eric's brother Godric saved her. They were the only two to survive . . .'

Blankly, he let himself be led. Most of her words washed over him like an incoming tide, leaving only a residue of scouring grit and the words *Rhosyn's dead* indelibly printed on his mind.

Judith gave him wine, lacing it liberally with usquebaugh, and poured a neat draught of the latter for herself. He sat down mechanically, looked at the cup, set it aside and raised disbelieving eyes to her.

'Tell me again,' he commanded. 'I don't know what you said.'

She swallowed her usquebaugh in one hard gulp and told him. His face never changed but, as she finished, he bent it into his slender hands and muttered something soft and indistinct against his palms. Judith bit her lip, put out her hand to touch his shoulder, but withdrew it again and folded it around her waist. She was at a total loss for words. Glib platitudes did not apply to rape and butchery. 'I am sorry, Guy,' she said miserably. 'Truly I am.'

He did not respond.

'At least you have Heulwen.'

He looked up at that, uncovering his eyes. They were dull, dark like those of a corpse. 'Yes,' he agreed tonelessly through the stiff lips of a death mask, 'at least I have Heulwen.' And

319

then he laughed and shook his head and buried it again in his hands.

Judith knelt beside him, her arm across his mail-clad shoulder. 'I wish I knew what to say, or how to ease the pain, but I don't . . .'

'Then don't say anything,' he muttered and, after a moment, withdrawing from her grasp, he stood up and moved towards the door.

'Where are you going?'

'To the chapel, where else?'

'No, Guyon!' She sprang after him. 'Wait at least until you have rested. I'll have a tub prepared and see to your comfort.'

'Do you think I care about that?' he demanded huskily.

'No, but I do.' She laid hold of his sleeve.

'Let me go,' he grated and, shrugging her off, continued on his way.

'Guyon, no . . . It's not . . . I mean . . .' She drew a shuddering breath and momentarily closed her eyes. 'She did not die cleanly.'

'Stop treating me like a damned nursling!' he snarled and lengthened his stride.

Tears prickled Judith's lids. She refused to give in to them and instead caught up her cloak and went after him. He might not be a nursling but he was inadequately prepared for what would greet him in the chapel. She knew, oh Jesu, she knew too well. It was imprinted on her memory forever.

Guyon looked at the row of shrouded pallets laid out before the altar, ten in all, white mounds of recent humanity.

Father Jerome hovered anxiously in the background, unable to gain a foothold on the expressionless mask of the young earl's face. 'A terrible business,' he ventured, 'but they are at peace now.'

Guyon drew back one of the sheets to look upon the face of Herluin FitzSimon, a promising young man from the Oxley holdings who had served with him during the Welsh campaign and who would one day, in his middle years, have captained a keep garrison. All wasted now on the edge of a sword. The linen shift in which he had been clothed did not cover the gaping wound in his throat or the sword slash that had laid his face open to the bone.

'At peace, are they?' Guyon enquired icily, replacing the sheet.

Father Jerome blenched. 'You must not doubt it, my son,' he said, putting out his hand to comfort.

Guyon stepped aside. 'I would rather you left me alone,' he said, tone flat and calm, with no indication of the raging current beneath.

The priest hesitated, but was forestalled from further effort by a gentle touch on his arm and, turning he found the lady Judith standing there. She was as pale as a winding sheet but at least her eyes were alive and he could see the thoughts within them.

'Go to,' she murmured. 'It may be that he will need you later. I will go surety for the nonce.'

Relieved, the priest pressed her arm and quietly left her alone with Guyon. Judith squared her shoulders and went to her husband. He was staring down at Rhys. The boy's eyes were weighted down with silver pennies, those retrieved three summers ago from de Belleme's saddlebags, for it had been impossible to close them by other means and the look of terror in them had frozen Judith's blood.

'If they had not overlooked Godric, the bodies would not have been discovered for some time. I was not expecting the escort back for at least three days and no search party would have been sent out before five.'

'You are telling me that this is fortunate?' he whispered, drawing the sheet back over Rhys's face, the cadence of his voice husky and dangerous.

'It could have been much worse. At least they were saved being despoiled by foxes and crows. Heulwen owes her life to Godric.'

'Sensible Judith,' he flung at her like an insult.

'Guyon stop it, stop shutting me out!'

'Do you interfere for pleasure or because you cannot help yourself?' he demanded savagely. 'In Christ's name, Judith, leave me alone!'

'In Christ's name, no!' she retorted with equal vehemence. 'I'll not be your scapegoat!' Going to the last pallet, she drew back the cover herself. 'Look and have done and come away!' she said brutally.

He flinched and went the colour of putty. Despite the work of Judith and the priest, Rhosyn's body was still not a sight for the squeamish. She had fought hard for her life and her beauty was marred by the livid bruises and distortions of strangulation. Her body beneath the shift was mauled and mutilated and her braids hacked off. Judith covered her up again.

Guyon swallowed jerkily. 'Where's Eluned?' he asked, fighting his gorge.

'De Lacey took her with him.' Judith compressed her lips.

Guyon went paler still at the implications. He did not need to imagine what de Lacey would do to the child. He knew. Too clearly and starkly he knew.

'My lord . . .' said father Jerome and was barged aside before he could utter more by a wild-eyed, travel-stained young man.

'Where is she?' he asked hoarsely, his French so thickly accented with Welsh and filled with raw emotion that at first Judith stared at him without comprehension. His gaze flickered over the row of bodies and the vigilant wax candles and his breathing stopped, then was drawn again in a harsh rasp. 'My Rhosyn, where is she?'

'*Your* Rhosyn?' Judith's expression sharpened. 'Then you must be Prys . . .'

'I went to fetch her father for burial and now I am told that I must bury her too, and the lad . . .' The wild eyes fixed on Guyon with bleak loathing. 'Couldn't you leave her alone? If not for you, she'd still be alive, aye and my wife!'

322

Guyon winced as his soul, flayed raw by the lash of guilt, took another brutal stroke. 'I did not know that she was coming to Ravenstow,' he defended. 'If I had, I would have stopped her. Christ knows, I tried to warn her.'

'You should have tried harder!'

'How much harder?' Guyon snarled. 'How much would you have tolerated? Short of locking her up, there was nothing I could ever have done to hold her.'

'Then what the hell was she doing here at Ravenstow?'

'She came to invite us to your wedding,' Judith said, trying to calm the sparks that were crackling in the air, threatening to flare into obscene violence and violate God's altar and the dead who sought sanctuary there, 'and to talk of Heulwen's future.' It was not the whole truth, but she felt no remorse at withholding what could not safely be said.

'Neither matter was so pressing as to warrant this!' Prys spat, gesturing towards the row of corpses, and it came to Guyon that the young Welshman was as filled with guilt as himself, for he too had not been there to prevent this dreadful crime and anger was a bolt hole to be dived into rather than face the unfaceable.

Prys pushed past him and Judith. 'Which one?' he demanded. Judith opened her mouth to say that he should not look, but Guyon stalled her by pointing to the nearest shroud. 'Walter de Lacey was the man responsible,' he said softly. 'I'm going to tear Thorneyford down stone by stone and make of that keep a burial mound.'

The young man drew back the sheet and fell to his knees at the side of the bier. 'Ah Rhosyn *cariad*, no!' he cried, aghast. Father Jerome came forward and set a comforting arm around his shoulders, although there was nothing that could comfort the sight laid out before their eyes.

After a moment that seemed to stretch into eternity, the priest gently covered up Rhosyn's corpse. Prys shuddered and crossed himself, the gesture blind, automatic. Then, body trembling, riven by the violent strokes of his heartbeat, he rose to his feet and stared at Guyon.

'I'm a merchant,' he said, voice unsteady with unshed grief, and savage. 'I wear a sword for my protection, but I'm clumsy using it . . .'

Judith drew a sharp, frightened breath, thinking for a mad instant that the Welshman was going to challenge Guyon to a trial by combat in order to assuage his agony. Guyon must have thought so too, for she felt him tense beside her, felt him shift his weight, ready to move.

'I want you to teach me to wield it properly. If you are going to march on Thorneyford, then I am coming with you. They told me outside . . . about Eluned. No worse can be done to Rhosyn, she's beyond it now . . . but God alone knows what that child may be suffering . . .' He choked, turned aside, spat.

Guyon compressed his lips, controlling his own urge to be sick. 'Be welcome,' he said, when he could speak. 'I'll lend you a hauberk from the armoury.'

The chapel was cold and almost entirely dark. The candles upon the altar and around the biers made splashes of light in the pre-dawn blackness. Guyon stared at the flames until his vision blurred and repeated the Latin words he had known by rote since childhood. Rote without meaning. The reality was the flagged church floor pressing cold and hard against his numb knees, the smell of incense cloying his nostrils and Rhosyn's stiff, waxen, desecrated body stretched out before him.

He had tried time and again to believe that it was a dream, nothing more than a nightmare from which he would awaken, sweating with relief. *Ave Maria, gratia plenia* . . . He had only to lift the linen sheet to know that it was not. Like a wolf he could feel it gathering within him, a raging howl to the moon, but he was a man and he subdued it, brooding upon revenge.

The candles flickered in a draught and light rippled over the bier, giving the winding sheet the momentary illusion of movement. The hairs rose along his spine and he stopped breathing. A gentle hand squeezed his shoulder and he jumped and stared round, startled at his wife, a smothered profanity on his lips.

'Guyon, come away,' she entreated softly. 'It is all but dawn now and if you are to lead the men, you need to be rested. Prys sought his pallet an hour ago.' She held out his cloak and he saw that she was wearing her own over the gold wool gown of yesterday. She had been kneeling in vigil with him most of the night, but he had not marked her leaving, or indeed Prys's, the world revolving around his own depth of pain.

'There is a tub prepared above. You must be frozen stiff.'

He was silent, staring at her. The words *sensible Judith* floated within the disjointed flotsam of the upper layers of his mind and he was suddenly aware of exhaustion seeping through his body as the coldness of the flagged floor was seeping into his knees. 'To the soul,' he muttered, genuflecting to the altar and rising stiffly to his feet. 'To the pit of my soul.'

Docile as a tame dog, staggering slightly with weariness, he let her lead him up the stairs to the main bedchamber. She dismissed the maids with a swift gesture and, as the curtain dropped behind the last one, knelt to unbuckle his swordbelt.

He stared down at the veil and circlet crowning her bent head and the snaking length of her braids. As the belt slipped into her hands and she rose and laid it aside, he turned her by the shoulder and tipped up her chin to examine her face. The dim rushlight concealed some of the ravages, but not all. Mauve shadows marred the clarity of her eyes and the bones of her face were sharp, suddenly reminding him of the first time he had seen her.

He was a sleepwalker, jolted awake. 'Jesu, Judith,' he said on a broken whisper and pulled her tight and close. She was crushed so hard against the iron links of his mail that she could scarcely breathe, but would not have broken the embrace for anything, needing the contact as fiercely as Guyon did.

'I met her on the day before it happened,' she said into his breast, the metal cold on her lips. 'God's love, Guy, I was so jealous, I wanted to scratch out her eyes, but I couldn't. She was so . . . so honest, and she did not deserve what they did to her! . . .' She burst into tears and gulpingly tried to stop herself, digging her fingers so hard into Guyon's hauberk that the rivets cut deep semi-circles against her knuckles.

'Judith love, don't!' Guyon pleaded hoarsely, kissing her wet face, his own eyes scalding and full. 'Do you want to break me?'

'I can't help it!' she sobbed. 'Since that night in Southwark, we have not had a moment to ourselves that has not been marred by fear and strain and war!' Her clenched fist struck his hauberk and split the bone-taut skin.

Guyon siezed her hand in one of his and clamped the other around her waist, holding her, aware through his own shuddering of hers.

At length, sniffling and tear-drenched, she pulled away to look at him. 'I meant to be calm and strong when you came home,' she gulped in self-disgust, 'and instead I shriek like a harpy. The tub is growing cold and you are still in your mail.'

'Never mind the tub, *fy cath fach*,' he said through chattering teeth, his whole body shaking with cold and the delayed reaction of shock and fatigue. 'I have lived without creature comforts for so long, that another night and day does not matter. Just help me unarm and come to bed.'

Judith considered him, wondering whether she should persuade him to eat some food and decided that, for the nonce, she just did not possess the energy. The battle could be taken up again once they had both slept.

'Judith,' he pleaded and stretched out his hand to her. She looked at his lean, tremor-shaken fingers and with a soft cry returned to his embrace, stood tightly enclosed within it for a brief moment, then set about removing his hauberk.

CHAPTER 27

THE DAWN SKY on the horizon was barred grey and cream and oystershell, striated like Italian marble. Smoke from cooking fires pungently hazed the immediate air. Fatty bacon sizzled. A loaded wain of fresh loaves from Ravenstow was creaking into the camp. Men were hearing mass, their bellies rumbling.

Guyon slitted his eyes and watched the mangonel launch another boulder at Thorneyford's curtain wall. There came the crash of stone splintering on stone and a high-pitched scream from within.

'It is a great pity to see such fine new defences reduced to rubble before we take them,' Eric murmured at his side.

'Do you have a better suggestion?' Guyon growled. 'If not, go and find out what's taking those sodding miners so long and get me a cup of wine before my throat closes!'

Eric lifted long-suffering eyes towards heaven and fetched the latter first accompanied by a mutton pasty and, face studiedly impassive, went in search of the sapper's foreman. Lord Guyon had been the very devil to please of late, the knowledge of what lay behind those walls goading him to frustrated rage like a dog-baited bear in a market place. Unable to come to grips with de Lacey, he vented his spleen on those around him instead. It was understandable, of course. All of them were sickened at what had happened to Rhosyn and her escort. Casualties of war were one thing; wanton destruction and rapine of a child were another, especially when the victims were people with whom you had shared companionship and hospitality and had always complaisantly assumed you would see many times again.

Having found the foreman of the sappers who had paused his endeavours to eat his breakfast, Eric asked him Guyon's question.

The small man wiped his earth-smeared hand across his mouth and grimaced. 'We been working all night fast as we can, see. What does he expect, miracles?'

These men were a law unto themselves, their invaluable skill setting them above the conventions of rank. Mainly Welshmen and brought up to the craft since birth, working open-cast coal seams, they were digging a tunnel underground to a point directly beneath the bailey wall, supporting their work with wooden props. Once completed, the tunnel would be filled with pitch-soaked furze and dry wood and bladders of pork fat, then set ablaze. As the props burned away, the tunnel would cave in, bringing down the wall below which it was dug, in this case a section of the eastern bailey wall. It was dirty, difficult work and the rate of pay reflected it. Dai ap Owain and the men literally beneath him earned a shilling a day, which was as much as a fully accoutred knight could expect to command.

'What do I tell him, Dai?'

'Tell him we'll be done by prime and that we need more oil and brushwood because the tunnel is longer than we thought.'

Eric looked doubtful. 'No sooner?' he mistakenly asked, envisioning Guyon's displeasure.

'If my lord desires such a thing, let him come down and dig himself. *A fo ben, bid bont!*'

Eric retreated. 'Prime,' he said to Guyon, 'and they need tinder and oil. I'll go and see to it,' and he disappeared before Guyon could flay him alive with the edge of his tongue.

By mid-morning, the first grey light of dawn had brightened into a strong blue heat and the arrows that swished between besieger and besieged were hard black shafts raining down from a cloudless sky. Guyon flickered a glance at his archers.

Half of them had set aside their bows and had begun preparing their short swords and round shields for the imminent assault. This was the lull, the still before the storm, a moment stretched with tension like the twisted ropes on a wound mangonel. Guyon's fingers twitched on Arian's reins. He made a conscious effort to relax them and as the stallion danced, soothed him with soft words and a smoothing hand on the sleek, silk neck.

It had taken a month to come this far, and not without trials. Walter de Lacey might be a fool in the political sense, might be a child-molesting murdering pervert, but it did not prevent him from being a skilled soldier and tactician. Their siege machines had been sabotaged by a daring night raid and a couple of attempts to take the keep with scaling ladders had been completely repelled. The enmity was intense, each foot-hold gained paid for in blood.

Guyon rubbed his sweating palms on his chausses. He had never wanted a thing so much in his life as to take Thorney-ford here and now and tear its occupant apart piece by little piece. He did not think of Eluned. To have done so now would have overset his balance completely and thus far he had kept it well on the level.

Over at the water butts two sappers were swilling down, their bodies lithe, hard and small. He had never met a man of the trade much above five feet in height. Indeed Dai, their foreman, frequently stood on a mounting block or a keg so that he could address Guyon at eye level. Fiercely independent and forthright, Dai saw no reason to back down from a point of view just because he lacked stature, and the men who knew him had long since ceased to make the mistake of patronizing him.

He was at the mine now, supervising the blaze which had been kindled half an hour since. Guyon switched his hungry gaze again to Thorneyford's defences, a muscle bunching and releasing in his jaw. The stone curtain wall had replaced a wooden palisade about ten years ago when Welsh raids had been particularly savage and the original wooden keep had been rebuilt in stone and now stood three levels high. It did not approach the impregnable grandeur of Ravenstow – few strongholds did – but it was certainly stout enough to repel the Welsh and several weeks of determined, conventional siege.

'It's going to go,' Dai ap Owain lilted, materializing out of nowhere to stand at Guyon's stirrup.

Guyon uttered a soft, triumphant oath and signalled his captains to take up their places if they were not already there and make ready their men. They knew what was to be done. Plans had been discussed last night and in more detail this morning while they waited for the miners to complete their work. If any man bungled now, it was his own fault, but Guyon did not anticipate problems. Eric, de Bec and Hubert Martin were all experienced, dependable men, quite capable of extricating themselves and those beneath their command if a crisis arose.

He looked over his shoulder. Godric was guarding his back, his sorrel fretting and dancing, as anxious as his rider for the action to be upon them. Beside Godric, astride one of the remounts, sat Prys ap Adda, sword drawn, shield held in tight to his body. For all his declaration that he was a clumsy swordsman, Guyon had found little lacking. The Welshman might not have the bulk of the men he would be facing, but he was as fast in motion and ferocity as summer lightning and he, too, had a personal cause to lend vehemence to his sword arm. Had the man been trained to war from birth, Guyon doubted that he could have bested him.

A dull rumbling sound like the roll of summer thunder grew gradually louder and the ground shook. Horses started and shied. The bailey wall collapsed, crashing down into the tunnel, sending loose stones and mortar bounding across the courtyard floor. Smoke and thick amber dust mingled upwards, obscuring the vision. Someone injured by a shard of falling rock was screaming thinly.

'There's pretty for you!' Dai breathed exultantly.

Guyon was not listening. 'Forward!' he roared, flinging all his pent up tension into the cry and, clapping spurs to Arian's flanks, he bolted for the gap.

Himself, Godric and Prys erupted simultaneously through the gaping hole, Guyon driving straight ahead, his companions to right and left. Eyes streaming, lungs choking on the boiling fog they breathed, Guyon rode down three of the defenders who were not swift enought to scatter before his rage. Arian barged past them, felling two among the debris. Guyon cut down the third. The stallion killed one man before he could rise. Guyon brained the other with his shield, dealt with another on a vicious backswing and swung the horse towards the inner bailey, the entrance of which was defended by two huge, iron-bound and studded gates, the thickness of four long fingers and secured on the inside by a massive bar which took the strivings of at least four stout men to lift from its slots.

'*Ravenstow à moi!*' Guyon bellowed and the men of his group disengaged as they could to run or ride with him, leaving those of Eric's command to take care of the outer ward. From the direction of the western wall walk, the wind fed them the yells of de Bec's group on the scaling ladders and the deadly whizz of arbalest quarrels.

'The ram!' Guyon shouted and the order was passed swiftly down the line. The huge oak trunk with its reinforced pointed iron head was run forward by fifteen men-at-arms, coughing and sneezing in the clogged air. One of them screeched and fell, an arrow in his leg. Guyon leaped down from the stallion and took his place, the exhilaration of battle coursing through his veins with the hard pumping of his blood.

'Heave!' he cried and the ram thrust forward and smacked against the gate, boomed and rebounded. 'Back . . . heave . . . back . . . heave . . .' And the rhythm was taken up and echoed down the line. Much to the appreciation of the men, Guyon began a crude song in English about the broaching of a difficult virgin.

A sword clanged on shield as Prys felled a defender. An arbalest bolt crashed into the ram hard by Guyon's thrusting shoulder. A moment later another one swished past his ear.

'Get that sniper! he broke off singing to bellow furiously. 'Before he gets me! No dolts, don't stop! God's death, you weren't as hesitant as this when you hit the London stews last summer!'

Bawdy guffaws, capping remarks and renewed efforts greeted his outburst. The polished, dinted head of the huge oak log pounded against the solid planks. Guyon began to sweat with effort. The breath grew harsh in his throat, torn in through a dry, dust-filled mouth. Through salt-stung eyes he glanced around, assessing the ward. Behind and around them many of the lesser combatants had begun to cry quarter rather than die and Eric's men were effectively dealing with those who preferred to fight on.

'Lord Guyon!' rasped the soldier beside him. Sunlight glinted from his helmet as he jerked his head energetically at the gates. Guyon squinted at him and then at their target, and abruptly stood up and raised his hand. The singing raggedly ceased. The men rested the ram and stared with their lord towards the scuffed, surface-splintered but otherwise intact gates. Guyon warded his shield, wiped his hand across his upper lip and commanded forward his two most accurate archers to train their sights upon the gap as the great, thick planks began to swing inwards.

A dour Saxon in a plain leather gambeson filled the entrance, grey-streaked hair falling to his shoulders, blue tattoos collaring his throat and banding his wrists. He was weaponless, not so much as an eating knife about his person and behind him, like the contents of a stoppered wineskin, cowered and goggled what seemed to be all the inhabitants of the inner ward.

'My lord, we yield ourselves and this keep to your mercy,'

he said formally, eyes betraying all the fear that his deliberate deep voice did not.

Guyon said nothing but gestured the men at his back to slip within and take up defensive positions. Prys spoke to him quickly in Welsh. Guyon answered with a single terse word and did not look away from the Saxon.

'It is no trick, lord,' the man said with dignity. 'I would rather open to you now and spare the lives of good men, than fight to the last drop of blood for such a one as lord Walter. If that is treason, then so be it.' His head came up proudly. There was a rumble of assent from the crowd behind him.

'And just precisely where is lord Walter?' Guyon asked in a hard voice.

He went over the west wall in the early hours of this morning, and his guard with him. I am Wulfwin, the constable's deputy and former bodyguard to lord Ralph. There is no-one else here of any higher authority. You killed the man he left in command on the first charge.' The Saxon shrugged his broad, leather-clad shoulders. 'Lord Walter knew he could not hold this place, not without aid. He's gone down the border to look for it, but with the King's forces stretched across Wenlock Edge, I doubt he'll find it my lord, unless it comes from Wales.'

Guyon's sword hand twitched and the blade came up in response to the rage that was choking his sanity. Over the wall and through his fingers like a fish through a hole in a net. 'Eric,' he said over his shoulder, voice soft and husky. 'Find out who was on duty at the west wall last night and bring him to me.'

Eric acknowledged, a chill running down his spine as if it was his own back that was laid bare to the lash.

Guyon returned his attention to the Saxon. 'What about the child?' he asked.

The man shook his head. 'He is here my lord, but not well, not well at all. He and his mother are both suffering from the bloody flux and like to die of it.'

Guyon gaped at him stupidly. In his mind there was only one child, his Eluned, but of course, to the Saxon, the query could only pertain to de Lacey's heir. 'Not the boy,' he said, 'the Welsh girl.'

The man sucked his teeth. 'My lord, she's dead,' he said with a troubled frown. 'On the first night he brung her. After he'd taken his first pleasure of her, she managed to escape him and jumped off the wall walk yonder.' He looked behind him at the clustered faces shielded by his bulk. 'Nick there was on duty and tried to grab her, but he was too late, just missed the edge of her shift.'

The young man nodded, his adam's apple bobbing up and down, partly at the memory conjured, partly at the expression on Guyon's face.

'No!' Prys denied, head going right and left in violent denial. 'He's lying. It is not true, it is not true!' He lunged at the Saxon who staggered and put up his hands to protect his head. Guyon moved mechanically to intercept, his mind aware of his body's actions, watching in detachment as he separated Prys from his victim and braced himself against the violence of the younger man's onslaught. Then Eric pinioned the Welshman's frenzy and led him aside. As if from a distance, he heard Prys being sick. His own body trembled with a deadly mixture of fury and fatigue. Somewhere at the back of his mind, he supposed that it was a mercy she was dead.

The old man wiped a streak of blood from the corner of his mouth, his eyes going sidelong to the retching Welshman. 'We buried her in the garth near the churchyard, me and Nick. Lord Walter said to throw her in the ditch, but we couldn't do that. Lady Mabel gave us a sheet to wrap her in . . . we did our best, lord.'

Guyon bit the inside of his mouth and forced himself past the white-hot burning barriers to rational thought. 'For which you have my thanks,' he acknowledged. 'It will not go forgotten, I promise you.'

They parted to let him through and he went across the ward and up the forebuilding stairs into the hall, his step no longer light with the spark of battle, but heavy, as though the spurs clipping his heels were fashioned of lead. It was all as nothing. De Lacey still owned life, limb and liberty. He was suddenly aware of the myriad minor cuts and bruises he had sustained in the heat of the fray. The keep had still to be cleared and inspected and shored up against a possible counter attack, and a report made to Henry whom he was to join as soon as all was finished here. Only it was not finished, and perhaps never would be.

Sitting in the rushes a few yards from where he stood, one of the servant's children was playing with her straw doll, expression intent as she decorated its ragged sacking dress with a necklace of delicate ivory daisies.

Guyon put his face in his hands and wept.

CHAPTER 28

WHEN JUDITH ARRIVED at Thorneyford in response to an urgent summons from her husband, it was sunset of the second day and work still hard afoot to repair the worst of the miners' ravages.

In the outer ward, scene of so much previous destruction, small cooking fires burned as normal, tended by serving wenches or soldiers' women and the smells of bread and pottage wafted enticingly on the evening wind. Judith guided Euraidd between the fires. A bat swooped low overhead, casting for insects in the gloaming. Broken arrows and lances littered the ground along with chunks of the curtain wall, sections of it slicked with the congealed fat that had poured molten over the stone during the fury of the siege.

A groom held her mare and Guyon himself stepped from the shadows to lift her from the saddle. His lids were heavy and dust-rimmed. Sweat and battle dirt gleamed in the creases of his skin, but the narrow semblance of a smile glinted before he stooped to give her a scratchy kiss.

'You made good speed, *cath fach*,' he approved. 'I had not thought to see you until tomorrow noon at least.'

'Needs must when the devil drives,' she answered lightly, her eyes full of concern.

The smile departed. 'Yes,' he agreed tonelessly and turned, his arm around her waist, to face the keep. 'Needs must.'

Judith eyed him thoughtfully. His letter had informed her of the victory and asked her to come quickly, little else, and his writing had straggled all over the place, sometimes illegible so that she had hailed the messenger peremptorily back from his refreshment to reassure her that Guyon was not wounded. First qualm of terror dissolved, she had set out to pump the man for the information not contained in the letter.

'I'm sorry, Guy,' she said softly and pressed his arm.

He made a rueful gesture. Faced by the thought of being unable to go on, he had felt a desperate need for the comfort of Judith's forthright, astringent presence and, despite its stilted brevity, the letter had been written straight from the heart. Indeed, had he paused for rational thought at the time of writing, he would have left her at Ravenstow rather than command her here to the shambles of a recent battleground, but yesterday there had been little room for reason.

'I suppose it is for the best,' he owned as they entered the inner ward. 'When you crush a flower it falls to pieces. God's eyes, Judith, if only I had . . .'

'Guyon, no!' She stood on tip-toe to press her palm against his lips. 'You must not shackle yourself with guilt. Rhosyn would have taken her chances on the drover's roads far more recklessly were it not for your warnings. At least you sought to protect her and the children.'

'But it was not enough.'

The stubble prickled her palm as his lips moved. Judith studied him narrowly. 'When did you last eat and sleep?'

Guyon slanted his gaze to meet hers and took her hand away to grasp it in his. 'You sound like my mother,' he said with a hint of weary amusement.

'Who by all accounts was a woman of sense,' she retorted smartly. Her brow wrinkled. 'Why send for me if you did not want to be nagged?'

'Because . . .' He drew a sharp breath as if to change his mind, then stopped and faced her, scraping a hand distractedly through his hair which was in sad need of cutting. 'Oh curse it, Judith, because you are the most infuriating, stubborn and capable woman it has ever been my misfortune to know!'

She burst out laughing. 'Is that a compliment or an insult?'

337

'To be honest, I do not know!' His own mouth curved. He set his hands on her shoulders. 'All I do know, *cath fach*, is that I need you as I've never needed anything in my life.'

Judith gasped and staggered. He was pungent with horse and sweat and smoke. His armour could have stood up of its own accord so strong were the mingled aromas. 'I might also ask you when you last washed!' she said with mock severity.

He slapped her rump. She yelped, looked round self-consciously and saw Eric grinning at them through a similar mask of grime. She turned again to her husband and rubbed her buttocks. 'And why precisely should you need me?' she demanded archly. 'Apart from the obvious.'

He grinned at that, shaking his head at her tart perception, but sobered quickly as they began to walk again. 'Apart from the obvious, *cath fach*, I need you to organize this shambles so that more than just cold pottage and dried meat graces the table. The servants don't know their heads from their heels and lady Mabel is in no fit state to organize them. I do not have the time.'

'Lady Mabel is here?'

'And her son.' A frown drew his brows together over the bridge of his nose. 'They are both sick with the bloody flux. Look at them if you will, but I reckon it is in God's hands now.'

There was something in his tone, a harshening that made Judith regard him with sharp curiosity. He paused at the foot of the forebuilding steps, fist gripped tightly on the hilt of his sword, as if holding it down in the scabbard.

'What is to become of them if they survive, Guy?'

He followed her gaze to his clenched fist and removed it carefully from the grip before he answered, his nonchalant shrug belied by the flaring of his nostrils and the pulsing of a vein in his throat. 'The lands will be forfeit because de Lacey has rebelled against his King, but they were only his by right of marriage anyway. I suppose that the child will inherit them when he is of an age to do so and in the meantime

Henry will appoint a warden. The convent is the best place for lady Mabel.'

'And de Lacey?' she asked softly.

'Is bound for hell!' he snarled. 'The reckoning is only postponed, not abandoned.'

Judith found lady Mabel and the child in a chamber off the hall. The floor was strewn with new rushes and the bed was made up with clean linen, but the air was still foetid with the stench of bowel sickness. Judith went to the shutters and threw them back, opening the room to an arch of cobalt twilight air. Helgund always swore that night vapours were bad for the lungs, but Judith had slept too often beneath the stars to give any credence to such superstition. Besides, night vapours were a sight more sweet-smelling than the human ones of the moment.

Sounds drifted up from the bailey; the good-natured railery of two serjeants, the outlandish Welsh singing at the miners' fire, the neigh of a truculent destrier.

The woman on the bed thrashed and moaned. Judith went to her and laid a gentle hand on the hot forehead. Mabel of Thorneyford raised sunken lids and struggled to focus, moaned again and clenched her lids in pain. Her head rolled on the pillow and a shudder wracked her wasted body. There were red stars of fever on the points of her flesh-stripped cheekbones and the breath was labouring in her lungs. A matter of time only, Judith thought, and short at that.

The child in the crib was awake and alert. As she approached him, his eyes locked on hers and tenaciously followed her movement. They were his father's eyes, ale-brown in colour, the tone echoed by the thick, straight hair. He drew his knees up towards his chest and wailed hoarsely. Judith bent and picked him up. He was hot to her touch, but not burning and, as far as she could see, his condition was still reversible.

'Poor little mite,' muttered Helgund as she set down

Judith's basket of medicines. 'What kind o' life is he going to make wi' the start he's had?' She came to peer into the infant's face and crossed herself at the marked resemblance to his sire.

'Better than the life he would have had otherwise,' Judith answered as she laid him back down and set about mixing a carminative potion to ease Mabel's pain. 'A mother who cannot speak, who never wanted him and a father who has bullied, deceived and butchered and who harbours a vicious lust for young girls. What kind of example is that to set a growing child? At least now he has a chance to learn honour and decency.'

'Aye, mayhap you're right, m'lady,' said Helgund, but a frown still furrowed her brow. 'Although I cannot help but think that wolves breed true.'

'He is only half wolf,' Judith said gently. 'And there is good blood on his mother's side. Come, help me lift her and then I want you to fetch the priest.'

'No hope then?'

Judith shook her head. 'There are others afflicted like this too. My guess is that the well water is to blame and that the weakest have succumbed. Guyon has set the servants to cleaning out the shaft.'

'I wondered why you had left the shutters wide.'

'What do you mean?'

'To let her soul fly free, m'lady.'

Judith said nothing. Let Helgund believe that she adhered to that old custom if it would stop her from lecturing on the ills of open shutters at night. Mabel coughed and choked on the bitter nostrum and most of it dribbled down her chin.

The infant was dosed with more success than his mother and his soiled linens changed. Unlike Heulwen, he was slow to smile and exuded not one iota of her engaging charm. His stare was solemn, almost old . . . but then, she thought, throat tightening, Heulwen had known only love and affection down the length of her short life and this child never had.

Mabel had rejected him so the maids said, and left him to the wet nurse who had been a dim-witted slatternly girl from the village with more interest in her trencher and the attentions of one of the grooms than in the child she was supposed to be suckling.

Judith blinked away the suspicion of tears and sat by the crib, smoothing the child's thick hair until his lids drooped down and his breathing came slow and soft and then she rose and, leaving him with Helgund, sighed and went to administer similar comfort to her husband.

Guyon stepped into the tub, hissing softly through his teeth as the hot water found cuts and bruises that he had forgotten he possessed until now. Slowly, he eased himself down into the herb-infused water until it lapped his shoulders and, tilting back his head, closed his eyes.

Clouded visions danced before his darkened lids. The imagined image of Eluned's death and the reality of the raw earth mound in the garth behind the churchyard. Rhosyn's mutilated body. Heulwen asking in bewilderment for her mother. Heulwen smiling at him through her lashes in the exact manner that had been Rhosyn's, her ruddy curls grazing his lower thigh, her hand curled tight and trustingly in his. He swallowed and swore, opening his eyes, and jerked forward in the water. Judith cried out and backed from him, almost dropping her basket of medicines.

'What's wrong?' She looked wildly around as if expecting some enemy to rush at them.

Guyon subsided with a shake of his head. 'Nothing,' he said and, tight-lipped, reached for the soap dish.

Judith scowled at him and set down the basket. 'Strange behaviour for a nothing,' she remonstrated. 'That's a nasty graze on your shoulder. You had better let me look at it before you dress.'

His mouth softened slightly. 'Yes, madam.'

She bent to sort through his baggage and find him some

341

presentable garments, clucking in irritation at the dismal state that a month without female attention had wrought on his clothes.

'What of lady Mabel and the boy?' he asked far too casually as he busied himself with his wash.

Judith looked round, a pair of cross-garters dangling between her fingers. 'Lady Mabel will die,' she said bluntly, 'probably before dawn. There is nought to be done. The child has a good chance of survival.'

There was a long silence. Judith came over to the tub in response to its quality. He looked up at her, then bleakly away into the middle distance. 'Do you know, Judith,' he confessed softly, 'when they told me that Eluned was dead and that the boy and his mother were still here in the keep, in my power, I wanted to kill them both?' He swallowed hard. 'The little boy ... he looks so much like his father ... I actually found myself unsheathing my sword and standing over him ... and then where would be the difference between myself and Walter de Lacey?'

Judith had put her hand over her mouth. Quickly she took it away as his gaze shifted towards her. Pale as a sheet, she knelt beside the tub, unsure if it was intentional or because her knees had become jelly. Gently, she touched his tense arm. 'You would have derived no pleasure from it, Guy, not like him.'

'You think not?'

'At least you did not do it, however much you desired,' she replied steadily, her insides turning over with fear.

His look was bleak. 'No,' he said. 'Eric stopped me in time, grabbed my wrist and wrestled it down, otherwise I'd have slaughtered that child in his innocence.'

Silence again. Judith wrestled with horror, forcing it not to show on her face. On the heels of horror came burning anger at Walter de Lacey, at Robert de Belleme, at this whole war and at how far Guyon had been pushed and pushed and pushed. Suddenly she understood his need of her and that she

342

must not fail him. 'You were overset and there is no point in brooding upon it.' She shook his shoulder. It was his grazed one and his breath caught. 'Guy, look at me.'

He turned his head. 'You would not have been to blame,' she said slowly and clearly.

'No,' he agreed in a toneless voice, gaze slipping wearily from hers and back to the middle distance.

'Oh, in the name of the Holy Virgin!' Exasperated and cross because she was frightened, Judith thrust to her feet. 'Go on then, wallow until you stick in your own guilt and sink! Just do not expect me to follow you!' She flounced away towards the flagon and reached jerkily for a cup.

Guyon shut his eyes and, with a soft groan, leaned his head against the rim of the tub. 'Judith, let be. I don't want to argue with you, not now.'

'And that is half the problem,' she diagnosed tartly. 'You are so tired that your wits are not serving you as they should. You don't want to argue with me because you dare not. You need time to rest and recover.'

He smiled crookedly. 'There is need and need, *cath fach*. Henry needs my report and then he needs me. My own needs can wait.'

'You will be worse than useless to him.'

'Stop pricking me, Judith. I'll manage.'

'And you have the gall to call me infuriating and stubborn!' she retorted, hands on her hips. When he chose not to respond, she narrowed her eyes and, mouth set decisively, reached for her vial of poppy syrup and carefully laced his wine with it, adding a hefty splash of usquebaugh to disguise the taste. Her eyes brightened with tears at the memory of the last time she had poured him wine while he lounged in a tub and she contrasted it bitterly with the present. This time there was no brimming laughter, no electric charge of sexual tension. This time there was only a fear-tinged determination and seeping weariness.

Returning to the tub, she handed him the spiked wine.

343

'Speaking of needs,' she said, changing the course of her attack. 'The men at least will have to be released for harvest very soon.'

'Such as are necessary,' he agreed. 'I suppose I will have to hire mercenaries to replace them. I'll send to Ravenstow for the strongbox.' He took a gulp of the wine and choked on the underlying bite of the usquebaugh.

'Drink it!' she commanded, eyes fierce, cheeks flushed, terrified that he would discover the taste of the opium.

His lids flickered wide at her peremptory tone and then he smiled slowly. 'Dare I? he asked. 'Last time you shoved a cup beneath my nose and commanded me like that, you were hellbent on torture.'

Judith felt her whole face scorch fiery red. 'I saved your life, didn't I?'

'Yes you did, *cath fach.*' His look became quizzical. 'Why are you blushing?'

Judith's heart did sick flip-flops. Her mind scurried to find an answer to the response of her treacherous flesh. 'I'm not,' she croaked. 'It is the summer heat.'

Guyon gaped at her over the goblet rim with undisguised astonishment. Hot without it might be, but the keep walls were several feet thick, the gaps filled with rubble and, even in the summer months, it was comfortable to have braziers in the private chambers.

'I'll fetch food,' she muttered breathlessly, and detached herself from his scrutiny to dive for the doorway.

Guyon shook his head and then ducked it beneath the water to wet his hair and clear his thoughts, wondering how on earth Judith had the temerity to suggest that his mind was not serving him as it should when her own was quite obviously addled. He pursued his wash and, frowning, took another swallow of the wine. That remark about the heat had been a flustered idiocy, her exit rapid before he could investigate further, or at least he thought, until she had invented a more plausible excuse for her blush than the one first offered.

It was after she had given him the wine, he thought. Until then she had been simmering at him like a cauldron on a blaze. After a moment, a glimmer of enlightenment caused him to taste the wine again and roll it experimentally round his mouth. Smooth, high quality Anjou and rough border usquebaugh and . . .! He spat it out into the bath water and swore with soft vehemence, staring with slitted eyes at the curtain through which she had vanished. Anger sparkled along his nerve endings, an enervating anger, buoying him up, subduing fatigue. Lace his wine, would she?

Judith returned with a tray of cold roast pigeon and manchet bread, a fresh flagon of wine and an excuse for her previous flustered behaviour ready and credible on her tongue, for it was in part the truth. She intended saying that she had been swept by desire at sight of him in the bath and the association of pouring him wine, and knowing how tired he was, had not wished to burden him further. It was therefore with a mingling of vexation and relief she discovered that he had fallen fast asleep in the rapidly cooling water.

Eyes raised heavenwards, she set the tray down on a clothing chest, gave Cadi a firm, low command that flopped the bitch down on her belly at the door curtain, eyes still cocked in distant hope on the food and went to the tub to pick up the empty goblet from the floor and study her husband with exasperation.

'In Jesu's name, Guy, you might have gone to bed!' she complained, aware that she would now have to summon two of the guard to lift him out and then she would have the problem of drying him without saturating the bed. She folded her arms, frowning, then shrieked as Guyon surged from the water like a striking pike and siezing her, dragged her down.

'And you might refrain from poisoning my wine, you witch!' he snarled as she tried to thresh out of his hard grip.

'I wasn't Guy, truly!'

345

'You deny there was poppy in that wine?'

'Only enough to give you a sound night's sleep. You need it.'

'You did it in deceit!'

'It was for your own good.'

'Ah yes, my own good,' he said silkily. 'Swaddle me up like a babe while you are at it.'

'Guyon please, you're hurting me!' Judith half-sobbed, more afraid of the cadence of his voice than the grip on her arm.

'I ought to beat you witless!' he growled, but let her go. She floundered from the tub, the front of her gown drenched and puddling water onto the floor, the ends of her braids dark bronze and dripping. 'Don't ever try that trick on me again.'

Judith took her courage in both hands and stood behind its wavering shield. 'I'll make sure that next time you don't know!' she gave back. 'My only fault was that in my haste I did not disguise the taste enough.'

Guyon jerked to his feet in a swish of angry water. 'Dare it at your peril,' he said thickly.

'Threat or promise?' she asked with a saucy confidence she was far from feeling, aware that she was playing with fire and that one step too far would ignite a totally different conflagration from the kind she was nurturing now. 'Will you unlace my gown? It's soaked and I'll catch a chill.'

'Your own fault. Call your maids.'

'I can't. Helgund's sitting with Mabel and the child and if you glare at Elflin like that, you will terrify her, not to mention what Brand will do to you if he thinks you have been making improper advances to his wife.'

'What?' Guyon knew by now that he was being led a merry dance, but was too interested in its destination to halt the devious steps of its progress.

'Well, if I sent for Elflin and she saw you in that condition, the lord alone knows what she might misconstrue. You know how timid she is of all men, saving Brand.'

'What cond . . .' Guyon followed the direction of her amused gaze, then flicked his own back to her face. Laughter was tugging at her mouth corners. She raised her eyes to his. They were round and innocent and she kept them on him as she raised her arms to remove her circlet and veil.

'Shall I leave that uncomforted, too?' she enquired with spurious solicitude. 'Or would you let me close enough to rub it better?'

'Judith!' Guyon choked, laughing despite himself. Half an hour ago he had been so weary and soul-sick that he could have lain down and died. Now the energy was flowing through him like a vigorous stream in spate. 'What am I going to do with you?'

'Get me with child?' she suggested, slanting him a provocative glance through her lashes. 'Woman are supposed to dote and soften when they are breeding.'

Guyon snorted. 'Since when have you ever done what other women are supposed to do?'

'There is always a first time. You might be pleasantly surprised.'

'For a change,' he said with a grin.

She gave him a lazy, answering smile. 'Unlace me, Guy?' she requested again, turning her back.

He reached to the top of her gown and began to pluck it undone. 'You are nought but a hussy, do you know that? Summer heat indeed!'

She stepped out of the drenched garment and turned in his embrace to twine her arms about his neck and meet his lips with her own. He reached to the drawstring of her shift. 'I have practised better deceptions,' she admitted impishly against his mouth. 'It's not knotted this time.'

'I did not think it would be,' he said wryly as the garment slid down from her shoulders and pooled at her feet and her body blended itself to his.

CHAPTER 29

GUYON STIRRED IN response to a dazzle of light across his eyelids and squinted them open. The chamber was dim, sunlight lanced across the bed from a gap in the warped shutter. He moved his head and idly watched the motes of dust hover suspended in its bright rainbow bars. It took him a moment to remember where he was and why. Then came the familiar feeling as of a cold stone sinking into his gut, immediately dissolved by the awareness of Judith's body curled at his side, sleeping with the innocent abandon of the kitten that was her nickname. Hard to believe in the scheming seductress of the nights.

He stretched and relaxed, smiling at the incongruity. Flowers and thorns. Sharp claws sheathed in softest velvet. He turned towards her and nuzzled his chin on the crown of her head. She made a soft sound and nestled closer. Her lips moved in a sleepy kiss at the base of his throat.

He glanced beyond the soft comfort of his bed and wife to the shifting strands of light and the smile still on his lips became rueful as he realised that it was the first time in three days that he had woken at dawn instead of noon. As usual she had been right, he acknowledged. He had not realized the depth of his exhaustion until he had succumbed to it, and succumb he had with a vengeance. The last three days had passed him by like distant scenes from an illuminated book of hours and he an illiterate turning the pages. He vaguely recalled rising to eat in the hall and speaking to people, although what he had eaten and what he had said were now a complete mystery. He also remembered going out to inspect the repair work on the curtain wall, but Judith had apprehended him with some specious excuse that had drawn him back within . . . and inevitably to bed where, by unfair means, she had enticed him to stay.

Restlessly he shifted his position, aware of a need to be up and doing that was born of renewed energy, not dull-edged desperation. The grief and anger and guilt were still with him, galling his soul like a hair shirt would gall his body, but no longer intruding upon his every waking thought. Raw, but bearable and probably a burden for life.

Lady Mabel had died on that first night, God rest her soul, since it had not had much rest on this earth. Judith had been tearful about that, although he suspected that the tears were more a relieving of tension than any deeper grief for the dead woman. The child still lived. His fever was gone and he had stopped passing blood, or so Judith told him. She kept the babe from his sight and he had no desire to go and see for himself – not yet, perhaps never.

He squinted down at his wife and thought of the incident with the spiked wine. He had always known that she was mettlesome, but sometimes she was almost too quick for him to handle. Get me with child, she had said. He was not sure that he could imagine Judith soft and doting. It was not in her nature, or at least not yet. Perhaps children would gentle her, but he doubted it. Kittens did nothing to make a cat less feral. In fact the reverse.

A blowing horn interrupted his ruminations, a hunting horn, but the notes were not in the sequence that summoned the dogs or blew the mort and they cut like a lightning jolt through his sense of well-being, bolted him upright in the bed and sent him reaching instinctively for his sword. In that same instant, Michel de Bec clashed aside the curtain without courtesy or preamble and strode into the room.

'My lord, it's de Lacey,' he said curtly. 'He's got lightweight siege equipment and an army of Welsh behind him and he's about to storm the walls.'

349

Guyon went grey. 'De Lacey?' he repeated. Beside him, Judith sat up, the sheet clutched to her breasts, her eyes filled with sleepy bewilderment.

De Bec wiped his hand across his beard and looked sick. 'We did not see them before. There was a thick mist at first light and they concealed themselves among a flock of sheep being driven up to the keep.'

'Sheep?' Guyon slanted his constable a look. 'Sheep?' he said again and gave a short bark of bitter laughter at the sheer irony of the situation. 'Do you think it is the same flock perchance? Thirty pieces of silver?'

'My lord?' De Bec looked at him sidelong and nervously.

'Hell's death, Michel!' Guyon exploded. 'He gets out over the wall without being seen and returns in the same wise. God in heaven, I ought to blind every last man on duty. It's quite obvious the bastards have no use for their eyes!' He flung back the bedclothes, tossed his sword on top of them and began swiftly to dress. 'Cadwgan's men, I suppose?'

'I do not know, my lord.'

'God's teeth, what do you know?'

De Bec swallowed. 'They came on us from the west, from across the border, my lord. I do not think they are part of the Shrewsbury force.'

Guyon pulled on his chausses. 'That doesn't make them any less likely to murder us all,' he said in a voice that was husky with curbed temper. 'How far are we outnumbered?'

'About three to one, my lord, but half of them at least are little more than bare-legged Welsh rabble.'

'Don't underestimate them,' Guyon said sharply. 'They might look like peasants, but they fight like wolves and a weakened keep, like a new lamb, is game for their sport.' He gave his constable a calculating look. 'They won't sit beyond a couple of days for a siege – it's all got to come on the first or second assault. If we can beat them back so that they lose heart, then we have a chance.'

'The women . . .'

350

Guyon followed de Bec's gaze. Clothed by now in a clinging white woollen undertunic, her hair spilling to her thighs, Judith was a sight to rouse the lust of any man in battle heat and rank was no impunity when Walter de Lacey was leading the assault.

Judith unsheathed Guyon's long poniard from his swordbelt. 'I can look after myself,' she said quietly, holding the knife in an accustomed, confident grip.

Guyon opened his mouth to tell her not to be so ridiculous, but snapped it shut again as she brought him his newly scoured hauberk. There was no point in telling her that most Welshmen were adept dagger-fighters and that she might strike once and succeed by dint of surprise, but not again. Probably she knew it already, but the die was cast and could not be revoked.

'The women will have to take their chance with the rest of us,' he said to de Bec as he fought the heavy hauberk into place across his shoulders, feeling that it was prison and punishment rather than security. He looked round at Judith again and held out his hand for his swordbelt. She fetched it and he stroked her cheek lightly with his knuckles.

'Organise the servants as best you can love. The women can care for the wounded and boil up whatever we have – pitch, oil, water. Let the men douse whatever is burnable and carry supplies to the battlements. I'll send you back word in more detail when I've seen for myself how the situation stands. At all costs, Judith, keep them from panicking.'

She nodded more staunchly than she felt. Panic was like fire when it spread – difficult to contain and very destructive. She would have to make sure that everyone was kept far too busy to give in to its ravages, including herself. Her chin came up. She looked Guyon proudly in the eyes and he drew her against him, arm hard around her waist. The swordbelt was between them, but for a moment they kissed without noticing. Her fingers tightened on his back, on the iron rings of war when not fifteen minutes before they had been resting contentedly on his warm, naked skin.

351

'Guy, have a care to yourself,' she whispered, feeling suddenly very frightened as it began to hit her. 'Don't go after de Lacey at the cost of all else.'

He released her to buckle on his belt. 'I'll take that as foolishness, not insult, *cath fach*,' he said softly. 'I know what is at stake.' He latched the ornate buckle, hitched the scabbard, then kissed her again, this time lightly and tugged a strand of her hair as had been his wont in the early days of their marriage.

She watched him leave, fear coiling like a cold serpent in the pit of her belly and squeezing her heart up into her throat. Death was so close. Its cold breath feathered down her spine, entering and numbing her soul. Jerkily, fingers icy and fumbling, she braided her hair and pinned it out of the way. The fear intensified and with it came a rallying anger. She yanked on her overtunic, belted it and thrust the poniard down against her left side. It was an act of bravado, but at least it gave her the confidence to stalk from the chamber like an amazon and begin organising the half-hysterical servants into something less reminiscent of a chicken run with a fox amok within.

Guyon peered down from the wall walk battlements on a scene of utter chaos below and, tight-lipped, rapped out several commands. 'Get the barrels of oil to the wall and stop that pick before that section of shored-up wall comes down . . . the same for the ram. And there aren't enough grappling hooks up here. De Martin, get one of the boys to fetch some up from the stores, and arrows too if we have them. Soak them in pitch and set them alight and see if we can get that mangonel.'

'Christ's bloody bones,' Eric cursed beside him. 'It looks as though half of Wales is howling out there for our blood.'

Guyon smiled grimly. 'Not quite,' he said, 'but enough to send us out of this world if they break through; de Lacey will make sure of that.' He drew up his mail coif and set his helmet on top of it and his expression, whatever else it held, vanished behind a broad nasal bar and patterned bronze brow ridges. His finger stabbed out. 'The ballista wants moving over there. It's not a sod's bit of good where it is now. Michel, see to it and you might as well command that section of wall. Choose the ten men that you think will best serve your needs. Eric, come with me.'

'Do we have a chance, my lord?' Eric looked doubtfully down on the ant's nest of Welsh below, their leaders distinguished by the circlets of gold binding their brows and the snakeskin mesh of link-mail hauberks. They were preparing an assault by scaling ladder with remarkable rapidity and making no attempt to conceal their intentions. Walter de Lacey was there, out of arrow range, talking with several of his captains and vassals.

'A fighting one, literally,' Guyon said, as he watched the small knot of men break up and take their positions and his eyes followed de Lacey with narrowed concentration before he turned and, hand on hilt, stalked to inspect the rest of the perimeter.

The attack came with the searing fury of a summer storm – fast and hard and wild, and as difficult to hold. Stones and molten pitch were dropped upon the ram and boiling oil was spouted down on the men scaling the ladders. An exchange of arrows swarmed the air. One sang past Guyon's ear, nicking his jaw. A slim trickle of blood ran down his neck and was lost in the rings of his coif. Another one tipped off his helm as he strove with Eric and another knight to grapple loose a ladder. Thirty feet long and set at an angle of about sixty degrees to the wall, they were extremely difficult to dislodge, particularly when loaded with fifteen determined, rapidly scrambling men.

'It's going!' panted Eric, face crimson with effort as he struggled for all he was worth. The foremost Welshman had reached the top and had begun straddling the wall, his round shield held before him, sword already swinging for Eric's throat. Eric was forced to duck and relinquish his hold on the grappling hook. Guyon swept beneath the Welshman's guard, slashing open his leather jerkin as if it were made of parchment and kicked him back over the wall to smash dead at its base, and slammed the sword pommel beneath the second man's jaw, snapping him backwards and screaming from his perch.

The ladder scraped and grated on the stone as it started to slip. Another of the enemy reached the top and met his death on Guyon's blade. His cry mingled with the shrieks of his companions on the rungs as the ladder toppled sideways and crashed into the ditch below. There was no time to congratulate each other, or even to lean weakly against the stone to regain breath and stop their hearts from bursting, for ladders were up either side of the one just dislodged and from one of these the Welsh had gained the parapet and were dispersing along the wall walk.

For a time the fighting was so desperate that Guyon could scarcely hold his own without time to think of the defences elsewhere; when there was a lull in his section, it was only because the wall had broken on the other side and de Lacey was drawing men away to force the breach.

Swearing fit to burn the ears off any priest alive, Guyon sprinted in full mail towards the danger and was tripped by a wounded Welshman. A knife glittered. Guyon blocked the descending wrist on the instinctive thrust of his shield and then slammed it again into the man's face, rolled and regained his feet. Eric bellowed a warning. He ducked and a hand axe connected with the side of his helm instead of splitting his face, and sent him to his knees. The second blow he caught on his shield which splintered beneath the impact. The third never landed, for he backswiped the blade across his opponent's shins and brought him screaming down. But there was another to take his place, and then another, and he could not break through.

CHAPTER 30

'I WANT THE WELSH put out of the reckoning, Miles.'

The lord of Milnham and Ashdyke set down the hoof he had been examining and slapped the destrier's powerful glossy shoulder, then looked round at the King. 'Easier said than done, sire,' he said warily. 'When we make war among ourselves, it is the time of their greatest profit.' He wiped his hands on his chausses and reached for his shirt.

'Perhaps I should have said the Welsh who are allied with de Belleme. The last thing I need when we march on Shrewsbury is for Cadwgan's rabble to come hurling out of Wales and attack from the side.'

Miles donned the garment and, hands on hips, signalled the groom to lead the destrier round so that he could assess how well the strained foreleg had mended.

'You want me to go to war against the Welsh, sire?' he asked with deceptive mildness.

Henry studied the stallion's long, fluid stride. His lips twitched into a shallow curve. 'I want you to negotiate with them Miles, bring them to the trestle and make them see sense.'

Miles snorted. 'Anyone who sits at a trestle with you, sire, usually ends up being the meal,' he said drily.

Henry's smile deepened and he made no attempt to deny the observation. 'They should be susceptible to bribery. Offer Cadwgan whatever he wants – within reason. He's not particularly intelligent, but he's greedy and astute with it. With your Welsh connections and other skills you should be able to persuade him off my back and on to de Belleme's.'

Miles glanced at Henry sidelong. 'And what happens to be in it for me?' he asked 'Apart from the warm glow of knowing that I am a loyal servant of my King?'

Henry pursed his lips and reminded himself why it was never wise to take anything or anyone for granted unless you wanted to fall flat on your face. Every man had a balking point, only some approached it with less warning than others. It occurred to him that perhaps he had been pushing Miles, and indeed Guyon, a little too hard for a little too long. Do that to a horse, he thought as he watched the roan, and it went seriously lame.

'A dispensation perhaps?' he said, raising his eyes to Alicia as she came down towards them, a packet in her hands.

Miles's mouth tightened. He nodded to the groom and the horse was led away. 'When do you want me to leave?'

'As soon as you may. I want possession of Shrewsbury before the winter frosts stop the grass growing.' He turned to Alicia with a gracious smile. Her braids were still as black as midnight and she smelled wonderfully of attar of roses. 'Worth it, isn't it?'

'It had better be,' Miles muttered obliquely.

Alicia lowered her eyes before Henry. Of a necessity he was occasionally a visitor, but she felt awkward before him and tried to keep their contact to a minimum. There had been desperate reasons behind her adultery. Henry's own need had been a simple, adolescent lust.

Mischievously, Henry reached for her hand to kiss it, but she evaded him and placed the packet in his grasp instead.

'What's this?' he enquired.

'I do not know, sire. The messenger has only just ridden in.'

Henry looked at the seal. It was Guyon's – a rampant leopard snarling on a motte. He slit the wrappings with his eating knife and quickly perused the contents. Alicia went to slip her arm through Miles's, seeking the reassurance of his body.

'He's taken Thorneyford,' Henry said with satisfaction. 'Says he'll shore up and garrison and move down to Bridgnorth via Ledworth and Oxley to gather fresh supplies.'

'What about de Lacey? Is he dead or prisoner?'

Henry grimaced. The writing was spider-like and straggling, quite at odds with the assertive, right-slanting hand of Guyon's that he had become accustomed to reading over the past year. 'No,' he said at length. 'Apparently he slipped out before the last assault, to Shrewsbury so one of the garrison said, but Guy cannot be sure. De Lacey's wife and son are at Thorneyford, both sick of the bloody flux.'

'Does he mention a Welsh girl?'

Henry shook his head and passed the letter to Miles. 'Some special concern of his? Didn't he have a Welsh mistress once?'

'De Lacey murdered her and her son and abducted her ten-year-old daughter to serve his lusts,' Miles said brusquely. 'Her other child, Guyon's daughter, is being cared for at Ravenstow. By a hair's breadth, she was spared her mother's fate.'

'I'm sorry, I did not know.' For a moment Henry's expression was stripped of its customary aplomb to show pity and complete surprise.

'Guyon would not make a parade of it,' Miles answered shortly. 'It was too deep and private a matter and it happened less than two months ago.'

Henry tapped a thoughtful forefinger upon his chin where he had begun to cultivate a neat dark beard. The wording of the letter was concise and clear, but the drunken appearance of the writing was cause for concern, as was this knowledge.

'Perhaps, in view of what you have just told me, it might be as well if you take a detour through Thorneyford on your way to parley with the Welsh, make sure that everything is all right.'

'I was going to do that anyway, sire,' Miles replied, spine stiff, eyes defensive. 'He is my son.'

Henry smiled. 'Well, now you have the royal sanction, don't you?' he said. 'It's starting to rain. Shall we go within and discuss what I want of Cadwgan in more detail?'

★

357

Miles stared in consternation at the serjeant he had sent ahead to notify Guyon of his imminent arrival, for the man was spurring his courser back towards the troop, not sparing the horse or himself in the late summer heat. Even if Guyon had returned to Ravenstow or already set out for Ledworth, there was no cause for this tearing haste unless there was serious trouble. His gut tightened and his stallion jibbed restively in response.

'The keep's being attacked, my lord, by the Welsh as far as I can tell, and it's going hard for the defenders!' Gasping almost as much as his labouring mount, the man gave his report and Miles's expression, grim at first, slowly brightened into savage amusement.

'The Welsh, eh?' His lip curled. 'And in search of a little Norman hospitality. Well, why not?'

'My lord?'

Miles shook his head and rode to the front of the column, increasing the pace from a steady walk to a ground-eating lope.

It still took them nearly an hour to reach Thorneyford Rise, by which time the defenders had reached a state of extremis. Miles took in the scaling ladders clumped against the wall, the lack of men on them, suggesting that most were engaged within the boundaries of the keep, took in too the broken section of the wall and heard on the breeze the sounds of desperate skirmish. Turning his stallion, he rose in the stirrups to address his men who were now expectantly threading their shields onto their left arms and readying their weapons for a charge.

'I'm not going to give you long explanations. You can see for yourselves what we're in for. You are all experienced, you should know the ways of the Welsh. Watch your destrier's bellies, they'll slit them open if you force them to fight in close. Remember, a Welshman does not wear armour. He's vulnerable, but he's faster than you. Kill if you must to save your own skin, but if you engage in combat with any man who seems important, try to take him prisoner. Lives will be useful to barter for Cadwgan's favour and whoever takes a useful hostage will find himself handsomely rewarded. Understood?'

As they acknowledged, Miles threaded his own shield onto his left arm, checked the secure fit of his helm, unlooped the morning star from his saddle bow and fretted the roan back on his hocks. The stallion jibbed and mouthed the bit. Simultaneously, Miles slackened the reins and, yelling, drove spurs into the roan's flanks.

The Norman charge burst into the outer bailey creating mayhem among the attacking Welsh. A bare-legged hill man flew from the roan's shoulder and was trampled by the destrier following on behind. The morning star caught in a Fleming's face beneath the brow of his helm, lodged, and tore away his flesh. He fell, screaming. The Welshman behind him tried to protect his head but was too slow and sprawled sightless in the dust. As Miles had said, very few of the Welsh wore armour and the Norman charge went through them like a scythe through a trench of ripe plums.

Miles spurred on beneath the portcullis. There was a sharp blow on his shield as he emerged into the daylight of the inner ward. He gasped as his left arm was jarred and rose in the stirrups to launch the morning star over his shield rim. A solid thud and a choked squawk were his reply. He twisted the reins and the roan plunged, hooves trampling over something soft that gurgled and writhed and then was still.

Miles swung his stallion around and, amid the renewed fighting and chaos, saw a bare-legged Welshman running towards a group of his comrades who were fighting furiously with something they had surrounded. Bare-legged the warrior might be, but the pommel of his short sword was set with uncut jewels, and his belt was tooled and gilded with gold leaf and a Norman helmet was set jauntily askew on his straggling black curls. With a yell of triumph, Miles rode him down.

359

The group of Welsh exploded outwards like ripples from a flung stone in a pool. One of their number rolled on the ground, clutching his ripped belly and screaming. Guyon followed through hard, iron shield-boss jabbing dangerously, sword swinging low at the enemy's unguarded legs. At his back, feet wide-planted, Eric's battleaxe hewed the air and any Welshman daring to venture within the path of the blade's glittering arc.

Miles's destrier ploughed into the Welsh and the morning star narrowed the odds. Guyon spat out a mouthful of blood from a cut lip and pressed forward. He was functioning on instinct now, not finesse and it took him a moment to recognise his father's stallion and even longer to realise that help, no matter how miraculously, was at hand.

Miles reined the stallion round to block the retreat of the Welsh noble he had marked. The young man's eyes flickered between the dancing shod hooves threatening to brain him and the suggestively swinging morning star. 'Throw down your sword and yield,' Miles commanded in Welsh. 'I promise that you will not be harmed.'

Guyon looked around the inner bailey, saw that the advantage of the battle had swayed back in his direction, glanced further and realised that the forebuilding doors had been broached. A terse oath issued from between his teeth and, commanding a handful of his soldiers to follow him, he ran for the keep.

Miles looked involuntarily towards his son and the Welshman thought he saw his opportunity and bolted for freedom. The horse got there first and the mace came down on the man's skewed helmet, rattling his wits round his skull and knocking him half-senseless to the ground. With a snort of disgust at the man's folly, Miles set about securing him from further attempts at escape.

Within the keep, Judith listened to the screams of men receiving a face full of scalding oil, the war cries, the death cries, the thud of the ram, and felt sick to the soul with fear lest one of those screams was her husband's last utterance.

She had done all that was possible for her to do, short of joining the men on the battlements; indeed, she might have even dared that were she not so fettered by her responsibilities to the wounded and those within the core of the keep who looked to her for guidance.

She knew that their situation was desperate. The Welsh alone they could have fought off, but with Norman leaders the thing was not so sure. Guyon had had to batter Thorneyford hard to take it and four days had not been long enough to shore it up to withstand the kind of punishment it was taking now. She could only thank Christ that she had left Heulwen at Ravenstow, for she had been in half a mind to bring her and only the doubt of what she might find here had made her leave the child behind . . . perhaps to be raised an orphan.

Judith's belly heaved queasily as she contemplated her future at the hands of Walter de Lacey should he prevail. He would force her into marriage in order to lay claim to the earldom. She swallowed convulsively. What had Guyon said about panic? The room started to close in on her, the walls throbbing. The wounded man she was tending groaned and jerked. Through stiff lips she apologized and, finishing with the salve, reached for a roll of bandage. There was none and a swift investigation among the maids showed that there was very little left. She took a swaddling band from Helgund to bind the man and, relieved to have an excuse, left the hall to raid lady Mabel's linen chest in the solar.

She was kneeling by the chest, cutting a linen tablecloth into strips with Guyon's poniard, when she became aware of how much nearer the battle sounded to the keep. The shouting was no longer an amorphous muddle of sound; she could distinguish actual words now and hear the blows and thuds of sword upon shield. From without there came a tremendous crash and then the screams of women and the grating screech of sword on sword. She ceased her task and rose, eyes widening, breath catching in her throat. Weapons clashed together outside the leather curtain. She heard grunts of effort and a hissing curse, and tightened her fingers on the leather grip of her knife, heart hammering as though it would flee her body.

There was a solid thud and a sharp cry followed by a low, bubbling groan and, hard on that sound, the curtain was clashed aside and her nightmare confronted her. Walter de Lacey blocked the light, mail glistening like snakeskin as the breath rasped harshly in and out of his lungs. His sword was edged with blood and the red of it seemed to reflect into his eyes which were aglow with an unholy joy.

Her throat closed, but not before a low, involuntary whimper had escaped her lips. Rape and a living hell. She could see her future clearly imprinted in that voracious stare.

De Lacey watched her, intoxicated with triumph and the terror he saw in her eyes. She was clutching some strips of yellowed linen to her bosom and above them her throat was working convulsively as she fought not to be sick.

'You're not properly attired for a wedding, but you'll do,' he mocked with a dagger-thin smile. 'And clothes only get in the way.'

'Keep your distance!' Judith snarled.

He shook his head and tutted at her. 'Is that any way for a wife to speak to her husband? It seems that I am going to have to lesson you into meeker ways.' Sheathing his sword, he advanced.

Judith backed. Her thighs struck the chest and pressed there. She was cornered, no retreat, and he was going to do all the things to her that Maurice de Montgomery had once done to her mother. She thought of Rhosyn and Rhys and Eluned, of what had happened to them. She thought of Guyon sprawled sightless in the ward, for surely de Lacey would not be gloating here otherwise and, as he reached for her, her eyes flashed and her chin came up.

★

Guyon ran, not feeling the weight of his mail or weapons, only filled with a dreadful sense of foreboding. A Fleming, intent on pillage, barred his way and was cut down. The maids were screaming and cowering. The wounded who had been unable to run away were all dead. A Welshman was swigging raw wine straight from the flagon. He was still clutching it to his chest when Guyon ran him through. Blood and wine soaked into the rushes. Guyon seized Helgund's arms. 'Where's your mistress?' he demanded.

'She went ... solar ... fetch more bandages!' Helgund gulped through a mask of tears and terror as around her men skirmished, chasing each other over and around trestles, hacking and slashing, killing or being killed.

Guyon released her arm and forced his leaden feet to run the length of the hall. Prys was sprawled across the solar entrance. He stooped and turned him over, but the life had flown, the blood-drenched body was as limp as a rag and beginning to grow cold, filmed eyes staring at nothing. Guyon's own blood seemed suddenly to congeal. The world plunged around him. He held on to the wall until his balance steadied, drew a deep breath and, parting the curtain, made himself walk into the solar.

A shaft of sunlight slanted across the room to the wall above the *prie dieu* and illuminated a splash of blood and a beadwork of sprayed drops above it. He followed the pattern up and then down to where it disappeared into the deep corner shadows beside the open linen chest, the napery it contained spilling untidily over the edge and embroidered erratically with great scarlet flowers of blood. Hesitantly he trod in the wake of his gaze until he was looking down on the body of Walter de Lacey and beneath it, the russet homespun of Judith's oldest working gown.

If his blood had congealed before, now he felt it freeze and for a moment was unable to move or to think, blinded and hamstrung by the power of his imagination. Something thrust at his hand, a nudging wet, cold nose and Cadi whined. Her tail swished against his chausses and he broke eye contact with what he dreaded to face to look involuntarily down at the dog. Her tongue lolled. She whined at him and then sniffed at de Lacey's hauberk.

Guyon discovered that the power of movement had returned to his limbs, although they seemed in part to belong to a total stranger. He stooped and, grasping de Lacey's shoulder, rolled him over and to one side. There was a jagged tear in his throat and his eyes were fixed in a sightless, baleful stare.

Judith was drenched in blood, but how much was her own he had no idea. Her face was unsmirched except for one small streak that only served to emphasize her pallor. Her eyes were closed and for one horrible moment he did not know if she was dead or alive.

'Judith?' he said softly and, kneeling, lifted her and braced her weight against his shoulders. 'Judith?' He patted her face and she flopped against him like a child's cloth doll. Frightened, he hit her harder and then, by pure reflexive instinct, shot out his arm and grabbed her wrist before she could do to him with the poniard what she had done to Walter de Lacey.

'Guyon?' Her eyes cleared of their cloudiness. She looked up at him and then at the knife and let it drop with a shuddering sob, turning in his arms to cling to him, shaking.

'Judith, are you hurt, love? I cannot tell for all this blood.'

'Hurt? . . . No . . . It is all his. He did not know I had the knife until I struck . . . I thought when I saw him that you must be dead . . .' The breath caught in her throat and Guyon smoothed her hair and kissed her. She kissed him fervently in return, then pushed him slightly away to look at him. 'You talk of my hurt, as if your own were of no consequence!' she said, pointing to a bloody rent in his mail.

'It's nothing,' he answered, not entirely telling the truth. 'I've taken worse in tiltyard workouts. And it doesn't matter now. It is all over.'

His tone was so weary that she panicked. 'What do you

mean? Surely with de Lacey dead, the Welsh will be willing to talk ransom?'

'Well, that is what I am hoping, although at the best of times they can be contrary bastards and I'm in no case to negotiate myself.' His eyes flickered to the doorway.

Judith stared at Miles in open-mouthed astonishment as he stepped over the corpse on the threshold and walked into the room.

'I thought you did not have the time to send for succour,' she said to Guyon in utter bewilderment.

'I didn't, love.' Guyon released her to wipe his sword on de Lacey's leggings, then wished he had not, for as he bent, the room swung back and forth before his eyes like the deck of a ship in a storm. He straightened slowly, feeling sick and carefully sheathed the blade. 'It was sheer good fortune, or the will of God . . .' He looked at his father. 'If you had not come when you did . . .'

'The will of the King, you mean,' Miles said with a wryly twisted mouth as Guyon fumbled to remove his helm. 'And as it happens, this situation could not have profited him better.' He stooped and fondled the fussy dog.

Guyon looked vacantly at his father. 'Forgive me. I've fought my way to the gates of hell and back. I can't think.'

Miles left the dog and went out into the hall, returning with a jug of wine that had miraculously survived the onslaught. 'Henry wants me to negotiate with the Welsh. Well, thanks to you and Walter de Lacey, I've a nice fat collection of caged birds to lure Cadwgan to the table . . . including his own son.'

'Cadwgan's son?' Guyon gulped the wine straight from the flagon, spilling more down his hauberk then he actually got into his mouth. 'You mean that idiot with the jewelled sword and no notion of how to use it is Cadwgan's son?'

Miles grinned wolfishly. 'The very same. Do you think that his father values him above his loyalty to Robert de Belleme?'

Guyon shook his head in wonder. His gaze flickered to the sprawled corpse of Walter de Lacey and a tremor ran through his body. He put the wine down. 'It is a pity he is dead,' he muttered. 'I would have borrowed one of de Belleme's greased stakes and let him dance on it awhile. He escaped too cleanly.' He rubbed his hand over his face and swore as his palm opened up the arrow-nick and it began to bleed again.

Worry in her gaze, trembling herself with the shock-waves of aftermath, Judith rose and went to him.

Torn muscles protested and shook as he reached out to stroke her cheek. 'Don't fret, love,' he said with his customary perception. 'The shoring up of Thorneyford will take some little while to accomplish this time. I won't be going to Bridgnorth just yet, so you can stop scheming as to how you're going to disguise the opium this time.' He tugged her braid, smiled at her and slowly slipped down the chest, unconscious, to the floor.

CHAPTER 31

Ashdyke
Autumn 1102

Below Ashdyke Crag, between it and the River Wye, the common grazing land was illuminated by a huge bonfire around which the people from the surrounding beholden villages clustered and capered.

The water glittered with scattered gemstones of firelit colour, the sharp autumnal breeze skimming the jet surface with creases and pockets of thick, ruffled gold. The burning wood from a sawn down beech tree crackled and spat, the pungent smoke alive with dashes of soaring molten orange.

Judith looked down on the scene from an arrowslit in the small wall chamber overlooking the river, and smiled as she replaced the hide screen. There was so much to celebrate that it was hard to believe that less than a season since they had been caught up in the violent ugliness of death and war.

She turned away and picked up her new, marten-lined cloak. Helgund was moving quietly about the chamber, tidying and setting to rights. The night candle softly illuminated the faces of the two sleeping children. The King had given Guyon the wardenship of Adam de Lacey and thus the infant and his inheritance were Guyon's responsibility until Adam should reach manhood. Guyon had balked at first, but she had managed to persuade him otherwise. The boy was not responsible for the crimes of his sire and in the years that they had him they could mould him to their own pattern and codes. Doubtfully, Guyon had consented, because at the time he did not have the strength to argue with her and she had taken shameless advantage of his weakness to install the child in their household. Adam was still slow to smile and solemn, but he had gained in flesh and confidence and followed Heulwen everywhere that she would tolerate him.

Heulwen. She looked so angelic and innocent with her rose-gold curls and delicate features that it was impossible to believe in the hellion of her waking hours. In all but her physical appearance and her ability to flirt, Heulwen might have been a boy. She romped and climbed and swung and already straddled a pony with more confidence than either of Helgund's grandsons.

'Are they asleep now?' asked Alicia, tip-toeing to look over Judith's shoulder at the children.

'Snuffed like candles,' she smiled in response. She considered her mother. Alicia was wearing a fetching gown of rich blue wool that turned her eyes the colour of hyssop flowers. Her hair was braided with pearls to match those worked at the neck of her gown and up the hanging sleeves.

'I suppose,' Judith said mischievously, 'that I ought to be organizing the bedding ceremony.'

Alicia's face grew slightly more radiant as she blushed and then laughed. 'Do not you dare!' she cried. 'It might be sport for everyone else but . . . well, the bedding ceremony with Maurice was enough to give me a lifelong dread of that ritual and with myself and Miles . . . it is hardly the first time, is it? We are not likely to repudiate each other.'

Judith embraced her mother. 'I was only teasing,' she laughed. 'I am pleased to see you so happy.'

Alicia returned the embrace warmly. 'I never thought to be. I was so frightened that I would lose him in this war.'

For an instant they clung, women aware of the fragility of their present joy, for even now it was not entirely over. Banished from England de Belleme might be, but for how long? Banishment could be revoked on the whim of a king.

Alicia was the first to step away. She looked Judith critically up and down. 'Does he know yet?'

Judith's hand went instinctively to her belly which was still tight and flat. It was early yet to be sure, the symptoms vague, more a knowledge of the body than of the mind.

'How did . . ?'

'You've put on flesh. Oh, not there yet, that will not show for some time I think, but you never filled your gowns so well before.'

Judith's gaze flickered down to her bosom. 'I suppose I ought to make the most before the rest catches up,' she sighed with false regret and smiled as they left the room and began to wind their way downstairs. 'No, Guy doesn't know. I suggested to him that the best way to handle my waywardness was to get me with child, and he took me at my word . . . literally.' The smile became a giggle at her weak pun, but then she sobered. 'I conceived at Thorneyford sometime between lady Mabel's death and the second siege. In a way, I suppose it is a new beginning, a light out of darkness and all the more precious for being so.'

She found Guyon standing alone by the riverside, watching the reflection of the flames dazzle in the water, and picked her way carefully over to him across the rank, autumn grass, the blades prickling through her hose. He heard the rustle of her approach and turned quickly, then his expression relaxed into a smile and he held out his hand.

'Brooding alone?' she asked lightly, but with a qualm, lest he was mulling over the private losses of the last year.

'Not now,' he answered easily enough, drawing her close. Their breath frosted the air and mingled. The water lapped near their feet, tipped with light. 'I was wondering what will happen in Normandy now that de Belleme is banished there.'

'It is not our concern now,' she said a little too quickly, fingers anxiously tightening in his.

He glanced at her sidelong. 'No,' he said, blanketing what he saw in the future with a half-lie. 'But I cannot help but pity Duke Robert and the rest of the Norman lords. He will

369

eat them alive.' And then Henry would interfere and there would be war again, but in Normandy not England.

'I do not care, just as long as he leaves us alone.' She looked up at him, seeing through his gentle avoidance and fully aware of what went unspoken. He had been very ill after the battle for Thorneyford – not unto death as the last time, thank Christ, but enough for Bridgnorth to have fallen and for Miles to have negotiated his treaty with the Welsh before he was capable of taking the field again and, in her ignored opinion, it had been too soon. He still tired easily. He had been at the bitter siege of Shrewsbury, one of the barons present to witness Robert de Belleme and his brothers ride out of the battered fortifications to exile in Normandy. For the nonce at least, they were safe.

'Are you tired?' She rubbed her cheek against his cloak.

He shrugged. 'A little.'

'Perhaps we should retire,' she suggested, then looked anxiously up at him as she felt him shudder, only to realize that he was laughing.

'Before the bride and groom? Shame on you, you hussy.'

Her lips twitched. 'Yes,' she sighed meekly. 'Shame on me.'

'Judith, you are never seeking to agree with your husband?' he mocked, grinning.

'Well if I am, it is all your fault.'

'Mine! Why?' he enquired with fine indignation.

'Why else should I grow soft and doting?'

That stopped him as if he had walked into a keep wall. He gaped at her like a peasant drunk on rough cider.

'Late spring, I think,' she added, eyes roundly innocent. 'Aren't you pleased?'

Guyon took her by the shoulders. A wondering smile gradually replaced the dazed expression on his face. '*Cath fach*, I love you,' he murmured.

She put her arms around his neck. 'Show me,' she said against his lips. 'I want to know.'

Elizabeth Chadwick's
next novel

to be published by Michael Joseph is

THE RUNNING VIXEN

England is threatened by civil war as King Henry has no
male heir. Adam de Lacey has been sent to accompany
the King's only legitimate child, Matilda, back to her
own country.

Now he returns to Ravenstow, where he has been
brought up as one of the family by Judith and Guyon.
But he finds his thoughts increasingly troubled by
memories of Guyon's daughter, Heulwen.

CHAPTER 1

The Welsh Marches
Autumn 1126

O
N THE DAY that Adam de Lacey came home to the
borders after an absence of more than a year, the
monthly market at Ravenstow was in full, noisy
cry, and thus it was that numerous witnesses watched and
whispered behind their hands as the small but disciplined
entourage wound its way through their midst.

The young man at the head of the troop paid scant
attention to their interest, to the bustling booths and mingling
of scents and stenches, the cries and entreaties to look, to buy
– not because it was beneath him to do so, but because he was
both preoccupied and tired.

He passed a woman selling fleeces and sheepskin winter
shoes and jerkins. The lilting cadences of Wales pleased his
ears, causing him to emerge from his introspection and look
around with a half-smile on his lips. In its place he had grown
accustomed to heavy, guttural German, spoken by humourless
men with a rigid, gilded sense of rank and order, their
lifestyle the complete opposite of the carefree, robust Welsh,
who owned few possessions and pretensions and set very little
store by those who did.

The outward journey to the mourning court of the recently
deceased German Emperor had been filled with the violence
and hardship of long days on roads that were often hostile;
the route home even worse owing to the vicious temper of
his charge. Adam was an accomplished soldier, well able to
look after himself where the dangers of the open road were

concerned. The lash of a haughty woman's tongue, and she the King's own daughter and dowager Empress of Germany, was a different matter entirely. Her high estate had prevented him from defending himself in the manner he would have liked, and the obligation of feudal duty had made it impossible for him to abandon her on the road, forcing her to bear with gritted teeth what he could not change; but then he was used to that.

A crone cried out to him, offering to tell his fortune for a fourthing. The half-smile expanded and developed a bitter quality. He flung a coin towards her outstretched grimy fingers but declined to wait on her prophecy. He knew his future already – the parts that mattered, or had mattered, until the pain of wanting denied had numbed them dead. Abruptly, he heeled the dun stallion's flanks and clicked him to a rapid trot.

Ravenstow keep, the seat of his foster-father's earldom, shone with fresh limewash on the crag overlooking the busy town. It had been designed and built during the reign of William Rufus by Robert de Belleme, former Earl of Shrewsbury and King Henry's prisoner these past fourteen years, his evil power a fading but still potent memory – too potent for some who had lost their friends and family to the barbaric tortures he had practised in his fortress strongholds.

His own father had been de Belleme's vassal and steeped in that same vile filth. Adam knew from servants' gossip, the tales whispered in corners of a dark winter's night or designed to frighten naughty children into behaviour, the kind of man his father had been – a murdering paedophile who had enjoyed watching a tortured man writhe the way a glutton enjoys sitting down to a feast.

The drawbridge was down, but the guards on duty were swift to challenge him and only rested their spears when they had taken a close look at his gonfanon and the face revealed to them by the thumbed-back helmet and unfastened ventail. Then they let him pass, with words of greeting and speculation rife in their eyes.

374

Eadric, the head groom, emerged from the stables to take the dun, and deployed his underlings among Adam's men. 'Welcome my lord,' he said with a white half-moon grin, 'It has been a long time.'

Adam stared around the busy bailey which looked as it always had. The smith's hammer rang out clear and sweet from the forge against the curtain wall. A soldier's woman was tending a cooking pot tripoded over an open fire and the savoury steam drifted tantalizingly past his nostrils like a houri's veil, reminding him that he had not eaten since well before prime. Hens pecked and crooned underfoot, doves from Countess Judith's cote cooing and pirouetting among them. A curvaceous serving wench carried a tray of loaves across the ward and was whistled at by a group of off-duty soldiers, playing dice and warming their backs against a sunny storeshed wall.

'A long time, Eadric,' he agreed with a sigh and the wary smile that the head groom so well remembered. 'I haven't been home to Thorneyford yet. Is lord Guyon here?'

'Out hunting, lord Adam, and the Countess with him.' The servant shrugged, looked apologetic, and then brightened. 'Master Renard is here though, and mistress Heulwen.'

The smile froze and then splintered. Adam's whole face changed. He set his hand upon his stallion's bridle as though he would mount up again, and twisted to look at his men. He could hear their groans of relief and see the way they stretched stiff muscles and rubbed sore backs. They were tired, had ridden a bone-jarring distance, and it would be both stupid and grossly discourteous to ride out now that their presence was known. The smell from the cauldron suddenly made him feel sick.

A young man with a stork's length of leg came striding towards him from the direction of the mews, stripping a hawking gauntlet from his right hand as he advanced – a broad-shouldered young man with pitch-black hair and strong

375

features just beginning to pare out of childhood's unformed roundness. It took Adam a moment to realize that this was Renard, Earl Guyon's third son, for when last encountered the lad had been a lanky fourteen-year-old with less substance than a hoe-handle. Now, although still on the narrow side, his limbs were beginning to thicken out with pads of adult muscle, and he moved like a young cat.

'We thought you'd gone for good!' Renard declared, greeting Adam with a boisterous clasp on the arm and a total lack of respect. His voice was husky, a trifle raw, for it had only broken in the spring.

'So did I, sometimes,' Adam answered wryly, and took a step back. 'Holy Christ, but you've grown!'

'So everyone keeps telling me . . . and not too old for a beating, mama always adds!' He laughed merrily, displaying white, slightly uneven teeth. 'She's taken papa hunting because it's the only way she can get him to relax his responsibilities for a day, short of spiking his wine – and she's done that before now! There's only myself and Heulwen here. She'll be right glad to see you.'

Adam dropped his lids, guarding his eyes, concealing what they held. 'Is her husband here, too?'

They went up the forebuilding steps and through the curtained archway into the great hall. The deep, sweet-scented rushes crackled underfoot and sunlight from the high, narrow unshuttered windows slashed them with yellow light and sparkled on the thread-of-gold embroidery on the banners adorning the walls. Renard crooked his finger at a serving girl, then tilted his visitor a sidelong look from narrow, dark-grey eyes. 'Ralph was killed at midsummer by the Welsh.'

'God rest his soul.' Adam crossed himself, the customary words and gesture emerging independent of his racing mind.

Renard shook his head. 'It was a bad business. The Welsh have been biting at our borders like breeding fleas on a dog's back ever since it happened. Warrin de Mortimer it was who interrupted them at their work, drove them off and brought what was left of Ralph home. Heulwen took it badly. Apparently she and Ralph had quarrelled before he rode out, and she blames herself.'

The maid approached them with a green-glaze pitcher and two cups. Her eyes flickered circumspectly over Adam. He stared straight through her, a muscle bunching and hollowing in his cheek. Mechanically he tasted the wine she poured for him. It was a rich, smooth Rhenish and he almost retched, remembering Heulwen's wedding day and how he had drunk himself into such a stupor on this stuff that lady Judith had forced him to be sick in order to save his life. Afterwards, the incident had faded into a memory recalled with wry chuckles by all saving himself. Sometimes he wished that they had been sufficiently charitable to let him die.